A DARK PLACE

A
DARK
PLACE

KEITH YOCUM

ACKNOWLEDGEMENTS

Writers need support; they work in isolation, have few resources except their imagination, and are often plagued with doubt and frustration. This project would not have been completed without Denise's constant intercession. She has been an emotional and editorial support system throughout. A special thank you also goes to a group of influential readers who provided critical guidance and feedback, including Michael, Jeannine, John, Louise, Lisa and Lyn.

CHAPTER 1

The older, heavyset man knelt down for the third time and held his thick fingers against her neck.

"Well?" the young man said.

"Yes. Finally," the older man said, standing up. He looked around the dense forest of beech, oak and ash. The damp soil was full of roots that made the digging difficult, but he let the young man do most of it.

"She is very pretty," the young man said, kneeling down. "I like her tan." He brushed a piece of dirt off the woman's face. "How much of that stuff did you give her?"

"A lot," the older man said.

"Are you sure she's dead?"

"There's enough in her to kill ten people."

"Do you think anyone is looking for her?"

"Someone is always looking for a lost person."

"She is very pretty," the younger man said.

"She was pretty," the older man said. "She's dead now."

"I think she's still pretty," the younger man said.

"You're getting on my nerves. Let's get going."

"Is the next part necessary?" the young man said. "Who will know?"

"You've done this before, so stop complaining. Help me remove her clothes. Look for tattoos. Then the hands, the feet, the head. It's the same. We take the hands, the feet and the head; we leave the rest here in the grave."

"I know how to do it, I just don't like it."

"If they find out we didn't do it right, there will be much pain and suffering, I promise you. You have no idea how cruel these people are. The body here, if it's ever found, will be nameless. We bag the hands, feet and head and bury them far away from here. Help me remove her shirt. And don't drop anything, like an earring or something."

They struggled to remove her clothing and underwear.

"See, a tattoo," the older man said. "Go get the razor. And don't forget the saw. You do the feet, I'll do the hands."

"I'm not going to help you with the head," the young man said. "Not this time. She's too pretty."

"I will do the head myself; you just shut up and go to work. It will be dark soon. And you're getting on my nerves."

◆

Dennis was uncomfortable and did little to hide it. This was his first meeting with Louise Nordland, his new boss.

"I know we have not worked together before, but I can assure you we'll get along fine," she said. "While I've been accused of looking young, I've been in the agency for thirteen years. I've had many overseas assignments in operations and moved to the Office of the Inspector General thirteen months ago. I was in the OIG's inspections group for one year and am now working in investigations. As you can imagine, I've heard a lot about you."

"You'll have to forgive me," Dennis said, "but you seem really, really young to be managing investigators here in OIG."

"What's 'young' got to do with anything?" she said.

"I'm just saying that, you know, my job is difficult," Dennis said, stirring in his seat. "This work can be kind of crappy. People inside the agency hate you when you come calling, and people outside the agency hate you because they think you're covering stuff up. It helps when you know your ass is being protected back here at OIG."

"You don't think I can cover your ass back here?" she said. "I told you I've worked at the agency for more than a decade. Just because I look young doesn't mean I'm not competent."

"So how old are you then?" Dennis asked.

Her brow wrinkled in two, long horizontal lines. "Cunningham, you know that's not an appropriate question. I was warned that you are irritatingly blunt, but asking my age?"

"Well, you brought it up. I didn't." He shrugged.

At five feet two inches, Louise had classic Nordic straight natural blond hair, parted down the middle and falling like lead weights to her shoulders. She wore the informal uniform of many agency female managers: an open-necked, starched white cotton blouse and a two-piece dark business suit. A simple gold chain circled her thin neck.

"You really are something," she said. "I'm thirty-nine. How old are you?"

"You can't ask questions like that," Dennis said. "I'll have to report you to HR."

"Ah, HR," she said, twisting her small mouth into a smirk. "Don't they run Langley? When I started here, I thought the director ran the agency, but it's actually run by HR. Who knew?"

Dennis laughed. "They said you were a straight shooter with a sense of humor."

"Who's 'they?'" she parried.

"You know, the faceless minions here, the great 'they,'" Dennis said. "There are twenty thousand of us going to work at the agency every day to make this country safe."

"Mmm," she said. "Safe from whom?"

"Ourselves?" He shrugged.

"Ain't that the truth."

Louise opened a dark brown folder and scanned a document. Dennis watched her pursed lips as she concentrated and wondered if that was why she ended up in OIG. She seemed incapable of disguising her emotions. As she read the document, her forehead wrinkled in concentration.

"Okay," she said, looking up. "We have a meeting with the IG in fifteen minutes. He'd like to speak with you."

"Come again?"

"We have a meeting with the inspector general in fifteen minutes," Louise said.

"We do?"

"Yes, what's wrong?"

"Well, I've never met the IG, for one," he said. "I mean, he doesn't want to talk about what happened in Australia and all that stuff, does he? I'm tired of talking about that. I'm back to work. I'm healed. Why the hell does he want to talk to me?"

"Which reminds me," she said. "How are you feeling? Physically?"

"I'm fine. It wasn't that big a deal. The bullet just grazed me here," Dennis said, pointing to his right temple. "You can't even see the scar."

"There was a skull fracture, correct?"

"Yes, but there were no clots or bleeding in the brain. I'm just left with a tendency to drool in public and wet my bed. Otherwise, I'm fine."

"God," she said, shaking her head. "You really are too much. Well, for the record, and I have to get this out of the way — you'll never hear me refer to it again — but I'm embarrassed and ashamed by what happened to you at the hands of your old boss Marty and his pals."

Dennis flicked his wrist upward as if he were brushing smoke from his face.

"Fine. I got that out of the way," she said.

"But the IG wants to see me? In his office?" Dennis said.

She exploded in a guttural laugh. "What is it with you and the IG?"

"Well, for one, I don't even know his name, because they change them every couple of years. And secondly, I don't like hanging with the brass. I like hanging with people like you, who keep me away from hanging with people like the IG."

"Relax, Cunningham," she said. "Chill. His name is Bill Richardson. Call him Bill."

◆

"Ah, the famous Dennis Cunningham," Richardson said, coming around the huge mahogany desk. "It's a pleasure to finally shake your hand. I hope you got the letter I sent you."

"Yes, I did," Dennis said. "Very nice of you to send it."

"Well, you went through a lot, and I'm not going to dig up the whole episode again, but I'm deeply sorry for what happened to you."

"Thank you," Dennis said.

"Please, sit," Richardson said waving to a round table with several, black Windsor-style chairs.

After they settled in, Louise said, "Bill, I see there has been an external request for Cunningham to be assigned to a specific project. That's a little unusual, isn't it?"

Dennis shot her a glance, but she kept her eyes on Richardson.

"Yes Louise, it is a little unusual. Awkward is probably the better word."

"Can you fill us in a bit more, since Cunningham has just returned to work? And he and I have not had a chance to discuss this issue. I want to make sure he is not disadvantaged in any way."

Dennis felt strange watching two people talk about him as if he were not in the room. And he was getting angry, which he knew from experience often led to trouble — mostly for him.

"Yes, well, this is what's going on," Richardson said. "Representative Daniel Barkley, the chairman of the House Intelligence Committee, has requested that we investigate the disappearance of the deputy chief of station in London."

"That was already investigated several times by operations," Louise said.

"Yes, and Barkley and his staff are not satisfied, for some reason," Richardson said.

"But he has no purview over the agency's investigations," Louise said.

"Of course he doesn't have direct authority, Louise. But you know how this works. He is extremely influential in our budgeting process, and it's good to have him on our side. When he makes an informal request through the director, and the director turns to me, well, we'd like to reduce any friction by just acceding to his request. Assuming, of course, that it's not harmful or illegal."

"Excuse me," Dennis said. "Did Representative Barkley request me specifically to work on a project? Is that what I'm hearing?"

"Actually, yes," Richardson said.

"By name?" Dennis said.

"Of course," Richardson said. "Otherwise we wouldn't be sitting here right now."

"Cunningham," Louise said, "we know you are familiar with Barkley because he was involved in the Australia incident. You apparently made an impression."

"I wasn't particularly fond of the congressman," Dennis said. "Thought he was a pompous son of a bitch."

As soon as the words tumbled out, he was sorry. When he was angry, his worst affronts came at the end of several sentences; the longer he talked, the more likely he was to offend. It was a problem of mathematics, he believed. When he was angry, uttering one less sentence was much better; it was always the last sentence that caused him grief.

Richardson winced, and Louise gave Dennis a surprisingly fierce stare.

"I'm sorry if that was too blunt," Dennis said.

"We're all entitled to our opinions," Richardson said. "We just need to remember who we're with when we express them. I think your opinion of the congressman might be shared by several people here. But there is the politics, as I pointed out. And we're in Washington, where politics reigns."

"Of course," Dennis said.

"So, do you mind if I just ask a few more questions, Bill?" Louise said. "I know this is delicate, but Cunningham is only just back in the office, and given his most recent episode, I was hoping we wouldn't expose him to any wasteful and unproductive case work. He's a valuable member of a very small investigative team."

"I understand fully," Richardson said. "But as I stated, Dennis here has been requested to do a final wrap-up of a controversial disappearance in London. I think we all know that Dennis not only has a reputation for being prickly at times—" he smiled wanly "—but has an extraordinary knack for finding people."

✦

The sadness had evolved slowly, picking up momentum as the days dragged by. She would find herself staring idly out the window of her car at a stoplight until someone hit their horn. Or at home she would lose interest in a book or TV show and find herself staring at the floor.

Her best friend Cilla finally confronted her. "You're depressed, Judy. And lonely. Let's just call it what it is," Cilla said as they ate dinner at a small Italian restaurant in Fremantle, Western Australia.

"No, I'm not," Judy said.

"Stop it," Cilla said. "You're depressed. And it's that Yank's fault. He lured you into a relationship; you flew to the US, saved his bloody life in that sordid CIA disaster. And now you're alone and depressed."

"I'm just lonely," Judy said, weakly swirling her wine glass. "I'm not depressed."

Cilla said nothing and stabbed at her pasta.

"All right, maybe I am depressed. A little. Perhaps."

"As your friend," Cilla said, "I'm not sure what to suggest. I feel as depressed as you about it. I know you want him. I thought he needed and wanted you enough to move here. With your son still in school, it's really up to him to move."

"Dennis says that he wants to move here," Judy said. "But he's just started back to work, and I'm afraid he'll get caught up in another one of those investigations."

Cilla held up her wine glass. "Here's to bloody men who promise one thing and do another."

✦

"I know, I know," Dennis said, dropping his right arm onto the soft fabric of the armrest. "I have to make a decision. I've tried, but I just freeze when I think about it."

"Well, it's not fair to her," Dr. Jane Forrester said. "And not fair to you either."

"Oh, please don't start the 'self-destructive behavior' thing," Dennis said. "Can't a guy just be stuck?"

"I thought you were madly in love with her?" Forrester said. "She risked a lot emotionally visiting you in the US, and without rehashing everything, she also risked her life in coming to your aid in that shooting."

Dennis slumped in his chair and crossed his arms over his chest.

"So?" he said.

"So what are you going to do about her?" she said. "If the relationship is over, then it's over and you should tell her. If it's not over, perhaps you should take some steps to improve the relationship."

"Like move to Australia?" he said. "I don't have a job there. I just started back to work here. I like what I do. What am I going to do there, play golf every day? I don't play golf. Take photos of kangaroos?"

"Dennis, as you well know, you are not the first adult on this planet that has to deal with a difficult choice about a relationship. But right now you're not dealing with anything. You're letting the situation deal with you. And it's sapping your energy and making you feel guilty. You shouldn't hide from your responsibility. This woman needs to be treated fairly, and you need to get on with your life. And I hate to say this, Dennis, but our time is up today."

✦

He surrendered his mobile phone, his wristwatch, wallet and a ballpoint pen and then walked through a large scanning device that resembled an MRI, was wanded with a hand-held scanner by a taciturn security official, and went through the retinal scanner outside the room. After being buzzed in, Dennis entered a large room that encased a smaller, glass-enclosed room in the center. Inside he could see Louise and two men talking at a table. The soundproofing of the glass room gave the scene a surreal quality, as if Dennis was watching a TV show with the sound turned down.

Louise waved at him and pointed to a door on the side.

"Great to see you, Cunningham," she said formally. "I'd like you to meet David Simpson, senior operations manager at the National Security Agency, and Tim Felton, chief of European signals intelligence at NSA."

Both men stood and shook Dennis's hand, and then they sat.

Dennis had been to Fort Meade in Maryland once before, a short visit to one of the outlying buildings. He had never been this far into the labyrinth office complex at the NSA's headquarters northeast of Washington, D.C.

"Well," Louise said. "Let's just dig in, shall we?"

"Of course," Simpson said.

"I'll summarize for everyone, if that's all right?" Louise said.

Simpson nodded.

"In April, the deputy chief of station in London, Richard Arnold, disappeared," she said, glancing at an open folder on the desk. "He is a twenty-two-year veteran of the agency and has spent his entire career in operations. As we all know, the London station is one of the most import-ant sites for the agency, given the newly resurgent Russian aggressiveness. Arnold is only the second senior agency employee to go missing in the last twenty years. It is highly unusual for a person of his stature to simply vanish. Usually, someone of his rank would be protected from foreign intelligence actions, since it could start a tit-for-tat cascade of disappearances. Britain's MI5 and MI6 have not been very helpful in the investigation of this case.

"Given the knowledge base that Arnold had of agency operations in Europe, there have been two separate, extremely in-depth investigations of his disappearance by the agency. The general consensus now is that Arnold's disappearance was carried out by a non-European foreign group, most likely an Islamic terrorist team.

"Recently, a request was made by a high-ranking member of Congress to reinvestigate Arnold's disappearance. The request specifically identified Dennis Cunningham, from the agency's OIG, to spearhead the effort. So here we are."

Simpson, Felton and Louise all looked at Dennis, who gazed down at the high-gloss tabletop. He looked up at her and said, "So why are we here?"

She looked blank. "I just stated why we're here. You've been requested to review the investigation of Arnold's disappearance."

"No, I got that part, Louise," Dennis said. "But what are doing here? At Fort Meade in Maryland, at NSA headquarters? Sitting in a high-security room with these two guys?"

"Oh, that," she said, turning to Simpson.

Simpson gave Dennis a brief, patronizing smile. "Arnold was the agen-cy's primary contact with the NSA in the UK," he said. "Arnold had almost full access at the NSA's Menwith Hill Station in North Yorkshire. I'm sure you've heard of the facility?"

Dennis shrugged.

"Does that mean you are or are not familiar with the facility?" Simpson asked.

Louise shot Dennis a sharp glance.

"I've heard of it," Dennis said. "Part of the NSA's vast network of digital vacuum cleaners, sucking in electronic communications everywhere to store in vast databases that no one will ever use. You mean that Menwith Hill?"

"Mmm," Simpson said.

Louise's mouth twisted sharply.

"Cunningham," she said, "it appears that Arnold visited Menwith Hill twice right before he disappeared. The last time was three days prior to going missing. The last visit was very unusual, and the NSA is rightly concerned. They've had their own investigation as well."

✦

To Judy, the yellow tape marked the limits of a demilitarized zone: the world outside the yellow tape was the normal, ordinary planet, replete with human beings who were nice to each other, waved at their neighbors, petted dogs and said "gidday" on the street. Inside the yellow tape was the world at war; the planet of evil, hostility and death.

Judy lifted the police tape and slid under it, walking with her partner Clive down the driveway toward the back of the house. She nodded to a uniformed policeman as she rounded the house and took four steps up into the kitchen, where she stopped immediately.

The bodies of two young men lay face down on the floor. One body was in front of the stove, and the other was awkwardly wedged under the kitchen table. Blood covered nearly half the floor.

A man wearing slip-on protective foot covers was on the far side of the kitchen taking photographs.

"Neighbors heard nothing, except for the barking of the dog, a great Alsatian that wouldn't let up," Clive said. "At around 2:00 a.m. someone called the police and complained about the dog keeping the neighborhood awake. This is what they found."

"No one heard gunshots?" Judy asked.

Clive shook his head. "Silencer."

At one time Judy might have been sickened by the site of two dead bodies that had bled out on the kitchen floor of a suburban house, but drug violence in Western Australia was now a common occurrence. Cheap heroin from Asia mixed with Chinese-manufactured fentanyl was devastating a segment of society here, and she was inured to it.

Now, it was just an unpleasant feature of her job in the Australian Federal Police. The AFP was partnering with an alphabet soup of government agencies, including the Western Australia Police Force, Australian Border Force and the Australian Criminal Intelligence Commission in order to beat back the scourge of drug smuggling.

"They leave anything behind?" she said.

"Not really," Clive said. "These fellows were tortured. The one under the table appears to have been stabbed through his hand several times. One of them must have told where the drugs and money were kept. We found a hiding place behind the wall in the upstairs closet. It's cleaned out."

"Mmm," Judy said. "Fun, fun and more fun."

"Indeed," Clive said, chuckling in the manner of all homicide detectives, coroners and funeral home operators.

✦

There was nothing to like about the NSA, Dennis believed; it had too much money, too little adult supervision, and was run by nerds: engineers, programmers and data analysts.

The American intelligence community once had two main tools: human intelligence, or humint, and signals intelligence, or sigint. Lately he was aware of new toolset called imint, or image intelligence, which combined satellite information with aerial photography. Dennis believed most assuredly in the old-fashioned humint side of the business: men and women, boots on the ground, using intuition, training and sometimes violence to get at the truth of a situation. The Office of the Inspector General had three operational groups: one did financial audits, another did inspections and Dennis's group did investigations.

Dennis thrived on digging out deception, graft and illegal behavior by agency employees, but only if it involved working with human beings and not spreadsheets. He could accost people, verbally harangue them and even threaten them to get information he needed. It was a visceral exercise that fit perfectly with his naturalistic view of the world.

The NSA, on the other hand, spent most of its resources capturing data and analyzing it. Employees were often former military people whose job it was to manage the nerds. Dennis found these individuals idiosyncratic, self-absorbed and irritating. Their work was more like playing chess or solving a mathematical problem than helping keep the world safe from bad people.

Or that was his bias, anyway. He knew bad people communicated by text messages and social media, and that they could be tracked and surreptitiously listened to in order to keep the world safe. He just thought there was too much emphasis on sigint and that it drained dollars and good people from the humint side of the business.

So he was not happy to be sitting across the table from a short, paunchy, prematurely balding man in his early forties named Fred Kaczka.

Simpson, the NSA official that Dennis did not like, had called Kaczka into the glass-walled office using a very odd-looking small desk telephone.

"Fred is a member of the NSA's Inspector General's Office," Simpson said. "He has been in the department for twelve years. He is a graduate of Georgetown undergrad and the law school and is one of the most valued members of the department. He will be the NSA's representative on the team to do this final review of Arnold's disappearance."

"What team?" Dennis said.

"The OIGs from all the intelligence groups commonly work together," Louise said.

"But I thought Representative Barkley requested me to do the final wrap-up?" Dennis said. "Did Barkley say anything about a team?"

"Not that we're aware of," Simpson said, flashing the condescending smile that Dennis was already worked up about. "Nevertheless, this is how the 'wrap-up,' as you call it, will proceed. It can't happen any other way."

Dennis looked at Louise for help, but the corners of her lips were pinched in what he took to be an attempt to control herself. His natural instinct was to strike out at their insistence that he work with another investigator. It was well known within his department that he was a solo practitioner who bristled at collaborating. They allowed him to work alone because he was so good at it. He knew Louise knew this as well. It suddenly occurred to Dennis that she either knew what was going to happen but didn't care how Dennis reacted, or that she had absolutely no control over the situation and was praying Dennis would not explode.

He cleared his throat in an attempt to gain a second or two to decide what to do. "I see," he said. "This must have come from high up. Okay, I see that." While Dennis and Louise had just started to work together, and they had already clashed, he decided not to embarrass her. It was not something he would have considered a year ago, but things had changed. A bullet one-eighth of an inch away from ending his life makes a man pause. Besides, his therapist said he needed to build relationships, not destroy them.

✦

"Of course I miss you," Dennis said, crushing the mobile phone between his left shoulder and ear. He was walking to his car from the mall with both hands carrying a heavy box. "You know I miss you. I can't believe you think I don't."

"I've heard you say it many times over the phone," Judy said, "but you have yet to visit me here. You know I can't just leave my son, with his father in prison and all that."

"I just started back to work, and I've got another case they've thrown at me," he said, awkwardly scanning the huge parking lot with his head tilted, still holding the phone against his ear. "I was wondering if we could meet maybe halfway for a short trip?"

The silence unnerved him, and he said quickly, "It was just an idea. I was hoping to make a work trip to London in the next couple of weeks. Is there any chance you could perhaps squeeze in a trip to the UK? I looked at the flights from Perth to London, and you have some options. Though it's not really halfway, it's longer for you. I'll buy the ticket. What do you think?"

"Is a trip to London going to resolve anything long-term for us?" Judy said.

Dennis found his car and placed the box on the hood, regaining his breath and his composure. "I'm not good at this stuff. I, I," he stuttered, "don't know how to proceed. But I know I think about you a lot. Probably way too much. But I guess I need some time to plan things."

"How can you think of me too much?"

"Well, I mean—"

"Dennis, that was a joke," she said. "I might be able to manage a trip to London. You don't have to pay for my flight."

"No, I insist. I want to see you."

Judy sighed. "When will you know your travel plans? My work life is very complicated these days. Western Australia is not the placid little backwater it once was."

"Which reminds me," Dennis said. "What's the latest on that bastard Voorster? Have they found him yet?"

Judy felt a chill whenever she heard that man's name. "No, nothing yet. We don't know how he got out of the country or where he went. I'm trying not to think of him."

"I'm sure he'll show up in a prison somewhere," Dennis said. "Just wish you knew so you could stop worrying."

Silence fell on the conversation, and Dennis squirmed.

"I can't stand being away from you." Judy blurted. "I know you don't like these emotional outbursts, Dennis. But I do miss you, and I wish I didn't feel it so strongly. I'm trying to figure out where our relationship is going, and I think we're running out of time."

Another moment of silence stretched between them.

"I wish you were here," Dennis said as he dodged a car backing out of the parking space next to him. "It's a gloomy, cloudy day in the Washington suburbs. I just bought a small hi-fi system to listen to music. I think I told you I moved into a condo. It's barren inside, and I realized that a TV set is the only form of entertainment I have. Shows what an exciting lifestyle I lead."

"Are you serious about London?" she said.

"I told you, I already checked the flight schedules."

"A man who plans must be serious," she said. "Men don't plan."

CHAPTER 2

You know, it would have been helpful if you had told me about the request from Barkley," Dennis said. "If we're going to work together, you can't be holding shit like that from me and let me go into a meeting completely unprepared."

Louise tapped the eraser end of an unsharpened school-bus-yellow no. 2 pencil on the top of her desk. She made little tap-tap-tap sounds, punctuated by pauses. Dennis found it irritating and stared at the makeshift drumstick to emphasize the point. But Louise continued to tap.

"Well?" Dennis said.

"I didn't mention it to you because I'd been warned that you can get pretty worked up over the smallest things. So I decided the best way to advance this effort was to keep you in the dark until the last moment." She shrugged, tapping the pencil again.

"Warned?" Dennis said. "What does that mean?"

"Please don't pretend that the OIG is clueless about its long-time employees," she said. "Your reputation precedes me and will post-date your retirement, I'm sure. Your surliness and difficult behavior have long been a subject here. As you can imagine, they've tended to look the other way because of your successes. Your former boss was quite hands-off with you."

"Marty," Dennis said. "Good old Marty. He's in prison now. But he knew how to point me in the right direction and was good at keeping the brass off my tail. So we got along great."

"Is that why he tried to kill you?" she said, giving the pencil a hard rap and then tossing it onto the table.

"Oh, God, we're not going there, are we?" Dennis said. "You swore you weren't going to bring that Australia thing up again."

"I lied," she said.

Dennis squinted at her. "Mmm," he said. "I think I like your sense of humor. But I'm not sure I like you."

"It's not necessary that you like me, Cunningham, but you have to respect my actions as your boss. Otherwise, this isn't going to work."

"You are correct," Dennis said. "Are we done?"

"No, not yet," she said, picking up the pencil again. "This guy from NSA — Fred Kaczka — is a very bright guy, and you need to work as a team. There's something going on over there about the Arnold disappearance, and NSA is not exactly coming clean with their concerns. As I stated, Arnold visited their listening post at Menwith Hill right before he went missing. See what you can get from Kaczka on this, because they're not telling us. Anything you can pull out of him would be greatly appreciated at the highest levels here. *Capisce*?"

Dennis nodded, stood up and paused. "I'm sorry for being a jerk sometimes," he said.

"No, you're not," Louise said.

"No, I guess not," Dennis said. "But I'm trying."

"Really?" she said, twisting her face into a smirk-smile-frown contortion.

"Yes, really. It's hard being a prick all the time. And my therapist says I need to stop."

"Mmm," Louise said.

✦

The room was brightly lit by exposed fluorescent bulbs; a small metal table was situated in the center. A laptop was placed in the middle of the table. There were no windows, no phones, no bookshelves, only two simple metal chairs without cushions.

Fred directed Dennis to come to the meeting wearing casual clothing; even a sweatshirt and sweatpants if that suited him. Dennis would be asked to turn over nearly every object in his possession, including watches, rings, coins, money clips and even eyeglasses. Fred had asked for his reading glasses prescription so they could supply a temporary pair. He would even surrender his shoes and go through several scans of various devices before being allowed into the examination room.

Dennis entered the room wearing disposable sandals and feeling like he was about to be operated upon. Fred sat at the table wearing a slightly stained and stretched white tee shirt. His chunky, hairy thighs were barely contained by a pair of old Georgetown University gym shorts.

"Hey," Fred said, smiling. "You made it through the gauntlet. We're pretty serious here, as I'm sure you can tell. Did you get the anal probe inserted? Frickin' thing hurts like hell in the beginning."

"What anal probe?" Dennis said, stopping in his tracks.

"Damnit, you didn't get it yet? Shit, we're in trouble." Fred stood up in alarm and looked at Dennis. Then he broke out in a huge laugh that resounded in the small room.

"Ha, ha," Dennis said slowly. "You NSA folks are pretty funny. Ha, ha."

"Oh, it was just a joke," Fred chuckled. "Has to be some fun in this business."

"I guess."

"I was told you had a good sense of humor," Fred said, "but a sour personality."

Dennis found himself frowning at the chubby, balding man about to split his ancient college gym shorts.

"Well, the sour part was correct," Dennis said, sitting. "Sense of humor part, well, that's still an open question."

"Sorry if I was a little crass," Fred said. "Shouldn't assume things like that."

"No, it was pretty funny. In fact, I'm going to requisition that joke for my own purposes one of these days."

"Well, it was great being with you folks tonight," Fred said, looking out over the table at the make-believe audience. "I'm here on Tuesdays and Fridays — eight to midnight. Stay safe and remember, I've been in love with the same woman for forty-one years. If my wife finds out, she'll kill me. Thank you, thank you, you're great."

Dennis burst out laughing. "Where exactly do you come from? Do they teach that at cryptology school?"

"Hell, no. That's just Freddie being Freddie. And that was a Henny Youngman joke at the end there. I'm not that creative."

"Do you always refer to yourself in the third person?" Dennis said.

"You want first person?"

"No, no, that's fine."

"Enough hilarity," Fred said, pushing a thick, bound volume of papers across to Dennis. "Let's get down to business."

✦

After ninety minutes Dennis pushed the pile of papers to the side and said, "Are we on rations here, or does the NSA have things like coffee, or water, and for that matter, toilets?"

"No toilets, just water," Fred said.

"Ha, ha."

"Fair enough," Fred said, "let's get out of here."

Dennis followed as Fred led him through two consecutive doors, where they encountered a taciturn young woman sitting at a desk. Both men had simple stick-on paper name tags plastered to their shirts. The woman reached out with a bar-code reader and scanned the name tags. She looked at her computer screen then at both men.

"Where are you going?" she asked Fred.

"The caf."

"For how long?"

"About a half hour or so."

She typed something into the computer and then opened a drawer and took out two small, gray metal squares that had safety pin-type catches on the back. Dennis followed Fred's lead by putting his on the front of his sweatshirt.

"Thirty minutes, men," she said and waved them through yet another door.

After five minutes of walking through a maze of corridors, Dennis found himself inside a small cafeteria, where he grabbed a cup of coffee and a pastry. Fred took a Diet Coke and a glazed donut. They sat at a small, round, Formica-topped table.

"How come there's no cashier here?" Dennis said. "This stuff free?"

"Of course it's not free; you're paying for it, and so am I, in our federal taxes. Our budget is about $10 billion, and yours is about $15 billion."

"Well, at Langley we have to pay for our food," Dennis said.

"Ah, we're not in the main cafeteria, where indeed we do have to pay," Fred said. "This is the high-security caf, and it would be too much trouble to have us go retrieve our cash or credit cards then have someone here to take the money ... you get my drift. No need for that kind of exposure here. Cheaper and safer just to let us get fat on bad coffee and stale glazed donuts, courtesy of US taxpayers."

"You know, I've been to a lot of facilities throughout the world," Dennis said, "and I've never been through this kind of security just to review case files. It seems kind of excessive, don't you think?"

"Ah, if you knew what we knew about the dangers lurking out there, your employer would be more careful," Fred said, taking an enormous bite of the donut. "But you lot at Langley really are neophytes when it comes to this stuff. We live and breathe it, so we're a little more careful. The number of breaches over there is hilarious; we'd just as well not be contaminated."

"That's bullshit," Dennis said. "We run a very tight ship. Everyone does now."

"Dennis, you have no idea what you're talking about. We won't even let you folks into our secure areas here at Fort Meade. You're one of the first in a long time, and it's only because of this particular case."

Dennis did not like a lot of things in life, but one that was guaranteed to push his buttons was being called out as stupid or uninformed.

"That's NSA crap," he shot back. "Part of the narrative you nerds love over here: those stupid agency idiots running around screwing everything up while we purists over here run a tight little ship and are above the fray, scanning teenagers texting each other in Finland and hacking Russian military facilities as the Russians are hacking our facilities. Come on, Fred."

"Oh boy, aren't we a wee bit sensitive," Fred said, finishing off the donut in one huge bite.

Dennis took a sip of coffee and tried to control his irritation; he took most negative comments personally, whether they had anything to do with him or not. It was a weakness and a sign of insecurity, he now understood, thanks to Dr. Forrester. Still, it rankled him, and he found himself scowling at his Danish pastry.

"So is this the Dennis the Menace I've heard so much about?" Fred chuckled.

"Why does that name follow me everywhere?"

"I give up, why?" Fred grinned.

"You're a pain in the ass," Dennis said. "You know that?"

"I know you are, but what am I?"

"You're a child in college kid's clothing," Dennis said.

"I know you are, but what am I?"

"Oh God, can you understand why we hate dealing with you jerks over here?"

"Lighten up there, kemosabe. All is right in the world," Fred said, displaying the grin that was getting on Dennis's nerves.

"You're not old enough to know who kemosabe was," Dennis said. "Jesus, where do you get this stuff from?"

"*The Lone Ranger*; ran on TV from 1949 to 1957. Clayton Moore played the Lone Ranger, and Jay Silverheels was Tonto."

Dennis put down his coffee and stared at his table partner. "Fred, you are one of the weirdest people I've ever met, inside or outside the intelligence community, which as you know is chock full of nutbags."

In complete contrast to what he expected, Dennis found Fred laughing hysterically and slapping his ample thighs. "Yer killing me," he laughed. "Absolutely slaying me."

"Can we go back to work now?" Dennis said.

"Sure, kemosabe."

"Stop calling me kemosabe."

"Okay, Dennis the Menace."

"Stop calling me Dennis the Menace."

"Okay, Dennis. But I have one question."

"And what would that be?"

"Are you going to finish that Danish?"

Dennis pushed the paper plate over.

"You know, I don't know if I like you, Fred."

"Oh, you'll like me, don't worry," Fred said, putting the rest of the Danish in his mouth. "I'm going to be your best friend. And I'll make you laugh, which is something I think you need more of."

Dennis sighed, partly out of exasperation, but also out of recognition that indeed, he did need to laugh more.

✦

The pistol still had the safety on, but Judy's finger was right on top of it, ready to flick it to life.

She, Clive and four uniformed West Australian policemen, along with a leashed drug-sniffing female dog named Halo, were spread out around a junkyard in Rockingham. The group was slowly making its way toward a large corrugated-roofed building. The drug task force had received reliable information that this nondescript graveyard for all kinds of vehicles was in fact a transit center for the synthetic opioid fentanyl.

The owner of the business had retired and left it to one of his sons, who used the facility to move the drugs to other distributors throughout the west.

The tip was that a shipment was concealed in a wrecked Toyota Corolla that had been towed to the junkyard that morning. The plan was to find the Corolla, put Halo onto the package and arrest the son and whoever was nearby.

Or that was the plan; Judy knew enough about the task force's intelligence unit to be wary of their predictions. She and Clive had been embarrassed by too many erroneous leads in the past to feel much comfort in this undertaking.

As she stepped closer to the building, she could see Clive about thirty yards to her right, making his way forward. Twenty yards to Judy's left was the dog handler, Marvin, and Halo, a six-year-old Labrador retriever. Halo's snorting was getting on Judy's nerves, as was the warning from the task force about the potential of guard dogs at the junkyard.

Judy did not like large dogs, nor did she much like dogs in general. But large dogs of any sort made her uneasy since childhood, and she was

unnerved when Captain Rogers of the WaPol had mentioned the possibility of Rottweilers running loose on the property.

The sun was directly overhead as the team made its way toward the
building, and Judy could feel her breathing grow labored. Clive suddenly
raised his right arm straight up, and she stopped, as did Marvin and Halo.
Clive suddenly stooped down and pointed sharply to his front several
times, as if he was hacking a piece of meat with a cleaver.

Judy turned to look and felt her stomach swirl as she saw a huge dog at
full speed racing toward Marvin and Halo.

"Hey," Marvin yelled as Halo stood on her hind legs, trying to get
loose of the leash. In seconds the Rottweiler had closed on Halo, oblivious
to Marvin and Judy.

There was a huge swirl of dust, saliva and deathly guttural growls as
Marvin let Halo loose to fend for herself. Judy barely had time to turn back
toward Clive as he yelled her name.

Another two dogs were racing from the building towards the dog fight,
and as the duo drew close to the quarrel, one of the dogs veered off toward
Judy. She raised her gun. Whether it was her fear of dogs or the fact that
it was — strangely — more disquieting to shoot an animal than a human
with a gun, she froze. The chaos of the dog fight to her left and the sounds
of Clive screaming at her finally broke through, and she pulled the trigger.

The safety was still on, and before she could flick it off, the dog was
airborne.

CHAPTER 3

A man like this does not simply disappear," Dennis said. "There's no narrative. I can't find the storyline. Guy is a pro, lives and breathes clandestine street craft. He knows almost everything that's going on in Europe, has access to the NSA's intercepts, lives a boring life and then, on a Tuesday morning, fails to show up to work. No surveillance video of him being hustled into a car. Nothing. Poof."

Fred was sitting far back in his chair with one chubby leg pulled up so his foot rested on the chair seat. "Putin's folks wouldn't touch him, that's for sure," he said, running fingers through his thinning hair for the hundredth time. "I'm with you, Dennis. No story line. No links, motives, no nothing. That's why this is so much fun."

"Fun?"

"Well, yes. It's a wonderful puzzle. I bet we can bust it. You and I. We can do this."

"Jeez, Freddie — I'm going to call you Freddie, and I don't care if you don't like it — I like your enthusiasm. But look at the other reports. You folks followed his emails, his web browsing history, you patched together what little CCTV you could find from London authorities. You've got his two trips to Menwith Hill fully accounted for on video and electronically time-stamped."

"Yeah, that's what makes this so cool. It's like he's defying us to find him, you know?"

"I guess I can't hold this back any longer: what's up with Arnold and Menwith Hill? Why's the NSA all worked up about him?"

"What do you mean?" Fred asked.

"Come on, you know what I mean."

"No, I don't."

"You're not telling me something," Dennis said. "I can smell it. I've been at this game for a while. As we old timers say, 'this isn't my first rodeo.'"

"You know that's the one thing I've always wanted to do," Fred said. "Go to a rodeo. Wouldn't that be awesome? Guys riding these huge bulls. Cowgirls riding their horses. Stuff like that."

"So you're not going to tell me?" Dennis said.

"Nope."

"So much for teamwork."

"It's not about teamwork; it's about me keeping my job."

"Now that," Dennis said stretching his arms and yawning, "is something different, and I understand completely. I'm done for today, Freddie."

He pushed his pile of papers over to Fred, who nodded and gathered them into a large pile.

"You want to do something completely out of the ordinary on this case?" Dennis said.

Fred stopped fussing with the papers and squinted. "What are you talking about?"

"I'm saying do you want to step outside the logical framework of this 'puzzle,' as you call it, and do something obtuse and not expected? I'm talking about the unexpected. Something your boss — who is your boss anyway? — would never expect you to do?"

"You're getting weird on me, Dennis, and my boss is Stephen Manfort."

"So let's say we shake things up a bit and follow an instinct I have, which of course could lead absolutely nowhere and down another rabbit hole of nothingness. Or maybe it could be the thread of a lead we need."

Fred avoided eye contact and resumed shaping the paper pile. "You wouldn't get me in trouble, would you?"

"No, why would I do that?"

◆

The dog's slobbering mouth hit Judy right below her sternum, knocking her backward with such force that she experienced whiplash as the pistol flew from her hand.

Everyone, it seemed to Judy, had some secret fear, like being torn apart by a shark or being bitten by a spider or snake. One of her friends would only go swimming at Cottesloe Beach for two minutes at a time then rush out onto the beach, frightened as she was by sharks.

For Judy, it was fear of dogs. It was why she barely heard the two rapid shots from Marvin's Glock as he hit the dog in full flight.

As she and the dog fell to the ground, Judy shoved the animal off her with all the dignity of someone running from a swarm of hornets. She pushed, shoved, screamed, kicked and crawled away from the inert animal as the sounds of gunshots and animals kept ringing in her ears.

Run, she told herself. *Judy, run!*

Getting to her feet, she took off and was instantly bear-hugged by Clive. "Judy! Stop!"

She shoved him like she had shoved the dog, but he kept yelling into her face until she sagged, out of breath.

"It's all right, Judy," he yelled, grabbing his cheek where Judy's fingernail had cut him. "Stop!"

✦

"I don't like this," Fred said.

"Oh, calm down," Dennis said, pulling into the driveway. "You should get out of the office and into the real world more often. Step away from your algorithms and databases. Talk to real people."

"I can't believe you got me into this."

Dennis turned off the car, got out and walked to the front door of the modest center-entrance colonial house in Alexandria, Virginia, a suburb of Washington, D.C. He waited until Fred trudged up to join him before ringing the doorbell. It was early evening, and the glare of the porch light was blinding.

An attractive woman in her mid-forties opened the door.

"Mr. Cunningham?" she said.

"Yes, and this is my colleague, Mr. Kaczka. May we come in?"

"Of course, I've been waiting for you. I appreciate you being prompt — as I told you on the phone, I have to meet some friends for a birthday party."

"We won't take too much of your time," Dennis said.

Dennis and Fred settled into a couch in the living room while the woman sat in a large, wing-backed chair, facing them.

"Well, Mrs. Arnold," Dennis said, "again, we appreciate you taking time out to meet with us. I know you've been interviewed before on this subject."

"Five times," she said.

"Really?" Dennis said, looking at Fred. "Our records show only three interviews."

"Five interviews," she said. "You're number six."

"In that case, we'll get right down to business and make this as quick as possible."

"That would be nice," she said.

"Your former husband has gone missing, as you're well aware, and because of the nature of his position, it's caused quite a stir."

"So I gather," she said. Dennis guessed that she was perturbed by this intrusion. *Six interviews?* he wondered. *Who were the others? Why were only three recorded?*

"The files show that you and your husband were divorced almost four years ago, and that you remained in the house with your teenage children at the time, correct?"

She nodded.

"And that Mr. Arnold moved into an apartment in Crystal City?"

She nodded again.

"Did you ever visit him in Crystal City to see the apartment?"

"No, why would I do that?"

"Did any of the children visit him there?"

She frowned, thought for a second and said, "I'm not sure about that. No, I don't think either of them visited him there. Why do you ask?"

"His apartment was very Spartan, as if he never really lived there," Dennis said.

"Well, you know more about his work schedule than I do, but he traveled a lot. And then he was stationed for quite a while in London." Dennis watched as she stiffened at this last statement; her face tightened slightly, stretching her lips taut at the corners into a barely perceptible frown.

"We don't have a record of this, but did any of your children visit him in London?"

"Good lord, no," she said. "He was working all the time. Don't you remember? That's all you folks do is work."

"Yes, it's a difficult job, and very hard on family life," Dennis said.

She stared at him.

"The records show that he had no known hobbies, like tennis, golf, photography, things like that."

"His hobby was work."

"Is there anything else that you think we should know about him, in the way of his personal habits or interests that wasn't already disclosed? Anything?"

"No. You folks have asked every question known to mankind. And to be honest, I hope you'll forgive me, but it's getting tiresome. I have no idea where he is or why he disappeared. He didn't gamble that I know of, barely drank alcohol, refused to even take aspirin, so I don't think he had a drug problem. You know I haven't seen him in four years, and I have nothing to add. We didn't keep in contact, which is not unusual for divorced couples. I'm sure you know that."

Dennis sighed. "Well, I just have one more question then, and we'll leave you be."

Fred shifted on the couch next to Dennis, as if he was going to stand up.

"Mrs. Arnold, had your husband been involved in an affair? Were you aware of another woman in his life?"

Fred made a little breathing noise that sounded like a wheeze.

"Ha," she said. "Hardly. Not his cup of tea."

"Excuse me?" Dennis said.

"If you're asking me whether he had an affair with another woman, I'd say I don't think so. But maybe every woman says that about her ex-husband. And you'll have to forgive me, because I have to leave now."

✦

Judy refused medical attention and did her best to pass off the entire event as if it were normal to have a 110-pound dog knock you to the ground as one of your partners shot the animal dead in midair.

"No, really, Clive, please don't worry," she said. "I'm fine. It was just a bit of a shock, that's all."

All three Rottweilers had been killed, and Halo, the drug-sniffing dog, had its right hind leg badly mauled as well as an ear nearly torn off.

They had waited until another sniffer dog was brought in, along with more police, and they scoured the property looking for the Corolla. When they found it, the new dog found no trace of drugs.

Judy fumed about the errant bust.

"For God's sake, you'd think they'd get better informers," she seethed to Clive. "Three dead dogs, a fourth wounded dog, no drugs and a complete bloody waste of time."

Clive put his arm around her shoulder and gave her a hug. "Let's get out of here," he said. On the drive back to Perth, he chatted endlessly about a football match that weekend, pitting South Fremantle against rival Subiaco. Judy barely paid attention and at one point raised her hand and felt a bruise at the base of her sternum where the dog's snout had hit her.

✦

"Do me a favor, don't ever ask me to join you on one of your 'gut instinct' forays again," Fred said when they were driving away. "I'll stick to my algorithms."

"You didn't pick up on the affair question?" Dennis said.

"I picked up on the fact that she was pissed off at you. That's what I picked up."

"Something happened back there," Dennis said. "It was about another woman. I could see it in her face. I wonder if Arnold was having an affair. The reports we read distinctly rule out an affair, right?"

"They ruled out an affair, yes, but there was nothing she showed in her living room that suggests she knew he was having an affair," Fred said, staring at the blur of lights on Route 50. "You're reaching on this one. I can see why they warned me about your investigative style. It's nutty, Dennis."

"Did you get warned about me?"

"Of course I did," Fred said. "You think they were going to pair me up with Dennis the Menace without warning me?"

"What did they say, exactly?"

"I don't want to get into it, and slow down, you're driving too fast."

"She was lying about the affair," Dennis said.

"Prove it."

"I will, you'll see."

"After you prove it, I'll declare defeat and embrace the confrontational mastery of the great Dennis the Menace. Meanwhile, I withhold judgment."

"She's lying."

"Right. And I'm going to be late. You told me I'd be home by 7:30. I have a bridge match tonight."

"Bridge? Like in cards?"

"Yes, like in cards."

"You play bridge?"

"I just told you I have a match tonight, didn't I? I'm on a team, and they'll be pissed that I'm late. And all to confront a divorced woman about her missing husband. Sheesh."

"It's our job to ferret out the truth of what happened to Arnold."

"Ha. I think you're the ferret. Ferrets are part of the weasel family. Did you know that?"

"No, I did not. But it makes sense."

The pencil was driving Dennis insane. Finally, he said, "Louise, would you please stop drumming the desk! I can't even imagine what the song is in your head that you're following."

"Don't try to derail the conversation," she said.

"I'm not derailing anything, but it's irritating."

"I think it's irritating that you haven't filed a single report on the Arnold disappearance."

"Well, Marty, my old boss, didn't much care when I filed reports, so I guess it's just a habit."

"For the record, please file a daily brief on this case; that includes weekends. That clear?"

"Yes, it's clear. I just don't know what all the fuss is about."

Louise sighed, threw the pencil onto the desk and leaned forward. "I thought I told you that the subject was very sensitive and that there is suspicion here that NSA is not coming clean on this case. Didn't we go through that? When the IG asks me whether I have an update on the case, and all I have is an email from you saying something like, 'working on it,' what the hell am I supposed to say? 'Cunningham's too busy to let us know what he's doing, if he's doing anything at all.'"

"I told you I don't like being micromanaged," Dennis said. "Freddie and I are reviewing the case files as a first step."

"Let's get clear on one thing: Representative Barkley specifically requested you to investigate this case. You are the last investigator we would have chosen to be attached to this wrap-up. The IG didn't like it, I didn't like it, no one liked it. We're still trying to figure out why Barkley wanted you. We don't know whether he knew you'd make the case even more opaque by screwing it up or whether he actually thought you'd get somewhere. But given your work so far, my guess it was the former."

"That's not nice," Dennis said.

"After working with you for two weeks, that's my professional judgment. Either that, or Barkley wanted to ruin my career. And why he would single me out for special treatment is only a wild guess."

"Louise, I think you're taking this thing a little too far."

"And I think you're not taking this thing seriously enough," she said, her straight blond hair bouncing wildly as she sat back in her chair.

A twitter of anxiety hit Dennis as the adrenaline flushed into his bloodstream. This was the old, defiant Dennis rearing his ugly face and getting the typical reaction. Dr. Forrester had spent the better part of two and a half years trying to get him to own the depression and anger he struggled with over his family's dark past and his wife's death. And now, after being back to work for only a couple of weeks, he was trapped again in another self-defeating cycle with a new boss that played by a different set of rules.

Louise suddenly shot forward in her chair, tore a lined sheet of paper off a pad, and grabbed a ballpoint pen. She furiously drew a black circle about an inch wide and then scribbled back and forth to darken the circle. Then she pushed it across her desk at Dennis.

"See that?" she said.

"Yes."

"Do you know what that is?"

"I have a lot of theories, but I'm going to say no, I don't know what it is."

"That's a reset button," she said. "We're going to have to reset our relationship. This is not working, and unless you're committed to working with me versus against me, you'll have to report to someone else in OIG. Like Nick Campbell, or even Nancy Klonowitz. I can't work with you, and I'll tell the IG you'll need another manager."

"I'm not going to work for that dope Campbell, and forget Nancy. Will never happen."

"Then get your finger over here and push the goddamn reset button, because I'm ten seconds away from walking into the IG's office and telling him to move you to someone else."

"This is kind of dramatic, Louise."

She stood up and struggled awkwardly to get around her desk. "We're done. I'll send you an email telling you who to work with next. Good luck, you'll need it."

Dennis used his thumb to press down on the drawing. "I pushed it," he said.

"It's too late," she said. "Get out. We're done."

"For God's sake, Louise, sit down," Dennis said. "You win. I'm an asshole. I'm difficult to work with. Maybe getting shot in the head was bad for my self-esteem. But I can adjust. You'll see. Sit down, please, you're making me nervous."

Louise looked down at him, her face twisted into something approximating a mix of fury and exasperation.

"Please," Dennis said softly. "Sit."

She returned to her seat and stared at him. Both of them were drained, and the room seemed frozen as neither moved.

"I'm good with all of this," Dennis said. "I'll post daily reports. Just one thing."

She took a deep breath. "What?"

"Can I take this with me?" he said, pointing at the hand-drawn reset button. "Be a good reminder for me."

✦

When did Starbucks become the preferred meeting venue for people in the intelligence community? Dennis wondered as he sipped his coffee.

He could see Connecticut Avenue traffic through the plate-glass window and marveled at the earnest and patriotic energy in the nation's capital that kept people like him busy. Undeclared wars in the Middle East, drone strikes everywhere, Russians making life miserable for everyone, Iranian and North Korean nuclear saber-rattling — perfect conditions for espionage activities. And, of course, malfeasance, theft, murder and lying in the performance of those duties, which was the bailiwick of OIG at the agency.

Dennis looked up and saw Peter Harbaugh walk through the door. Several minutes later, the retired agency senior director settled into a chair next to him.

"Always good to hear from you, Dennis," Harbaugh said. "Margaret says hello."

"She's a great person," Dennis said. "Nice to see some agency marriages survive."

"Well, let's not make it sound too perfect; there were storms along the way," Harbaugh said. "And speaking of storms, how are you feeling? I can't even see a scar on your scalp."

"Fine; seems like a blur now, the whole thing. But I'm feeling fine and back at work."

"Everything going okay? You sounded a little stressed on the phone," Harbaugh said.

Dennis had a long relationship with his fatherly mentor, and though the elder statesman had spent his career in the clandestine operations side of the agency, their friendship seemed to satisfy both men. Dennis desperately needed someone to provide counsel on agency nuances and personalities. Harbaugh felt a fatherly interest in helping the mercurial Dennis survive the byzantine organizational fights. Plus, Harbaugh liked to feel the thrill — albeit at a retired distance — of the hunt.

"Well, my new boss is a hoot," Dennis said. "Very controlling. She seems pretty uptight, and we've already had a couple of run-ins. Kind of a pain, given this new case I'm on. Seems like a high-profile situation that's got everyone in fits. Barkley on the House committee picked me to do a wrap-up on a disappearance, which seems very strange. And they've got me paired with this goofball from NSA. I mean, the entire thing is just plain nutty."

"Barkley?"

"Yes, can you believe it? Asked for me specifically."

"Wait," Harbaugh said putting down his coffee, "this isn't about the London station, is it?"

"Um, Peter, I'm not supposed to be discussing this, and I think you know that."

"It is about the London disappearance then."

"Christ, Peter, how the hell do you know so much about what goes on there still? I'd love to know who you talk to. Anyway, I can't get into it, if you don't mind."

"Of course," Harbaugh said, picking up his coffee again. "But can I just say one thing?"

"I suppose."

"If it's this particular case that I referenced, I can absolutely say without hesitation that this is possibly the worst thing you could be doing. Can you reject it? Is it too late for that?"

Dennis put down his coffee and stared at his table partner. They looked at each other in silence, the sounds of people laughing and the hiss of a milk steamer providing a backdrop.

"I'm a little stunned," Dennis said. "You've never reacted like this to anything in our years of gossiping. In fact, I can see something in your face right now that I can't figure out. And I'm not confirming for a second that I'm involved in the London disappearance."

Silence again fell on the table.

Harbaugh reached into the inside pocket of his blue blazer, withdrew a fountain pen and then pushed a brown Starbucks napkin toward Dennis. He drew a circle about an inch wide. Then he drew a larger circle surrounding the first one.

"There are two governments at work in intelligence," Harbaugh said. "See this inner circle? This is the real intelligence organization, made up of about twenty thousand bureaucrats who live and breathe intelligence work. They control everything, including all of the assessments, findings, reports — everything, really — that the elected government sees."

Harbaugh moved the pen tip from the inside circle and touched the outer ring. "This is the elected government. When a new administration takes over, there are only about five hundred total appointed government positions. That's all. These folks here—" he pointed to the outer ring "— think they're in charge, but it's these folks here that are actually in charge. Do you see that?"

Dennis nodded, but he was not sure why Harbaugh was droning on about a state of affairs he already knew. "Um, okay."

"And right here," the elder statesman said, putting the pen tip in the gap between the inner and outer circles, "is where you are. You work for the bureaucrats that actually run the intelligence business, but you also work for the other group, the elected officials like Barkley who think that they run intelligence. So you're nowhere. Neither of these groups own you, nor do they trust you. You're all alone, and no one is invested in protecting you. The problem you ran into with the Australia case was just a tiny reflection of the clash between these two governments. Do you see that?"

"I guess so," Dennis said. "I mean, I appreciate the overview, Peter, but not sure what you're getting at. I've been doing this for a while, and I've been able to negotiate the space between these two entities pretty well. Or at least I think I have. And I don't know if this is a good thing, or a bad thing, but you're the second person who's drawn a circle for me recently."

"What's that about a circle?"

"Nothing," Dennis said. "Sorry, go ahead."

Harbaugh frowned. "I'm not getting through, am I?"

"Yes, you are, but I'm trying to say that I don't think any of this is new to me."

"Didn't your former boss try to kill you because you stumbled upon something this inner group didn't want you to find?"

"Yes, but that was a rogue operation, and it was a one-off disaster, not a reflection of the entire intelligence structure."

"Ah, well that's my point," Harbaugh said, screwing the cap back onto the pen and returning it to his blazer pocket.

"What point?"

"That you're wrong. It's a reflection of the entire intelligence structure. You've always been a believer that the system is inherently good at its core, and that problems occurred when a couple of bad people acted up. I mean, I loved your enthusiasm for digging out the miscreants, but it was always a tad naïve. This London thing is eminently more complicated than you could ever know, because it is precisely at the intersection of the two governments. Someone is going to get hurt on this one, and I don't want it to be you."

"Peter, one thing I've never been accused of is being naïve," Dennis chuckled. "Please don't misconstrue what I'm about to say, but perhaps you're overdramatizing the state of affairs? And I'm not confirming there is something going on at the London station."

"Of course," Peter said, smiling softly. "I'm not really in touch with folks there anymore."

Dennis knew that was not the case, but he let the moment pass. They sipped their coffees.

"What's up with this new boss thing?" Harbaugh finally said. "Who is he?"

"It's a she. Her name's Louise Nordland. I think she washed out in operations, and HR felt they needed a good balance of male/female, young/old, dumb/stupid in the OIG. So they gave her this position. I'll get through it okay."

"Nordland?"

"Yes, have you heard of her?"

"Wait. Is she the one who was injured in Lebanon several years ago? You know, the car bomb that Hezbollah set off at that safe house?"

"No, you must be mistaken. I don't think Louise was involved in anything like that."

"Well, if it's that gal, she's pretty decorated. Don't you remember the incident? I mean, it was in the papers. *Washington Post* covered it. Pretty tawdry, even by our high standards."

"I have absolutely no idea what you're talking about," Dennis said, draining the rest of his coffee.

"You must pull your head up out of OIG and look around every now and then," Harbaugh said, chuckling. "Does this Nordland woman have a limp?"

"Mmm, you know that's a good question. She does walk funny. I don't know if it's a limp. Seems to have difficulty navigating tight places. Almost thought she had a bad knee. Why do you ask?"

"Well, if it's the woman who survived the car bomb at one of our safe houses in Beirut, then you should be a little more respectful. That woman lost a foot in the blast and was buried under a ton of rubble for something like two days. Or that's what we heard. Everyone else was killed in the blast, including the station chief and two Mossad guys."

"That couldn't have been Louise," Dennis said.

"Well, maybe not. But if you ever meet the woman who survived that blast, tell her a Langley old-timer salutes her."

He often felt depressed when he was in a shopping mall, but strangely, he also longed to be there at other times. A shopping mall — especially the larger ones in the Washington, D.C. area — was an artificial city where masses of people congregated for the purpose of commerce. They offered the illusion of connecting with people, but they were in fact excellent venues to be alone without feeling alone.

Dennis sometimes ate dinner at the Cheesecake Factory in the Tysons Galleria in McLean, Virginia. The shuffling shoes of shoppers, the crying children and piped-in music muted his loneliness.

The last French fry had been consumed and a burger rested uneasily in his stomach when he raised his right hand and mock scribbled in the air for Sally, his favorite bartender. She nodded on her way by, and Dennis put his napkin on the bar.

A man sat down on the open stool to his left. "Hello there, Mr. Cunningham."

"Oh, hello," Dennis said as his expression quickly faded from inquisitiveness to alarm.

"You don't mind if I call you Dennis, do you?"

"No, that's fine, Representative Barkley. Dennis is fine."

"Well, please call me Dan, if you don't mind, Dennis."

"Sure, Dan. Is this an accidental meeting," Dennis said, scanning the crowd milling behind the bar, "or something more planned?"

"Oh, I think it's planned. My driver is waiting outside, but you were not hard to find. My chief of staff is behind us somewhere, probably shopping for his wife. I guess you like the hamburgers here at the Cheesecake Factory."

"Yes, I do. Thanks for asking." Sally dropped the bill off as she whisked by.

"So how's the investigation going?"

"What investigation?"

"Come now, Dennis. You know what I mean."

"No, I don't. Sorry, but we're not allowed to chat about work. I think you know that, sir."

"Please call me Dan."

"Okay, Dan, we can't talk about our work."

"Well, there's one project you're working on that I'm very interested in. You don't have to say a thing. Just listen. This project is very, very important to me. And I'm thrilled you're working on it."

Dennis reached into his back pocket for his wallet, pulled out a credit card, slapped it on top of the bill and pushed it forward.

"If at any time you think there's something going on that I should know about — something that's not quite right in the community, feel free to let me know. Please don't be alarmed that I'm reaching out to you like this. Your work on the Australia case showed that you have little patience for bad behavior, even if it's on our side. I like that. We elected officials govern from a profound lack of insight into your organization. This London thing is troubling. Something is not quite right. If you find yourself with information that is troubling and would like another set of ears, please reach out to me through my chief of staff."

Sally returned and slid the credit card and receipt to him. "See ya, Dennis," she said. "Can I get you something?" she said to Barkley.

"No, thank you."

"Bye, Sally," Dennis said, signing the bill and pocketing the duplicate.

"One more thing," Barkley said. "I can be very influential. You'd be surprised how I can throw my weight around. For instance, I could get you posted to Canberra, if that's what you wanted."

Up to this point Dennis had avoided eye contact with Barkley and showed his discomfort by staring at the row of bottles behind the bar. At the reference to Australia, he turned abruptly to face the congressman, but Barkley had already stood and disappeared into the horde of busy, happy shoppers.

CHAPTER 4

*S*hit, Dennis said to himself. *Shit, shit, shit. I can't believe it. What an idiot.*

He picked up his desk phone and dialed.

"Are you free right now? Good, I just need to stop by."

He poked his head into the doorway, and Louise waved him in.

Dennis sat and said quickly, "We have not come up with anything new on the Arnold case. This guy from NSA is pretty good, and he thinks the theory of a rogue unit from the Middle East is as good a theory as any. We would like to interview two people in the UK, though."

"Who?" Louise said.

"The chief of station in London and Arnold's contact at Menwith Hill in Yorkshire. Maybe after that we might be able to close this up."

"Well, that would be a welcome bit of news, given the rocky start to this investigation," she said. "I'll give Bill an update that he can pass along to Barkley's staff."

Dennis chose not to divulge his meeting the Barkley. He knew enough to leave this one alone. To bring it up with Louise would complicate his assignment immeasurably.

"Oh, and another thing," he said. "I didn't know you were the one who survived that car bomb in Lebanon."

She stared at him.

"I just wanted to say that you were pretty courageous. And I feel kind of stupid for giving you a rough time."

She stared at him long enough for Dennis to squirm.

"What if I told you that I'm not that woman," she said. "I have a twin who works in operations, Dennis. It was her that got injured."

He started to speak, then stopped, then started again. "I guess that I'm doubly stupid, then. Maybe I should just go right now. Anyway, that's the latest update on the London thing."

Dennis rushed out the door and was several steps down the hallway when he heard her calling him. He pushed his head back into the doorway.

"I don't have a twin."

"Oh," he said.

They continued to look at each other as Dennis felt his palms moisten with sweat.

"I suppose it was mean of me to say that I had a twin," she said. "But I felt like I had to get you back for being such an asshole."

"Well, I'd say you accomplished your goal pretty well," he said carefully. "I felt like a jerk when I first mentioned it then felt like a major jerk when you said you had a twin. Now I'm feeling completely jerkified, if that's even a word. But I can promise you one thing, Louise.""And what would that be?"

"I will never underestimate your toughness again. Nor will I misjudge your ability to seek vengeance."

"Well, we will get along just fine then," she said.

"Can I leave now?"

"Please do," she said.

✦

"It's just that you look like you need a break," he said. "We all need breaks now and then. We are fully staffed, and this seems like a good time to go on holiday."

Judy looked at her boss, Calvin Miller, and sighed. It was no use accusing him of patronizing one of the few female investigators in the AFP's Perth office. In fact, she was indeed drained and exhausted.

"Really, Calvin, I'm fine," she said. "I don't need a holiday; I need to stop snarling dogs from ripping me to shreds."

"A holiday would be brilliant," he said, ignoring her response.

She stared out the window behind Calvin and could see the top of the ornate brick façade of the West Australian Art Institute across the street.

"I suppose a brief holiday might be nice," she said.

"Oh, I nearly forgot. Interpol had a possible hit on a sighting for Voorster," he said.

She stiffened. "Where?"

"Well, it was a fake passport, but the face-recognition software picked it out as a possible match. The individual landed in Ireland about two months ago on a flight from Rome. It was a very poor match, but I thought you'd want to know."

"Still can't believe we didn't get him the first time around," she said.

"We tried, Judy. I don't think you have anything to worry about. I know he threatened you and your family. But he's been on the run ever since, if he's even alive. You broke up a very large drug ring and should be proud of that. We certainly are."

"Yes, but he is a very dangerous man, Calvin. He threatened to get back at me and my son. He's a cruel, dark man."

"I'm sorry I brought it up. I wanted to reassure you, not distress you. Please, just forget it and think about a holiday."

She nodded.

"Brilliant," Calvin said, standing. "I'm sure Clive can cover for you while you're away."

Judy lumbered back to her small office and fell into her chair. She was exhausted. And lonely. And maybe depressed. Her friend Cilla was right: she missed her Yank but needed to get over him so she could find someone new. An Aussie in Western Australia would be a good start. An American in Washington, D.C., had been a bad idea from the start, but what was a woman to do when she fell in love? She missed Dennis and wanted him dearly, but she was now aware that their halting and awkward phone conversations were a sign. Translation: the relationship was over. They should just finish it and say goodbye. The world was full of possibilities, but only if you looked for them. Wallowing in self-pity was unhealthy; even she knew that.

✦

He bolted forward in his chair as if there was an electrical charge in his seat.

"Come again?" Dennis said.

"I think it's time for us to stop meeting," Dr. Forrester said.

"Are you firing me? Can you do that? Therapists can't fire patients, can they?"

She smiled. "Dennis, relax. I'd like you to consider that we don't need to meet any longer, that's all. You've made incredible progress over the two-plus years we've been meeting. There's a time when therapy is no longer required, when the patient is self-sufficient and there's nothing more to be gained by meeting. You should feel good about this, not discouraged or alarmed."

Dennis sat back in his chair and winced. "Are you serious?"

"It's something I'd like you to start thinking about. I'm not talking about today being our last meeting; I'd like you to be thinking about it, that's all."

"So you think I'm healed? Is that it?"

"We don't talk like that," she said. "Healing is a process; it's not an end state. You're more than ready to deal with life's challenges without coming here to talk about them. We don't need to revisit your painful childhood, your wife's passing and even your recuperation from the shooting. You're well enough to handle things on your own. And you should feel good about that."

"You're firing me," he said.

"Dennis." She smiled. "Please. That's not true."

"That's what it feels like. And how am I supposed to deal with Judy now? You're the only person I can talk to about her."

"Ah, well, that's a perfect example of why we don't need to meet any longer. You know how to manage the situation with her. You're both adults. People figure out how to move forward. It's in the nature of things."

"I'm feeling abandoned," Dennis said. "You always encourage me to express myself and not bottle it in. So here I go: I feel like you're tossing me out."

"Like I said, Dennis, we should start talking about it. We don't have to rush."

✦

The flight was smooth from the start, and Dennis was thrilled, since turbulence unnerved him. In fact, the business class flight to London's Heathrow Airport would have been glorious except for the fact that he was seated next to Fred.

"So what are we supposed to ask the station chief that hasn't already been asked of him?" Fred said. "He's been interviewed a ton of times on this case. What do we do that's different?"

"Leave that to me," Dennis said. "We'll test his mettle. Just stick by me on this one."

"You're not going to submit him to one of Cunningham's famous interrogations, are you?"

"What are you talking about?"

"Come on, everyone knows about your methods. I'm sure the station chief has already been briefed on what to expect from you. You're famous for accosting people. Even when they haven't done anything wrong."

"I wish people would stop talking about this stuff," Dennis said. "It sort of takes away the surprise and makes it harder to tease out the good people from the bad when they know what to expect."

"Are you pouting now?" Fred said. "You look like you're pouting."

"I'm not pouting. I just wish people would stop talking about me so I could do my job."

"You're pouting."

"And you're a pain in the ass. Go read your in-flight magazine or watch a movie."

Fred laughed and started to push buttons on his personal TV screen. "I have a new bit of information," he said, adjusting the channels.

"What?"

"I wasn't going to tell you, because it's only a slight correlation, but you never know," Fred said.

Dennis turned to look at him. "Correlation? What are you talking about?"

"About Arnold. Just a theory, but I don't think you believe in the science of this stuff, so I was reluctant to mention it."

"Try me," Dennis said.

The flight attendant stopped and asked if either man needed anything.

"Single malt," Dennis said.

"Light beer," Fred said.

After she left with the order, Fred said, "What a great-looking woman. God, what I'd give to have someone like that pay attention to me. I noticed she was all smiles with you and kind of treated me like an eighty-year-old toad. You blue-eyed, rugged guys get all the action."

"Where the hell did that come from?"

"Look at me," Fred said. "Women just ignore me. I'm this balding little slob who has zero sex appeal. But I'm used to it, sort of. Resigned to it, more like. I bet you have a hundred girlfriends."

"No, I don't," Dennis said. "Just one. And she probably won't be my girlfriend for much longer. It's not as easy as you think to have someone you care about live so far away. And not for a minute do I believe you don't have a girlfriend."

"I tried all the online dating sites, and I used a photo from when I was in college. When I was thinner, you know, and had more hair. But when they see me, you can tell, they're like, 'Ugh, what a troll.' So I've given up. I just have buddies now."

Dennis frowned. "Buddies? Are you gay?"

Fred exploded in laughter as the flight attendant returned with the drinks. "It would be better if I was gay," he said, taking a huge pull of his beer. "I mean I thought about being gay, but I don't think you can think yourself into being gay. I like women. But they don't like me. So I have buddies."

Dennis shook his head. "Fred, it doesn't surprise me that you're from NSA, the center of the nerd universe. But you still haven't told me about your buddies."

"I have a movie buddy and a classical music buddy. The movie buddy is Cathy; she's sixty-six years old and is on my bridge team. Her husband died years ago. We're not attracted to each other, because, well, there's like twenty years separating us. But she likes movies, and I like movies, so we have this relationship based on going to dinner and seeing a movie. No sex, just conversation and a movie. And maybe a drink afterward. Do you have buddies like that?"

"No," Dennis said, taking a sip of his Macallan. "Never heard of the buddy thing. Kind of find it interesting. And the classical music buddy?"

"Oh, that's Jennie. She's really sweet. About fifty-five, I think, though you'd never know it. She retired from the Library of Congress like two hundred years ago or so. Never married. Lives on Wisconsin Avenue. We go to concerts together. Same thing. Dinner, concert, drinks afterwards. Great women. Just no sex, you know?"

"No, I don't know," Dennis said. "You mean you can't find a woman your own age to date?"

"Didn't I just tell you that? I don't have those blue eyes you've got, Mr. Casanova. You have no idea how lucky you are."

"I don't like this conversation, so can we go back to something else?" Dennis said. "What about your theory? You mentioned a theory."

"Oh, that. Yeah, well it goes like this: we can run massive amounts of data to look for patterns and correlations."

"So?"

"I asked for a run of Arnold's cell phone tower pings — you know, a tracking of his movements using his phone. This isn't tracking his conversations, it's tracking his physical movement using cell phone geolocation. And we ran his geolocation against all of the surveillance data we had in London. And there was an odd match, or a wisp of a match."

"Come on, Freddie. I don't speak 'algorithm.' Help me out."

"Yeah, okay. So MI5 and you folks track thousands of suspicious people in the UK. Some are suspected spies, some are friends of suspected spies, and some are friends of friends of suspected spies."

"Fine, I got it. So what?"

"We track analog follows and digital follows of all of these people."

"Analog follows?"

"Physical surveillance with agents; you know, old-fashioned tails with a human being following another human being. Very quaint stuff. All goes into a database. Got it?"

"Go on."

"Now this may be nothing—"

"Just tell me, for chrissakes!"

"All right, all right. So there were two proximity matches between Arnold and a Ukrainian named Pavlychko. MI5 has been following this guy Pavlychko for about three years. He's suspected of being connected to a guy who is connected to the Russian FSB, their intelligence service."

"Maybe it's the altitude or the single malt, or just you, but I have absolutely no idea what you're talking about."

"Right. It goes like this: Arnold was physically in the same location that Pavlychko was. Twice in the last six months. One was a Premier League soccer match, the other was a department store."

"Were they seen talking to each other?"

"No, nothing like that. Just in the same location. Pavlychko is not a priority target, so sometimes there's only a single tail, and sometimes guys like Pavlychko lose their tail. But Arnold and the Ukrainian were at the same soccer match at the same time. Second time was one week before Arnold disappeared. Harrods department store in London."

"That's it? Two matches? No evidence they met each other, just two proximity matches?"

"Yep. The probability of the two geocode matches in six months was extremely low. It's a small flag, not a big red waving flag. Could be random. But I've been told by one of the analysts that it's still a flag."

"I think you're a big flaming flag," Dennis said. "I'm going to try to sleep."

"Well, just thought I'd mention it."

"I have a headache. Stop talking to me."

"Roger that."

◆

"You really need to go see your father," Judy said, cradling the work phone against her shoulder. "It's been almost a year and you've never visited."

"Mum, he's in prison! For working with drug dealers!"

"Yes, I know that. But he sent me a letter saying he misses talking to his only child. He knows he's done something wrong, but you haven't written to him or visited him. He's lonely. He's lost his career, his family and his friends."

"You expect me to feel bloody sorry for him?"

"Trevor, don't talk like that. I'm just asking you to visit him. I can take you out of school and drive you. Or your grandfather can."

"No, I won't go."

She sighed. "Fine. I was passing along a request. I would just like you to think of it. Your father and I don't talk to each other, given the circumstances and the divorce. But he is your father."

"Can we please stop talking about it, Mum? I have to get to practice. Can't be late."

"Ta," she said.

"Love you, Mum."

She hung up and leaned back in her office chair. Her arms flopped down at her sides and her neck bent back so far that she stared at the ceiling.

Judy was not wild about pressing Trevor to see his father, but Cilla had told her that all sons need fathers, even incarcerated fathers.

"What are you afraid of?" Cilla had asked Judy. "That Trevor will become a criminal? Don't be daft. You said yourself that Trevor seems a little lost these days. Let him see his father and deal with that bit of tragedy, and then he'll move on."

And Judy had relented, albeit not without reservations.

Her mobile phone vibrated. The number was blocked, and she guessed who it was.

"Hello, Yank."

"Judy, how are you?"

"I've had better weeks. Lots going on. Copper stuff."

"I'm in London and was wondering if you could visit like I suggested? I can buy you a ticket. I know it's a long way to go for you. I need to talk to you in person. No more phone chats."

She sat up. "What's on your mind?"

"Us. You and I."

"Is it really necessary for me to fly to London for us to have the conversation?" She could feel her tone growing sharp and aggressive. Arguing was never her strong suit.

"Can you please come to London? I think we should talk face to face. These things are better in person."

✦

"I swear to God," Fred said, leaning over and whispering, "if you dare act like an asshole to Chandler, I'm going to walk out. I'm already friggin' nervous about sitting in with you."

"Stop it, Freddie," Dennis said. "I told you this will be quick."

"Quick and friendly, not quick and insulting."

"Then stay here in the waiting room, you baby."

"Did I tell you that I hate you sometimes?"

"Now look who's pouting," Dennis said.

"Okay, officially for the record: I hate you. I know you're going to do something stupid. I can feel it."

"Jeez, will you stop? I can see why you guys like sitting in front of computer screens instead of in front of people."

The door opened, and a surprisingly young man greeted them. "Please come in, gentlemen," Phillip Chandler said.

They entered a medium-sized office that had no windows and very little furniture.

Dennis and Fred settled into uncomfortable wood chairs facing the London station chief's spartan desk.

"So I gather this is yet another go-around regarding the Arnold disappearance," Chandler said, putting his hands together as if in prayer. "I guess I don't blame the folks in D.C. for feeling unfulfilled. Strange case, even for us."

Dennis and Fred had reviewed all of the prior interviews with Chandler and his staff; the results were redundant and useless. No one noticed anything unusual about Arnold's behavior prior to his disappearance; he was a veteran agent with a stellar reputation and a proclivity for signals intelligence and was the agency's designated NSA contact at the London station. Arnold's clearance level was Top Secret, with a separate clearance for TCI, or Top Level Compartmented Information because of his access to sigint from the NSA facility at Menwith Hill. In the parlance of the intelligence community, Arnold was cleared to have access to nearly every bit of secret information and in some cases had access to information not even available to Chandler.

Dennis and Fred, by contrast, did not have TCI clearance, and so, like the earlier investigators, they were blind to the details of some of Arnold's assignments, though a summary of his activities was available.

"We've thoroughly reviewed the prior investigations," Dennis said. "There are so few leads to follow, but I'm sure you know that."

"Yes, lamentably, that is true," Chandler said, looking down and reading from an open folder. "On June 14th he fails to show up to work, doesn't answer his phone. By 11:00 a.m. protocol called for a standard alert, and two agents were dispatched to his apartment. We have keys, of course, and they entered his apartment. He was not there, but his phone was still in its charger, his car keys were there, his clothes and personal belongings were left behind. No sign of struggle. We put out an instant alert, MI5 and MI6 were told and Arnold's picture was widely disseminated. All available closed-circuit TV in the area was requisitioned and analyzed. The night before he disappeared — and I know you've already seen this — it rained particularly hard in London and video results were poor and indistinct. In short there is one, slightly opaque possible match of Arnold walking down St. Thomas Street at 8:43 p.m. That's it, a single unconfirmed sighting."

Chandler looked up at the two investigators. "That's an outline of his last evening. I know that in this day and age, it may seem unlikely that a high-ranking agency employee can disappear like this, but there you have it. Gone. Pfft. Many of us have spent more time reconstructing Arnold's days and weeks prior to his disappearance than we have fighting our enemies here. Very frustrating. If we catch the bastards that grabbed him, I'd like nothing better than to be there to do some freelance waterboarding. I have a lot of frustration to vent. Emotionally, that is."

"I don't blame you," Dennis said. Chandler looked exhausted, he thought, with a mild redness to the whites of his eyes. His dark hair showed premature gray hints above his ears, and the corners of his eyes were creased into a permanent squint.

Chandler was cut from the same mold of all station chiefs, Dennis thought; taciturn, highly intelligent, obedient men and women who were often introverted and reserved. Even when pressed, they were rarely flustered, and the London station was at the epicenter of the intelligence vortex, with a resurgent Russian intelligence operation, a surprisingly clever Chinese presence and the myriad teams of agents from Eastern Europe and the Middle East.

"Just one question, really," Dennis said. "And by the way, we appreciate your time. I'm sure this has been difficult for the entire team here."

Fred swung his head to look at Dennis, suddenly confused about his companion's gracious pandering.

"Six days prior to disappearing, Arnold visited Menwith Hill. To the best of our knowledge — and this has been widely noted, of course — Arnold had no appointment at the Yorkshire facility that day. His usual contact there, Nathan Sorenstam, did not know he was coming, nor did he even see him. Arnold's visit to Menwith Hill was captured on video in its entirety, and he apparently did nothing but go to the bathroom, visit the reading room to see the most recent analysis of sigint between an Iraqi immigrant in the UK and a Syrian expat in Paris. Arnold spent ten minutes scanning the report, left the reading room and was tracked on video getting a bottle of water from the cafeteria, and then leaving the facility."

"Yes, that's pretty much what we have been told," Chandler said.

"So here's my question," Dennis said. "You're on record saying that you had no idea Arnold was going to visit Menwith Hill that day. He did not record it in his electronic calendar and did not tell you he was going there. Yet all of his other visits were recorded, and you knew about them in advance."

"What is the question?" Chandler said, sitting back in his chair. "I hear a statement, not a question."

"Are you sure you didn't know he was going to Menwith Hill that day? I was a little confused about your log book the morning of Arnold's visit. There was a fourteen-minute meeting vaguely catalogued in your log about a 'standard briefing.' Your log typically showed something titled a 'standard briefing' every morning at 8:30 a.m. local time. On this particular day you had a standard briefing at 8:30 a.m., then another one at 10:05 a.m. I looked at several months' worth of your log book, and you never had two mentions of a standard briefing on the same day. Ever."

Fred readjusted himself in the chair, the fabric of his slacks brushing the polished wood surface of the chair made the only sound in the room.

"Your point?" Chandler said.

"That you lied."

Fred cleared his throat.

"I lied?"

"Yeah, you lied. You knew he was going to Yorkshire that day. He told you when he met with you at five minutes past ten o'clock that morning."

"Mmm," Chandler said, focusing his dark brown eyes on Dennis.

Absolutely nothing happened for thirty seconds; Chandler stared at Dennis, Dennis stared back at Chandler. Fred stared at Dennis, then back at Chandler, then back at Dennis.

Finally, Fred said, "Do you have any water? I'm thirsty and would love a glass of water." To add to his discomfort, Chandler said nothing and continued to stare down Dennis.

"Water?" Fred said. "The drinking kind?"

"Well, thanks again for meeting with us today," Dennis said. He stood up, and Fred sprang from his chair as if catapulted.

Chandler neither said a word nor moved a muscle as the two men left his office. They took the elevator down to the first floor, signed out in the lobby then showed their IDs to two men near the front entrance of the building in Margate.

"I hate you," Fred said. "I really do." But Dennis was not listening, busy mulling over their visit.

✦

The drive north was dreary and depressing, and Dennis guessed it was the famous English winter weather. The moment they hit the M1, it started to rain, smearing the view of the countryside and making Dennis feel claustrophobic. The fact that they were driving on the left side of the road unnerved him further.

Fred had stopped talking early in the trip.

"I think you're being passive-aggressive," Dennis said.

"I'm not talking to you," Fred said.

"My therapist says that particular behavior is called passive-aggressive."

"Leave me alone."

"I guess I don't blame you," Dennis said, looking at his watch. "How long is this drive going to take?"

"I already told you, about four and a half hours. You said you didn't want to fly, so here we are."

"Do you know why people are passive-aggressive?" Dennis said.

"Yes, because they hate the person they're sitting next to."

"No, it's because they are uncomfortable expressing their true feelings of anger. It's easier to let the silence express those feelings. You get it? That's what my therapist said. Or my soon-to-be former therapist said."

"Oh, is he fed up with you too?"

"Actually, it's a she. Yeah, she might be fed up with me, now that you mention it. But the official reason is that I'm better and don't need to go in for regular tune-ups."

"I'd be tempted to file a complaint with the licensing board that she's not competent to provide mental health services if she thinks you're better. Just sayin'."

Dennis laughed and idly looked at his phone. "I'll have to tell Dr. Forrester that. She'll get a kick out of it."

They drove on in silence. until Dennis's phone rang.

"Hey, Judy. How are you?"

Fred took a sideways glance at his companion.

"When? Perfect. Yes, yes. At the St. George. Room 1201. No, this is not going to interfere with my work here. No, not at all." He shot Fred a glance. "Yes, we do need to see each other face to face." Dennis chatted on for another five minutes and then hung up.

Fred said, "So what's up with Judy?"

"Ah, she's the girlfriend. Lives in Australia. We met on an investigation. She's Australian Federated Police, sort of their FBI."

"And?"

"And what?"

"Your voice sounded nervous, and excited at first, and then kind of let down or something at the end."

"Remind me not to have phone conversations with you in earshot. I think you're interpreting things that aren't there. It was just a conversation."

"Now look who's being evasive. I thought your therapist wants you to be more open with your feelings."

Dennis frowned. "I thought you didn't want to talk."

"I changed my mind."

"I'm not sure I want to talk about her."

"Well, if you remember, Casanova, I don't have girlfriends. Last time I had a real girlfriend was in my senior year of college. Let's just say I'm basically jealous, and if nothing else, I'm curious about relationships. I don't get to have them; you do."

"Stop calling me Casanova."

"I will if you tell me what's going on with this Judy. You sounded happy, then sad. All in the same conversation."

Dennis sighed. He looked out the left side of the car as more dark-green fields blurred by in the soft rain. "Okay, it's like this. We met on an assignment in Australia. She hated me at first."

"Gee, that's surprising."

Dennis turned sharply.

"Totally uncool thing to say. Sorry. Go on."

"Like I said, she hated me at first, but then we both went through a lot of crazy stuff in our personal and work lives. And we kind of found each other. Not entirely sure how it all came together, but it did. And we helped each other when we needed it most. To be honest, she saved my life."

"How the hell did she do that?"

"It's a long story, and I can't talk about it. I had to sign one of those special nondisclosure forms the agency has. But let's say she was at the right place at the right time. And knew how to handle a Glock."

"No shit."

"Yeah. For real. Saved my sorry ass. I took a round right here," Dennis said, pointing to his right temple. "Grazed me and put me out of action for a while."

"No one told me that," Fred said. "Not in any reports I've seen. So what's the problem then with this Judy?"

"Well, she can't leave Australia right now because her son is in school there, and her ex-husband is in prison — don't ask. And she sort of thought I was going to move there to be with her, but I was, well, recuperating. Then when I got back to work, I got thrown into this case."

"What's that got to do with Judy?"

"Good question. Doesn't have anything to do with Judy, except that I've been stalling about moving to Australia. She can tell it. And if I'm not moving to Australia, and she's not moving to the States, then I don't think we have a valid relationship, if that's the right term."

Fred turned the wipers up to high speed as a large truck passed them in a hurricane of wind and water.

"Gee, I'm not exactly the expert on these things," Fred said. "Maybe you should just let it go and be honest with her."

"You sound like my therapist."

"Is that what she says?"

"Something like that."

"So is Judy coming to London?"

"Yeah, next week. I'd appreciate it if you didn't say anything, unless somebody asks. Won't interfere with this project."

"What are you going to tell her?"

"I think we both know that it's over."

Fred drove north into the rain, the windshield wipers and water spray from the M1 were the only sounds for a while.

✦

By the time they turned right onto B4561, the weather had cleared and they could easily see the huge, dimpled, golf ball-shaped antenna domes in the distance. The sight even took Fred by surprise.

"God, there must be at least thirty domes," Fred said. "And look, there's a flock of sheep. Weird."

"You've never been here before?" Dennis said.

"Nope. I'm sure you know that this is one of the most closely guarded sites in the world. It sits here in the middle of the English countryside. Locals know what goes on here, and there are regular demonstrations at one of the entrances by some loonies, but by and large, this place is a self-contained NSA listening post. Got their own baseball fields, bowling alley, crap like that."

Fred pulled the car onto the side of the country road next to a bank of hedges. He put the car in park and turned toward Dennis. "So here's the drill: you shut the hell up when we're in there talking to Sorenstam. You got that? Nothing from you; no confrontational interrogations, no wise-ass stuff. This is NSA territory, and I'm the investigator from the NSA's Office of the Inspector General. You're from OIG at Langley. This is my turf. Are we clear on this?"

Dennis crossed his arms. "You're kidding."

"Nope."

"I can't ask a single question?"

"Nope. Otherwise you can get out here and wait for me. Just don't bother the sheep."

"Freddie, come on. What if I think you're missing something?"

"You can tell me what I missed later. I'm deadly serious about this."

Dennis opened the car door, got out and leaned in. "You sure about this?"

"Close the door, I'm late. Like I said, leave the sheep alone."

"God, you're such a pain in the ass," Dennis said, sitting back in the car.

"Give me your word."

"Yes. I agree. Won't say a damn thing. Just hope you know what you're doing."

"So help me, if you go back on your word, I'm going to stand up and ask Sorenstam for security. And by the way, you have no idea how serious they are about security here. So once I call for it, you will be escorted to a clean room, and if you thought I was kidding about an anal probe earlier, wait till you see what they'll do to you in that room. Meanwhile, I will have finished my interview and be waiting for you in the car. Maybe eating a cupcake from their cafeteria. And drinking a Diet Coke."

"Got it; can we go now?"

They drove down several country roads until they came onto a small roadside sign with the words "RAF Menwith Hill, Nessfield Gate." Pulling up to the brick guard shack, an RAF policeman packing a submachine gun asked for their identification cards. He consulted a list on a clipboard and waved them five feet farther ahead to a glass-enclosed guard station. They went through the same drill and were told to drive to a small parking area after the metal gate was opened. At the parking area, the car was thoroughly inspected by four men in blue overalls, one of whom slid under the car on a rolling sled. Dennis and Fred were told to walk to an adjacent building.

Inside, they were again asked for identification and were directed to a small room. There they were physically searched while being monitored by several CCTV cameras.

Dennis went through a metal detector, was wanded by two different devices, asked to empty his pockets of everything and told to take off his shoes, his belt and watch. His phone had been turned over already. After his shoes were scanned separately, all of his personal belongings except his eyeglasses were put into a clear plastic bag with his name on it.

He joined Fred in a meeting area, and they were told their car was to be parked a hundred yards away in a special parking lot, and they would be driven to their destination in a golf cart.

"Is all this really necessary?" Dennis said while they were driving to the parking lot.

"Yes. Try not to let it bother you. Just remember: you'll be under electronic surveillance while you're here, including audio and video tracking. Everything you say — and you promised you wouldn't say a goddamn thing — will be recorded. Even a whisper. Got that?"

"What if I burp?"

"Then they'll shoot you."

"Okay. I got it. Let's get going."

CHAPTER 5

Sorenstam was a very ordinary-looking man in his mid-fifties. His gray-flecked brown hair was cut short, Dennis noticed, in the habit of former military men. He wore a gray fleece vest over a polyester long-sleeve white shirt.

"So Arnold never asked for you on his last visit?" Fred said. The interview had been going on for forty-five minutes, and Dennis was unimpressed with his companion's questions. Still, he felt like he owed it to Fred to remain silent. Plus the anal-probe warning thing bothered him.

"No," Sorenstam said. "You've seen the records, I assume. He said he had an appointment with me, and it's recorded on his intake forms that day. But he never stopped by, never called me, and as far as I was concerned, he was never here."

"But isn't it protocol that once he checked in at the gate and reported he was meeting with you, that you would have been called and told your visitor was here?"

Dennis was surprised by Fred's question and looked closely at Sorenstam.

"Yes, that is normal protocol, but he'd been here so often that security just let it ride."

"That is a serious breach of security," Fred said. "None of the earlier reports mention this, which leads me to believe that there was not a thorough investigation of Arnold's last visit here."

Why the hell didn't he tell me about this? Dennis wondered.

For the first time since the interview started, Dennis noticed Sorenstam's demeanor change from attentive but bored to attentive and agitated.

"That has been corrected," he said. "The man responsible for not alerting me has been sent home."

"Why didn't it come out in the earlier interviews?" Fred asked.

"It might have, I just can't remember. I don't have access — as you well know — to reports from the earlier investigations."

"Okay, let's move on," Fred continued. "Arnold was here for thirty-three minutes. His every move was recorded, and I know you must have gone over it a hundred times."

"Maybe a thousand times," Sorenstam said.

"According to the reports we've seen, Arnold drives all the way up from London in four and a half hours or so, goes through security, and instead of seeing you, he goes to the men's room in Building 4C, checks into the reading room there, spends ten minutes reading sigint, then stops by the cafeteria and picks up a bottle of water and leaves the facility for a long drive back to London."

"That is correct," Sorenstam said, shifting in his seat and looking bored again.

"Cunningham and I do not have the appropriate clearance to read the sigint that Arnold perused that day, but we have been told that we'll get the clearance soon. Have you looked at the data he was reading that day?"

"Yes."

"Anything jump out at you that you want to share with us? Reports show it was a routine telephone intercept he looked at."

"When you get clearance to read the intercept and have an analyst explain the context of the phone call, then you're free to reach your own conclusions."

"I'm asking about your conclusion," Fred said.

"My conclusions are irrelevant," Sorenstam said.

"Not to me."

Dennis watched as Sorenstam struggled to control his anger. Dennis was more than a little impressed with Fred's persistence.

"My own personal judgment," Sorenstam said, "was that the intercept was important information regarding the geolocation of a person being targeted by a unit at Langley. Again, if you insist on pressing me on this issue, I would have to say the sigint he read that day was important. But I think everything we do is important."

A brief period of silence fell on the room as Fred looked at a small notepad in his lap.

"Did Arnold ever complain to you about being watched or feeling like he was in danger for any reason?"

"We didn't have the kind of relationship where he might divulge that," Sorenstam said. "I'd check with his station chief on that kind of information."

"One of the theories floating around is that a rogue unit from the Middle East snatched Arnold, presumably for the intel he had or just to be assholes. What do you think of that theory?"

"I don't think anything; that part of the business is not my bailiwick. Why don't you ask your partner there about what Langley thinks happened to him?"

Dennis was about to speak, but he glanced at Fred and saw his "Don't-you-friggin-dare-talk look" and shrugged instead.

"Does this guy talk?" Sorenstam said.

"I don't want him to talk," Fred said. "He can be a real asshole, and I'm trying to save you."

Sorenstam laughed for the first time. "You serious?"

"Yep. Best let sleeping dogs lie," Fred said.

"Now you've got my curiosity. What can someone from Langley say or do to rile us up here at NSA?"

"You'd be surprised. Can we continue, please?"

"No, I'm serious. These jerks from Langley are not equipped to know how or what we do; all they can do is take our intel and screw it up. How is this guy any different from the other idiots we have to deal with there?"

Fred's cheeks suddenly developed small red circles the size of silver dollars, and Dennis realized he was getting angry, which impressed him.

Fred turned to Dennis. "Do you have any questions for Mr. Sorenstam here?"

"You're going to let me talk?"

"Do I have to ask again?"

Dennis looked back at Sorenstam. "Okay. I have just two questions. First, given the voluminous — and boring, I may add — reports I've seen on this case, including Arnold's phone activity, his geolocation tracking, his every digital move in the past two months here, why is it that you guys don't know what happened to him? I mean, my understanding is that right now your analysts and programmers here are tracking text messages between jihadists in Afghanistan talking about their girlfriends or hedged trades they made on the New York Stock Exchange, but you don't know what the hell happened to a very important intelligence official right in your own backyard. Why is that?"

Sorenstam looked at Fred. "I see what you mean, they are assholes over there."

"Well, you started it. And by the way, could you answer his question?"

"No, I can't answer his question, because as I stated, I don't know what happened to him or why he stopped by here for thirty-three minutes that day. You guys at Langley may think we have all the answers here, but we don't. And neither do you."

"We have women at Langley, so it's not appropriate to say 'you guys,'" Dennis said.

Sorenstam glared at Dennis and was about to speak when Dennis interrupted.

"And my second question is: Can we see the video of Arnold's visit? It's not in the reports."

✦

The monitor was a large flat-screen in a small room with a laptop to the side. Dennis, Fred and Sorenstam looked at the blank screen while a fourth man typed into the laptop.

"Got it," the man said.

A black-and-white video flickered on the screen, which was time-stamped in the top right corner. The camera looked down at a sharp angle and showed Arnold driving up to the gatehouse; a video splice occurred, and Arnold was now going through the security inspection building, being wanded, removing his personal belongings and being inspected closely. Another splice occurred, and Arnold could be seen in the men's room going into a stall and closing the door. The angle of the camera prevented a view into any of the stalls.

"Why are these videos in black and white? You can't spring for color? Looks like it's circa 1928."

"Too much data packed into color video; black and white is fine for our purposes. Remember, we have to store all of this crap."

"I thought you had terabytes of data storage," Dennis said.

"Ha, we have petabytes of data," Sorenstam said. "But we're not going to waste it on color video."

Dennis had noted the time stamp when Arnold went into the stall; after three minutes Dennis said, "Jeez, guess he had to really go."

"It was a four-hour drive from London," Fred said.

When Arnold came out of the stall, six minutes and forty-two seconds had elapsed. In the video he washed his hands laboriously and then exited.

The next splice showed Arnold entering the reading room; he sat down in the small room with his back to the camera. He typed a few items into the computer and then settled down to scroll through the contents.

"What was he typing in just then?" Dennis asked.

"Password," Sorenstam said.

"You sure?"

"Yes, we track key strokes. It was his password."

Even though Arnold spent ten minutes in the reading room, Dennis realized after the first four minutes that nothing was happening. Arnold sat with his back to a video camera barely moving.

"Is this it for ten minutes?" Dennis asked.

"Pretty much," Sorenstam said.

"Does he take any notes?" Fred asked.

"You can see he has a notebook with him, but he does not appear to write anything down."

"Did he take notes on his prior visits?" Fred asked.

"Sometimes."

"Can we speed up to the end?" Dennis asked.

Sorenstam nodded to the man on the laptop and the motion on the screen sped up until the time stamp showed ten minutes had elapsed.

With less than a minute left in the reading room, Arnold suddenly stood up and hunched over his notebook. Because the camera was behind him and elevated, his body obscured his actions.

"What was he doing just then?" Fred asked.

"He was logging out."

"Standing up and logging out?" Fred repeated. "When he logged in he was sitting down. Why would he stand up to log out?"

"If you find him, ask him that question," Sorenstam said.

On the screen Arnold finally turned toward the door to his left with the notepad in his right hand and left.

The next splice showed him walking down a hallway, then another hallway into a crowded cafeteria. Another splice showed the same cafeteria from another angle, and Arnold's body was identified with a white circle to show where he was in the room. He purchased a bottle of water then left. More splices showed him walking down halls, then retrieving his belongings, then driving away from the front gate.

The screen went blank, and Sorenstam nodded toward the door and the video operator left the room and closed the door.

"Who assembled the video into a single file?" Fred asked.

"Myself and two other people. We did it together, and there is a record of our work. You're welcome to review it."

"No thanks," Fred said. "I think we're done here."

✦

"He seemed like a warm and fuzzy guy," Dennis said as they drove south in a light drizzle.

"Shouldn't be too harsh with these folks," Fred said. "Their lives are pretty dull, and we can't get anyone else to do this stuff. You think dragging your wife and kids to live on a locked-down RAF base in the middle of the English countryside is a great duty assignment?"

"No, I guess not. Anything jump out at you back there?"

Fred said nothing for a few moments and then shrugged. "Not sure."

"Not sure about what?"

"Not sure of anything."

"Come on."

"I'm confused, that's all. Think we're missing something. Just don't know what it is."

"When you find it, would you let me know?"

"Sure thing, kemosabe."

"Hey, I told you not to—"

"Yeah, yeah, okay. You sure are sensitive for an agency guy who gives everyone else shit."

Dennis fell back into his seat and watched the gloomy and wet English countryside slide by in a long, continuous depressing smear. It had been a while since he had fallen into one of his funks, but the dreary weather and diffused light were wearing on him. And the fact that Judy was going to show up in a few days further agitated him. His response in circumstances like this was to grab on to work and dive in so deep that he couldn't possibly be depressed or anxious.

"What was it you said about that Russian guy? You said something about a correlation?"

"Pavlychko. He's Ukrainian."

"He's in London?"

"Yes. Under surveillance. But that was just a correlation of geolocation points. You know, same place, same time stuff."

"You said something about probability."

"An analyst friend suggested the probability of them being in two locations in the same timeframe was statistically very low. So the two matches are higher than pure chance, but it's all probability. In reality it doesn't mean much. Don't know why I mentioned it to you. Don't focus on that."

"Let's visit Pavlychko."

"I think one of those radar domes back there fried some of your brain cells. We can't visit him. He's under surveillance by MI5."

"Who gives a shit if he's being watched? We'll just show up at his house and freak him out."

"Freak him out? You're freaking me out."

✦

Judy settled back into her seat and looked out the window as the plane taxied at Perth International Airport. It was a warm spring day, and she worried whether she'd brought the right clothes for the gloomy London weather. She already dreaded the layover in Singapore, and knew she'd look like a rag doll by the time the flight was over.

If she kept thinking about the clothes, she would stop thinking about Dennis and how they were going to settle their relationship. She bit the inside of her lip and for the hundredth time vacillated between just wanting the relationship to be over and just wanting to be in Dennis's arms again. The former thought was the mature wish; the latter was the romantic but childish wish.

She sighed and pressed her forehead against the cold window as the jet screamed down the runway.

CHAPTER 6

'm afraid it's going nowhere," Dennis said. "There's no thread. Can't find the story line that pulls it together. Might be a random criminal act that's totally unrelated to his work life."

"How much longer are you going to be there?" Louise asked.

"Maybe a week; no longer than that."

"What should I tell the IG?"

"Well, you can say that we met with the folks at Menwith Hill and are going to revisit some people at the London station."

"Okay. You're not holding anything back, are you?"

"No. Nothing substantial."

"What does that mean?"

"It means that I don't have anything solid, just a hundred dumb hunches. And I don't think you want to hear all my dumb hunches. It'd be like watching one of those French movies without the subtitles. Wouldn't make any sense."

"Please don't start this crap, Cunningham. Give me one of your hunches."

"All right. Chandler. Something's up with him. Don't know what it is, but he's holding something."

"Maybe he's just trying to save his career; this is not good thing to happen on his watch, you know."

"No, I don't think it's that. Feels like we're not getting the story."

"What story?"

"You know what I mean, Louise. You were in operations for years. You know what I'm talking about. He's probably a good guy, but he's not going to let OIG in on his little secret, because he doesn't have to. I mean, we'd like him to believe he's required to tell us, but they lie to us all the time. I just get the feeling he's sitting on something. And it's the kind of lie that he's okay with, if you get what I'm saying. He's not authorized to tell the IG, and he's just following orders. It's a hunch."

Silence.

"Louise?"

"I'm thinking."

"Let me in on it, maybe?"

"No."

Silence.

"Okay," she said. "Got to go."

"Um. Bye then."

◆

The bar was loud with early evening drinkers pouring out into the streets from the service industries powering the London economy. East Europeans, Africans, Germans, Chinese and even Yanks had settled into the booming city to fuel its growth as one of the world's financial powerhouses.

"I'm not going to give you his address, so stop asking for it," Fred said, hunched over his beer. "You're talking like a crazy man."

"Well, I'll get it through my own channels then," Dennis said.

"And what do you intend to do, even if you do find out where he lives?"

"I'll just leave it up to my intuition to guide me," Dennis said, waving his left hand dramatically.

"I think you've had too many single malts, my friend."

"I'm going to head over there tomorrow; come if you want or stay in your little itty bitty hotel room and surf the web for pick-up bridge games in the neighborhood."

"I hate you most of the time; like 99.9 percent of the time."

Dennis slapped Fred on the back. "You don't hate me. You just don't want to get outside your comfort zone. As long as you have a computer screen in front of you, you're comfortable. But people in front of you, well, not so much. People to people; that's where the real truth comes out, not with algorithms. There's too much reliance on that stuff, and you know it."

"Oh, please, let's not take on the entire intelligence establishment, if you don't mind. If we didn't scrape this stuff out of the digital universe, we'd be in much worse shape, believe me."

"So why don't you join me then tomorrow? You did a good job — though I hate to admit it — on the Menwith Hill guy. I was impressed. Thought you were going to play footsies with him, but you got him going there."

"You think so? Honestly?"

"Yes, you were pretty damn good. My type of interview."

"You don't think I was too hard on him?"

"Hell, no!"

"You're just saying that so I'll go with you tomorrow."

"Never crossed my mind."

"And you might be drunk," Fred said.

"Not true. After an eight-plus hour drive into sheep country, I'll admit to being tired. But drunk, no."

"Well, I still think it's nuts to confront the Ukrainian."

"I told you, stay here," Dennis said. "It'll be fine."

"Suppose it wouldn't hurt. And so what if we'll be watched by MI5? We can explain it."

"Fucking A, we can."

"Maybe you are drunk."

"Fucking A, I'm not."

✦

The dog sank its teeth into her forearm first, then her elbow. It wasn't the pain that bothered her or the saliva-frothed teeth clamping down; it was the evil of its large black eyes that drove her insane with fear.

She awkwardly jerked her right arm away from the dog and in the process slapped her tray table, which was down.

The woman sitting next to her was snoring slightly, so Judy was relieved at not being observed in a nightmare.

She sat up and tried to stretch away the awful vision of that dog. The lights had dimmed throughout the huge jetliner, and she could see the random signs of wakefulness: a flickering movie being watched here or a book being read there.

Reluctantly, she turned on her overhead light and reached for a book she had brought along. It was a mystery by a Norwegian author whose main character, a police inspector, seemed haunted by both a villain and his own frailties. She liked its authenticity.

✦

They took a cab until it was a block away and got out.

Dennis told Fred that he could probably pick out the car the surveillance agents were sitting in, watching Pavlychko's house. Dennis guessed the surveillance on the Ukrainian was more for show than substance. More serious surveillance would not be noticeable. Public surveillance was designed as a nuisance; you know we're watching you, and we know you know we're watching you.

Fred said nothing in the cab, and Dennis guessed he was having second thoughts but was too embarrassed to tell him. Dennis had developed a strange fondness for his frumpy fellow investigator, and although it was completely out of character, he was concerned about him.

So he stopped walking.

"Got an idea," he said, grabbing Fred's arm. "You stay here. Maddox Street is the next corner. I'll go up to the front door by myself and ring the doorbell. He's probably not even at home, and there's no use two of us showing up on the surveillance report and having to explain ourselves when the Brits complain. Just stay here."

"Nope. Came this far, and I'm not backing out. You said yourself last night that I spend too much time in front of a computer, and I think you're right. Plus I trust you. Don't ask me why I trust you, but I do. So there it is. Let's go."

Dennis considered arguing more vigorously, but he liked the sudden spunk his pal showed. *And hell*, he thought, *isn't this work a contact sport and not a video game?*

"Let's go then," Dennis said.

They turned the corner on Maddox Street and made their way slowly down the opposite side of the street toward the townhouse. Dennis scanned the street for parked cars and vans but could only see a small white utility van ahead. As they passed the van, Dennis looked in and saw two older gentlemen in the front seat. The man behind the steering wheel had his head back and appeared to be sleeping; the other man, closest to the sidewalk, was reading a newspaper.

Dennis and Fred crossed the street, walked up a half-flight of stairs, and Fred pushed the button next to a huge, ornate, glossy red door. They waited three minutes before Dennis rang the doorbell again, but this time he pushed it in a strange pattern of ring-pause-ring-pause-long ring.

"Why'd you do that?" Fred whispered.

"To get his attention. He'll think it's a friend or a prostitute."

"Very funny."

Inside, Dennis could hear the heavy thud of footsteps and then an explosion of mechanical sounds from locks being turned and hinges swinging. The door opened, and behind it stood a very large man, perhaps six feet three inches, with broad shoulders and a block-shaped head with longish brown hair. He was barefoot and wore an old pair of sweatpants and a white tee shirt.

No one spoke for several seconds.

"Who are you?" the man said in heavily accented English. "What you do want?"

Dennis had known what he was going to say all along but had not told Fred. And he was going to say it to whoever opened the door, whether it was a valet, a girlfriend or Pavlychko himself.

"Hello. We're looking for Richard Arnold. He's an American official who's been missing for a while here in London, and we thought you might be able to help us."

Fred's head swiveled sharply toward Dennis then swung back to look at the man in the doorway.

"Who?" the man said.

"Arnold. Richard Arnold. An employee of the Central Intelligence Agency."

For the first time, Dennis noticed the chill London air, and he reflexively hunched his shoulders inside his khaki-colored raincoat.

The three men looked at each other; from the interior Dennis could hear a television announcer. A large lorry passed behind them in the street, creating a momentary crescendo of sound.

Dennis did not like the fact that the man in front of them kept passing his eyes from Dennis to Fred, then back again. Was he memorizing their faces? Looking for a joke? Gauging their sincerity? What was he doing?

And then, in slow motion, the man closed the door but did not take his eyes off Dennis.

"Let's go," Dennis said, and they crossed the street and walked by the two men in the van, who were both staring.

Dennis waved at them.

"Stop it," Fred said. "If they're who you think they are, why piss them off? Maybe no one's watching this guy's house, and these jerks are utility workers. Sheesh, can't believe I just did this."

"You were great," Dennis said. "I liked the way you stared him down."

"Shit, I didn't stare him down; he pretty much made me shit my pants. Did you see those eyes?"

"He wasn't that bad."

"And thanks for being subtle with your questions," Fred said. "'Hey, Mr. Ugly Ukrainian, have you seen our missing CIA employee? We'd really appreciate it if you could help us out.' I don't know what I thought you were going to ask the guy, but I didn't expect you to be so direct. I mean, what was the point of that?"

"Just wanted to see how he responded. No need to dance around."

"Well, how did he respond, in your careful judgment, being a professional pain in the ass that you are?"

"Thought he was pretty pissed off."

"Pissed off because he didn't know what the hell we were talking about, or pissed off because he knew exactly what we were talking about?" Fred said.

"The latter, not the former."

"You could tell that just by his response?"

"Yes, that's what I'm saying," Dennis said.

"I find that hard to believe."

"Well, don't believe it then."

They walked for ten minutes until they found a cab to hail, during which time the chilled air continued to penetrate Dennis's thin raincoat. He shivered.

As they got into the cab, Fred said, "Now that you mention it, I think I like computer screens better than knocking on the doors of Ukrainians living in London."

Dennis laughed. "Come on, you did great."

✦

"Are you crazy?! Jesus Christ, Cunningham, what the hell has got into you?"

"Louise, take it easy. Fred said he discovered some kind of geolocation link between this guy Pavlychko and Arnold. So I decided to just stop by and say hello to the guy."

"Number one, you didn't say a damn thing to me about it, so I was completely blindsided and was made to look like a fool with the IG; number two, if you would have told me what you were doing, I would have told you not to dare visit the guy; number three, what in God's name did you think the Brits were going to do after seeing you show up there?; and number goddamn four, what the hell is a geolocation link?"

"Well, to answer the fourth question first, Fred says there was data showing this Ukrainian and Arnold were twice in the same location at the same time; to answer question three, I would have expected MI5 to identify Fred and me and then go through channels to complain or at least ask what the hell was going on. Which they did, and it's the reason we're talking right now. To answer number two, well, I was certain you'd tell me not to knock on Pavlychko's door, so I avoided you on purpose. And number one, well, I knew I was going to blindside you, but I thought afterward you'd cut me some slack because I was on to something strong. Anyway, that was my thinking."

"Your thinking is not particularly linear," Louise said. "I'm going to cut you some slack, but not more than an inch of rope. Never, ever blindside me again on something as important as this. Got that?"

"Yes, got it. Can I say something else?"

"What?"

"How far have we got on Pavlychko? I'm telling you he was freaked out to see me and Fred standing in front of his home asking about Arnold."

"You'd freak me out if you showed up unannounced at my home," she said. "Why are you so damn sure this guy is part of the Arnold disappearance?"

"I can tell; I saw his face. He was half pissed off and half-worried. What do we have on him so far?"

"Operations is putting together a report now, though I have no idea what they're going to tell us. And officially MI5 says to stay away from Pavlychko's home or they'll file a complaint. Do you know what that would mean?"

"Something not good?"

"Yes; something not good for you. Have to be honest, Cunningham, if it wasn't for Barkley offering you cover on this, the IG would have yanked you off this assignment. Next time you stumble, he's already promised to go to the congressman to get you reassigned to a desk job in Buffalo, or maybe Anchorage."

"Snows a lot in Buffalo," Dennis said.

"Yup."

"Okay, got the message. And I mean this, Louise, but I'm sorry I put you in a bad spot with the IG. I just had to go this route. I think we're on to something, and if I would have asked permission, I wouldn't have been able to confront him. You see?"

"You can't tell, because I'm in my office in Langley, and you're probably in a pub in London somewhere, but I'm yawning. That's how bored I am by your promises."

"No, honestly, Louise. I promise."

"Oops, another yawn."

"Okay, I deserve it. But you'll see."

"Yawn."

"Man, you are a tough one," Dennis said.

"I'm actually falling asleep, I'm so bored. Goodbye."

✦

"I'm getting cold, Freddie. You said you were going to show me something important. 'A slice of London history,' you said. I'm freezing."

"Now look who's the baby," Fred said.

They walked for another block, and then Fred stopped, looked at his iPad and then pointed at a long building on Shardeloes Road.

"Notice anything?" Fred said.

Dennis looked around at a row of three-story, modern brick buildings. "I give up. They look like apartments."

"We just passed other homes on this street back there," Fred said. "You don't notice anything different about these buildings?"

"I'm trying to work with you here, Freddie. I mean, they look just like the other buildings. Well, actually they look more modern. Maybe."

"Very astute," Fred said. "November 1, 1944. German V2 rocket shattered this part of the street. Killed thirty-six people. After the war they rebuilt the buildings in this block."

"You play bridge, have 'movie buddies,' and walk around London finding World War II missile strike sites," Dennis said. "I'm going to have to report you for being the weirdest NSA employee I've ever met. And there are a few really, really strange ones."

"Ah, but Dennis, you're missing the story," Fred said, closing his iPad. "The V2s were modern history's first terror weapon. They were shot sixty miles up into the stratosphere then came barreling down at three times the speed of sound with a thousand-pound warhead. No warning sirens, no nothing, except a crack as the sound barrier was broken. At least 1,400 of them fell on London. One hit a Woolworths Department store and killed 160 people who were shopping."

"I thought World War II was over," Dennis said.

"But the lessons are still there."

"Besides the lesson that it's cold in London in November, what other lesson were you thinking of?"

"Technology has made it possible to deliver death and destruction completely out of the blue. These people killed here years ago were just having tea around the table or reading a newspaper, and this missile comes in at 2,300 miles per hour and takes out the whole block. No warning siren. When the first missile hit in London, they had no idea what happened and thought it was a gas explosion."

Dennis looked at the buildings, stamped his feet to stay warm, and said, "Can we go now?"

"Sure, just thought you'd be interested in this bit of history," Fred said.

"I find it a little depressing, actually."

"Governments at work doing what they do best."

"Which is what?" Dennis said.

"Faster, cheaper, more efficient ways to kill their enemies. The machinery of war, honed to a knife's edge."

"And this from a guy who works for the NSA."

"Yeah, and that should tell you something."

"It tells me you ate something bad for breakfast."

CHAPTER 7

There is no need for you to see the actual content Arnold read," Chandler said. Dennis, Fred, Chandler and a small, rail-thin, gray-haired woman named Cecilia Francis sat at a round table in an interior room in the London station.

"Why not?" Dennis said.

"Because it's simply a disjointed, hardly intelligible transcript of a phone conversation," the woman said. "Arnold was part of an interagency group tracking and identifying high-priority targets in the Middle East."

"Targets for what?" Dennis said.

"Neutralizing," the woman said.

"Drone strikes, you mean," Fred said.

"In most cases, correct. In rare cases, we need boots on the ground to grab the target."

"So was this particular intercept that Arnold read critical?"

"No, not really," Chandler interjected. "Sally here and the rest of the team have been tracking this target for seven months or so. It was not important what the target was saying, but it was vital to know the location of the person he was talking to. He was talking to someone in Mosul. Caught us a little by surprise. But the contents of the message were not so important; it was the location."

Dennis looked down at the transcript summary, which was a bunch of salutations and odd phrases about friendship and family.

"Is this what you folks do all day, listen in to this stuff?" Dennis said to Fred.

"Don't look at me, I'm not an analyst."

"Mr. Cunningham," the woman said, "we did analyze this conversation, and you have to understand that in many cases these men know they're being listened to, and they talk in a kind of code that we don't completely understand. This conversation lasted for about four minutes and appears to be about confirming a meeting or an exchange of money. We're not sure, but that's our guess."

"But as I look at this," Dennis said, tapping the sheet of paper, "I can't understand why Arnold sat for ten minutes reading a more detailed version of this. I timed myself when you let us in here thirty minutes ago. It took me about a minute to read the summary. What am I missing? Why did he spend this much time reading a nonsensical transcript?"

"We're not sure," Chandler said.

"That's all? You're not sure?" Dennis said.

"Afraid so," he said. "We've checked with the folks at Menwith Hill, and Cecilia here works extensively with the same material. It's not clear why he sat staring at this material for so long."

"Is there something special in the transcript that you noticed?" Fred asked.

"Not that we're aware of," she said. "I mean, there's always a possibility that we're missing something, but there's not a lot of conversation, period. Little bit of a mystery why Arnold sat there for so long looking at it. You'd be interested to know that we had our crypto team look at it, and they drew a blank."

"Crypto team?" Dennis said.

"Cryptologists," Fred said. "Code breakers — those folks."

"Oh. And they saw nothing?" Dennis said.

"Zip," Cecilia said. "Sorry."

Dennis tapped the table absently with his right forefinger. *What am I missing?* he thought. *What the hell was Arnold doing for ten minutes? Daydreaming? Plotting?*

"So what's the story on the target?" Fred said. "What happened to the guy on the other end of the intercept? Did we get him?"

"No. He's still roaming around somewhere. His voice hasn't been found on an intercept since."

"Is this unusual?" Dennis asked.

"No, not unless the target completely disappears. And we won't know that for a while yet. But if you're asking if we've heard from him since this intercept, the answer is no, we haven't."

✦

A text pinged on his phone.

"u won't believe it. get down here now"

Dennis did not prefer texting, but Fred had insisted on staying in contact using this channel, and the government's encrypted messaging system was considered safe and reliable.

"why?"

"hottest woman ever seen. loves my accent. can u believe it? at bar downstairs. come now"

"can't, waiting for call from judy"

"she can wait. not kidding. gorgeous!!!"

"behave yourself"

"she wants to go to club and wants me to bring friend"

"can't go!"

"your loss kemosabe"

✦

"My God, I can't believe how exhausting these long flights are," Judy said. "I should have flown business class."

"I told you I'd pay for a business class ticket, but you wouldn't let me," Dennis said.

"I know, I know. Bloody silly of me to turn it down. Feel like a sardine."

"So you'll be here at around 2:00 p.m. tomorrow?"

"Yes, unless we're late."

Judy sat in Singapore's Changi Airport, waiting for the next leg of her flight. She wondered what she was doing flying all the way to London in order to break up. Was it her immature hope that Dennis would change his mind? Or was she just punishing herself in order to get over this Yank once and for all?

"Listen, Dennis, I need to get down to my gate. I've got a room at the Clarendon, two blocks from your hotel. I'll call you when I get to the hotel."

"Okay."

"Bye."

✦

Dennis lay on the bed and felt a strange loneliness seeping through the pores of his skin. It was an early warning sign of depression, and he recognized it well enough. Dr. Forrester had trained him in self-observation, but she wasn't able to stop it from starting in the first place.

He felt he had no choice but to end the relationship with Judy. It was not fair to try to maintain a relationship across two continents and a very big ocean. She was energetic, tough, smart, very attractive and a great lover. But she was too far away. *Why prolong the misery? She deserves better,* he thought. *God, I'm going to miss her.*

where r u? Dennis texted Fred. *changed mind*

But Fred never answered, and after watching a rugby match on television that he could not comprehend, he went to bed sullen and depressed.

He dreamed that night of the Australian outback. In the dream he was standing on a small rock formation looking out over acres of arid red soil and sparse vegetation. In the distance he could see a small cloud rising from the ground. A large truck was barreling through the desert toward him, throwing off sand and dust. At first he was confused about the truck, but as it grew closer he began to feel menaced, the kind of fear that made his palms sweat and his stomach flip. In the dream Dennis turned and ran as fast as he could, but as in so many of these dreams, his legs did not work and he could hear the truck bearing down on him from behind like a force of nature.

✦

"You look like shit," Dennis said, scooping his scrambled eggs onto his fork. "What time did you get in?"

"I think it was around two; yeah, something like that. You wouldn't believe the time we had. Wish you would have come. She kept asking if I had another American friend, but I told her you couldn't make it."

"What did you do?"

"She took me to some kind of dance club."

"You? A dance club?"

"Dennis, I'm not kidding, she is a model. From either Bulgaria, Lithuania or Slovenia. I could barely understand her, the accent was so strong. She would dance and rub up against me. I mean, for a guy like me, you can't even pay for that kind of attention."

"Well, you could pay for it, actually."

"Oh, shut up. You're jealous."

"Well, I am kind of. I talked to Judy last night, and she didn't want to talk much. I actually texted you to see where you were, but you never answered."

"I think I was a little drunk. Damn, she could drink vodka."

"Well, you should get some sleep. We'll catch up later."

"Oh, before I forget," Fred said, "I got a message last night from the same guy who pulled out the geolocation connection between Pavlychko and Arnold. He thinks — mind you, he just thinks — that he might have found out that Arnold regularly used another cell phone."

"How would he know that?"

"Voiceprint and textprint; everyone has a distinct audible voice, but they also have a distinct way of texting and emailing. The machine learning tools we have allow us to detect an individual's digital communications fingerprint. The texting piece is not an approved tool, or a completed product, but my friend ran it anyway. He created a profile for Arnold and then ran it against something like eleven petabytes of data we have stored.

"So?"

"So he thinks that someone matching Arnold's textprint used a cell phone that we didn't have registered. Once he found the phone number, you know, he worked backward and then ran a report on that cell phone's activity."

"Wouldn't Arnold know that as well? That he'd be profiled like this?"

"No, not texting. He wouldn't know that because the software is still in beta trial here. Again, this is just a tip from a friend who's snooping around. Probably nothing. Thought I'd mention it to you. Damn, I'm tired. And hungover. I'm going to lie down. I sent you my buddy's report by email. See if anything jumps out at you. Otherwise trash it. He's breaking the rules by letting me see it."

◆

At first Dennis could not understand how to read the report; there were strings of numbers intertwined with what he took to be text messages. After a few minutes he determined that the numbers were phone numbers, and next to them was a date stamp, followed by the text message itself.

In the forwarded email, Fred pointed out which phone number his friend suspected was Arnold's. Dennis followed what looked like minimalist interchanges — even by text messaging standards — to another number. Both appeared to be UK telephone numbers.

It started out the prior December from the phone they suspected was Arnold's.

"hey" the maybe Arnold started.

"bored?" mystery person responded.

"yes, u?" from the maybe Arnold.

"drink?" from mystery person.

"8:30?" maybe Arnold.

"OK" mystery person.

Dennis rubbed his forehead. He felt a headache coming on but was unsure whether it was from trying to decipher all of the numbers and texts on the laptop screen or whether it was due to Judy's expected arrival that afternoon.

He quickly scanned the rest of the report and found the text exchanges grew more intimate, or at least it seemed so.

Farther down the list, Dennis saw exchanges like *miss u* that suggested something was going on between the two. One of the last texts came from the mystery person: *hungry for u*; the maybe Arnold responded: *yummy*.

Dennis reread Fred's email; it appeared that there was no other activity on these two cell phones other than the texting between them. Interestingly, Fred noted in his email, the activity stopped completely two weeks before Arnold disappeared. Lastly, there was almost no important geolocation data on the two cell phones that Fred's friend could find. Typically, a phone pings cell towers nearby while it's turned on, and that can be recorded and tracked after the fact, but these two cell phones were nearly always turned off after an interchange. And when they were turned on, the locations were in crowded venues like Paddington Station or a street corner at rush hour.

Dennis picked up his phone and called Fred. "Hey," Dennis said, "how you feeling, party hound?"

"Like crap," Fred said. "I'll never drink vodka again."

"Would have paid money to see you grinding against that woman."

"You could have come, and she was mightily disappointed that I didn't have another friend with me. She even offered to use my phone and call you."

"Well, like I said, I texted you later, but you were having too much fun."

"Fun that comes at a cost, my friend. Next time I'll stick to light beer."

"Got a question for you," Dennis said. "I looked at those texts that your friend pulled out of the atmosphere. Wondered whether you thought we should pursue this or not?"

"Been thinking about that. Sent him an email asking if he could give some percentage of confidence that Arnold was one of the people texting, and he replied that he couldn't offer an opinion."

"Meaning what?" Dennis said.

"Meaning that he has no idea how to evaluate the accuracy of this software."

"Is that enough to go on for us? I mean, I have no idea how to attach importance to this stuff. What do you think?"

"I'd say perhaps," Fred said.

"That's it? Perhaps?"

"Yep. I mean these matching algorithms are new, and as I told you, the textprint project is in beta, and that's just for the English-language version. God knows how long it will take them to come up with a Farsi version."

"Okay, let me ask you this then: do you think Arnold — if this was even Arnold — had a girlfriend? Some of these exchanges are a little romantic, if you get my drift."

"That was my thought, to be honest. But I was waiting for you to put your two cents in. Yeah, I think there was some boy-girl stuff going on here."

"Strange that the exchanges end two weeks before Arnold goes missing," Dennis said. "Could just be coincidence."

"Yeah. Odd coincidence. My friend says the phones have gone dark. Either turned off or thrown away."

"Can we get authorization to ping those phones?" Dennis asked.

"Well, that's a possibility. But we'll need to make a request through the Brits, and they're a real pain in the ass on these things. Let me think about that."

"All right. Meanwhile, feel better. I'm seeing Judy this afternoon. She gets in around 2:00 p.m. Kind of nervous."

"Oh, stop that silliness," Fred said, coughing. "I can tell you're nuts about this woman."

"No, you can't."

"You think I'm dumb and blind? Maybe dumb, but not blind."

"You can't see shit."

"I'm telling you, she's got you hooked. The word is 'smitten,' I think."

"The word is: 'leave me alone.'"

"That's three words."

"Go to bed."

"Roger that."

◆

She was not going to be overly emotional, Judy told herself. Nor was she going be standoffish. She was just going to give Dennis a hug and a peck on the cheek, something neutral and preserving of dignity.

When she stepped into the lobby of the Clarendon, he was reading a newspaper.

Damn, he's handsome, she thought. *Hold it together. This is the beginning of the end of the relationship; don't make it worse. Weakness will only lead to more pain.*

Dennis dropped the newspaper when he saw her and bolted to his feet. He nearly knocked the porter sideways getting to her. He engulfed her in a bear hug then held her briefly at arm's length before pulling her face into his in a furious kiss.

"God, you look great," he said after they parted. "I'm so glad to see you."

She had trouble fashioning the correct facial expression as her heart beat a little too fast and the freshness of his kiss lingered. She tried to muster a dispassionate but friendly face, but she found the corners of her mouth twisting into a smile that she could not hide.

"Dennis, for heaven's sake," she said. "You caught me by surprise. I, I—" she stumbled "—wasn't prepared for that."

The porter stood awkwardly by as they looked at each other.

"Dennis, let me check in, please, and I'll be right down," she said.

"I can carry your bags," he said.

"No Dennis. You sit right here. I'll be back in fifteen minutes or so. Go sit."

She could see his disappointment, but she was glad to wrestle back control of the situation.

After she disappeared up the elevator, Dennis sat down and struggled to understand what had just happened. He had practiced a somber, break-up monologue that was mature and sensible.

But the moment she'd whisked through the hotel door, his insides had fluttered. She was beautiful in that girlish way: the slightly upturned nose, the tan, the confident stride. And suddenly all of the good times they'd experienced seemed magnified, the loneliness and distance between them evaporated.

Dennis stood up and then sat down in confusion.

What the hell is going on with me? I feel so stupid thinking that I could rid myself of this woman. Damnit, damnit.

CHAPTER 8

'm throwing up, and I can't stop. What should I do?"

Dennis sat in the lobby talking to Fred on the phone and was stressed; he was waiting for Judy to come downstairs, but he had Fred on the line, complaining of a terrible hangover.

"Jeez, Fred, if I wasn't busy right now I'd take you to an ER. You want me to come over? You sound like you have the flu or an *E. coli* infection."

"No, stay where you are," Fred said. "I'll call the front desk and ask them to call a cab to get me to an ER. I'm sure I'll be fine."

"Will you call me from the ER?"

"Sure. Just my friggin' luck."

Dennis hung up as Judy came out of the elevator. He waved, and she hustled over, smiling gently.

"Feel like taking a walk?" he said.

"That would be brilliant," Judy said.

And so they walked in the late afternoon through the bustle of an early rush hour. Judy was hoping that Dennis would start the conversation they both dreaded.

Instead, he acted like an excited adolescent; he held her hand and tugged her through the crowd until they found one of the many small parks in London, where they slowed their pace and talked nonstop.

He kept talking about work and would hardly let up. While she and Dennis were not strangers, much of their relationship existed around a series of dramas in Australia and one brief period in Arlington, Virginia, involving a shooting. Her prior experience with Dennis had swirled around emergencies. Their romance had grown exponentially around

these incidents, but it had also fallen off precipitously after they were separated by distance.

Her memories of him did not exactly coincide with the reality of the
man holding her hand. She remembered him as taciturn, rebellious, confrontational and moody, though also vulnerable, charming, and a little
self-conscious.

This Dennis would not shut up and kept chattering about his new
assignment, a funny fellow investigator named Freddie, a visit to a government electronic listening post in the north of England and even his
new boss.

"And what's this you said about dogs?" Dennis asked, as he stopped at
an empty park bench.

"Oh that," Judy said. "Well it started out as a routine search of a sal-
vage yard — I think you Yanks call them junk yards." Judy spent the next
twenty minutes reciting in precise detail the dog attack, the shooting and
the aftermath. She was surprised at how much emotion she brought to the
story, and as an afterthought, wondered whether she had been downplay-
ing the trauma to herself.

"That's awful," Dennis said when she finished. "Can't say I'm surprised
about poor intelligence. You'd think with our multibillion budgets that
our folks would know where the hell a deputy chief of station disappeared
to. It's all the same; guesswork and luck. They'd have you believe it's technology and science, but to me, it's just guesswork and luck."

The late afternoon weather was pleasant, with a mild breeze from the
east, rustling the bare branches. The sun — a rarity, Dennis noted, for
London during his stay — had moved behind the buildings and cast long
shadows.

"So, Judy," Dennis said, "what do you think of us?"

"Us?"

"Us as a couple? What do you think of the chances of us being a
couple?"

Now that he had brought up the subject, Judy froze. She had rehearsed
a couple of variations of the 'there's-a-good-time-to-end-a-relation-
ship' talk, but now she couldn't make her mouth work. It was not that
she had lost her nerve, it was just that she found Dennis so engaging and

comforting. He engulfed her two hands in his on a London park bench, using those damned blue eyes to penetrate her defenses.

"Dennis," she said, slowly, flickering her head sideways to remove a wisp of her hair from her mouth, "we simply can't be a couple this far apart. I think we've been over this on the phone. I can't move until Trevor goes on to uni. And I feel unsettled about leaving my mum and dad and sibs. And you don't seem interested in leaving the States. I mean, honestly, how can we be a couple? I'm not saying I don't miss you or want you; that's not the case at all. But we can't do this any longer. It's not fair to either of us."

As the words tumbled out, more or less like she'd hoped they would, Judy found herself feeling immensely sad. She stared down at the ground to avoid his blue eyes.

There, I said it, she thought. *God, that was awful.*

"Well, I don't think that's going to be a problem going forward," Dennis said. "I'll just move to Australia."

Judy frowned in disbelief. It had never occurred to her that Dennis would really join her in Australia. She considered every other option, but she never seriously thought he'd move so far away from his home.

"You're joking," she said. "That's not funny, Dennis."

"No, I'm serious. I'll leave the States and see if I can get a transfer to Australia. Won't be the same job, but I think I can swing that. Someone important has offered to help me get assigned there."

She sat looking intensely at his face, seeking a clue to what was happening. He beamed a smile back at her, though the longer she remained silent, the more his smile wilted at the edges.

"Isn't that what you wanted?" he said. "Or has something happened in the meantime that I don't know about?" He let go of her two hands. "Never occurred to me that you'd meet someone else. Jeez, what a dope." Dennis leaned back on the bench and stared off across the park.

"No! Dennis, that's not what I mean. There is no other man in my life. I just didn't expect you to want to move to join me. I guess I'm shocked. But in a good way."

She reached out quickly and now grabbed his two hands in hers. "Look at me, Dennis. There is no other man. You're the one I wanted, but you caught me off guard. I'm still processing what you just said. Can't you see that?"

Judy leaned forward and kissed the corner of his mouth.

He turned. "We're okay? As a couple?"

"Of course we are," she said, kissing him again. "But Dennis, you exhaust me sometimes! You're so unpredictable. But like I said, in a good way."

✦

Fred's face was yellowish, and his thinning hair looked almost translucent.

"You still look like shit," Dennis said, pulling up a chair.

The emergency room was more cluttered than what he was used to in the States, but Dennis was able to find someone to direct him to a bed where Fred was being kept in a curtained-off area.

"Flu. Can you believe it? Friggin' flu in London."

"Were you making out with the Serbian or Lithuanian model?"

"No, we just danced. And drank vodka."

"When are they going to let you leave here?"

"They pulled some blood and are running tests. Have to wait to see that I don't have bubonic plague or ebola."

"Have you told anyone back at Fort Meade that you're in the hospital?"

"Yeah. Told my boss. I called him an hour ago. He's all in a tizzy. Wants me out of here ASAP. If they keep me over, he's going to get me moved to the Royal London Hospital. Says they have a special unit there for idiots like me who should be protected from themselves."

"I'm sure it's fine," Dennis said. "Can I get you anything?"

"No. You should go. You got your old girlfriend here, right? The one you said you were going to break up with."

"We're not going to break up after all."

"Ha. I'm shocked."

"Well, it just happened. I'm going to move to Australia after we wrap this one up here in London."

"I guess congrats is in order, then. Am I going to meet this Judy?"

"Sure, but get your ass out of the hospital first. Is there anything I can get you before I leave?"

"Nothing. Actually, you can bring back one of the models to snuggle up with."

"I thought you'd be looking for a bridge game."

✦

Dennis spent the night in Judy's hotel room. They had dinner in the hotel restaurant then a couple of drinks at the hotel bar and barely made it through the door before the clothes were ripped off and they went at each other.

Afterward, Dennis lay on his back staring at the ceiling while Judy turned on her side, toying with the hair on his chest.

"You're serious about moving to Australia," she said. "Right?"

"Of course," he said.

"But you didn't tell me when."

"When would you like?"

"Tomorrow?"

He laughed. "When this assignment is over, I'll put in a request. They're treating me with kid gloves, as it were. My guess is that they'll want to keep me happy, and if I request it, they'll just move me over to operations and then post me to Canberra. But I'll work out of Perth."

"They'll just do that? Just because you ask?"

"Well, if you remember, the Australia event and the aftermath was a huge embarrassment. And it appears I have another benefactor, an influential congressman."

Dennis explained how he was attached to the current case and the role that Representative Barkley played in it.

"I'm impressed that he picked you out," she said, yawning and resting her head on his shoulder.

Dennis could feel her thighs and breasts press against him.

"Did you notice something?" she said.

"Notice what?"

"You didn't notice then," she said.

"Did you get your hair done? Did I miss that?"

She laughed. "No, not that. I got a tattoo."

He gently pushed her off his shoulder and sat up on his elbow.

"A tattoo? You?"

"Yes, but you didn't notice."

"Where is it?" he said.

She turned away from him and pointed to the base of her spine, just below her panty line. Dennis bent forward and laughed.

"It's a rising sun, isn't it?"

"Yes, it's the Australian military badge. I did it to remember my dad. Couldn't think of anything else. Just thought I'd be daring. I lead such a dull life."

She turned back around and snuggled against his shoulder.

"I think it looks cute," he said.

"It's silly, but a woman has to be silly every now and then." She yawned. "You going to sleep?"

"I'm exhausted," she said, her voiced muffled with her face pressed against his chest. "You fly in sardine class halfway 'round the world and see how you feel."

Dennis had not felt a naked woman pressed against him under the sheets since the last time he'd slept with Judy nine months ago, and he was having trouble hiding his arousal.

"God, Dennis," she said. "Don't men ever get tired?"

"Apparently not tonight," he said.

"Before I acquiesce," Judy said, "can you tell me how much longer you're going to be on this case here in London? I'm hoping it's not going to be for long."

"At this rate, I'd be surprised if this thing isn't closed up in a couple of weeks. I keep thinking we're stumbling onto something, but they're all dead ends."

"In that case," she said, reaching for the light, "game on, as you Yanks say."

CHAPTER 9

No, sir, he checked out late yesterday. He's been transferred to another hospital, but I'm not at liberty to disclose it to you," the woman said.

"Was it the Royal London?"

"Please, sir, I'm not able to provide any further information."

Dennis hung up and wondered who he could call to find out where Fred was but realized he had no contact information for anyone at the NSA, including Fred's boss, Stephen Manfort.

"What's wrong?" Judy asked, buried under a comforter in bed.

"Oh, my pal Freddie got sick, and they moved him to another hospital and won't tell me where he went. Ridiculous. And I don't know who to call."

"He'll be fine, I'm sure," Judy said, pulling back the covers. "I don't think I've ever slept completely naked before. Dennis, you sure make a woman do strange things." She jumped up, grabbed some clothes from the bureau and went into the bathroom. "I'm going out for a jog. I need some exercise."

"I thought we had enough exercise last night," he said.

She opened the door several inches and said, "Well, I need *more* exercise then."

"I'm going to head over to my hotel," he said through the closed bathroom door. "I'll call you after I take a shower. I may need to do some work. That okay?"

"Of course," she said.

✦

His cell phone rang while he was shaving in his hotel room. He walked out of the bathroom and looked at the number. It was an agency number he recognized.

"Hey, Louise," he said.

"Where are you?"

"I'm in my hotel room, why?"

"The same hotel as Kaczka?"

"Yeah, same as Freddie's."

"Pack your clothes and get out. We're taking you somewhere else."

"Wait! Louise, give me a second. What kind of place are you taking me to?"

"A safe house. There will be some medical personal and technicians waiting for you. They'll explain everything. Hurry, the hotel you're in is being shut down."

"Wait! I don't understand. Can you at least—"

"Damnit, Dennis, will you please just do as I say and quit asking questions. Go now. There is a silver utility van waiting outside for you with the company logo of Wilshire and Sons, electricians. Just knock on the back door and they'll open it. Get in and do exactly what they tell you to do. Got it?"

"Got it, I guess."

✦

Dennis hurriedly packed and left the room. In the lobby he saw several policemen and two men in white overalls behind the counter talking to one of the employees. As he approached the receptionist, she said, "Oh, Mr. Cunningham, no need to check out. We're all set. Your stay was on us. Goodbye."

The two men in overalls stared at Dennis.

"Are you serious?"

"Yes, sir. I'm sorry, but the hotel is being closed unexpectedly and will not be charging our guests for their stay. Thank you and have a good day."

Dennis pulled his roll-on suitcase to the entrance and pushed through the revolving door. He spotted the utility van but stood still while he called Judy.

"Hey, it's me. I know you're out jogging, but something has come up and I'm being moved out of this hotel. Not to worry. Will contact you soon. Please don't stress about this stupid change of hotels. Hope you had a good run."

Dennis put the phone in his pocket, went up behind the van and knocked.

The two doors opened. Inside sat a woman and a man on one side of the van, both wearing what looked like Tyvek overalls that covered their shoes. They wore caps, breathing masks, goggles and purple medical gloves. They pointed to where Dennis should sit on the other side of the van. The man closed the door and the woman tapped on the Plexiglas shield to signal the driver, who took off.

The woman held a white instrument the size of a cigar box in one hand and a long wand with a wire attached to the instrument in the other hand. She leaned over and ran the wand slowly over Dennis's body, starting at the soles of his shoes, up to his crotch, down the other leg, up the outside of legs, then across his chest, his face and hair.

They never spoke.

"What are you doing?" he asked the woman.

She shook her head, which he took to mean, "Don't talk."

But he was in no mood.

"Come on folks, talk to me. What are you doing?"

"Shut up," the man said through his mask.

"No," Dennis said. "Tell me what you're doing."

The man and the woman looked at each other, with, Dennis determined, a can-you-believe-this-dope look.

The woman raised the forefinger of her right hand over her mask-covered lips in a universal sign of "shush."

Dennis sighed and leaned back in disgust as they used the same device to go through his suitcase and belongings.

Dennis's cell phone rang in his inside jacket pocket, and he pulled it out. He saw that it was from Judy and was about to accept the call when the man across from him plucked it out of his hand and turned it off.

"Hey!" Dennis yelled, reaching for the phone.

The man held it over his head out of reach, and Dennis stood up to grab it. In a surprisingly quick maneuver, the woman jumped forward with all her momentum, hit Dennis in the chest with her outstretched arms in the middle of his chest and slammed him back onto the bench. Dennis flashed with anger and was about to jump up when he noticed the man now held another device that Dennis recognized as a Taser.

"You've got to be kidding me," Dennis said.

The man and woman simultaneously shook their heads back and forth in the universal sign of, *No, we're not fucking kidding.*

Judy had mapped her run beforehand using an app for her smartphone. She stretched in the hotel room, took the elevator downstairs, and then started to run paying close attention to the street signs. She did not see any other runners until she got to the large park, where she encountered several other runners and commuters flying by on bikes.

She ran faster than her normal pace, but it did not bother her because she was so happy. In the nine months or so she had struggled through so many issues that happiness had seemed a thing of the past. But today she was thrilled, and the exuberance took her by storm as she swept past commuters and mothers pushing strollers through the park.

Dennis was whisked through the safe house's garage and into a room with several more people in white Tyvek suits and masks. No one spoke to him — they only gestured and continued to push wands over his entire body, including down his underwear.

He was asked for a urine sample and was followed into the bathroom by a man who watched everything closely.

Finally, a very small woman pulled off her mask and said, "He's clean. We're okay here."

Her command was met with the rustling sounds of the synthetic material being ripped off. "I was sweating up a storm in that damn suit," one man said, stepping out of his overalls.

"Can someone tell me what's going on?" Dennis said.

No one spoke as they looked at the small woman.

"You've been checked for contamination, Mr. Cunningham, and are clean. You're lucky, and I guess we are too."

"Damn right," someone said.

"I'm not a complete idiot, folks. I figured those were Geiger counters," Dennis said, "but what the hell do they have to do with me?"

"Follow me, please," the woman said, walking away through a door as the other people in the room ignored Dennis.

She walked into a well-appointed living room, where several people were sitting talking in hushed tones. They looked up at him.

Dennis recognized Chandler from the London station and Sorenstam from Menwith Hill, but there were three others he had never seen before, two women and a man.

"Pull a chair over here, Dennis," Chandler said. "I think you know Sorenstam, but this is Mary Martinson from MI5, Signey Colpitt from our Russia team at Langley and Bill Clarkson, from the London station."

Dennis did his best to appear calm and matter-of-fact as he grabbed a small wooden chair and dragged it across the oriental carpet, but he was entirely confused. In the past twenty-four hours he had visited his pal in the hospital, rekindled his relationship with Judy and spent a glorious night with her, been kicked out of his own hotel by strange people in white protective gear, whisked away in a van and poked and prodded aggressively in a London safe house.

"Dennis, I just want to make sure that we acknowledge that you report through the Office of the Inspector General, and as such, take orders from his staff," Chandler said. "The law is pretty clear about separation of church and state, as it were, regarding OIG and the rest of the group at Langley. But given the severity of the situation, we have been in contact with the IG and he has authorized us to move ahead with you directly."

"Ahead with me," Dennis repeated.

"Yes, that is correct," Chandler said.

"What does 'ahead' mean?"

"It means that we are to debrief you and explain the circumstances as they now present themselves. It is up to the IG to decide what, if anything, he chooses to do with your current assignment."

"I really hate to say this," Dennis said, "but someone better start explaining what this is all about or I'm getting up and leaving. And you'll have to Taser my ass to keep me here."

CHAPTER 10

can't explain it right now, Judy, but I'm caught up at work. It's kind of important, and I've been in meetings all day. I'm not sure we'll be able to have dinner tonight."

"Oh God, what happened?"

"It's so complicated — and confidential — that I can't talk about it. I'm sorry, Judy. But I'll call you later this evening after I finish up here. It's been a very strange day. But don't fret, it'll be cleared up soon."

Judy hung up and looked at herself in the mirror. She was happy until about fifteen seconds ago, and now those old fears of insecurity and hurt began to work themselves into the corners of her eyes.

How strange, she thought. *One moment I'm on top of the world, the next I'm falling. I wonder if I should just return to Perth. Dennis has no intention of following me to Perth; he's married to his silly, stupid job.*

◆

Dennis paced back and forth across the room, unconsciously wringing his hands as if washing them. They had given him a break, during which he'd called Judy, but then it was back at it.

"You're absolutely sure," Dennis persisted. "There is no doubt whatsoever?"

"None," Chandler said. "It was pure luck that one of the physicians at Royal London overheard someone talking about the case. Otherwise, we'd never have known why he was sick. It's so rare. It's pure serendipity that the physician overheard the discussion. The tests are positive. No doubt about it."

"What is it again?"

"Polonium-210," Martinson from MI5 said. "It's a rare radioactive substance. Almost certainly Russian, since they're the only ones who still manufacture it."

"And it's inside Freddie?"

"Yes," Chandler said.

"And there's nothing we can do? Nothing?"

"We're flying over two physicians from the US right now, but we've been warned that it's causing something called 'acute radiation syndrome,' and that is impossible to stop."

"He's going to die?" Dennis said.

"Almost certainly, yes," Sorenstam said. "It would have been much better if you would have avoided confronting Pavlychko. Or if you had to do it, you could have left our guy out of it."

"Nathan!" Chandler said. "Is this the time for that?"

Dennis slumped in the chair. He was so agitated and filled with guilt that he had trouble concentrating.

"Can we do this one more time?" Dennis said, avoiding Sorenstam's comment. "I want to make sure I got this. So, Arnold disappears, several prior investigations are completed, and it's determined that the only likely scenario is a Middle Eastern jihadist group nabbed him. Is that part one of this thing?"

Chandler nodded.

"Okay, part two is that Freddie and I are sent to take one more look at Arnold's disappearance. And in the process, Freddie stumbles across two possible geolocation matches of Arnold and a Ukrainian named Pavlychko."

"None of this information he bothered to share with Fort Meade," Sorenstam said.

"Nathan, can we just take it easy? Go ahead, Dennis."

"So Freddie stumbles on this potential long shot with Pavlychko, and we make this visit. We know MI5 is probably watching this guy, but we go anyway. Pavlychko answers the door, says almost nothing, and then closes the door. Part three: couple of days later Freddie has a woman drape herself over him at the hotel bar. She begs him to bring his good American friend along, but the American friend declines. She parties with Freddie, and as I understand it, she slips a minuscule amount of Polonium-210 in his drink. He comes home, gets sick and now we know he's dying from radiation poisoning."

Everyone except Sorenstam nods in agreement.

"And we can't find the girl?" Dennis said.

"No match anywhere," Martinson said. "We have a few CCTV shots, but she was probably wearing a wig. We have hundreds of thousands of foreigners living in London. And of course some are illegal. I'm afraid we haven't had much luck so far."

"So, number four," Dennis said. "Our best theory is that Pavlychko freaked out when Freddie and I showed up, somehow figured out where we were staying, grabbed some polonium-210 that he kept in his refrigerator for special moments like this and sent someone out to poison Freddie."

"And you, if you would have gone with them," Chandler said. "I think that's pretty clear. Fred admits that the woman pressed him pretty hard on bringing his American friend."

"Number five: the only reason we can think that our Ukrainian friend would go through the trouble to poison US intelligence personnel is that he's nervous we're on to something worth killing for. And he does it in a manner that will not look like the Yanks have been poisoned. No one is supposed to suspect this polonium stuff."

Martinson nodded. "Seems that way."

"And Pavlychko?" Dennis said.

"He hasn't left his house yet," Martinson said. "We're reluctant to be aggressive on this since our suspicions are circumstantial. But I believe the consensus is that we're ready to bring him in for questioning today."

"Does Freddie know what the prognosis is?" Dennis asked.

Martinson nodded.

◆

"Hey, kemosabe, you look like shit," Fred said.

Dennis wore a surgical mask, overalls and a hair guard. He was glad that much of his face was covered, because he felt like it was melting into a grim, depressed pool of muck.

"Well, you'd look like shit too, if you felt as guilty as I do."

"Oh, don't start. You had no idea what was going to happen. I mean, who could predict anything like this? Not in a million years."

Dennis stood next to the bed looking down at Fred, who was losing most of what hair he had left. His face was an odd shade of yellow and his cheeks sagged. His eyes, though, were still bright.

"They have some physicians coming from the States," Dennis said.

"Yeah, I heard."

"You in much pain?"

"They're giving me some stuff to get rid of the pain. Makes me sleep all the time. Great dreams, though."

"Are they going to fly you back home?" Dennis asked, even though he knew that was too dangerous.

"Don't think so. They're just going to leave me here. For a while. See what happens."

Dennis could not stand to look at him and walked over to the window. "What kind of view do you have here? Charming. Looks like an alley about eight stories down."

He put his forehead against the cold glass and stared at the asphalt alleyway.

I could break this window right now, he thought. *I could jump. They wouldn't be able to stop me. Would be over in maybe ten seconds. No more pain, no more guilt. Nothingness.*

"What are you doing?"

"I'm checking out your neighborhood," Dennis said.

"No, you're not. I know what you're doing."

Dennis turned.

"You're trying to figure out how to find that bastard Pavlychko."

"Yeah. You're right, Freddie. The Brits finally go to bring him in for questioning, and he's gone. They search his home and find lots of cash, couple of guns, and traces of you-know-what. Total incompetents, the Brits."

"Well, you must feel pretty good about it."

Dennis frowned and moved toward Fred. "What are you talking about?"

"That your hunch was right. That Pavlychko had something to do with Arnold's disappearance."

"Oh, that. Given the circumstances, Freddie, I'd just as well have been wrong on that."

"Do me a big favor, would you?" Fred said.

"Sure. Whatever you want."

"Stop being a baby."

Dennis stared.

"I mean it. You're acting like a child. All droopy-eyed. I can only see your eyes, but they're bloodshot and sunken. Don't beat yourself up over it. I'm sure my name will go onto the plaque of heroes at Fort Meade. At least I'll be remembered for something there. I mean, I'm getting more attention now than at any time in the last fifteen years. I got a call from the director. Can you believe it?"

Dennis shook his head and looked away. "It's not funny, Freddie."

"Everything's funny if you try."

"Not for me. Everything's fucked-up right now on my side of the fence."

"Come here," Fred said. "Closer. Want to tell you something."

Dennis walked over and looked down on Fred. He was beginning to feel the petrifying sadness again and tried to fight it by biting his lip.

"The video," Fred said.

"The what?"

"The video."

"What video?"

"Menwith Hill."

"Sorry, Freddie, I'm not getting it. What video?"

"Arnold's video. His last visit."

"Oh, that."

"Yeah. It's not right."

"You mean it's been edited? Something like that?"

"No."

Dennis leaned forward and looked closely at Fred. *Is the poor guy hallucinating? Is he too drugged to make sense?*

"We missed something. I asked if they'd let me see it again, and they said no. You need to watch it again. See what we missed."

"Sure, Freddie. I'll look at it again. Good idea."

"You know it's the alpha rays that are doing all the damage."

"I, I, I'm not sure—" Dennis said.

"Polonium-210 doesn't have gamma rays, just alpha. The rays can't penetrate a piece of paper. But they can do a job on your organs, you know?"

"Oh, okay. I didn't know that."

"Has a half-life of about forty days. Clever."

"I guess."

"What are you going to do when you find Pavlychko?"

"Um, well, I'm going to make him pay."

"Good. Not that I hate the guy. But I thought I had some more bridge games left in me, and he's pretty much put the kaibosh on that."

Dennis looked away.

"Hey, Dennis?"

"Yeah?"

"Can you get the nurse for me? Don't feel so good right now."

"Sure."

✦

"They just poisoned him with this stuff? And it could have been you too?" Judy said.

"It should have been me," Dennis said. "Poor Freddie was just going along for the ride."

Judy had tried several times to distract Dennis, but he was depressed. She remembered his dark moods in Australia and was struck by how she'd buried those memories. *He is a very complicated man.*

"What are you going to do about the video?"

"I think Freddie was just acting goofy with all those drugs in him."

"But what if he wasn't? You said so yourself that he was a pretty bright fellow."

"I don't think it's worth reviewing. If you would have seen the shape he was in, you'd come to the same conclusion."

"Ah, Dennis, come on. He could be on to something important."

"I doubt it."

"But you owe it to Freddie to look at it," she said, leveraging the only thing she knew could move him away from his gloom: anger.

Dennis sighed. "Well, he did ask me to look at it. And I don't give a shit what that idiot Sorenstam says. I'll demand he show it to me."

Judy would have preferred introspection or self-awareness as a motivating factor in her Yank, but she knew by now that anger focused him in a way that other emotions did not.

"To hell with Sorenstam," she said.

"Bastard."

✦

"Don't think it's a good idea," read the email from Chandler. "Sorenstam is pretty sore about the whole thing and is being a pain. Do you really think it's that important?"

"Yes, please persist," Dennis typed back.

Dennis signed off his clunky encrypted laptop, the ones all agency personnel were ordered to use in the field. He could hear Judy in the shower after one of her jogs and then heard her yelp.

"Damnit!" Her voice was muffled behind the bathroom door.

"You all right?" he yelled.

"Damnit," she said over the running shower.

He opened the bathroom door.

Judy had just turned off the shower and pushed back the curtains. Dennis marveled at her sexy, shiny and slick skin, like a candied apple.

"Hand me some tissues," she said, pointing at the box next to the sink.

He grabbed several and gave them to her.

She pressed them hard against the inside of her calf. "Damn, damn," she said. "These bloody razors are so sharp these days. Why must women shave their legs, anyway?"

"I don't know," Dennis said. "You tell me."

"Because men don't like women with hairy legs or hairy underarms. That's what we've been told."

"Well, this man could care less."

"More tissues," she said, holding out the bloodstained pile.

"I don't like the sight of blood," Dennis said, resisting taking the stained tissues.

"You are such a baby."

Dennis grabbed the tissues, tossed them in the trash and gave her another handful.

She stood bent over in the bathtub with the foot of the cut leg up on the tub rim, pressing the wound.

"I hope you don't take this the wrong way," Dennis said, "but I'm getting pretty aroused just looking at you soaking wet in the shower."

"Out," she said.

"Okay, it was just an observation."

✦

The dread was overpowering as he put on the protective clothing. Sorenstam had called and told Dennis that Fred's organs were failing, and he would not survive for more than a couple of days. Since Fred insisted that he see Dennis one more time, the medical staff had relented.

Dennis did not want to face Fred again, but Judy had insisted.

"You can't run from this," she said. "He wants to see you. Go see him. Say goodbye. I know this is tragic, but it's not your fault. And he needs you. Go."

"You sound like my therapist," he said.

Dennis stepped into the hospital room, the protective clothing making him sound like a walking paper bag. He was barely recognizable as the Freddie that Dennis knew. This new Freddie was completely bald, his skin had a dusty yellow hue, and his face had lost that chubby boyishness. His eyes were closed, and Dennis thought for a second that he was dead. He began to panic.

There was a nurse in the room, also in protective clothing, adjusting a device attached to a drip line. She gave Dennis the practiced, polite half-smile employed by all nurses attending to end-of-life patients: part welcoming, part somber.

How do they do it? he thought. *Why would you want to do this for a living?*

"Is he...?" Dennis said.

"You'll need to wake him," she said. "He's heavily sedated."

She left the room with her eyes lowered, as if participating in a religious ceremony.

Dennis looked down at his friend and instead of waking him walked over to the window and peered down at the alley as he had days earlier. The sun had furiously battled the gray, steel-wool clouds all day over London, but the clouds continued to win out.

The alley behind the hospital looked down on several brick buildings of varying ages. Dennis could see the alley open into the busy street to his left and watched pedestrians and cars whisk by, oblivious and uninterested in Fred's plight.

He stood there for several minutes and finally turned and walked over to the bed.

"Hey, Freddie. Hey there. Can you hear me?"

Fred opened his eyes slowly and appeared not to be able to focus. "Hey, kemosabe," he said.

"How you doing?"

"*Comme ci, comme ça.*"

Dennis smiled at his friend.

"So now you speak French?"

"*Oui.*" Fred smiled, but it was distorted as his skin stretched awkwardly over his cheekbones.

"You comfortable?" Dennis did not know what to say and felt stupid for uttering banalities.

"Whatever they're giving me feels great. Only problem is that I sleep all the time. Don't like that," he mumbled.

"I'm sure it's for the best," Dennis said.

Fred closed his eyes and took a labored breath.

Dennis bent down in alarm and watched Fred's nostrils, then his chest to see if it was moving. He could not detect the slightest activity and bolted upright.

"Hey," Fred said suddenly. "Forgot."

"You forgot something?"

"Yeah."

"What was it? Do you remember?"

"Yeah." But Fred kept his eyes closed and didn't speak.

"Freddie."

"Yeah. Got something for you," Fred said with his eyes closed. "My friend."

"Your friend?"

"My friend."

"What about your friend?"

"You need my friend."

"I do?"

"Yeah."

"Okay. Who is he? Be glad to meet him," Dennis said.

"He's NSA in London. Not Menwith."

"Do you want me to talk to him?"

Fred nodded, his eyes still closed. "He'll find you. Very smart guy. He helped me find the Ukrainian. Told him to help you."

"I don't need help, Freddie."

"Ha. Make me laugh."

"Don't bother with this stuff, please, Freddie."

"Friend not supposed to talk to anyone. Do what he says. He'll help you."

"Sure."

Dennis waited for Fred to continue, but he appeared to be asleep. He heard the door open behind him, and a young man in a white coat said in an American accent, "You'll have to leave now."

Dennis reached out and touched Fred's pasty, hairless arm.

"You're not supposed to touch him," the man said.

"Fuck you," Dennis said.

After several seconds Dennis turned and left the room, removed his protective clothing in an adjoining room, was tested for radioactivity by an older man and then walked down the wide hospital hallway.

After several steps he stopped amid the hospital bustle and did something he had not done in many, many years.

He turned to the wall on his left and hit it with his fist as hard as he could. He knew that if he hit a wall stud, which he'd done years ago, he'd break his knuckles. This time he hit plaster and felt nothing but satisfaction as the fist disappeared past his wrist in an explosion of sound and dust.

When he turned and continued walking, he did not notice the stares and silence that followed him.

Outside, he looked up and noticed the sun was not going to win; the day was going to remain cloudy, with a slight chance of showers.

CHAPTER 11

I don't know, Cilla," Judy said, sitting in her hotel room and cradling the phone while she put on a coat of maroon nail polish. "Yes, he said he will move to Australia, but he's in some kind of trouble with work here, and he's very unhappy. I forgot how moody he is. I suppose that's not unusual when you're separated for so long; you only remember the good things."

"What are you going to do?" Cilla said. "Do you still want him to move to Australia?"

"Yes, I still do. I'm just nervous that he's going to change his mind the moment I fly back. I don't think he means to be this way, but his work here is so complicated. And he's complicated."

"When are you coming back?"

"I fly out in two days. I need to get back to work, and I miss my family. I called Trevor yesterday, and he finally visited his father in prison. I know it was difficult for him."

"Hopefully it will help Trevor move on with his life," Cilla said.

"I suppose," Judy said, delicately twisting the nail polish cap onto the bottle with fingers splayed to prevent smearing. "Poor Trevor. He seems so protected and yet so isolated at the boarding school. I can't wait for him to go to uni and have a normal life."

"Just get home soon. I'll treat you to a nice night out for dinner, and we'll split a bottle of wine. Or two."

Judy laughed and signed off.

My confused, moody Yank, she thought. *Will he follow me to Perth? Is he lying to me or lying to himself? I wish I knew how men thought. They are a mystery to me, and even after falling in love, I'm still not sure what I'm supposed to do, or why.*

✦

The envelope was mailed to the hotel and delivered to the room by a bellboy.

"What is it?" Judy asked.

"I'm not sure, exactly," Dennis said, reentering the room. He held the oversized manila envelope up to the light of the window. "I can't see into it. Strange to get something sent to me here. Has a stick-on label that was done on a printer. It's my name and your room number. Who would know that I moved into your room?"

Judy stood up, walked over and took the envelope from Dennis. She shook it. "Seems like a letter or piece of paper inside. But I don't think you should open it."

"You think my Ukrainian friend is trying to finish the job?" Dennis said.

"Well, it's at least a possibility," she said. "Please don't open it, Dennis. Give it to your folks to open."

Dennis reclaimed the envelope from Judy and put it on the writing desk. They stared at it.

"Could be a poison or anthrax or something," Judy said. "I don't like it being here."

Dennis sat down on the edge of the bed and continued to stare at the envelope.

"What are you doing?" she said.

"Thinking."

"About what?"

"My letter."

"Please don't tell me you're considering opening it?"

He continued to stare at it, moving his head slightly every now and then.

"Dennis?"

He stood up and walked over to the desk, turned on the desktop lamp, picked up the envelope and held it to the light from the lamp. He shook it again.

Judy had seen Dennis like this before, and it made her uncomfortable. A year ago, when they had traipsed over the Western Australian desert in search of a hidden government facility, Dennis had often grown strangely focused, pensive and quiet. Those moments were often followed by what Judy took to be reckless behavior. Dennis often defended his impulsivity by referring to his instincts.

Judy did not believe as strongly in the power of instinct; it was the most worrisome thing about his behavior, and watching him now she was reminded of it.

"Please tell me what you're thinking," she said quietly.

"If it's my Ukrainian friend, he knows that I wouldn't open something like this. It's too obvious. On the other hand, the operating theory about the polonium is that we're not supposed to know it was radioactive poisoning. So now that I think about it, it could be from Pavlychko."

"I agree."

"But I don't think so," he said.

"Dennis, I don't mean to be the note of paranoia here, but is it possible that he found out you Yanks discovered that Fred was poisoned with polonium? And therefore his train of thought is that you would not expect it to contain poison since it was too obvious?"

"Perhaps."

"In fact," Judy said, standing up, "I think we need to get this room tested for radiation right now. My God, why didn't I think of it earlier?"

"Hang on, Judy. I hear what you're saying, but this just doesn't work. I think this letter is something else. I can't be sure, of course, but I don't think we need to be alarmed."

"But I am alarmed!"

"Yes, I can see that, and I don't blame you. But I think I'd be making a mistake by turning it in."

"God, you'd be making a mistake not to turn it in! Dennis, let's get out of here. Leave the bloody thing here, call your folks and get this room tested. Let's go, please."

"I have a better idea," he said. "Let's both leave the room. I'll call in and tell them that I need your room here tested for radiation because I'm just nervous or paranoid. That will be our backup test."

"No, I'm paranoid and being sensible. You're being reckless and silly."

"After I make the call you get the hell out. I'll take the envelope with me, go to a pharmacy and buy a mask, protective gloves, the whole works, and I'll open the envelope outside, away from anyone except me, of course. It's too light and flexible to be an explosive, and I don't see any powder floating around when I hold it to the light. And I was told you need to ingest polonium to make you sick."

"You've lost your mind," Judy said. "Listen, I know you feel horrible about Freddie. Hell, I feel horrible about the man, and I don't even know him. But this is stupid."

She stepped in front of Dennis and cupped her hands on both sides of his face.

"Look at me, Dennis. I've come a long, long way to find out what was going to happen to us. I feared the worst, but I was gifted with the best news in a long time. This capricious Yank I've fallen in love with has agreed to move to Perth. And now all of that is being put at risk because of your guilt. Or maybe it's not the guilt — maybe it's just your stubbornness. Or your 'instinct,' whatever that is. But please don't do this. Don't open that damn thing. Turn it over to your people. Let them see what's inside. If it's nothing harmful, then there is no problem."

Dennis reached out, put his arms around Judy's waist as she stood and tugged her body to his. She dropped her hands and felt him gently wrap his arms around her.

"I'm not doing a good job of protecting you," he said. "Why is it that just when we get close to each other, things start to fall apart *out there*? *In here*, I feel great about you and us. But the *out there* is what keeps getting in the way. I feel like it wants to destroy us sometimes."

Judy gently rubbed the back of his neck and let her eyes rest on the wallpaper three feet away. She focused on the simple repeating pattern of yellow and white lines.

He is going to open the envelope, she thought. *He is correct. It is the* out there *that is ruining our relationship.*

She slowly released her hands and stood back to look into those deep blue eyes.

"Do whatever you think is best," she said. "But I'm not going any-where, and neither are you. You want to open the envelope and risk your life, then do it here. Don't run away. Take responsibility for what you're doing. I'm not Freddie. I know what I'm doing. I can't stand being away from you, more than I can't stand your recklessness. Open the damn envelope here and now."

"For chrissakes, Judy, what has got into you?"

"You have got into me, that's what. Do you think I like being this way? Do you have any idea what you mean to me and how it's driving me crazy that we can't be together?"

She turned, leaped at the desk, snatched the envelope and ripped it open as Dennis tried to grab her arms.

They stared at the torn envelope and the folded piece of paper inside that Judy had tossed on the desk.

"I can't believe you did that," Dennis said softly.

"Me either."

Dennis reached for the hotel pen and used it to clumsily move the folded paper around as if it were a dead insect.

The paper appeared to be a trifolded, cheaply printed brochure with some religious lyrics. At the top in red ink were the words: "Silence is kept, after which all stand with the choir."

Underneath that sentence was the headline: *Nunc Dimittis*, followed by "The Song of Simeon (occasionally sung in Latin)."

And beneath the headline were lines of text, attributed at the bottom right to "Luke 2:29-32."

Dennis pointed the pen to the first line of text, and they looked at each other. The single line of words appeared to be covered by a bright fluorescent yellow highlighter ink.

The line of text read: "Lord, now lettest thou thy servant depart in peace."

Dennis reached across the table for another pen, and using both like chopsticks, he flipped the brochure over.

The first page had a logo at the top showing crossed swords and "D" between the blades of the swords. Next to the logo were the words "St. Paul's Cathedral."

Below that was the headline "Evensong," with an explainer: "Christian worship has been offered to God on this site for over 1,400 years. By worshipping with us today, you become part of this living tradition of prayer and thanksgiving. You are most welcome."

The entire word, "Evensong" was also highlighted in yellow.

Dennis dropped the two pens and used his hands to open the first flap of the brochure.

"Don't do that, Dennis!" Judy said.

"No, I think this is fine. I have an idea of what might be happening. See," he said, pointing at the two open facing leaves of the brochure. They bent over for a closer look. Individual letters — not the entire word — were highlighted on both pages.

He picked up the trifolded brochure and quickly turned it over, looking at each page. It was a brochure from St. Paul's Cathedral in London describing a recurring prayer service at the famous church. There were only a few highlighted words and letters.

"Judy, can you write these letters down?"

She took one of the hotel pens and pad of paper.

"The letter 'n,' the letter 'o,' the letter 'v.'" He stopped.

"That's it?" Judy said.

"Wait." Dennis scanned the opposite page and noticed the citation at the bottom of the text from the "Magnificat." It read "Luke 1: 46-55." The "1" and the "4" were delicately highlighted.

"Shit," Dennis said looking up at Judy. "November 14."

"I'm not with you, Dennis."

"This is a message."

"What's the bloody message, besides scaring the hell out of me?"

"I think the person who sent this is Freddie's friend. You remember I mentioned that? This must be his friend who works for the NSA here in London. Look, the sentence he highlighted about 'letting thy servant depart in peace' is in reference to Freddie. And he wants to meet at Evensong at St. Paul's on November 14, which is tomorrow. What the hell is Evensong, anyway?"

Dennis pushed the brochure aside and opened his laptop. While he logged in and searched online for St. Paul's, Judy picked up the brochure and unfolded it, reading every word.

"They must hand this out at Evensong," she said. "This describes the service and the liturgy, including the music. Hey, you missed something."

Dennis looked up from the computer.

"Here," she said, pointing, "isn't this word highlighted?"

Dennis took the brochure and held it close up. In the *Nunc Dimittis*, on the sixth line, the word "light" appeared to be highlighted.

"I think so," Dennis said. "I mean, you can barely see it. But I think so."

"What does that mean?" she said.

"I have no idea. The website says St. Paul's has Evensong Monday through Friday at 5-5:45 p.m. So this guy is saying 'Meet me at Evensong tomorrow evening.'"

"What's the part about the 'light'?"

"Not sure about that."

Judy spread the two-sided brochure out on the table. "And we missed this," she said, pointing to the bottom of a page showing an image of a camera with a red circle and diagonal line through it. She read the text: "No form of visual or sound recording, or any photography, is permitted during this service. Please ensure that all mobile phones are switched off."

She fingered the first word "no," which was highlighted, and slid her fingertip along the rest of the paragraph to the highlighted words "mobile phones."

"And what is this supposed to mean?" she said.

"I think it means don't bring a cell phone," he said. "If you think I'm paranoid about eavesdropping, you should see how crazy these NSA folks are."

Judy looked at Dennis as he scanned St. Paul's website. His face was taut and his blue eyes jumped around the screen as he navigated. She admired his intensity and laser focus but also lamented it; would he ever be able to show her that kind of intensity? Was he just some kind of attention deficit disordered adult addicted to the action who would always be leaving her for the chase?

"Would you be upset if I rained just a little on your parade?" she said.

"No, go for it. Maybe I need a little rain to cool me down right now."

"Just for a moment, did it occur to you that your Ukrainian friend is behind this letter and that you're being lured to something bad? Hang on, don't smirk. What if you don't tell your folks about this letter and you go to this meeting, and an 'accident' occurs? Especially if you don't take your cell phone; there will be no way to track your movements and location. The end effect will be that the two investigators that came closest to cracking this missing person's case have died. And I lose the one man I've been stalking around the planet."

She didn't mean to cry, and in fact she didn't break out in sobs. But her eyes welled up, and she looked away.

"If this is how ordinary couples spend their time romancing each other, then I'd rather not bother," she said.

Dennis closed his laptop lid, sighed and said, "I don't think we're ordinary people."

CHAPTER 12

The phone rang, and he looked at the time. It was 3:23 a.m. He felt Judy's body tense as he reached for the phone and untethered it from its charging chord.

"Hey, Louise," Dennis said.

"Sorry, I know it's late there. You should know, though. Fred Kaczka passed away about two hours ago. They'll be an autopsy and an official inquiry, of course. We'll have plenty of time to prepare for it. Not to worry. I'm sorry, Dennis. I gather you were fond of him."

"Will there be a service for him?"

"It's private. Family only, or that's what we've been told."

"Would have liked to attend." Dennis held the phone to his ear but did not know what else to say.

"You okay?"

"Yes, fine," Dennis said.

"There's some confusion right now about what all this means in relation to Arnold's disappearance. There is a growing consensus that Pavlychko had nothing to do with Arnold, and you just scared him about some other illegal activity he was involved in. And he reacted accordingly."

"Are you serious?"

"Yes. Operations thinks there's no real link between Arnold and Pavlychko. And they want you to close out the investigation pronto."

"I need to do one more thing," Dennis said.

"Nope. Can't do it."

"Louise, please? Just one more thing?" Dennis was aware that his voice had slid an octave higher and that he sounded emotional. He was doing his best to manipulate Louise, even if it meant sounding vulnerable and desperate.

"Nice try," she said. "No go."

"Louise," he said slowly. "Please?"

Dennis heard a man's muffled voice and realized that it was Louise's husband.

"If I say, 'no,' will you accept it and move on?" she said.

"I guess I'd have no choice," he said. "But it would be a huge mistake."

"Fine. Then do your 'one thing.' I'll cover for you here, but it has to be fast. By the way, what is your 'one thing?'"

"I need to review the video of Arnold's last visit to Menwith Hill. That's all."

"Then do it, for chrissakes. End this damn thing."

He hung up.

Judy turned and rested her head on his shoulder.

"What is this Louise woman like?"

"I'm not sure," he said. "Check with me when all of this is over."

✦

"You can't see that now," Sorenstam said. "Out of the question. If you have any requests, go through channels. I'm going to report this call."

"Go right ahead," Dennis said. "I'll see the video again, regardless of what you think."

After Sorenstam hung up he called Chandler's office.

"He's not available right now, Mr. Cunningham," his secretary said. "Do you want him to call you?"

"Yes, please. Tell him it's important."

"Certainly."

Dennis heard the passkey unlock the hotel door, and Judy came in with several shopping bags.

"Trinkets for the natives?" he said.

"Of course," she said, dropping the bags on the bed. "Can't go home without some gifts."

They had not talked about Dennis's decision to go to St. Paul's. She argued with him that morning at breakfast, but gave up quickly. It was Judy's last night in London and she preferred peace, not war at this time.

"Did you make reservations?" Judy asked.

"Yes; they only had 7:45. It's supposed to be a very nice, cozy restaurant. Can't say that I'm happy to see you go tomorrow. You can't stay a little longer?"

"Lord, no," she said. "I had a call from Clive this morning, and he's begging for me to return. He's got two new cases."

"Oh, well," Dennis said.

He looked out the hotel window and was surprised to see the sun shining, casting long shadows across the busy street below.

"The sun sets so early here," he said. "Something like 4:00 p.m. Seems like a gloomy, cold, rainy country."

"Ah well, I'll be flying back into spring Down Under, and I bet the sun doesn't set until around seven thirty this time of year. Think what you're missing."

"Not for long," he said as his phone rang.

Judy put away the shopping bags and listened as Dennis argued with someone.

"No, I told him I wanted to see it one more time, that's all," he said. "Damnit, Chandler, the investigation is still ongoing and I'm requesting another look at the video. And yes, that is all I need at this point."

✦

Judy pulled on her running shoes and slid her room key in a small pocket on her running shirt. She checked her watch. It was 4:35 p.m. and pitch-black outside, with the usual crush of London rush-hour traffic.

"Do you have to run at night?" Dennis asked. "You'll be hit by a car."

"Don't be silly," she said, stretching out on the hotel carpet. "I need to burn off some nervous energy. And you're the one that has to watch out this evening. I'm going to walk you partway to St. Paul's then run a long route through the park back to the hotel and wait for you to tell me all about your skullduggery during our romantic dinner this evening. I decided to stop wasting my time worrying about you. I'm just going to go with the flow and assume you're correct that this meeting you're having is not dangerous. There, I've said it. I feel better already."

Dennis laughed. "Really. Judy, I think you're in more danger running the streets of London than I am at St. Paul's tonight."

"Let's go," Judy said, getting up off the floor. "I'm getting hungry and nervous, even if you're not."

They walked out the hotel into the hordes of Londoners on their way home. They took a left, then a shortcut through a small side street that could pass for an alley, then onto another busy thoroughfare.

"Are you sure you know how to get there?" Judy asked.

"Yep. See you back at the hotel. Wish me luck."

"I'll need the luck," she said. "You're giving me a nervous breakdown."

✦

Even though he did not remember it raining during the day, the streets had a damp coating that magnified the garish reflections of car lights and street lamps. He fought his way through the pedestrian crush, crossed two busy intersections, and then saw the spire of St. Paul's. The cold, damp air made the evening feel unpleasant against his face, and he pressed forward.

Dennis was not entirely sure he was going to meet Freddie's friend; Judy had planted just enough doubt about Pavlychko that he was nervous. And of course he was blind to whomever he was supposed to meet; he felt vulnerable and unprotected.

But he was also curious. Somewhere deep in his psyche he was being driven by a remarkably powerful force that he suspected was part guilt and part revenge. It was not going to be enough to punch a hole in a hospital wall; somehow he needed to find the perpetrator. If this meeting could advance that cause, then so be it. If he had duped himself into lowering his suspicions about the Ukrainian because of his guilt, well, so what? Either way, something was going to happen at St. Paul's. Dennis just wanted to get on with it.

An elaborate statue of a woman — perhaps a queen — ringed by iron bars stood near the base of the steps leading up to the cathedral doors. He could make out tourists being directed to a towering door to the right and followed them up and into the cathedral. The service had already started in the cavernous building, and he followed the small group of people forward.

The choir appeared to be a hundred yards ahead in a narrow section of the church; choristers wore white frocks and faced each other on both sides of the long alcove where the altar was situated. The music was somber and seemed to get lost in the huge, vaulted ceiling covered in gilded religious paintings. There were two sections where people sat; one section was closer to the altar, and another was farther back. Dennis took an open seat in the back.

He was not a religious person, and his only experience with church ceremonies was funerals and weddings. He tried to appear serious and respectful. There were many open seats, and tourists of all ethnicities and nationalities filtered in, sat for a while and then slid out through the back of the cathedral.

He wondered who was watching him; was it the Asian man in his mid-forties sitting two rows up to his right? That man periodically scanned the area, checking out everyone. Three rows up to his left sat a stiff-backed woman in her sixties with snow-white hair pulled into a dignified bun at the back of her head. She wore a beige raincoat. Was Freddie's friend a woman?

Just wait. It will happen. Don't rush it, he thought. *You're in a house of worship. What could go wrong?*

The service went on far longer than Dennis had hoped, with more people filtering in and out. There were prayers and more songs. He might have enjoyed the solemnity of it all, if it weren't for the fact that he knew someone was observing him.

Dennis scanned the enormous space, looking at the ceiling and lighting fixtures. The word "light" was somehow part of the message, but he saw numerous lights that could be important. The service went on until the choir and minister left the chamber to resounding organ music.

The service was over, and the crowd made its way to the back door. No one sat next to Dennis during the service or made an attempt to contact him.

He stood and filtered to the back. In a minute he'd be outside on the dark steps. Perhaps he would be met outside? Was there a large light fixture outside he missed?

Docents ushered churchgoers to a door to the right. Dennis lagged behind as the place emptied. At the back of the hall he saw two women and a man lighting votive candles that were lined up in five parallel tiers in front of a painting of Christ.

Dennis walked back to the candles and lingered. A tall man in a short blue wool coat to his left bowed his head as he lit a candle. Dennis heard the tourists behind him being pressed to vacate the cathedral. He turned to leave when the tall man said, "That was for Fred. A very good man."

The man turned without looking at Dennis and proceeded to join the sparse crowd as it left the church. Dennis followed at a distance as they exited into the night. The man made his way down toward the statue, where a group of tourists were taking pictures, their camera flashes giving the scene a strange, strobe-like effect.

The tall man walked across the street and entered a hotel bar; Dennis followed and saw the man sitting on a stool at the bar. Dennis sat a barstool away.

Dennis ordered a single-malt Scotch while the man perused the menu. The rush-hour crowd was boisterous, and Dennis realized if the man spoke to him across the open bar seat he would not be able to hear him, so he slid over. The man said nothing but suddenly put down his menu, took out a pen, grabbed a drink napkin and wrote something on it. He slid it to Dennis.

Fred said you needed help.

Dennis nodded and pushed the napkin back.

The man wrote again and pushed it over.

Only meet me at church. Send date/time in postcard to: occupant, PO 20199, Westminster 02110.

Dennis pulled out a pen and wrote *email or text?* and pushed it back.

The man gave a short, sharp laugh and tapped his finger on the address. Dennis looked down at it, memorized it and nodded. The man stood up, took the napkin and left.

✦

Dennis had expected Judy to be out of the shower when he got back to the hotel room, but she had not returned from her run. He couldn't wait to alleviate her fear about the meeting at St. Paul's.

He looked at his watch. It was almost six. He called her cell phone, but it rang on the desk next to him, and he remembered she thought it was too cumbersome to run with.

At 6:22 he started to wonder why her run was taking so long. He distinctly remembered that she liked to run between four and five miles per outing, depending on her whim at the moment. During their stay together in London, she had never been gone for more than forty-five minutes or so, always returning slightly winded, her cheeks pink from the cold. When he saw her off at the end of the alley earlier that evening, it had been 4:50.

He called the front desk and asked if anyone had tried to call his room, or if there were any messages for him. The answer was no.

He was not sure why, but he started going through Judy's belongings. He looked through her purse and her clothes hanging in the closet. He looked at her phone, and while he did know her password, there were no missed calls or texts that he could see on the home screen.

It felt like a small, agitated rodent was clawing the inside of his stomach. He sat down. His breathing grew shallow, so he stood up and for the fifth time in last hour opened the door and looked down the empty hallway.

He left his room and took the stairwell down to the lobby, walked around and looked into the bar area. He asked the woman behind the check-in counter whether she had seen a female jogger in the lobby. The woman said she had not.

Dennis went out the front door and looked up and down the busy street. By the time he got back to the hotel room it was 7:14. Judy had written down the restaurant name and number on the hotel's note pad. He called the restaurant and cancelled the reservations; Judy had told him it was rude and thoughtless not to cancel restaurant reservations. In truth, he was just doing anything he could to keep busy one moment to the next.

The rodent continued to rip away at his stomach.

Why would she do this to me? Is she purposely trying to frighten me? Surely she'd be aware of how crazy I would be? Damnit, Judy, where are you?

CHAPTER 13

The woman wore a traditional Muslim black headscarf covering most of her head, including her ears. Only the area from her forehead to her chin was visible. She wore a long-sleeved white cotton shirt, black pants and a black vest with the words "Metropolitan Police" stitched in white lettering across the chest. She had taken off her fluorescent yellow coat and laid it across her lap.

Her male partner left his coat on. He was about fifty years old, with silver hair at the temples and a large, florid nose. His gray eyes kept a tight focus on Dennis as they sat in the hotel room.

"How long did you say she's been missing?" the male officer said.

"Are you deaf?" Dennis said. "Haven't I told you already? It's been almost three hours since she went out for a jog. Jesus Christ, why haven't you started looking for her yet? She could have been hit by a car or mugged. Neither of you have picked up your radios since you've been here. Do something!"

"Mr. Cunningham," the woman said. "Please remember we have to make sure we ask the correct questions so that we can proceed. You said you called the local hospitals already, yes?"

"Yes, yes, yes. I called, but I don't know if someone took her to another hospital. I don't know what your emergency procedures are here."

"Mr. Cunningham," the male officer said, "you work for the United States government? Is that correct?"

"I already told you that! You've looked at my passport, haven't you?"

"And Judy White, she is a police officer with the Australian Federated Police?"

"Yes!"

"Have you contacted anyone in Australia about her disappearance?"

"No; I don't know anyone she works with. I'm sure you can call their office in Perth and find out if she's called them, can't you?"

"Of course we can," the woman said.

Dennis ran his right hand through his short, bristly hair. "Don't you folks have closed circuit cameras everywhere?" he said. "I read there are more cameras here in London than any city in the world. Isn't that true? Get on your monitors and see if you can find her. I showed you her passport. Take a copy of her picture. Send it out. Just do something, now!"

"Yes, we do have cameras, but it's not so instantaneous to get access to their videos," the man said. He looked at his partner, and they both turned and looked at him.

"Does this happen a lot in London?" Dennis asked. "Do women just disappear?"

"There have been some disappearances," the man said. "Mostly young foreign women. We don't know why. But we're looking into all of the disappearances, I assure you."

"So you know about these things?"

"There have been three instances in the past eighteen months," the female office said. "We are not sure they are related at all. There have been no bodies found, and we're not sure why these women disappeared, but some are undoubtedly runaways."

"Jesus, there may be a serial murderer out there!" Dennis said.

"That's not clear," the male policeman said. "You're jumping to conclusions. London has eight million residents. People go missing all of the time, as they do in New York City."

"But why do you seem so lackadaisical about this? She's an Australian woman; an Australian policewoman, for God's sake. Do something!"

"We have the report, and we will contact you for a more formal interview in our offices tomorrow," the man said. "Meanwhile, if we get any new information we'll let you know as soon as possible. And of course if you hear from her, please let us know."

"What formal interview?" Dennis said.

"Well, you were the last person who saw her," the man said, standing. "I'm sure the detectives would like to ask a few more questions. And of course, I think we'll be reaching out to her family and the AFP office in Perth."

✦

He did not sleep. Dennis could smell Judy's odor in the bed; perhaps it was the shampoo or cream rinse on her pillow. He wrapped his arms around the pillow and hugged it, but there was no sleep. Just turmoil. Like a small craft at sea in a gale, Dennis's mood swayed back and forth in wave-like rhythm from fear to gloom. Back and forth it went, and at one point around 4:00 a.m. he found himself physically swaying in bed, holding Judy's pillow, as if matching each wave.

The phone rang, and he grabbed it without looking at the number.

"Judy?"

"No, mate," a man answered. "Is this Dennis Cunningham?"

"Yes, who is this?"

"My name is Clive Smith. I work with Judy here at the AFP office in Perth. I'm sorry for calling at this time. I believe it's 4:00 a.m. there in London, but it's important. We've received notice that Judy is missing. Is that correct?"

"How did you get my number?" Dennis asked. Right away he knew it was the wrong question, but he was exhausted, confused and was not even sure if this was really the Clive Judy had spoken about.

"Ah, well, Judy has a close friend here named Cilla, and she had your number. Like I said, I'm sorry for calling, but we're all quite concerned here. Is she still missing?"

"Yes," Dennis said. "She went out for a jog last night and never returned. I can't get anyone here to treat it seriously. What is wrong with these London police?"

"Well, mate, they certainly contacted us, I can tell you, and asked a lot of questions. They asked a lot of questions about you, Dennis, but to be honest, none of us has ever met you. Though of course we've heard a lot about you and that unfortunate incident in Washington."

Dennis did not know what to say, and at least five seconds of silence ensued.

"So she hasn't called in there?" Dennis said.

"No, mate, nothing. We just thought we'd ask you directly."

"She just went out for a jog, and she never came back. This is a huge city. People just don't disappear in London."

"I would think not," Clive said.

✦

Chandler looked across the desk at Dennis and rocked gently in his office chair.

"You there, Louise?" Chandler said.

"Yep," she said, her voice artificially amplified through the phone speaker.

"I guess you could say we have a situation; the one I spoke to you about this morning. I've got Cunningham here now. The man seems capable of creating trouble wherever he goes."

"That's not appropriate, Phillip," Louise barked. "Think you could take it down just a notch?"

"Only if Cunningham stops causing trouble."

"Jesus, Phillip."

"Fine. Whatever."

"So what are we looking at?" Louise asked. "They want to interview Dennis as a person of interest? Is that it?"

"Something like that," Chandler said. "I'm sure you know the drill. Cunningham does not work for the embassy or the consulate or the military here and has no official diplomatic immunity. But through international rules of protocol, we can request that he not be interviewed by local authorities in an investigation. I mean, you know all that."

"So what's the big deal?" Louise said.

"Well, I was wondering if we should let Cunningham talk to the Metropolitan Police? To be honest, I'm kind of curious how this woman disappeared. You know she's Australian Federal Police?"

"So, let me get clear on one point," Louise said. "Dennis, you believe there is no connection between what happened to Kaczka and the disappearance of this woman, Judy?"

"Well, I've thought about it a million different ways, and it just doesn't connect," Dennis said, absently rubbing the unshaved stubble on his chin. "The team here at the London station has poked and prodded the issue as well. It just doesn't seem like there would be any reason for the Ukrainian to grab her. If anything, it would bring a ton of bricks down on his stupid head and would heat up an investigation. And apparently there have been some disappearances."

"What disappearances?" Louise said.

"Police say several women have gone missing in the last eighteen months or so," Chandler said. "No bodies. Just missing women."

"How many?" she said.

"Maybe three," Chandler said, "but police say one of those might be a runaway."

"So this is not related to our case then," Louise said.

"Nope. But like I said, Louise, I think we should let the Metropolitan Police talk to our intrepid investigator here. Who knows, they might find something."

Dennis narrowed his bloodshot eyes on Chandler across the desk and swore that he saw something akin to hatred cross that man's visage.

"Hey, Phillip," Louise said, "do you have a tumor? That's the stupidest fucking thing I've heard in a long while. There is no way Dennis is being interviewed by London police."

"We've already lost one guy who was working with this clown, and now his girlfriend is missing. I don't know why you insist on protecting him, Louise. The guy is toxic, or maybe worse."

"The answer's no," Louise said. "Do me a favor. Send Cunningham back to his hotel, and you call me back in five. We need to get something straight between us."

"Whatever," Chandler said, hanging up. "Oh, and by the way, Cunningham," he said. "The AFP is sending two people here from Perth, and they want to talk to you as well. You going to dodge them too?"

It would have felt wonderful to lean across the desk and hit Chandler as hard as he could, but Dennis's knuckles were still a little sore from his hospital wall incident. Besides, he was drained of nearly every ounce of energy, and it took a lot for him just to keep his head steady. He stood up slowly, looked down at Chandler and sighed.

"You," Dennis said.

"Me?" Chandler said.

"You," Dennis repeated, turned and left the room. He did not know what it meant, but the "you" sounded good and mysterious. And besides, it was better than hitting the London head of station.

✦

"I need to talk now! Right now," Dennis said.

"I can't talk now, Dennis, I have a patient in the waiting room. And besides, I can't talk to you unless I use the encrypted phone they gave me for agency patients. You've never called me like this before. Is everything all right?"

"No. I'm losing my mind."

"Dennis, just sit down and relax. Give me your number and I'll call you back."

When Dr. Forrester called a few minutes later, Dennis gave a rambling, sloppy and emotional description of Judy's disappearance. But he also worked in the poisoning of Fred and the police requests for an interview with him.

"Dennis," she said, "slow down. You told me earlier that you were in crisis. What do you mean that you're losing your mind?"

"I can't seem to calm down," he said. "I mean, Judy's missing! Just gone like that. Pfft. And Freddie. Holy shit."

"Dennis, does the agency have psychiatric services available in London? Do you know how to check on that?"

"I don't need psychiatric services, I need Judy," Dennis sputtered.

"I'm going to check on my end about services," she said. "Dennis, you're in crisis, and I can hear it in your voice. Do you feel like you're going to hurt yourself or someone? Are you capable of that right now?"

"If I find the bastard that hurt Judy, you bet I'd kill him right now!"

"Dennis, no one knows what happened to Judy yet, isn't that right? So you shouldn't think like that. Do you feel like you could harm yourself?"

"Me?"

"Yes, you. Are you despondent enough to harm yourself? Just answer that question," Dr. Forrester said.

"No, I don't think so."

"You don't think so? Is that a definitive answer? Are you carrying a weapon?"

"No, I don't carry weapons."

"What kind of medications do you have near you?"

"I don't have any medicines," he said. "I stopped taking that stuff you wanted me to take a long time ago."

"The Zoloft?"

"Yes."

"You have nothing else?"

"No, I told you that already, Dr. Forrester! I'm just feeling like the whole world is upside down. Things are confusing. And Judy's missing. And I think they think I did something to her."

"Who said that?"

"The police."

"The agency?"

"No, London police. I think they want to interview me. Can you believe that? Instead of looking for her, they want to interview me. Idiots!"

"Okay, Dennis. Please do me a favor, and do not drink alcohol right now. Just go for a long walk, go back to your hotel room and try to get some sleep. I'm going to try to find an approved physician for you to see in London. It will take me a while. Just hang in there."

"Why do I need to see a physician?"

"I need you to get a scrip. Something to calm you down. Very mild stuff."

"I don't need any damn medicine, I just need to find Judy."

✦

He took a long walk, keeping his eyes out for Judy at every street corner, through every shop window and on every park bench. It was useless, of course, and Dennis knew it, but at least it was something active. After an hour and a half he was back in the hotel room, lying in bed, staring at the ceiling.

Dr. Forrester was right, he thought. *I'm calmer now. Maybe I can sleep.*

But before he closed his eyes, his phone rang.

"Yes, Louise," he said, looking at the incoming number.

"This is the drill. You ready?"

"Yes, I guess."

"Before I go on, I want to make something perfectly clear."

"Okay."

"What I'm about to tell you is not a negotiation, it's an order. There is no variation you are allowed to take in regards to these directives. If you break any of these orders, you will be subject to very serious disciplinary actions, including arrest. These orders come right from the director to the IG, and then to me. In shorthand, this is no bullshit. I know you're going through a very tough period right now, but I'd like you to focus on the fact that if you screw any of this up, you'll be arrested, handcuffed and flown back to the States in a military transport and be incarcerated. Tell me you understand."

Dennis lay in the bed, his right hand holding the phone against his ear, his left arm splayed out across the bed where Judy had slept. His eyes were closed and he breathed slowly.

"Dennis?"

"Yes."

"You didn't answer me."

"I'm thinking, Louise."

"Don't think; just say yes, and let's get going. I'm trying my best to save you and your career, but if you screw this up, you're done here."

"That bad?"

"Yes, that bad. I have no idea why the director is involved; all I know is that you are a very hot potato, to use a stupid metaphor. Just tell me you're on board."

"I'm on board," Dennis said slowly.

"Dennis, are you drunk or taking drugs? Your voice is slurred."

"I haven't slept properly in thirty-six hours. I'm tired. And confused."

"Just tell me you're on board."

"I'm on board."

"Good. Ready?"

"Ready."

"Pack your bags only; leave Judy's stuff exactly as it is. Do not touch anything of hers. Just pack your own stuff. There is a flight to Dulles that you've been booked on at 6:00 p.m. London time. Take that flight home and call me when you land, regardless of the time. Got that?"

"Why can't I pack Judy's stuff?"

"Some Aussies from their embassy are coming, and they want to pack her stuff and search the room."

"Sounds like they're looking for some evidence or something," he said.

Louise said nothing.

"Do they think I did something to her?"

"I have no idea what they're thinking. All I know is what I've been told to do to get you out of there."

"Why do I have to leave London?"

"That's none of your business. Just follow orders."

"Louise, please. Help me out just a bit. I'll do everything you ask. Just tell me why I have to leave London."

"This is unofficial, and I'll deny telling you this, but the London station has requested you be pulled out due to Kaczka's death and now the disappearance of Judy. They have made the case that you are damaged goods and need to be relieved, and they went to the very top, and the director of the agency has suggested to the IG that you be pulled out. Simple as that. The IG agrees that there's something wrong."

"What if I decide to stay and keep looking for Judy?"

"Then they'll find you, arrest you and return you in chains to a US military prison."

"Ridiculous," he said.

"Get some sleep and be on that plane. Please don't do something stupid. There will be no good outcomes if you fail to get on that plane, I promise."

CHAPTER 14

It happened so fast and with such spectacular ferociousness that Judy was incapable of resisting.

She had made the same run several times during her stay in London, although they had been during daylight hours. There was one part of the run where she ran two loops around the walking path of a large park, then followed the path as it existed onto a side street, where she took a hard right and ran on the edge of the sidewalk for another half mile. By this time in her run the endorphins had usually kicked in, and she was in glide mode, alert to her surroundings but also contemplative. She thought about introducing Dennis to her parents and friends and wondered how he'd respond.

This time, after the second loop, she started to exit the park and was about to make the right turn when she noticed a white van stopped on the street about ten feet in front of her. The door was open and the interior light was on. A man with a ski mask pulled over his face sat inside, looking directly at her.

She had been daydreaming about Dennis, so she was confused about the van. But at the moment she slowed up, two people came up behind her, lifted her by the arms and threw her into the van.

Judy fell on her knees and could feel hands grabbing her. She started to scream as the van roared off, but a gloved hand covered her mouth. At nearly the same instant she felt something sharp pressed against her neck and then a stun gun discharge.

✦

First, there was a vague feeling of discomfort, which was followed, inexplicably, by a soaring euphoria and a lightness of being.

At some point Judy opened her eyes and tried to focus on her surroundings. There was a gauzy quality to her consciousness, as if she was under a huge white tent of cheesecloth flapping in the breeze.

She tried to move her right hand, but it would not budge. Suddenly, the pleasant feelings were overwhelmed by a dark fear. Her memory suddenly started working, replaying up to the moment she was thrown into a vehicle.

Judy struggled to move her legs and arms, but she seemed bound.

"Ah, you are awake," she heard a woman say. "Please don't struggle, you will hurt yourself. Relax, please."

Judy's focus returned, and she found herself looking up at the ceiling, which held a single light bulb surrounded by a faded, metal shade. Looking left and right, she saw that her arms and legs were firmly bound with a very heavy cloth-like rope.

A woman sat in a chair to her left and repeated soothingly, "Just relax." The woman was perhaps in her twenties and had long, straight black hair that was parted down the center. She was attractive and thin, with long, arching eyebrows, a small, pointed nose and perfectly round mouth.

"Where am I?" Judy said hoarsely.

"You are here with us," the woman responded. "My name is Agata."

Judy scanned the room, taking in the bare cement walls, the bulb hanging from the ceiling, what looked like an open toilette, and a small sink and shower against the far wall. She turned back to Agata.

"Why are you holding me like this? What do you want?"

"Ah, everything is fine, you will see," Agata said.

"Where are you from?" Judy said.

"Serbia," she said, smiling broadly.

Judy found Agata's welcoming behavior confusing, given that she was bound to a bed and in a bare-bones room.

"What do you want with me?" Judy pressed.

"Me? I want you to be happy."

"How can I be happy if I'm tied up, Agata? Can you untie me, please?"

"Ah, no. I am so sorry. I cannot do that." Agata proffered a sympathetic smile and gently squeezed Judy's forearm.

"Who can untie me then?"

Agata sighed and shrugged. "So sorry," she said. "I go now and get them."

"Get who?" Judy said.

Agata smiled, stood up and walked in small delicate steps around the bed and out the door into a hallway.

She tried the bindings again, but they were expertly attached to her wrists and ankles. The sense of powerlessness was barely surpassed by dread.

Where am I? I think I was grabbed and thrown into a van while jogging. Is that what happened, or did I just imagine it? Why am I so foggy? What in God's name do they want with me?

Judy turned her head toward the door as the sound of footsteps came from the hallway.

✦

He boarded the flight as if weighted down by a thousand bungee cords; he moved slowly, each step farther from London stretching the cords to their limit. Dennis wondered vaguely if he was being observed, but it was not important. He'd decided to accede to Louise's dictum, even though it ran counter to his desire to search the entire city of London by himself.

But he was also very disturbed by the swirling events that had occurred in a short span of time in the United Kingdom; Freddie poisoned and deceased, and now Judy missing. An investigation of a missing agency official had spawned a cascade of violence and loss. Now he was being recalled and prevented from doing the only thing he wanted: looking for Judy. How could this be happening? *Why* was this happening?

✦

"But I'd like to talk to those folks," he said. "Why can't I?"

"Dennis, it's simply not something we do," Louise said. "It's bad precedent. We can't let those investigators talk to you. Months from now the

Aussies will bring it up again as justification for interviewing another agency employee on some cockamamie case, and we'll have to dance
around a denial. It's just not done. And by the way, you look like shit.
When was the last time you shaved?"

"The day Judy disappeared."

"I see."

"I know you think I'm being a pain in the ass," he said, "or worse, that
I'm off my rocker, but Judy is still missing, and I think I could get something out of talking to these investigators."

"What do you mean?"

"I mean that these folks worked with Judy in Perth. They have some
questions about my relationship with Judy, and I have questions about
Judy that I'd like them to answer. Each day that goes by with her missing is bad, Louise. You know that. You've grounded me, taken me off the
investigation and put me in limbo. I'm just trying to warn you that I did
my part by getting out of London, but at this point I don't care about my
career. In fact, I don't care about anything except finding Judy. And after I
find her, I'm going to find my Ukrainian friend."

"Jesus, you are a wreck. You can't just go off running back to London.
And stop mentioning the Ukrainian. You're not in operations, and if there
was a directive for action against him, it would not include an OIG investigator, that's for sure. You're not a contract killer, for God's sake, you're a
simple investigator."

"Louise, how long have we worked together?"

"Couple of months. Seems like a couple of centuries."

"Okay. I'm trying to communicate to you that I'm about to skedaddle
out of here unless you do something to help me. I'll resign and go back to
London."

"That won't do, and you know it. They'll cancel your passport."

"I have several passports."

"It doesn't matter. They'll find you in London and arrest you. It's an
island, Dennis. You know they'll find you. I told you there is nothing I can
do. I can't single-handedly change agency policy, for God's sakes. What is
it you expect me to do? Get myself fired for you?"

"I have an idea," he said.

"And what would that be?"

"Why don't you tell the powers that be that you suspect I had a hand in Judy's disappearance and that you think it would help confirm your fears if the Australian investigators got a chance to interrogate me?"

Louise's head tilted left, then right. Each time, her straight blond hair flopped to the side, exposing a delicate, gold starfish earring. "You're a very odd person," she said slowly. "I'm not sure I've ever met someone quite like you. And I've met a few questionable people."

Dennis waited. She stared at him. Her phone rang, and she ignored it until it went to voicemail.

"You understand this is a pretty dangerous game you're playing, right?"

"What else am I to do, Louise? I'm going nuts sitting here worrying about her. Help me out, would you? You're covered on this. If this thing turns sideways, it's my ass, not yours."

"I'll let you know," she said.

"Soon, please."

"Go now."

✦

Agata entered the room first, followed by two men. The first one was short and thin, with medium-cropped black hair, a thick mustache and a long, thin nose. The second man was bulky, fat-fingered and bald.

"Hello," the small man said. "How are you today?"

Judy said nothing as they entered the room and stood on the right side of the bed near the door. Agata walked around and sat next to Judy on her left. She gently stroked Judy's hair, but Judy shook her head and said, "Stop it."

"How are you today?" the small man repeated.

Judy stared at the two men who stood to the right of the bed. Her mind whirred with anxiety: *What did they want with me? What am I doing here? Was I grabbed randomly or was I targeted?*

"Not feeling so well?" the small man said. Judy noticed his accent; it was Eastern European, perhaps. "That is understandable. It happens a lot.

Agata here will bring some food and water for you. Please make sure you stay healthy. That is very important."

The burly man opened a package covered in black cloth and tied together by a black ribbon. Agata began to gently stroke Judy's forehead and hair.

Judy arched her back and tried to pull her arms free of the constraints as she saw the small man fidgeting with the syringe. Agata cooed softly to Judy as she yelled and whipped her head back and forth on the pillow.

The burly man sat on the bed and tied a rubber tube around Judy's right bicep; his hands were so large and powerful that she could not move her arm, though the rest of her body writhed. She saw the small man lean forward, she felt a very sharp prick, a tiny amount of pain, then the most amazing feeling of pleasure cascaded from the top of her head down to her toes.

"Ah, yes," she heard Agata purr as Judy's eyelids fluttered. "Isn't that nice?"

✦

Dr. Forrester sat impassively listening to Dennis, nodding and taking a small note every now and then.

"There is no new information on Judy?" she said.

"Nothing. She's vanished. And I'm going back to look for her. I don't care what my new boss thinks."

"But the consequences seem very severe, Dennis, don't you think?"

"Who cares?"

"This man, Freddie; you sounded very fond of him. It must have been very hard for you to see him suffer."

Dennis had been seeing the agency-approved psychologist for several years, and while he grudgingly agreed that his self-awareness had improved greatly, he was also growing tired of her efforts to get him to express emotion. She was doing it now by drawing him out on Freddie.

"Yes, of course it was tough to watch. Especially since it was my idea to bring him along to visit that Ukrainian."

"Do you feel guilty for his death?"

"Of course I do!"

"Are you sure you were responsible? You said there is no hard evidence it was the visit to the Ukrainian that caused the poisoning. And even if it was related, Freddie agreed to go along, didn't he? You didn't force him."

"Yes, that's true, but it was all because of me," Dennis said. "I could have left him back at the hotel. And now he's dead."

"When you called me from London, you sounded like you were in crisis, but I've seen you twice since, and you appear more controlled. What's happened to calm you down?"

"I'm more focused now. I have a plan."

"What kind of plan?" Dr. Forrester asked.

Dennis frowned. "A plan."

"Do you intend to hurt someone, or even yourself?"

"Hurt myself? Of course not."

"Dennis, I feel like you're manipulating me right now. That's not how we've interacted in the past. We've always been truthful with each other, as hard as that has been at times."

"I'm being truthful now. I have a plan. I feel focused. I feel calm. I've always been better when I'm mission-oriented. I don't think that's a surprise."

"No, that is not a surprise," she said. "But the plan thing worries me."

"A man without a plan is not a man. Nietzsche said that."

"Heavens, Dennis. Nietzsche?"

"Great Hall of Fame player. Played second base for the '42 Dodgers. Hit for power."

"I think our time is up today," Dr. Forrester said.

◆

The room was too large for four people, but it was just as well in order to defuse the tension, Dennis thought.

"Thank you for permitting us to visit," Clive said to Louise. "I gather that there were official objections to the request, but again, we appreciate your cooperation. Meeting here at Langley is quite impressive. Never thought I'd ever be inside the inner sanctum of the CIA. My colleague Phil and I were hoping to ask Dennis just a few questions and leave you busy folks to your work."

Louise nodded politely. "Well, we're not in the inner sanctum. This is the public area at Langley. But please proceed."

"Ah well, then," Clive said, "let's get going."

Dennis did his best to appear polite and calm during his recitation of the events surrounding Judy's disappearance. The Aussies had placed a small digital recording device on the table, and Dennis attempted to speak toward it, as if the device was a person. The questioning was moving along in an orderly fashion when Phil suddenly said, "Do you normally go through Judy's personal belongings?"

"Pardon?" Dennis said.

"You know, do you typically browse through Judy's purse and wallet?"

"I don't get you."

"Your fingerprints were discovered on every item in Judy's purse, including her credit cards, compact, nail file, comb, everything," Phil said.

Dennis felt Louise's head swivel a modest degree in his direction.

"No. I believe I looked through her purse to see if I could find anything that would explain where she was."

"But her credit cards? Her passport?" Phil said.

Dennis felt a sudden surge of anger, and he knew it would be a bad decision to show it, so he used a small trick to distract himself. He focused on a tiny freckle on Phil's forehead, above his right eye.

"Like I said, I looked through everything I thought might provide a hint to why she was missing."

"I see," Phil said.

Clive picked up the questioning and pressed on Dennis's efforts to find her, including checking with the lobby, his calls to local hospitals and the police. And then, just when Dennis felt the session was drawing to a close, Clive said, "Did you cut yourself in the hotel room?"

"What?"

"Did you cut yourself?"

"No, why?"

"Did Judy injure herself or cut herself in the hotel room?"

"No," he said, too quickly, as a surge of anger bubbled up and overrode his caution.

"Well, the hotel maid reported that one day when she emptied the waste bin in the bathroom, there were several tissues with large blood stains on them. Of course, it was too late to find out where the trash was sent to, so we could not corroborate it."

"Judy cut herself shaving," Dennis said. "I forgot that."

Again, he felt Louise's head twitch minutely in his direction.

"But I thought you just said neither of you cut yourselves," Clive said.

"I said I forgot. She cut herself shaving her legs."

"What else might you have forgotten?" Phil said.

"Well, I forgot how idiotic AFP investigators are."

"Dennis," Louise said.

"Sorry."

The two men looked at each other and then back to Dennis.

"Is there anything else you left out that we should know?" Clive asked.

"Yes, actually. Have you looked into her recent cases that raised any red flags? Had she received death threats?"

"None that we know of," Clive said. "We worked together on most of our cases, and she would have notified the group if she had been threatened. But it's not impossible that a disgruntled criminal might try something stupid."

"Like who?" Dennis asked.

"There are so many cases she worked on over the years that it's impossible to guess. But we are looking into that. And there was the famous Voorster case, which you know all too well."

"Who's Voorster?" Louise said.

"A South African gangster," Phil said. "Judy broke up a drug ring, with help from yours truly sitting next to you."

Louise looked at Dennis. "You?"

"It's a long story," Dennis said.

"What happened to this Voorster guy?" Louise said.

"He disappeared," Phil said. "There's every reason to believe he's dead. We get false reports of his reappearance all the time, but our best guess is that he's dead or in prison."

"She mentioned something about a botched raid on a junkyard," Dennis said. "It involved dogs that had to be shot. Was that case ever cleaned up? She said she was pretty shook up by that."

"Ah, yes, you are correct," Clive said. "I wouldn't say the case was botched, per se. But we did not find what we were looking for at that time, so the case was closed."

"Did she get knocked to the ground by a pit bull?"

"Yes, she did, unfortunately. She was quite upset about it."

"And her former husband is still in jail?"

"Yes, for several years more."

✦

Judy had stopped fighting; it was pointless. She did not know how many days she had been there. The big man was too strong, and the sensation of the drug hitting her bloodstream was pleasurable beyond belief. The sensation was so overwhelming that she began to justify not resisting.

The big one will just hurt me, she thought. *I can't do anything except lie here. It will end soon, so why resist? If they wanted to kill me, they wouldn't bother me with these drugs. I'll wait them out.*

And perversely, the presence of Agata during the injections was reassuring and vaguely sexual. Agata had taken to kissing Judy's forehead and stroking her hair and whispering things like, "You are so beautiful," or "Isn't that a nice feeling? You deserve to feel this way."

Judy knew they were addicting her, but she no longer cared or even wondered why. For most of the time she was no longer tied up to the bed. She sat on the bed or chair and waited patiently for the next injection. Agata had brought Judy a bright blue silk bathrobe and clean underwear. Three times a day, she also brought food and drink; Judy used the small toilet and sink. Had she been there a week? A month? She had no idea. The confusion and strangeness of her time there evaporated into the background; all she thought about were the injections. They were so nice; she loved them and was no longer self-conscious about wanting the next one. Her dreams at night were milky and indistinct. There was nothing in her life now except the injections.

But then something happened to alter her small world of pleasure.

The first time they held back on the injections, Judy began to feel ill. It was a sickness that slowly began to gnaw away at her skin, teeth and brain. She started moaning and moved toward the locked door, pressing her ear against it to see if they were coming.

They didn't come.

She pounded on the door.

They didn't come.

She suddenly started to vomit and raced to the toilet. Judy had never felt so sick; every molecule in her body began to ache with a pain that was unbearable.

Steps could be heard coming down the hallway, and Judy could barely stand. The door opened, and Agata came in first.

"Ah, you poor thing. Come here and lie down."

Judy rushed to the bed, flopped down and put her right arm out. There was no struggle any longer; the big man was not there, just Agata and the small man. They injected her, and she welcomed it, her eyes fluttering and finally closing.

Agata kissed her forehead, then her lips gently. "You rest for a while."

✦

It was not something he'd intended to do at the outset, but it was clear that it might be his only chance.

Representative Barkley's chief of staff, Chuck Morton, was a surprisingly young man, perhaps no more than thirty-five, Dennis thought. He waited in the outer office for thirty minutes before he was ushered into his office.

"So, how can I help you?" Morton said. "You said you've talked to the representative before? You work in OIG in Langley?"

"Yes, that's correct. And Representative Barkley and I have an understanding," Dennis said.

"What kind of understanding?"

"An understanding that we will communicate with each other when there are pressing issues to discuss."

Morton cleared his throat, unscrewed the cap of a plastic bottle of water, took a short sip, then slowly and deliberately screwed it back on. His hand on the thin plastic water bottle made a crinkling sound.

"I see. And am I to presume you would like me to mention to the congressman that you have a pressing issue to discuss?"

"That is correct."

"How may I get in contact with you?"

Dennis handed him a business card. "I've written down the number of a private cell phone."

"And if he does not wish to discuss anything with you, you'll not hear from him. And I would appreciate you not pressing the issue. If the representative does not wish to talk to you, I hope you'll honor that wish."

"Of course."

Dennis had found a public parking space on the National Mall. After he got into his car, an incoming text message pinged his phone.

tomorrow same place/time as last

CHAPTER 15

The sandwich was on white bread with curried egg salad and lettuce. Agata smiled as Judy sat on the bed, eating.

"You are so pretty," Agata said.

"Why am I here?" Judy asked.

Agata shrugged.

"What do they want with me?"

Agata made a face that Judy could not interpret.

"Is it heroin I'm getting?"

"Yes, and some fentanyl. Do you like?"

Judy ignored the question. "Why?" she asked again. "Why me?"

Agata shrugged again.

Judy looked at Agata's arms and could see the pinpricks.

"How long have you been here?"

"I don't know," Agata said, smiling. "A long time. A short time. One doesn't count the days."

"Did they grab you too?"

For the first time, Judy noticed Agata's demeanor change from pure, unadulterated complacency to confusion and conflict.

"Mmm," Agata said. "You are not eating well. You must eat. The medicine will make you not hungry, but you must eat."

"It's not medicine, Agata."

She smiled and stood up, taking the plate from Judy.

After the door was locked, Judy got up and began to pace the floor. She had developed a small workout routine out of boredom and a desperate attempt to regain some control over her strange life. She walked around her room for what she estimated was thirty minutes. Then she stretched and completed a sequence of exercises on the cold cement floor. She was in control of the walking and the number and duration of the exercises. At the end of each session, she felt winded, sweaty and healthy.

But there was also a sickness that had infected her body and mind; each day in the room had broken her down just a little more. She was vaguely aware that her workout routine was a lie; it *seemed* like she had more control. But she didn't, really. They were starting to delay her injections, and the mere thought of those delays made her break out in sweat. She noticed that her nose was running, and the injection sites at the crook of her arms were beginning to bruise.

Do all addicts lie to themselves? Is this how they trick themselves into believing they are in control? Perhaps there are now two Judys, the addict Judy and the Judy who is in control. Or is there just the one Judy who lies to herself?

Not long after her workouts, she found her focus invariably fell to those glorious and wonderful injections.

✦

Dennis ordered a Chinese chicken salad from Sally at the Cheesecake Factory.

"Haven't seen you for a while," she said. "Business? And what's with the beard?"

"I'm trying to look older."

She laughed.

"And yes, I was traveling for work."

"Fun, I hope," she said. "I just work here, go to school during the day, study on my time off. And then repeat."

"What are you studying?"

"Political science, or that's my major. My minor's in philosophy."

"Philosophy? Really? Why that for a minor?"

"Don't ask; I can't even explain it to my boyfriend. I just like it."

"Do you have a favorite philosopher? Aristotle?"

"If I had to choose, it would probably be Paul Ricœur. Yeah, I'd say Ricœur."

"Ha. Never heard of the guy."

"He was French. A little obscure, but very interesting."

"Okay, so in twenty words or less, tell me why he's your favorite philosopher."

"Wow, that's a tough one," Sally said, laughing, placing her hands on her hips and raising her head in thought. "Let me think. I'd say something like, he's not dogmatic and angry, like a lot of the twentieth-century European philosophers. And he believes we strive to make our lives intelligible, and you can't divorce the body from the mind like Descartes suggested; they're the same thing. Or something like that. Boy that was hard!"

He laughed. "My head's spinning, Sally, but not my body."

"Very good!" she said, moving down the bar to attend to a couple that had just sat down.

Dennis toyed with his salad for a while. He had lost weight and was fighting the tug of depression that had followed him for many years. With Dr. Forrester he had made great progress in tracing his sordid family life as the origin of his illness, but Freddie's death and now Judy's disappearance had shaken him. His mission was to get back to London immediately, sanctioned or not. Today was his last attempt to make it legal.

"Barely recognized you," Barkley said, sitting down on the open stool to Dennis's left.

"It's my mountain-man look," Dennis said.

"So what's going on? I have my daughter's birthday party this evening, so talk fast."

"I got yanked from the Arnold investigation," Dennis said, putting down his fork and grabbing his glass of water.

"I heard someone got ill and died. But I hadn't heard they'd pulled you out. Why?"

"We were getting close to something," Dennis lied. "Guess they don't want me poking around there."

"Can I get you something?" Sally asked Barkley.

"Ah, yes. How about a glass of red wine? Cabernet?"

"You got it," she said.

The two men stared in silence at the bottles of liquor on the wall in front of them. Sally brought the glass of wine and placed it in front of Barkley.

"Thank you," the congressman said.

The two men sipped their drinks.

"When you say you were on to something there, can you be more specific?"

"Something is wrong with the head of station there," Dennis said. "Can't quite figure it out, but it has something to do with the last visit by Arnold to Menwith Hill. I just need more time and another look at the video."

"What video?"

"Closed circuit of Arnold's last visit. They won't show it to me."

"Who won't show it? Fort Meade or Langley?"

"Not sure, to be honest."

More silence.

Barkley took another sip of his wine and then looked at his watch.

"Do you know why I insisted you get involved with this case?" Barkley said, staring straight ahead.

"No."

"I thought you could unearth something."

"That's what I'm trying to do."

"No, I don't think you're close. I don't think you know what's really going on there."

"Well, if you know something, you're not helping me much."

Barkley smiled briefly, looked down at his wine, took another sip and pushed it away. "I only have so many chits I can call in, and I'm willing to use one more. But that's it. Maybe I was wrong. Maybe you're not the person to shock these bastards."

Dennis turned toward the congressman, taken aback by the sudden anger in the man's voice, but he had already stood up.

"Do you mind picking up the wine?"

"No, not all. Good evening, Congressman."

✦

Richardson drummed his fingers on the tabletop, waiting for Dennis and Louise to sit down. For a man with a reputation for being unflappable and even-tempered, he was remarkably agitated, Dennis thought.

"You know, I don't appreciate what's going on here," Richardson said.

"What do you mean, Bill?" Louise said with a small flip of her hair.

"Something is going on behind my back on this Arnold investigation, and I don't like it. I'm greatly disadvantaged on this account. I have one boss, the director here, telling me to do one thing, and I'm getting pressure from another boss in the House of Representatives to do another thing. I thought the investigation was over after a man from the NSA was lost, not to mention that our investigator here was ordered back to the States for creating a ruckus in jolly old London, including the disappearance of his Australian girlfriend." At this point Richardson raised his hands into the air in an isn't-that-right gesture.

"And what is it with the beard, for God's sake, Cunningham? Have you gone completely native?"

"No, sir," Dennis said. "Just a change in appearance. I didn't think the IG was interested in my facial hair, sir."

Louise's good left foot kicked Dennis's right foot under the table.

"And now an insolent bearded investigator to boot. Great. Just great."

"Bill, Dennis here has been under a lot of pressure, as you well know. He and his NSA partner, Fred Kaczka, were very close to breaking open the Arnold case when a series of deadly events occurred. We believe that they were all related to getting Dennis here off the trail."

Dennis shot Louise a glance.

"Wait," Richardson said. "I thought the two events were not connected? It specifically states in the report that the Kaczka's death and the woman's disappearance are independent of each other. You told me that in person."

"We now believe the woman was taken precisely to accomplish the goal of driving Dennis back to the States and off the Arnold investigation. And you'd have to admit it was brilliant. Because here he is, sitting in your office right now, Bill, and he's not in London tracking down what happened to Arnold."

Richardson's face crumpled into a frown. He started to speak to Louise and then stopped and pivoted to Dennis.

"I don't think I like you very much, Cunningham. My job is difficult enough without this kind of trouble. And I'm getting pressure from the House chairman, of all people. Why the hell does he care about this?"

He turned back to back to Louise.

"Fine! Great! Send him back to London. Just get him the hell out of here. Louise, would you mind staying behind for a moment?"

"Certainly, Bill."

Dennis stood up and hustled out of the room. He raced back to his office, closed the door and opened the small notebook in which he kept his investigative notes. He turned to the pages where he had listed all of the circumstances around Judy's disappearance and reread them. He closed the notebook and tossed it on the desk.

Someone knocked at his door.

"Come in."

Louise poked her head in.

"Got a second?"

"Of course."

He watched her navigate awkwardly around the single chair he kept for infrequent guests and was reminded about her prosthetic right foot.

"I just got in trouble back there."

Dennis sighed. "I guessed as much. I'm sorry, Louise. You should have just let me resign and try to sneak into the UK. Why are you putting yourself out there on this one? You have a family and a career. I have nothing to lose."

"My husband asked me the same thing," Louise said, staring at her hands as they fidgeted in her lap. "The odd thing is, I don't have an answer, for him or you. There are too many moving parts in this one, which to me translates to something very serious. I'm not prepared to let this one go quite yet."

Dennis tried to figure out where Louise was going with her comments; she had never dropped her guard like this before in his presence, and she appeared oddly vulnerable but heroic at the same time. They were enviable qualities that Dennis did not share. Perhaps it was the same qualities of loyalty and grit that put her in harm's way in Lebanon but also kept her alive in the rubble. He felt a sudden affinity for the small, blond, disabled warrior on the other side of the desk.

"How can I make your exposure go away on this case?" he asked. "I don't want another person's life or career on my conscience."

She stiffened, raised her chin and focused her pale blue eyes on his.

"I'll cover you as long as I can back here," she said. "I'll only ask two things."

"Name them."

"You keep me informed — like, really informed."

"You got it."

"And you work on the Arnold case while you're looking for Judy. I mean *actually* work on it."

"I will do that."

She stood up.

"Can I ask you a question?" Dennis said.

"Shoot."

"Was that a ploy back there to link Judy's disappearance to Freddie's death? I liked it. Very convincing. But was it just a ploy, or do you really think they're related? You never said anything to me about them being connected."

"You know," she said, tilting her head in the way that she did, "for such a good investigator, you really suck sometimes."

"Yes," he said, frowning, "I guess I do."

CHAPTER 16

They no longer locked the door, which she found odd.

Judy would sometimes stand by the open door and peer down the poorly lit hallway. She could hear voices, some male, some female. There was often laughter and whispering, but no screaming and no violence. Everything seemed normal, yet she was being kept in a Spartan room, in a silk robe, being fed and given opioid injections on a more or less regular basis.

Agata had told her that under no circumstances was she to leave her room, and Judy had obeyed. Only once had she yelled down the hallway when they were late with an injection.

She slept a lot and experienced wonderful dreams after the injections. She was no longer scared or even angry about what was happening to her. Her world had become very small.

But there was also discomfort when they delayed an injection, and the aching and physical pain was extraordinarily powerful.

This day Judy decided not to do her physical workout. She lay in bed, staring at the cement ceiling, following a small crack as it spread out toward the wall.

She looked at the inside of her right elbow; there were many small prick marks and two large bruises where the vein had hemorrhaged. She gently ran the tips of her left hand across the wounds and felt a sudden chill and ache in her stomach.

They were late again.

Why do they do this? Just come down here and give it to me. Don't they know I'm going to get sick? This hurts!

Her mouth felt dry, and she rolled out of the bed and shuffled over to the sink. Cupping her hand underneath the faucet, she drank the trapped water as it trickled out. Then she walked over to the open door and put her head out into the hallway. Her stomach hurt, and her body began to ache, so she clutched her arms around her chest and started to walk around the room.

"My God, come on! Let's get going," she said out loud.

She returned to the doorway. "Hey!" she yelled. "Hey. Please?"

No one answered.

Judy could feel herself getting sicker by the seconds, and she rushed to the toilet and dry-heaved over it. Out of breath and in pain, she went back to the door and clutched her thin robe around her. She called again, and this time stepped outside the door into the darkened hallway.

"Hey!" she yelled.

There were muffled voices far away, so Judy timorously stepped down the hallway in her bare feet. She began to shiver from the cold floor and the drug sickness. Her nose began to run again, and she wiped it on the back of her wrist.

The hallway was twenty feet long, leading to an L-shaped turn to the left. She slowly pushed her head around the corner when she got to it and saw a small room with an oriental carpet, several cushioned chairs, a small table and a floor lamp. The small man sat smoking a cigarette. Across from him sat Agata and another young woman, a thin blonde wearing what looked like an elaborate kimono. All three looked at Judy. Agata showed a restrained, sad smile, and the small man rose and walked toward Judy. His face was expressionless, and as he got closer, Judy pointed to her crooked right arm and said, "Please?"

He hit Judy so hard in the stomach that she jackknifed forward and her chin made contact with her bony knees. The man grabbed her hair and dragged her down the hallway.

She screamed and held on to his wrists as she felt some of her hair coming out. He pulled her into the room and dropped her on the floor. She sat up and yelled, "Please!"

He slapped her hard on the side of the head and stomped out.

Judy lay on the cement floor and sobbed, her cheeks against the cold floor.

Agata came in and caressed Judy's shoulders and finally helped her up onto the bed. Judy clung to Agata and continued to cry.

"Why?" Judy sobbed. "Why don't they give it to me? Why?"

Agata stroked Judy's hair, comforting her as best she could.

Judy heard steps coming down the hallway and she turned, already putting her arm out for them.

The thin man entered the room, and Judy's eyes focused on the blessed black cloth-wrapped package.

"Up," he said.

Judy got to her feet.

"Come," he said, and she shuffled over to him. She flinched as he put out his hand and undid the silk belt holding her robe. He pulled the robe off her shoulders and it slid to the floor. Judy had stopped wearing underwear days ago, preferring the feeling of silk on her ravaged body.

He walked slowly around her and put his hand on her right buttock, squeezing it briefly. When he completed the circle, he stared at her breasts, putting his hand under her right breast and lifting it slightly. Judy could barely breathe; the drug sickness and physical fear were making her shiver. He dropped his hand from her breast and whipped around and yelled to Agata in a language she could not understand.

Agata nodded and spoke quickly to him. She rushed over, gathered the robe off the floor and put it on Judy. She led her to the bed, gently pushed her down and pulled up her sleeve to expose her pocked arm.

"You must eat more," she whispered. "You like ice cream? I get ice cream, yes?"

Judy could only concentrate on the black bag the man was unfolding; the syringe was the only truth in the world at that point. Nothing held more clarity for her than the syringe as she watched the tube being tied to her bicep. The needle hurt a little as it navigated around some damaged tissue, but the pain was just fine. The plunger drew in some blood then was pressed down, and she waited.

Her mouth fell open as oceans of pleasure flooded her brain, and she floated to the place that no one could bother her. No one.

✦

Dennis mailed the postcard before he boarded the plane and spent most of the six-hour trip to Heathrow going over his notes on Judy's disappearance. His research on police jurisdictions in London was more complicated. The City of London, which actually encompassed only a 1.1-square-mile area in the center of London, had its own police force. Dennis had originally spoken to two constables from this force, presumably because Judy was assumed to have disappeared in that part of London.

The larger area of London was policed by the Metropolitan Police Department, with a separate police structure.

Langley's refusal to allow the London police to interview Dennis had complicated his approach to finding Judy, since he could not go to them directly. His plans to find her — Dennis would not entertain the prospect that she was dead — rested on two people: the first was Freddie's mysterious NSA employee, and the second was a distant acquaintance from MI5 named Ian Fletcher-James.

MI5 was the closest equivalent to the FBI, and MI6 was similar to the CIA, but there were many overlapping responsibilities regarding terror investigations and surveillance of suspects. From earlier work with both MI5 and MI6, Dennis knew they were beset with precisely the same internal tensions and ridiculous layers of authority as the US security organizations, only their mutual distrust seemed more refined due to their charming Downton Abbey British accents.

✦

"It's a bit complicated, Dennis," Ian said. "You do realize that there was an investigation, and it stopped with you. The Australians are very angry, as you can imagine. They think you might have had something to do with her disappearance."

"Yes, yes, I know that, Ian. I don't care what they think. I'm trying to find her. I think — I *know* — she's alive. Can you help me with a few things?"

"It depends," Ian said, sipping his coffee. They sat inside a small coffee shop two blocks from Paddington Station. "What can I possibly help you with? It would be difficult to get my hands on the investigative reports without leaving my fingerprints, as it were, all over it. Surely you can see that I'm limited in this matter?"

"Can you at least ask someone to summarize the report? Even that would be helpful."

"Well, I've already done that."

"What did you find?" Dennis said, taking out his notebook.

"You're not going to write this down, are you?"

"No," he said, putting the notebook away. "Of course not."

"Right. From what I understand, your friend Judy left for a jog during the early evening hours and was never seen again. Because it was at night, and there were so many pedestrians and heavy traffic during the London rush hour, they have very few hints of her presence."

"I thought London was one of the most heavily monitored cities in the world with closed circuit TVs?"

"Ah, well, that is technically true, but what is not well known is that many of those cameras are not functioning. They're too expensive for the city to maintain, so only a modest percentage are active. And they do apparently have a snippet of video of you and this woman Judy walking down the alley outside the hotel. You both had your heads down. And that is it, really."

"That's it?"

"Please remember I did not see the report, Dennis. This was a verbal explanation from someone who had seen the report. This person said there might be additional footage of her, but it's murky and not reliable."

"Jesus, you'd think they'd have more than that."

"And, well, there were the blood-stained tissues the hotel maid mentioned. And the fact that you apparently went through all of her belongings."

"I'm getting nowhere," Dennis said, looking around the coffee shop.

"Sorry, but it was the best I could do on that one."

"And my Ukrainian friend?" Dennis asked.

"Well, that's more up my alley. Pavlychko has completely gone to ground. I'm surprised, frankly. We typically do a good job of monitoring people like him."

"How did he get away?"

"Appears there was a side door leading to the pathway through some private gardens and out to the street behind. Our guess is that he and his girlfriend just slid out one evening."

"Did you go through his place?"

"Of course. And you'll be interested to know there was a trace of radioactivity in his kitchen."

"Shit. Have you turned that info over to the folks at the London station?"

"Of course. Didn't you know that?"

"No. When was it turned over?"

"Perhaps a week ago. They didn't share that with you?"

"No."

"I see. Very odd. This whole thing with your fellow Arnold is quite the talk in our circles."

"What do you think happened to him?"

"Haven't the foggiest idea. I mean we knew he was of that persuasion, but in the current climate that's no longer a leverage point for an intelligence agent."

"What do you mean leverage? What are you talking about?"

"Arnold."

"What about Arnold? What do you mean persuasion?"

"I mean he was gay, of course. He was quite public about it. You can do that these days. It's not the Cold War any longer, when gays were blackmailed for being, well, gay. The London station certainly knew; we all knew. It's not such a big deal any longer if you come out."

Dennis concentrated on holding his paper coffee cup steady, though he could feel his fingers itching to crumple it in one huge stroke and throw it against the wall.

✦

Dennis walked for what seemed like miles in the cool December air, past busy Londoners taking lunch breaks. Quite a few were smoking cigarettes in hunched, furtive groups outside pubs. He was angry and knew by painful experience that he should not talk to anyone until he calmed down and developed a plan.

Arnold was gay, but that was not in any report that Dennis had been given. Presumably Freddie had not seen it either, or he would have mentioned it. Those strange text messages that Freddie's beta program had turned up between a "maybe Arnold" and his lover were now clearer.

The agency was hardly pristine in its treatment of LGBT employees. But President Bill Clinton's executive order in 1995, which stated security clearances could not be revoked or denied based on sexual orientation, had opened the door to a more open era. Dennis knew several, mostly younger LGBT employees and could not have cared less about their sexual orientation. The only contempt he harbored was for employees of any orientation that were cheaters and thieves. And liars.

As he stalked the cool streets, he could not understand why the agency had left out the fact of Arnold's sexual orientation; it was a fact, not an accusation. No one was supposed to care about sexual orientation, of course, but when a senior operative went missing, you would look for all leads, including girlfriends. Or boyfriends.

And there was the additional information that Pavlychko's house had traces of radioactivity. No one had forwarded that information to him; Chandler had even made the case that Freddie's death probably had absolutely nothing to do with the Ukrainian, which was now fully refuted.

Dennis stopped at a street corner and started to cross when an automobile horn roared to life in front of him and tires screeched. Someone yelled, and he looked to his right, where a taxi driver was gesturing wildly at him.

Damnit, he thought. *You friggin' idiot. You're not in the States; they drive on the left here. You'll get yourself killed before you even find what happened to Arnold. And Judy. Where the hell is poor Judy?*

He waved apologetically at the taxi and stepped back onto the sidewalk. He stood on the street corner and took a deep breath; the car horn had been a welcome clarion call. His natural hunter's instinct had been distracted by new information on Arnold, but in truth he didn't care at all about the guy. Judy was his mission. *Find Judy.*

He crossed the street, now looking carefully to his right, and sauntered past shop windows and bundled pedestrians. He had slipped into a kind of cruise control and was refocused on Judy. He simply prowled, looking for inspiration. He could feel something emerging; a hint, a wisp of a lead perhaps.

Dennis often took long walks in shopping malls or crowded city streets to clear his head and wait for some inspiration to solve a problem. It was never a perfect tactic, but allowing introspection and intuition to go to work was often effective.

He smelled food and found himself in a dimly lit pub. Scanning the plastic-coated menu, his eyes fell to something he'd never seen before. He put his finger on the word: "Boerewors."

Dennis pointed to the word and asked the bartender, a young man of about thirty with long brown hair, "What is this? I'm not familiar with this food."

"Ah, that's Boerewors. It's sausage. Best sausage you've ever had. From South Africa. You want an order?"

But Dennis was already halfway out the door into the brilliant glare of a December sun in London.

Of course! he thought as he pulled his phone out of his pocket.

CHAPTER 17

'm not supposed to be talking to you, unless it's on the record and being recorded," Clive said.

"I could give a shit what you do with our conversation," Dennis said. "Broadcast it on the BBC or whatever you have there. I was just hoping you could help me with a couple of questions about Judy."

"No, mate, can't help you in any way, and you'll need to call me back on my work line so I can record the conversation. And we have the ABC, not BBC here."

"What happened to Voorster, the South African gangster who escaped a couple years ago when Judy busted that ring? What happened to him?"

"Dennis, you're not hearing me. I can't talk to you like this—"

"Judy told me that he hadn't surfaced. Is that true?"

"I told you before that we think Voorster is dead," Clive said. "There was one nonconfirmed match on a passport, but we don't believe it. He had many partners in his drug business, and they were not happy when it all came tumbling down. Forget him."

"I think Voorster had something to do with Judy's disappearance, but I've racked my brain for how he would know Judy was in London, and all I come back to is Phillip."

"Her husband? That Phillip?"

"Yes, of course. I know he's in prison there, and all I can think of is that he found out Judy was visiting London. And then Phillip told someone."

"Wait, Dennis, you must be joking. How would Phillip know that? And even if he did find that out, how would he communicate with Voorster?"

"Here's what I'm thinking," Dennis said. "Like most prisoners, I would think Phillip has some telephone privileges. And that after finding out about Judy's London visit, he communicated with someone during one of his weekly calls."

"But London is a very big city, Dennis, and even if I follow your theory, it's not possible that Voorster would know where Judy was. Surely you must have thought of that?"

"Of course, that's why I need your help."

"Bloody hell. Judy warned me about your persistence. Can't say I like it much."

✦

"You must eat," Agata said. "Please eat the ice cream. You must not lose weight. It is bad."

Judy half-heartedly ate a spoonful of the chocolate ice cream, though her teeth were beginning to ache. All she knew was her bed, the cracks on the ceiling, Agata and the injections. She could no longer muster the enthusiasm to fight back or even complain. Earlier during her imprisonment she had begged Agata to help her escape, but now she did what she was told.

So she silently ate the ice cream, coaxed by a nervous Agata sitting next to her on the bed.

There were footsteps from the hallway, and Judy stopped eating, turning her head reflexively toward the door. She felt her stomach swoon a little at the thought of another glorious injection.

The small man walked in first, and Judy locked her eyes on the black bag that held the precious implements.

But it was the second man that startled her; she was confused initially, because he was new. He had dark brown hair, a long face and small nose. He was perhaps in his late thirties or early forties. Judy could feel Agata tense as she got off the bed.

There was something familiar about the stranger, but as much as she wanted to investigate his features, Judy found her gaze focusing on the black bag.

"Are you ready for your little gift this afternoon?" the small man asked, waving the bag.

Judy nodded, but she grew wary. He had never acted like this before when it came to injections; he rarely spoke and simply relied on Agata to tie off the tube on either arm. Now he was acting odd. The stranger leaned against the wall with his arms across his chest, watching carefully.

"Before you get your free gift," the small man said, "first you have to earn it. That is the way it will be in the future. You must prove your worth."

Confused, Judy shot Agata a glance, but the young woman looked away.

"Come here," the man said.

Judy got up off the bed and walked slowly over to him.

"Get down on your knees," the man said as she approached.

Judy did not like this idea, and she resisted.

He waved the black bag into her face. "You want me to go away?"

"No," she said.

"Then get on your knees."

She slid down, and her bony knees dug into the cement floor. She sat back on her haunches and looked up at him, half expecting to get slapped.

Instead, he put the bag under his left armpit, and using both hands, he pulled down the zipper on his pants.

"Go ahead," he said. "Pull it out. You know what you need to do."

Judy rolled back on her heels. She looked back at Agata, but the young woman would not look at her. She turned back and shook her head at the man.

The man pulled up his zipper and said, "That is too bad. Let's go." Agata rushed by with the ice cream container. Judy, who was still on her knees, watched them leave. They slammed the door behind them.

✦

This time the choral music seemed morose. The night was gloomier than he'd anticipated, and the misty, cold rain had reduced the volume of tourists.

Dennis sat farther back in the public section of the Evensong at St. Paul's and tapped his foot impatiently, waiting for the service to end. He pulled his raincoat tighter around his chest. He decided not to scan the visitors looking for his nameless NSA contact, since it was not important.

Dennis had followed the instructions about a postcard and expected to be contacted much the same way as last time.

At the end of the service he sauntered back to the painting. He lit a candle and waited, but his contact never appeared. Finally, he was approached by a docent and told that the cathedral was closing for the night.

He went outside and stood under the covered entrance to stay out of the rain. Looking around the steps, he saw very few people.

Damnit, he thought. *Did I mess up the postcard process? Where the hell is he?*

After fifteen minutes Dennis walked across the street to the hotel bar where he had first met the NSA employee.

Dennis did not see his contact sitting at the busy bar, but he managed to grab a stool. He asked the bartender for a menu and then ordered a hamburger and a beer.

"You an American?"

"I guess so," Dennis said warily.

"Name isn't Dennis, is it?"

"What if it is?"

"I have a message for a Yank named Dennis who might be stopping by. I've been given a couple of quid to deliver a message."

Dennis absently pulled at the hairs of his new gray-blond beard and thought a little about this. "Who did you say gave you this message?"

"Another Yank. Don't know his name. I mean, if you're not Dennis, no worries, mate."

"I am Dennis."

"Well, here you go then," the bartender said, reaching into his pocket and pulling out a folded drink napkin.

Dennis looked around the bar and opened the folded napkin. In block letters he read: *Next time lose tail. Flush down toilet now.*

The bartender brought Dennis his beer, and he took a sip. Standing up, he found the men's room, went into a stall, tore the napkin into pieces then flushed it away.

Back at the bar, Dennis wondered who would have him under surveillance. London police? Australian Federated Police? The NSA? CIA? The Ukrainian?

He desperately needed this NSA employee to find Judy, and being followed was yet another obstacle. Dennis ate half his burger before he bolted back to his hotel. If he was being tailed, he did not notice, nor did he care much. He needed to send another postcard immediately to resume contact with the only person he felt could help him find Judy. While he convinced himself that she was still alive, the fear was sinking in.

✦

"Yes, I know you are very concerned, as we are, Trevor," Clive said, using his shoulder to press his work phone against his ear. "Believe me, we have been in very close contact with the London authorities. I talked to your grandfather, and he says the family is heading to London tomorrow, is that correct?"

Clive doodled on a writing pad in his office as he listened to Judy's distressed teenage son explain the family plans. Her disappearance was so depressing that he and the rest of the staff in the AFP's Perth office could barely discuss it.

His police experience told him that after fifteen days without a trace, it was likely Judy was no longer alive. Yet, after talking to the Yank, Clive was intrigued. He did not believe Dennis was responsible for her disappearance.

He was also angry, and the policeman in him wanted some kind of closure, including the burning desire to get hold of the bastard who took Judy. If the Yank's instincts were correct, Phillip might have something to do with it. That's why he needed to tease a fragment of information out of the poor teenage boy on the other end of the line.

"So, Trevor, I assume your father knows about the family's plans to go to London?" Clive froze his doodling as Trevor answered.

"He does? I see."

Trevor explained the details of the London trip, including the London Police and Australian embassy employees the family were meeting with and when.

"Tell me, Trevor," he said, holding his ballpoint pen absolutely still, "your mum said that you hadn't been in contact with your father while he was in prison. Is that so?"

Trevor admitted that he had not seen his father but had been pressed to do so by Judy and relented.

"Ah, well good on ya for seeing your dad, Trevor. Tell me, do you remember when you saw Phillip? Do you remember the date, by any chance?"

Clive wrote down a day of the week and date then slowly circled the date several times.

"When you met with your dad in prison that day, it must have been difficult, I'm sure. I mean, all the publicity about his crimes working with that drug ring. Must have been very rough, but Judy said you were a strong young man."

He consoled Trevor as the boy admitted his distress at seeing his father in the prison meeting room. But he also admitted that when they got talking, it was sort of like old times.

"And so did you get a chance to tell Phillip about your mum's trip to London? Ah, he was surprised? Yes, I suppose he would have been. He didn't happen to ask where your mum was staying, did he? Oh he did, did he? Ah, yes, Judy would have told you the hotel. Perhaps he was just a little envious, you know, being in prison and all. London is such a grand city."

✦

Judy had thrown up the ice cream and was now dry-heaving.

She crawled back to the bed and wrapped herself around the pillow, hugging it tightly as she fought the sickness that made her skin crawl, her teeth ache and her muscles cramp up. Briefly, she thought she was going to die, since it was impossible to confront this much agony and not expect to die.

She had initially resisted banging on the door to ask for an injection, because she knew now what they wanted her to do. The thought of performing oral sex on the small man made her sick in its own right, but the drug sickness was a thousand times worse, and she eventually started hammering on the door.

Rocking back and forth on the bed and moaning, she heard them open the door. She sat up as the small man, Agata and the stranger came in. Agata looked nervous.

The small man said, "Come here."

Judy rushed over.

"Kneel."

She kneeled, keeping her eyes on the black bag.

"Pull down my zipper," the man said.

Judy felt her stomach swirl with hatred and sickness as she fumbled with his zipper.

"Take it out," he said. "Gently."

Judy closed her eyes and felt like there was another person in the room that was kneeling in sexual supplication before a man she loathed. She fumbled with his underwear, trying to find out how to navigate the fabric, when she heard the stranger speak.

"You were not joking, Stefan," he said. "It always works. This is something I've waited a long time for."

Judy froze. The voice. It was *him*. She looked up.

He laughed. "Yes, it's me, you bitch. You thought I was going to let you get away with destroying my business?"

His Afrikaner accent was crystal clear.

"Hey," the small man said. "Be gentle. I want to see you take it nice and slow. It is part of your training here."

Afterward, she recollected very little of what happened next. Pain and trauma do strange things to a person's memory.

CHAPTER 18

Yes, I hate to admit it, but you were correct. He told his father that Judy was going to London. And yes, he asked Trevor where she was staying."

Dennis's jaw tightened as he took in this latest piece of information. It was that son of a bitch, Phillip. He had turned Judy over to Voorster, the thug who had escaped into thin air after she busted his drug ring in Western Australia.

"I'll kill him," Dennis said.

"Hey, mate. I'm not supposed to be talking to you. This is privileged information, and I'd be in very serious trouble if they knew I was talking to you."

"Come on, you guys weren't even looking at this angle! Shit, if you would have jumped on it earlier we might have found her!"

"I'll admit that we thought he was dead, but now we can start with Phillip. I need to turn this over to my boss right away. And I don't have to remind you that this new information does not prove Voorster is involved."

"Wait, you can't talk to your boss until you get me two pieces of information," Dennis said, opening his notebook.

"I can't do any more sleuthing for you, Dennis. I have to turn this over."

"What are you, about eight hours ahead of the time zone in London?" Dennis said.

"Well, yes, but what does that have to do—"

"It's 1:10 a.m. here, so it must something like 9:10 a.m. there in Perth. Is that right?"

"Yes, but—"

"All I need from you — and I bet you can get this stuff pretty quickly — is the precise date and time that Phillip used the telephone for an outbound call from prison immediately after he met with Trevor. I'm sure he has weekly access to a phone there in prison. So I just need the date and time of that call. And then I need the prison telephone number he made the call from. Got that?"

"Dennis, you're not hearing me. I can't do anything more for you on this. I need to tell my superiors immediately."

"Do you want me to find Judy or not?"

"Of course I do."

"Then simply get those three pieces of information for me: the time and date of his call after meeting his son, and the number he called from. And then you can chat with your supervisors until the cows come home. I mean, you could get that stuff in less than an hour, I bet."

"Judy told me you were persistent to the point of boorishness."

"Yes, I'm a royal pain in the ass — just please get me that information. Call me at any time. I'm either going to find Judy alive or I'm going to find the person who took her and kill them."

"I didn't hear that last part."

"Get going, Clive! Go, go! We don't have time!"

✦

When Judy knelt in front of the small man her plan was simple and she acted fast. The purity of her hatred momentarily overwhelmed her desire for the drugs, but she knew the battle would tip in favor of the heroin in a millisecond if she didn't act.

She leaned forward on her knees, used her left hand to push his thighs apart — which he accommodated nicely by spreading his feet — and with her right hand made a fist near the floor and rammed it up as hard as a drug-addicted waif could.

Judy felt her knuckles crush his testicles, and he collapsed like a giant ragdoll on top of her.

He made a very odd shrieking groan and fell onto his side, clutching his groin. Judy heard Agata scream. From her right she saw a boot flying toward her face, and she gamely tried to block it with her wrists, but Voorster was strong and fit, and his boot easily made it through her feeble arms, catching her on the side of her head and knocking her backward.

She slid easily across the cement floor up against the bed. She felt her hair grabbed and her head yanked upward. The first blow glanced off her temple, with little damage. But the second one hit her squarely on the side of her jaw, and she went out into an unpleasant blackness.

She wondered whether she was dead. *What were those screams? Was it the drug sickness or something else that made her whole body ache? Why was she so cold? Who was crying?*

Opening her eyes, she found herself on the cement floor. Her eyes were wet.

She had been crying.

Even before she felt the crust of blood around the corner of her mouth, the drug sickness roared to life, sending her into small, rolling convulsions.

✦

"Louise, I'm telling you that the London station is just a pack of hyenas. It's probably that jackass Chandler who's doing it. Complete asshole."

"Who told you that Arnold was gay?" she asked.

"My friend in MI5."

"Well, I looked through the file, and I didn't see any mention of it, but I have to tell you, Dennis, that we're not supposed to have that kind of notation in personnel files any longer."

"But he disappeared Louise! What if he got snagged in a honeypot? I mean, how would we know to look for a male instead of a female?"

Dennis knew that a honeypot scheme was one of the oldest tactics to compromise a target in an intelligence operation. The target is typically seduced by someone working for the opposition and either blackmailed or coerced into gathering intelligence.

"Yes, I suppose so," Louise said. "I'll look into it on my side. But what's this about radiation found in the Ukrainian's home? Are you sure about that? Nothing's come through on that, and there has been no update to the Arnold file."

"I'm telling you, something is wrong in the station here, and I think it's Chandler."

"Why would he hold out on this?"

"You tell me."

She sighed. "Jesus, this Arnold thing is a cesspool that keeps running deeper."

Dennis started to sign off when Louise interjected. "How's your other task going?"

"You mean Judy?"

"Yes."

"I think I found something; could be nothing but right now, the flimsiest thread is better than nothing."

"Well, good luck on that front. But promise me that you'll keep me the loop on the Arnold thing?"

"Yes, of course. I smell a giant rat named Chandler."

After hanging up, Dennis felt relieved. He had fulfilled Louise's part of the bargain, albeit just barely. Dennis did not care about Arnold, Chandler or anyone except Judy. Every ounce of energy would now be spent on finding her.

◆

It was not something he could articulate, but Dennis had the undeniable sensation that Judy was disappearing from his world forever. He refused to consider that she might be dead, and knowing that she was alive — actually, feeling that she was alive— kept him going.

But something had changed, and he struggled with uncertainty.

His phone rang. "This is the last time I'm talking to you about this subject, so get a pen ready," Clive said.

Dennis rushed to the hotel desk, grabbed a pen and wrote down a time, a date and a phone number.

"Thanks," he said, but Clive had already hung up.

◆

This time Dennis employed every trick he knew to shake a tail. Though he was not a trained field agent, he had absorbed many of the secrets of the trade over the years of investigations. He knew that he needed to temporarily alter his clothing while in transit, use public transportation, move through the rear of restaurants or hotels, if possible; anything to throw his tail or tails off his track.

He left his hotel wearing a faded blue Boston Red Sox baseball cap and a thin tan windbreaker; he took several different lines on the Tube, walking slowly, then faster. Twice he barged through the kitchens of pubs out the back door, all the while taking off his baseball cap and putting on sunglasses.

Two hours after taking off from his hotel, Dennis found himself inside St. Paul's at Evensong with his baseball cap bundled up in his windbreaker, which lay in his lap. The blue wool sweater was not as warm as he had hoped, but it was enough. He could barely wait for the service to end.

He waited in vain at the back of the cathedral and managed to light two candles before leaving. Dennis decided to visit the restaurant bar.

The NSA employee sat at the bar, reading a newspaper and drinking a beer.

Dennis sat next to him and ordered a beer. Neither spoke or looked at each other.

Finally the man said, "No phone?"

"No phone," Dennis said.

"No electronics at all?"

"Just my Seiko watch."

"Get a real watch."

"Ha."

"What do you want from me?"

"Fred said you could help. You created a beta program of some sort."

The man said nothing and toyed with his beer while looking down at his newspaper.

"He was not supposed to mention it. I'm disappointed."

"Too late, he did. And I need your help."

"To find who killed Fred?"

"In a roundabout way, yes. First I need another problem solved."

"I don't care about your other problems. Forget it." He closed the newspaper and raised his hand. "Check please."

"The two things are related," Dennis lied. "I need one to get to the other. Don't go dark on me now. I'm close to getting his killer. These things are complicated."

The bartender slid the man his check.

Dennis pulled a folded piece of paper from his pants pocket and pushed it across to the man.

"Here's a date, time and a phone number. It's a prison phone. The man in prison made a call to someone at precisely this date and time. I need the number that he called. That's what I'm calling phone number alpha. Then I need the first phone number that alpha called right after getting the call from prison. I'm calling that follow-on phone number beta. This beta number is critical. I need to know its geolocation. My guess is it's in the UK."

The man said nothing, put some cash on the bar and slid the folded piece of paper into his palm. As he stood he whispered, "You're fucked if this isn't to help solve Fred's murder."

✦

She was shaking and bent in a fetal position on the cement floor, rocking gently to take her mind off the sickness. Though she was very sick, she also felt a glimmer of hope. She had taken charge and acted against her jailers, although she was paying a price. Somewhere amidst the agony created by her brain receptors aching for opiates, Judy felt a wisp of empowerment.

She crawled to the door and slowly opened it. Sticking her head out, she looked down the dark hallway and heard raised voices. Feeling sick but strangely emboldened, she crawled down the hallway on her bony knees, the silk dressing gown making a thin whooshing sound, like sand falling onto a tabletop.

Near the end of the hallway she stopped and listened.

"Why don't you just take care of her," the small man said. "This is stupid. Let's just be rid of her."

"You told me you could break anyone," Voorster said.

"That is true, and we can break her, but you are rushing things. I told you that already. It takes time, and you are impatient. This is too personal for you, and I don't like it. Just take care of her. Get it over with. We have a stable of women who are compliant and work very well. We don't need her. And she is losing weight; our paying customers are very wealthy and discriminating. They don't want to have sex with emaciated drug addicts. Let me get rid of her."

"Not until I see her broken and working. She has cost me many millions of dollars, and just putting her in a grave is not satisfaction enough."

"I don't like it," the small man said.

"You don't have to like it. I pay you plenty. Break her."

Judy rolled on her side and put her left cheek onto the cold cement floor.

That is why I'm here, she thought. *How odd that Voorster enjoys seeing me suffer so much. How does a person get that evil? Can I survive this nightmare? What will I have to do to survive?*

Judy got back onto her knees and crawled to her room, closing the door silently behind her. She got off the floor and onto the bed just as Agata opened the door with some food.

"Agata," Judy said. "Can you help me?"

"Yes, of course. Please eat. You are too skinny."

"No, I mean can you help me get out of here?"

"No. That I cannot do."

"Why?"

"They will kill me."

"But they are killing you slowly here, don't you see that?"

Agata put down the food tray and stared at the wall on the other side of the room.

"Please do not ask this," she said. "It is bad for both of us."

"Do you help them break the girls? Is that what you do?"

Agata gave a sharp, angry look at Judy and stood up.

"Please eat your food," she said, walking out and closing the door behind her.

Judy looked at the sandwich, grabbed it and took a small bite.

CHAPTER 19

D ennis had taken many long walks through London, both to satisfy his irrational hope that he'd see Judy sitting on a park bench and his need to burn off energy. He was growing angry and restless in his hotel room, wondering if the NSA employee would ever help or whether Judy was even alive.

Louise had called once, telling him that Fort Meade agreed to let Dennis see the Menwith Hill video again, but only under supervision at the London Station. He did his best to act enthusiastic about this latest twist, but Dennis could care less about the Arnold case and was no longer interested in seeing the video.

Dennis's hotel gave guests the option of having a newspaper delivered to their door each morning, and he had chosen *USA Today*, though he rarely read it. This morning he decided to eat in the hotel restaurant instead of using room service. He picked up the newspaper and took it with him downstairs.

He ordered scrambled eggs and toast and opened the newspaper. A yellow sticky note was attached to the top of page three of the newspaper. Reflexively, he looked around the restaurant and then ripped the note off the page.

In block lettering there were three items listed: at the top, the word Alpha was followed by a phone number with an Australian country code. This was the phone number of the person Phillip called from prison after seeing his son. The next line started with the word Beta, and listed another phone number with a UK country code, which was the follow-on call by the person Phillip had called from prison. The last line was an address in London that received the follow-on call.

Dennis pulled out his phone, opened Google Maps and typed in the address, which was in the affluent Mayfair neighborhood. For the first time since Judy disappeared, he felt buoyant. A thread had emerged that might actually take him to her. He took a large sip of coffee and looked at his watch: 7:44 a.m.

The waitress put his breakfast in front of him, and Dennis asked for the bill right away. He wasn't hungry. He pushed the plate away and again scanned the small restaurant, looking for evidence of surveillance, but only saw a young couple cooing over their pastries and an elderly gentleman methodically stirring his cup of tea.

Dennis paid the bill and rushed back to his room. He put the yellow sticky note on the small desk and opened his notebook.

On a blank sheet he drew a diagram with the prison phone number on the left, Alpha in the middle, and the Beta number to the right. He drew arrows as he followed the suspected chain of phone calls: Phillip found out from his son that Judy was going to London and was staying at a particular hotel. The next time he had access to the prison phone, he called Alpha, which was in Australia. Phillip knew better than to try to contact Voorster directly and probably had established an intermediary.

Dennis guessed that the intermediary would immediately contact Voorster, which was why he not only needed the Beta number but its geolocation. Leave it to the NSA to have the metadata of nearly every international phone call.

He prayed that his instinct was correct and that Judy was still alive, albeit at the mercy of Voorster. And — he felt sick at this thought — if Judy were not alive, he would simply kill Voorster.

As an investigator with the agency's inspector general's office, Dennis was a far cry from a trained street agent and had only a passing knowledge of weapons and hand-to-hand combat. He had never been trained to kill.

But today, sitting in his hotel room and using his finger to trace the suspected trail of communications that led to Judy's disappearance, he felt he could easily kill someone if they had hurt Judy. He just needed to find Voorster, and he was nervous enough about the fact that phone number Beta was probably a mobile phone with a geolocation that moved.

Dennis assembled his kit into a small black backpack, including two different colored nylon jackets, a second red St. Louis Cardinals baseball cap, a small pair of binoculars and his cell phone charger.

✦

It had been almost thirteen hours since the last injection, and Judy felt the dread of the sickness, along with the fear of what they were going to do next. Out of thin air she had finally found a powerful motivating force to keep her focused: she needed to stay alive long enough to kill the small man and Voorster.

Granted, she had plenty of reasons to stay alive, not the least her son, her parents and even Dennis. But those goals were based on love and affection; they made her sad and listless.

Hatred and enmity were perverse flip sides of that coin, and for some strange reason Judy could not understand, they motivated her to action. The mere thought of killing these two men had provided the only boost in concentration during her incarceration. Her rudimentary knowledge of drug addiction, gleaned during her time on the drug task force in Australia, suggested that they were accelerating her addiction by spiking the heroin with fentanyl, a synthetic opioid a hundred times more powerful than morphine. And the gap between injections had been consistently less than twenty-four hours, so her brain chemistry was rapidly dumping and depleting her endorphins. The onslaught on her brain chemistry change was so furious that she was now going into withdrawal faster and more painfully than a maintenance addict might.

She found herself picking at her skin, her mouth had become permanently dry, she was constipated and she fell into sudden and severe depressions, unlike anything she had experienced before.

And she could not stop thinking about the little black bag that the small man carried under his arm. The pleasure emanating from the thin little syringes in that bag was otherworldly. But how to stay alive long enough to kill these two men? She fantasized how she might kill them, and the perverse pleasure it gave her only sometimes overcame her sickness.

Judy heard footsteps that she recognized as Agata's and turned to see the woman carrying a small tray with a sandwich and a bowl of ice cream.

"You look healthy today," Agata said, putting the tray on the bed. "That is good."

"Yes, I feel a bit better. I'm trying to eat. But I'm starting to feel sick again. Will he come soon?"

"Yes, perhaps," Agata said.

"Perhaps?"

"Soon, I'm sure."

Judy took a bite out of the sandwich.

"Why are they doing this to me?" she asked nonchalantly, as if it were an idle conversation.

"Why?"

"Yes, why? Do they expect me to be one of their prostitutes? To work for them?"

"Perhaps."

"Do they have lots of women working for them?"

"They have some, yes. But it is a good life with plenty of fun. All the women like this life."

"How about you? Do you like this life? Were you one of the girls that worked for them?"

"Yes, for a little."

"How did they find you?"

"You know, they just find me. My friends were not careful and some got into drugs."

"But don't these women have families that go to the police?"

"Like me, many are illegal."

"You mean undocumented?"

"Yes, it is not hard to get into this country without a passport. I'm from a very poor country. Serbia is small. My friend and I come here to work as models. But we get trapped." Agata shrugged. "It's not so bad here."

"Can you help me a tiny bit?" Judy asked.

Agata winced. "Not so much. I cannot help you get out."

"No, I mean can you help me with my sickness? Perhaps some times you could bring me a little bit extra of the drug when I'm feeling sick? It would help me."

Agata shook her head violently. "No, I cannot do that. You will resist more of the training."

"What will they do with me if I resist?"

Agata got off the bed. "The ice cream is melting. You need to eat the ice cream."

"Will they kill me?"

"I don't know anything. Please eat. Get strong and healthy."

"So I have no choice?"

Agata turned away, walked slowly to the door and leaned against the door jam.

"I don't know why that man want you. He is crazy. My boss is frightened of him. This is not good."

"I can tell you why he wants to break me," Judy said, mashing the ice cream down distractedly with the plastic spoon.

"Why?" Agata said. "You steal from him?"

"Well, in a way, yes. I'm a policewoman. From Australia. We broke up his drug ring."

Agata bounced off of the door jamb as if shocked with electricity.

"Who is policeman?"

"Me. I'm a policewoman."

"*You*?"

"Didn't you know that?"

"No one tell me that. Oh my God." Agata turned and walked out the door and down the hallway but quickly returned to retrieve the tray of food.

"You lie," she said, her brow furrowed in deep horizontal lines of anger.

"No."

"You lie," she repeated, grabbing the tray and rushing out of the room, this time careful to close the door behind her.

✦

The rental car was small and awkward to drive. And of course he was required to drive on the left, but after several close calls and many florid verbal and gesticulating exchanges with cabbies, Dennis managed to find the address listed as the location of phone Beta in Mayfair.

He parked in a no-parking zone and retrieved his binoculars to glance at the building. It was a swank section of London, and there was not much traffic through the neighborhood. Dennis locked the car and sauntered down the block across the street from the address, turned around at the corner and then walked back up the street directly in front of the house and back to his car.

He sat in the December chill, the windy day sending puffy small white clouds skittering across the landscape. He started the car every now and then to keep warm.

No one entered or left the house during the five hours he sat there. He periodically got out and walked nearby, each time changing his hat or jacket.

As the afternoon sun accelerated and dipped behind the buildings, Dennis realized how silly this exercise was. There was no telling if Voorster was living in this building, whether Judy was in there, whether the geolocation was correct at all. As he settled into despondency, someone banged on his car window, startling him.

A traffic warden pointed to the sign and raised her ticket book.

Dennis started the car, pulled out and drove around the block. He took a series of turns and after ten minutes managed to return to the same no-parking zone. The sun was setting, and some of the homes twinkled with festive Christmas lights.

Dennis did not feel festive; he felt frustrated and gloomy as he stared at the building a half-block away. He tugged absently at his beard, twisting a couple of strands into a point and then brushing them back.

He opened the cap of a plastic water bottle and took a swig. Putting the cap back on, he tossed the bottle onto the passenger seat and yawned. He rubbed his eyes, yawned again, and then watched in amazement as the door of the home opened and two men and a woman walked out and down the steps to street level.

CHAPTER 20

She rocked back and forth on the bed, clutching a pillow around her stomach as if it were a child. The sweat had already beaded up on her brow, and the sickness was in full force. She dreaded what was going to happen next but tried to focus on how she might kill the small man. The hatred was strong enough to occasionally break through the sickness, but only slightly.

And she thought about Dennis, the blue-eyed American who had brought her to London in the first place. *Would he save me?* she thought. *Could he piece together clues to recognize it was Voorster? And if he did save me, would he forgive me for what I'm going to do to stay alive?*

They had started to leave her door open again, since she had shown increasing compliance. The small man's attitude toward Judy had changed, of course. He was visibly cold and angry toward her, sometimes being reckless with the injection site and damaging already hemorrhaged veins.

Agata and the small man wheeled quickly into the room.

"Come here," the small man said. "Kneel."

Judy jumped off the bed and kneeled in front of him. This was the first time since her attack on the man that he had tried to force her to perform. But this time Voorster was not present, and Agata stared at Judy with wild, nervous eyes.

"Let's go," the man said. "You know what to do."

Judy's fingers could barely work the man's zipper, she was shaking so badly.

And then she did it; though she did not remember it afterward because she was elsewhere. In the imaginary place she went to, there was just a knife in her right hand, and the small man. And she did bad things to the small man with the knife, since the knife was so incredibly sharp.

✦

Dennis had left his car quickly and followed the three people as they went down the block to the main thoroughfare. The maelstrom of early evening rush hour made it difficult for him to follow. His attempt at nonchalance was tested by the salmon upstream-run of pedestrians as he shoved through to follow from twenty yards behind.

And before he knew it, they were gone.

"Shit!" he said out loud. "Goddamnit!"

Several passersby gave him a wide berth as he cursed and spun around, looking for the group.

Dennis raced ahead for a half block and could not see them, though it was difficult in the darkness and crowds. He retraced his steps to where he'd last seen them. He was in front of an upscale pub and decided to look inside.

The place was busy, and the smell of beer permeated everything. Dennis quickly canvassed the interior and did not find them. Stepping into the cool air, he moved next door to an Italian restaurant.

He was too nervous to be careful and simply walked through the dining room as if it was his own house, staring at everyone with wild-eyed panic.

The threesome was seated at a back table, looking at menus and laughing. Dennis caught his breath and went past them to the men's room. He stared at the bearded madman in the mirror and washed his hands, dried them and walked past the group to the bar, where he could watch them.

He ordered a beer and asked for a menu so he could hide his face behind it. The woman in the group was attractive, tall with short blond hair, an angular face with high cheekbones. Dennis concentrated on the men, one of whom he thought looked familiar. He took out his small black notebook and turned to the back, where he had glued several pictures of Voorster downloaded from a database. All of the photos were of a blond-haired man; neither man at the table was blond.

But there was something about one of the men that resembled Voorster, and Dennis kept glancing down at this open notebook on the bar top and peering over the top of his menu to stare at the threesome.

After his second beer, Dennis had convinced himself that one of the men was Voorster. It was not inconceivable that the South African, who was on the lam from international law enforcement, would dye his hair and eyebrows.

It was the nose that Dennis convinced himself was the telling feature; the Voorster in the three photos he had pasted in his notebook sported a slightly off-kilter nose, perhaps the result of a fistfight or a wayward elbow in a rugby match. And one of the dark-haired men at the table had a little notch at the top of the nose and a slight twist to its shape.

He needed a clean, head-on photograph of this man in order to certify he had his man.

Dennis took out his iPhone, opened the camera app and played with the settings to turn off the flash. He stood up, making an overly dramatic attempt to act like he was using two hands to type in a text message as he walked to the bathroom, all the while taking still photos as he fake texted a message.

After his third beer, Dennis decided to leave the restaurant before he did something stupid. He was a little tipsy, and worried that he might do something crazy like use the large beer pitcher on the table next to him to crush the skull of this man.

But what if it wasn't Voorster? And what if it was? Attacking him would get Dennis no closer to finding Judy.

Dennis paid his bill and stepped out into the sharp, cold air. A biting wind was rushing down the streets of Mayfair, pushing a candy wrapper and a single forlorn oak leaf skittering along the pavement. Dennis got back to his rental car and barely made it back to the hotel without injuring a pedestrian or motorist.

He went to the hotel's business center and spent almost an hour reviewing the still photos he had taken of the Voorster lookalike, then picked three and printed them. He went back to his room and filled out a prepaid postcard. Before retiring for the night, he managed to mail it.

✦

The next three days were one of the worst periods in Dennis's life. According to the protocol established by the skittish NSA employee, Dennis could expect to meet him exactly three days after the postcard was mailed. There was no way to speed up the process, and it infuriated him.

Dennis passed the three days by periodically driving by the house he suspected Voorster lived in. It was a useless behavior and even potentially reckless if someone in the house noticed the same car passing by. Still, he did it, mostly out of nervous energy.

The morning of the third day his cell phone rang.

"Hi, Louise," he said. "How's things back at the ranch?"

"Fine. Same crap, different day."

"Ha, sounds like my life."

"Have you been looking at your emails?" she asked.

"Um, not closely."

"I'm guessing not at all."

"Maybe that is correct," Dennis said, opening his laptop and letting it run through its security scanning protocols. "Guess I was busy on the other thing."

"Thought we agreed you'd work on the two projects simultaneously."

"I guess I dropped the ball on the Arnold project. I'm sorry. I think I'm close to getting a resolution on the other project. I'm a little crazy right now because of it."

"The IG has been asking about the Arnold project, and I've been lying about our progress. There's been no progress because you haven't done anything. I've been emailing you, and I finally realized you weren't even checking."

Dennis quickly scanned a host of emails from Louise.

"So the London Station came through with the radiation report on the Ukrainian home," Dennis said. "It was polonium. Well, that's about as close to a straight line from Pavlychko to Freddie as we could hope for."

"I gather you're looking at the emails now," she said. "Let me save you the time. Your contact at MI5 was correct: Arnold was gay. It appears that it was well known and public at the London Station. The official reason it was not included in his file, even anecdotally, was that the information was irrelevant."

"That's bullshit."

"Of course it is. But why don't you read the last email I sent you yesterday. Just scroll to the bottom of the list."

Dennis scanned the email and said nothing. He reread the email.

"Hello?" Louise said.

"I'm here."

"So?"

"So what?"

"Stop it, Dennis. I thought we had a new understanding of how we were going to work together. No more bullshit or cuteness. Just answer the goddamn question."

"I have to think about it," he said.

"What's there to think about? Either you met privately with Barkley, or you didn't."

"Where did you get this information?" he asked.

"It doesn't matter where the information came from. Did you meet with him?"

"Your email says that the IG wanted clarification, so I'm to gather that someone squealed to him."

"So it's true."

"Yes."

"And you decided not to tell me."

"Barkley told me to keep it quiet. What was I supposed to do?"

"You meet privately with the chairman of the House Intelligence Committee, you're a lowly investigator with OIG, and you don't disclose it?"

"Yes. And what's this 'lowly investigator' stuff?"

"Christ, Dennis, you think anything stays secret here in D.C.? Someone tipped the IG that you met with Barkley. He came to me, and I said it wasn't true, or you would have told me. Now I find out it is true and you most decidedly withheld that information."

Dennis tugged at his scraggly beard with the fingers of his right hand as he pressed the phone to his ear with his left hand. He said nothing; Louise said nothing.

"I'm sorry," Dennis said. "Barkley asked me to treat it confidentially, and I did."

"I'll be there tomorrow around 10:00 a.m. Let's chat in person."

"You're coming to London?"

"Didn't I just say that?"

"Is it necessary?"

"Yes. I have your hotel info. Meet me for lunch in the restaurant there at eleven thirty."

"Okay."

✦

This time Dennis did not bother going to Evensong; he went across the street to the hotel bar and found his contact already sitting there.

He took a stool next to him and ordered a beer. Dennis had brought with him a folded edition of *The Guardian* and placed it between them.

"No electronics?" the man asked, staring ahead.

"Yup."

"This is getting tiresome," the man said. "I don't think you're chasing Fred's killer. You're bullshitting me."

"Not so," Dennis said, taking a long sip of his beer. "Inside the newspaper is an envelope. Inside the envelope are three pictures of a man whose identity I need to verify. I have written down his name on the front of the envelope; or at least who I think he is. Last name is Voorster. He's altered his hair color, but I just can't be sure. I need someone like you to run these pictures through face-recognition software to verify his identity."

The man frowned and shook his head slightly. "Give me a break. You could easily run that through Langley."

"No I can't. I'm being blocked back there. They want me to drop it."

"Bullshit."

"Why the hell am I sitting here with you in this fucking London pub? I don't even know who you are, and getting hold of you is so dated it feels like *The Spy Who Came In From The Cold*. If you don't want to help find Freddie's killer, fine."

Dennis had lost his cool, but he did not care. He stood up and asked for the check.

"Jesus. Take it easy," the man said. "Sit down."

Dennis settled back onto the stool.

"Is this guy's identity important to finding Fred's killer?"

"Yes. I already told you that."

"Then I'll run the pictures."

"Thanks," Dennis said. "I'm sorry for being a pain. I've got to move fast on this thing. Speaking of that, isn't there a quicker way to contact you than sending a friggin' postcard?"

For the first time the man chuckled.

"Next time use a pay phone and call this number. Let it go to voice-mail. When it does, hit the number three on the phone and hang up. I'll meet you here that evening. If I don't show up, try it again. If I don't show up a second time, you'll never see me again."

Dennis took the business card the man had slid across the bar. It stated simply: *Frederick Singletary, Solicitor*, with a London phone number.

"Fine. Help me on this and we'll get Freddie's killer."

"Why are you getting blocked at Langley?"

"I don't know, but I'm guessing Freddie's death is inconveniencing someone."

"Fuckers."

"Yup."

✦

He opened the hotel room door, bent down, picked up his *USA Today* and opened it to page three. The sticky note read: *It's him.*

Dennis got dressed, brushed his teeth and was about to head out to get his rental car when he stopped.

What the hell am I doing? he thought. *What would I do if I got my hands on Voorster? I don't give a shit about him, I want Judy! Am I going to threaten him? Shoot him? I don't even have a weapon.*

Dennis sat down at the desk, leaned back in the chair and placed both hands on top of his head.

Shit! Louise is going to be here in a couple of hours. I can't ditch her, she'll have me hunted down and arrested.

After several minutes of tugging at his beard, he called the valet for his car to be brought up, grabbed his backpack and left. If nothing else, he would keep an eye on Voorster's house. There was nothing to lose. Besides, he was sort of coming around to the idea of torturing the man.

✦

Judy was so depressed, ashamed and despondent that she had stopped eating. Agata had berated her, warning that she was going to lose favor with her boss, and that would lead to a very unhappy ending.

Judy daydreamed about Dennis; she choreographed elaborate fantasies of him coming to save her and the two of them hunting down Voorster and the small man and killing them in various grisly ways.

Her favorite fantasy was to use an ice pick on Voorster; her only confusion during these fantasies was which man to kill first, the small man or Voorster. Mostly, she picked the small man to go first.

The passage of time had been so disrupted that Judy had no idea how long she had been kept in the room. There were no windows, and the only regular activity was Agata's visits, the injections, and the "training" that she was undergoing.

They had introduced a young, dark-haired man to the mix who never spoke but was ordered to have sex with her. The young man was not particularly interested in having sex with Judy but seemed to accept it like she did; he too had marks on his arms.

The small man had taken to coaching Judy on pretending to enjoy the sex so that her customers would be more enthused and satisfied. He slapped her once when she yawned during one session, but Judy only glowered back at him.

"Why do you fight this thing?" Agata once asked. "Do you want to die? I tell you many times already that they are getting angry at you for not eating and not liking your training."

"Aren't you ashamed of what you're doing?" Judy asked.

"No, I am not ashamed. I have no choice."

"You always have a choice, Agata. Always."

"You are wrong. None of us have a choice. I am just trying to survive. But you are not. You act like you want to die. And you will soon. My boss can see the hatred. He has told the other man — the one who brought you to us — that you are no good."

Judy stared for a long moment at Agata.

"I think you're right," she said slowly. "Perhaps I want to die. But not before I kill someone."

Agata got up off the bed, grabbed the food tray and started to leave. "You are crazy now," she said.

"Stop," Judy said. "Leave the food. I will eat it all. I'll get strong again. I don't want to die. Yet."

CHAPTER 21

Dennis had just turned off the ignition when Voorster came out of the building, walked down a flight of steps to the street and got into a cab that was waiting out front.

He started the car and pulled out. The drive was harrowing for Dennis, navigating small streets, driving on the left and trying to keep up with a cabbie that flew through London like an Exocet missile. Twice Dennis ran through red lights, and he prayed that he was not going to be chased down by police.

Just when he was getting used to the chase, the cab stopped in front of an elaborate building with a curved blue awning covering the three short steps up to the landing area. Voorster got out, gave a quick glance around and then bounded up the stairs. A well-dressed doorman let him in.

Dennis drove past the building and pulled over. He adjusted the rear-view mirror so that he could look at the building. He could not tell whether it was a hotel, because there was no sign on the front. But there was certainly a doorman, and the awning was very formal and new. He looked at his Google Maps app and figured out the address.

He had been parked no more than five minutes when a late-model Bentley pulled up to the building, and the driver hopped out and opened the door. A well dressed, portly gentleman, perhaps in his late seventies, got out. The driver helped the man up the steps while the doorman held the door open for him.

After another ten minutes, Dennis did a U-turn and drove back past the building to make sure he had the correct street number and pulled over again farther down the street.

He dialed a number on his phone and got a voicemail. Dennis left a hurried message, looked at his watch and realized he needed to get back to the hotel to meet with Louise. He started out following the audible driving directions from Google Maps when his phone rang.

"What's up, old chap?" Ian said. "You just called."

"Have a big favor. Should be easy for a guy like you. I'm trying to figure out what type of place this building is. I know it sounds funny, but I'm going to give you an address and perhaps you could tell me whether it's a private club or something. There's no sign out front and yet there's a doorman."

"Well, just go up to the bloody doorman and ask!"

"Can't do that. Can you at least tell me what the building is? You have contacts."

"Well, I'm not Google!"

"Just text me or call me on that new mobile phone number I gave you. It's important. Please hurry!"

"My word, Dennis. I have a job, remember?"

"Please!"

"Fine. Goodbye."

✦

"Jesus, you look like a caveman," Louise said as Dennis sat down in the restaurant.

"Ah, yes, well, I'm going through a stage."

"And what kind of stage would that be? Early Cro-Magnon?"

"Ha, more like late sixties," Dennis said, holding up a weak peace sign.

Although he had grown to like Louise, he was still shocked about how schoolgirlish she appeared. Her straight, almost white-blond Nordic hair, deep, glacial-blue eyes and wrinkle-free face combined to suggest a senior in high school. Maybe a sophomore in college. But her fierceness always dissolved those impressions once she started talking.

"No, I'm not kidding, Dennis. You don't look so well. Do you still eat, shower, stuff like that?"

"Do I look that bad?"

"Yes, actually."

"I've been a little out of it lately. Things are kind of coming to a head on this other thing."

"Can we park that 'other thing' for a minute and talk about the Arnold case?"

"Of course. By the way, why did you have to fly to London to talk about this?"

"Where's your phone?" she said.

"In my pocket."

"Hand it over."

He sighed, pulled it out and gave it to her. She opened her purse, pulled out a metallic mesh bag and put his phone in next to hers.

"Good. You realize every electronic communication we have is being monitored?"

"Yes."

"I want to be clear that we cannot discuss anything sensitive about the Arnold case unless we do it in person or using burners. Got that?"

"Yes," Dennis said, wincing. Burners were cheap, prepaid cell phones that could be purchased almost anywhere for cash and thrown away for new ones. They were a pain to use because the phone numbers were always changing.

"If we're talking on the phone and I repeat the name 'Arnold' twice in succession, that's the flag that we need to go to a new burner. Buy a couple today and give me the number of the one you're using; I'll do the same. That clear?"

"Yes, ma'am."

"Don't be a wise ass, Dennis."

"Sorry, was just trying to lighten things up."

"And why are you fidgeting so much? My God, your eyes are darting like minnows, and I can feel your foot tapping the base of the table. Are you all right?"

"I'm, I'm … just trying to find Judy. Think I'm close."

"Do you think this side project is almost done? I mean, I can imagine this is pretty damn personal and important for you, but you promised you'd help me finish the Arnold case. I'm not trying to make light of this poor woman's disappearance, but we have jobs to do. And the London Police are supposed to be very good so we need to let them do their work."

"Yes, yes, I'm on it. So let's get going. What do you want to talk about?"

"Barkley."

"Fine, ask away."

Dennis rushed through his interactions with the congressman, holding nothing back.

"And the last time you saw him, he agreed to lean on them to get you back to London?"

"Yes, but as I said, he seemed to think I wasn't getting the inside story. He sounded disappointed. Or pissed off. Or both."

Dennis noticed Louise did her tilting head thing where she moved her head one way then the opposite way, as if it was an old-fashioned weighing scale.

"Doesn't make sense," she said. "You're not telling me something."

"No. That's it, Louise. Scout's honor."

"You're bullshitting me."

"Listen, I'm just as confused as you are. He originally forced the IG to put me on this case, remember? And when things went south, he listened to me and agreed to send me back. Obviously, he didn't know why I wanted to go back to London. But the strange thing is that he seemed kind of disgusted that I didn't know what was really going on here."

Louise took a sip of coffee and stared at the tabletop, fussing with her spoon.

"So what do you think?" he said.

"I think he's right."

"And what does that mean?"

"I think you don't know what's going on with the Arnold case any more than I do. My guess is he thought you'd figure it out. Since you were this hot-shit investigator, he thought he could point you in the right direction, and you'd stumble onto something. But what's got me intrigued is that he seems to know what he wants you to find, but he can't publicly do anything to point it out. He needs to keep his hands clean. But I'm gathering you're not following through with his plan; you haven't found a damn thing."

"All I've done is get Freddie killed."

"Stop that, Dennis. Not your fault."

"Easy for you to say, Louise."

"Grow up a tiny bit, would you? This is how this stuff goes down in No Man's Land."

"Louise, do I need to remind you that I'm a friggin' OIG investigator, not a field agent? This is your world. Freddie and I don't run around with burner phones or get poisoned."

"Well, for a guy who says he's not a field agent, you appear to act like one."

"Osmosis. You slum around with enough of them, you pick it up."

"Someone has to do it, Dennis. There's nothing wrong with field work. Call it a necessary evil, but it needs to be done."

Dennis saw her raise her chin slightly in defiance and instantly thought of her missing foot.

"Sorry, Louise. I know that. I'm just cranky today."

"Just today?"

He laughed the first time that morning.

"Listen, I know you're shattered by the disappearance of Judy, but I need you to pay attention to the Arnold problem. Can you do that?"

"Yes."

"Okay. Have you seen this video that you insisted on reviewing? The one from Menwith Hill?"

"No, not yet."

"You said it was a big deal, and you made a fuss, but you haven't bothered to see it?"

"Not yet, no."

"Well, we're going to see it together while I'm here, got that?"

"Yes."

"Arrange it with the London station."

"Okay."

"Here's where I'm staying," she said, writing the name of a hotel near Trafalgar Square. "When you get the burner, leave a note for me at the front desk with the number. Got it?"

"Yes."

✦

"It's a what?" Dennis yelled.

"Keep calm there, Dennis," Ian said. "Why is this such a big deal?

"A brothel?"

"I didn't say the building was officially a brothel. I said it was a private club — which, by the way, are numerous here and in your lovely cities like New York — that we suspect is a high-end brothel. At least that's what I've been told."

"Why haven't you busted it then!"

"Hold on there, Dennis. You seem quite exercised. I said it was suspected, and I gathered this from a contact I have in the London Police, so don't go arresting the doorman there!"

"Okay. Sorry."

"Is this important to you? Why are you taking such umbrage at this notion of an exclusive men's club?"

"Don't pay any attention to me. Sorry, Ian. Long day for me. Thanks so much for your help. Please let me know if I can help you any time. Just call me."

"Perhaps you need some time off there. You seem a little strained these days."

✦

It was 10:20 p.m. when his new burner rang.

"Louise?"

"Yes. I just checked my messages. What's this about an emergency?"

"I need a gun."

"Excuse me?"

"A gun. A pistol. Can you help me get a gun in London? We're not in Northern Virginia, where you can just go buy a gun, even if you've just been released from an insane asylum."

"I wasn't worried before, but now I am. Weren't you seeing a shrink? Did I read that in your file?"

"You're not listening, Louise. I think I've found Judy. Well, I haven't found Judy, but I found the guy who grabbed Judy. He's either got Judy somewhere in this building, or he's killed her. Either way, I need a gun to get in there and to settle this."

Louise stopped talking, and Dennis heard the drone of a TV in the background at Louise's hotel room.

"Louise?'

"Why don't you meet me in my hotel bar in forty-five minutes. Just bring the burner. Bury the other phone. That clear?"

"Yes, on the way."

Dennis hung up, rushed over to the desk and unplugged his agency iPhone from its charger. He turned it off, put it in his hotel safe and locked it.

CHAPTER 22

It was just a hunch, albeit a gauzy, white, indistinct hunch, but Judy felt that the small man was going to get rid of her. He had stopped the brothel training completely and only administered the injections with Agata in attendance. She guessed that he insisted on giving the injections because he suspected Agata might take some for herself.

Even the schedule of injections had increased somewhat, which she guessed was because they no longer needed her to be sick. They were going to kill her, and the less she complained the better. The only reason they hadn't done it already, she imagined, was because her sponsor Voorster had to be consulted.

Dennis, where are you? she mused, staring at the crack in the ceiling. *You were always the strong one, the clever one. Why haven't you saved me? I tried to save myself. I really did fight it. But I'm too tired to continue. I've done bad things. I'm so ashamed. But I have one fight left. I hope you'll understand that I did fight them. But you can't always win. I'm not like you, Dennis. You keep pressing ahead against every obstacle. Somehow I hope you'll know that I fought them. I really did.*

✦

"You followed this man to the brothel?" Louise said. "Are you sure it was him? What did you say his name was?"

"Voorster. South African. I told you, my contact at the NSA confirmed it."

"Isn't that the fellow the Aussie cops mentioned? They said he was dead."

"He's alive. I saw him."

Louise sat at the bar wearing a pale blue blouse and jeans and nursed a sauvignon blanc. Out of her official agency uniform, she looked even younger, though no less fierce when she started to process information.

"Okay, and your plan is what exactly?"

"Well, you get me a weapon that I can use. And I'll follow Voorster to this place again," Dennis could not use the word brothel, "and I'll just go in there and do whatever it takes to find him. Then I'll beat the shit out of him until he tells me where she is. Or what happened to her."

"You're completely delusional," she said, shaking her head. "Number one, you won't get past the doorman. Number two, if you did get past him, you'll get no farther than the lobby. If this place is what you say it is, they'll have people there that can keep the peace, if you know what I mean."

"I'll kill them all," he said. "I don't care."

"You? Ha, you're a Boy Scout. Like I said, you'll be lucky to get past the doorman."

"Don't underestimate me, Louise."

"Don't you underestimate them. You're all emotion right now, which means it's going to end in disaster."

"Can't you just get me a weapon? You must have knowledge of safe houses here and where you might get a gun."

"Won't happen, Dennis. I'm sorry. I know you're going through agony at this woman's disappearance. I can see that, and I feel bad for you. But you're acting crazy right now, and if I helped in any way, the blowback for me would be career-ending. Can't you see that?"

Dennis swirled his single malt in the small glass, raised it quickly and downed it.

"I understand. You're right, I am crazy. No need to take someone else with me."

He stood up off his stool, reached out, grabbed her right hand and shook it. "I'd give you a peck on the cheek," he said, "but my guess is you'd think that was silly. So thank you for all you've done. If I come out of the other end of this thing with Voorster, I'll help you get the Arnold case resolved. If I don't, then keep looking at the video. Freddie said we missed something."

She held on to his hand and would not release it. Dennis felt her tiny, pale fingers clamping. He frowned and looked down at his captured hand.

"You're a dead man, Dennis. They'll find your body in a dumpster somewhere. You understand that, right?"

He put his left hand on top of Louise's and gently pried away her fingers.

"Well, I hope it's a nice dumpster."

✦

Dennis spent the next twenty-four hours observing the brothel, waiting for Voorster to return. He had purchased a telescoping metal baton and two knives, a three-inch folding blade and six-inch fixed blade. They didn't sell firearms in London, but he'd noticed you could buy a blade of any length, even a sword, if needed.

He periodically moved his car around to avoid being spotted, he hoped, and managed a few hours of sleep in the early morning hours. Dennis was surprised at the discreet but constant traffic to the building. Men came and went at all hours; he saw several women visit as well. But no Voorster.

The morning of his second day, his burner rang.

"You still on your mission of mercy?" Louise asked.

"Yes."

"I've been thinking," she said.

"About what?"

"About your mission."

"I told you: don't worry about it. Doesn't involve you."

"If I lose you, I lose the Arnold case. You're the only one who can figure it out. I haven't the faintest idea how to proceed or what to look for in the video. With Barkley involved, I think it's a bigger deal than anyone realizes."

"You'll figure it out."

"No. I need you alive."

"I don't intend to die."

"With your stupid plan, it's almost certain you'll never come out of that building alive."

"Thought we've been through this. Not your problem."

"You're my problem. I don't want to lose the Arnold case."

Dennis sighed. "Louise, you're a very smart person. Please. I've got to get going."

"So here's my plan," she said quickly. "We'll go in together the moment Voorster goes in. We'll get Voorster and Judy, if she's even in there. It'll be a professional operation, not a chicken-shit pretend operation. You can't kill Voorster or do anything to loosen his tongue, if you get my drift. We'll turn him in regardless of whether Judy is there or not."

"Stop it, Louise! Now you're acting crazy. And for the record, you have no idea where this place is or where I am, and I have no intention of telling you. Go for a walk. And stay out of this."

"You dope, I'm parked two cars behind you."

Dennis reached up and adjusted he rear-view mirror.

"Christ, Louise. What the hell are you doing?"

✦

The push-ups were very hard on her shoulders and vein-damaged arms, but she persisted. The cold cement floor was almost painful on her ravaged nervous system, but Judy kept at it. She had managed to put on a few pounds of extra weight, but she was still almost skeletal.

Agata's attitude toward Judy had altered considerably in the past two days.

Judy was certain she had heard the small man and Voorster arguing several days ago. She knew what the argument was about; the small man wanted Judy gone, and Voorster was not quite ready to give in on his plan to convert her to his personal concubine.

"She is no good," she heard the small man yell. "No good. No good."

Judy could not hear what Voorster yelled back, but his voice sounded less emphatic. Her time there was coming to an end.

She had one more scene to act out in this strange tragic play, and she was ready.

✦

Dennis sat in the front seat of Louise's rental van. She was dressed in loose-fitting gray slacks and an equally loose-fitting black wool jacket. Her hair was pulled back into a stubby ponytail, and she wore wraparound sunglasses.

"You're pissing me off," he said. "I mean really pissing me off. I have enough guilt on my goddamn head right now for Freddie and Judy, and now you! Not going to happen. Get the fuck out of here right now."

Dennis closed his eyes and put both hands on top of his head, as if he could keep it from exploding. He took several deep breaths and finally opened his eyes. He spoke quietly, as if explaining something important to a child.

"Louise, I appreciate what you're trying to do, but I have a lot of baggage I'm carrying around in my stupid head, and I have no more room for additional luggage."

Louise said nothing for a long time, and Dennis finally turned to look at her. She stared out through the windshield into the glare of the cold December morning. She did not turn to look at him but spoke with an alarming fury.

"You know, they said I was one of the best trainees they'd ever run through Camp Peary in Virginia. They said I was smart, agile and intuitive. I bested all the guys in the group, and the two other women as well. Top of class. They started me in Ankara, then briefly in Israel, where I killed for the first time.

"Then it was on to Iraq, where I led a small team of men — a hulking Seal Team of assholes — reporting to me. We ran fourteen targeted killings — fourteen! All successful. Only lost one man, and that was because he was a fucking idiot. The men stopped hitting on me, or making fun of me, and treated me like a leader.

"Then Beirut. The bomb brought the building right down on top of us. My partner had his chest crushed and died the most painful death imaginable. I couldn't move or help him. I thought about cutting off my own foot that was trapped and withering, but I didn't have a knife or anything sharp.

"So they pull apart the rubble and nearly crushed me to death doing it. Sure enough, my foot needs to be amputated. I'm the only survivor, of course. And guess what? They give me a medal, a new prosthetic foot and say my days in the field are over. I'm like, 'What? How can they keep me out of the field? What the hell does a foot have to do with it? I was great out in the field. They convert me to an analyst, and there I am in Langley, calling in drone strikes in Afghanistan operated by flyboys in Nevada using joysticks. Everyone is so complimentary. 'Nice job, Louise. You're fantastic. Such a leader.' And each time I ask for reassignment to the field, I'm told that I'm not eligible because of my disability.

"My husband Phil — he's an analyst at the National Security Council — is begging me to take it down a notch, but I'm getting madder and madder. Finally I blow up at my supervisor — a real condescending prick from Utah — and next thing I know I'm detailed to OIG with a little pat on the shoulder. 'You'll be better suited here, Louise.'"

Dennis watched her closely, though he felt disadvantaged by her sunglasses. The eyes are the real windows into a person, not the fingers or facial expressions — the eyes. And he could not see Louise's eyes.

She turned to look at him. Dennis could see his distorted, wide-angle reflection in her sunglasses.

"So here's the deal, Dennis. This operation is what I was trained to do. This is what I loved doing, if that's possible. And I'm not going to turn down the chance to do some heavy lifting in the field. You want revenge and hopefully to find your Judy, and I want to mix it up like the warrior they trained me to be. Simple as that. I'm running this operation, and you'll do what I say. You have a problem with that?"

"No ma'am," he said softly. "It's your call. I'm in."

"Then listen closely, and keep an eye on the building."

"Okay."

"In the back you'll find a standard skinny Kevlar vest; that goes on under your jacket. There are two pistols, one 9 mm, one 32-caliber, both with stubby silencers, and two extra clips. They're for you; the larger one goes tucked into your belt at the back under your jacket. The smaller one goes in the right-hand pocket of your jacket."

Dennis listened dutifully as Louise detailed the weapons, the plan of attack, the primary goal, the secondary goal and the exit plan. She had apparently already scouted the back of the building and the fire escape.

Then she made Dennis repeat everything back to her. Several times she stopped and berated him for missing some detail. Oddly, he did not feel angry or frustrated. Louise had a commanding air about her that he found comforting in the circumstances.

When they had finished the second go-around and he had satisfied her, Dennis could not resist.

"What's the palm pump you keep talking about? I have no idea what it is. And where did you get all of this stuff?"

She turned, leaned toward him and used the tip of her right forefinger to tug down her sunglasses. "Don't worry about the equipment or where it came from. Got it?"

"Not a problem. Just thought I'd ask."

"You know, you have some weird-colored blue eyes, do you know that?" she said, squinting. "That's not a come-on, Dennis, just an observation. Anyone say that to you before?"

"Yes, I've heard it mentioned before. It means I have the power to see through bullshit."

She smirked and pushed the sunglasses up again.

"You think I'm full of shit?"

"No, not you. Especially not you. Chandler here at the London Station, absolutely full of crap. But not you."

"Mmm," she said.

"You didn't answer about the palm pump."

"There's an agency weapon that is very useful in situations like this. I've used it once before, long time ago. It fits in the palm of my hand under my glove and has a small barrel that sits snugly behind my extended right forefinger." Louise closed her right fist loosely and pointed her forefinger at Dennis like it was a gun.

"Once we start shooting, even with silencers, all bets are off. So we'll avoid guns as long as possible. The palm pump is in my hand, and when I point my finger nonchalantly at someone, I squeeze the disk in my palm with my closed fingers and it shoots a tiny glass pellet that can penetrate most clothing. It injects a substance into the skin of the person and initially creates cognitive confusion, then quickly unconsciousness. Please don't ask what the friggin' substance is; they won't tell us and I don't give a shit. It works, and we can make our way forward without killing people or announcing our presence. Got it?"

"Yes, got it."

Dennis's phone rang.

Louise frowned. "Don't answer it," she said.

"I have to," he said. "Hello?"

"It's Ian, Dennis. Have some news I thought I'd share."

"What do you have?"

"Well, I don't know how you're going to take this, and I don't mean to alarm you unnecessarily, but thought I'd tell you regardless, old man."

"Well, tell me then."

"Ah, yes then. The police found some bodies north of London. In a public forest. Some fellow was walking his dogs and found them."

"What bodies?"

"Bodies of women. A tad grisly, I'm afraid."

"Jesus, Ian. Can you please cut to the chase?"

"It appears that there are three bodies, but not in the same grave. Each buried separately. Two of the graves are older, perhaps a year old. But the third one is recent. Perhaps a week or two old."

Dennis felt like a shade had been pulled down in a sunny room, casting everything in a dark, gray lifeless sheen.

"Is one of them Judy?" he said quietly.

Louise turned to look at Dennis.

"Not sure, since there's a problem with the bodies."

"Problem?"

"Ghastly, but it's meant to prevent them from being identified quickly. Or at least until we can use DNA. But if we don't know who they are to start, we don't know who to match the DNA with. You with me on that?"

"I don't get it, Ian."

"The bodies don't have hands and feet. They've been removed. And the heads are missing too. Just the torso left. No clothes. Some folks at the Yard think they're women who have been used up, as it were, as prostitutes in a human trafficking scheme. Or they overdosed, or there's a serial killer loose. But the recent grave, well, I gather they think it might be this Aussie woman Judy. The timing seems to suggest it might be linked. But of course it's not certain. They're sending to Australia for a DNA sample from this woman's son."

Dennis swallowed several times and twisted his beard with his left hand.

"Dennis, you there?"

"Yes, still here."

"I didn't say it was this woman Judy, you understand. I just thought you'd want to know. Might be totally unrelated."

"Would you let me know about the DNA test?"

"Of course. But don't forget that this may be unrelated."

"Sure."

Dennis hung up and put the phone on his lap.

Louise stared out the window. She had heard enough of the one-sided conversation to remain silent.

✦

Judy heard them walking down the hallway and sat up on the right side of the bed so that she could force them to use her left arm for the injection. She had loosened the sash on her gown to make it easier to move.

Judy was startled to see Voorster with Agata and the small man. He had not shown up in person for an injection since the last incident.

She held out her left arm as Agata tied the tube around her bicep, and the small man bent over and opened the black bag on the bed next to her.

"You disappointed me," Voorster said in his clipped South African accent. "I had plans for you. Good plans, you and I. Not to be, Judy. You are a fighter, and you're wasting away. My friend here says you are not breakable. Says he's never seen it before."

Judy watched the small man fill the syringe, and then he looked briefly for an open spot on her damaged left forearm. As he leaned forward, Judy glanced up at Voorster, then ripped the syringe out of the small man's hand in one swift movement.

She knew they would not expect it, and her only fear was that she would be too weak to actually grab the syringe. But it worked as planned; the syringe was in her right hand, her thumb was on the plunger, and as the small man jerked back from her, she leaped forward and stabbed him in the left side of his exposed neck, as close to the jugular as she could get, plunging her thumb down at the same time.

Agata screamed and fell backward to the floor. Voorster stood still, momentarily stunned, while the small man staggered back against the wall, ripping the syringe out of his neck and throwing it on the floor. Judy, Agata and Voorster looked at the small man, who roared with fury and stepped forward to take a swing at Judy.

She rolled away to the other side of the bed and felt his fist glance off her shoulder.

"You bitch," Voorster yelled as he grabbed the small man by the shoulders to hold him up, but it was too late; the small man made a small sighing sound and then collapsed onto the floor.

Judy had planned this meticulously, and it had worked so far; she knew the injection would put the small man down and that Agata would cower and scream. But she had not counted on Voorster being there and had no plan to deal with him. Perhaps she might land one weak punch at his Adam's apple, if she could muster that much. But he could easily strangle the life out of her or crack her skull with several stiff kicks.

"Damnit!" Voorster yelled. "Help me get him on the bed."

Agata scrambled to her feet, and they clumsily got the small man onto the bed. Voorster checked for a pulse on the man's neck, then on his wrist.

Finally, he looked up at Judy in pure rage and shot around the bed to get at her.

CHAPTER 23

Shit, Louise, it's him."

She turned and looked at the man walking up the steps to the doorman.

"Are you absolutely sure?"

"Yes!"

"Let's get suited up, then. Get back there now."

Dennis barely remembered what he was doing; the call from Ian had drained him of energy. Was Judy dead? Was that her headless body in a shallow grave north of London? He was not really surprised; the chance of finding a missing person alive weeks after an abduction was extremely low. Still, he had persevered with the thought that she had beaten the odds. But now, with Ian's call rattling around in his head, he was growing morose.

"What's wrong with you?" Louise asked, ripping off her sunglasses to glare at him.

"Huh?"

"What the hell has gotten into you? You forgot your vest. And your gloves. You have to wear gloves. Didn't we go through this already, for chrissakes?"

"Yes, sorry. Got it," he said, taking off his jacket to put on the Kevlar vest.

She grabbed his arm and dug her fingernails into the skin.

"Listen, Dennis, I'm not going into this thing with a weak partner; we'll never make it out. Either you're focused and ready, or we're not going. Seems that phone call took something out of you. From the part I heard, they found a body, but it's not clear whether it's Judy or not. So why are you suddenly a fucking mess? I thought this was the guy who did it?"

"Yes."

"And is there a slight chance she might be in this building?"

"A tiny chance, yes."

"Then are you going to grow the fuck up and be a reliable member of this team, or do we bag it?"

Dennis thought he'd seen all the sides of Louise's personality, but he had not seen this person before. Her pale blue eyes were almost too luminous to look at, and her expression was hardened into a fierce block of pale granite.

"Don't worry about me. I'm ready."

They got out of the van from the rear. Louise wore a red beret and her small ponytail jutted out behind. She wore a pair of gray wool gloves. Dennis noticed that her right forefinger was stiffly extended.

Dennis wore dark blue slacks, a light brown jacket and a logo-less maroon baseball cap. They both wore sunglasses.

They crossed the street and walked arm and arm toward the building, just as she directed, they were to act like an affectionate couple on an afternoon stroll.

When they got to the awning, Louise suddenly looked up at the doorman.

"Excuse me, is this a hotel?" she said, leading Dennis up the steps.

"Ah, no, miss," the burly doorman responded in a thick accent. He wore a full-length double breasted navy blue wool coat, blue slacks and black polished shoes. He also wore a pair of black leather gloves, but his shaved head was hatless.

"I thought this was a hotel," she repeated. "Are you sure? I saw it on a brochure at the hotel."

Dennis smiled, as he had been directed, and kept his eye on the doorknob of the huge, ornate glossy black door.

Louise reached into her inside coat pocket and pulled out a brochure, unfolded it and pointed at something.

"See, it says so right here."

The doorman frowned and took a step closer to look at the brochure. As he leaned forward, his chin exposed, Louise pointed her extended right forefinger under his chin. There was a small whoosh of air and the man yelled, "Ow!" and grabbed his throat as if stung by a wasp.

Angry, he grabbed Louise by the shoulders and yelled, "What the bloody hell was that!"

Dennis released her arm and reached for the doorknob, turned and pushed it open, leaving the hulking man and Louise behind him. He prayed that this silly palm pump weapon was going to work as she promised.

Inside the plush, ornate foyer, Dennis saw a startled, well-dressed, dark-haired man in his thirties behind a counter. A very attractive, very tall blond woman, also well dressed, stood next to him.

Before they could speak, Dennis did as Louise instructed.

"Excuse me," he said, holding the door open. "There appears to be something wrong with your doorman. He might be sick."

Both rushed from behind the counter to the door as Louise led the doorman inside.

"Philippe," the woman said, "what is wrong?"

But Philippe was not doing well. He was still ambulatory, and Louise did her best to direct him to one of the sofas, where he collapsed, his eyes rolling around. He made a guttural sound and gestured to his throat.

"I think he had a heart attack," Louise said.

Dennis furiously scanned the foyer, looking for hallways, doors and any obvious CCTV cameras. Louise told him there would be no cameras in sight, but she was convinced they would be there somewhere.

"Philippe!" the young man said, leaning into the doorman's face. "What happened? Are you all right? Can you speak?"

Dennis stepped backward behind the woman and slowly withdrew the 32-caliber from his coat pocket. He heard the faint whoosh sound again as Louise fired another glass pellet into the side of the young man's exposed neck.

"Ahh!" he screamed, holding his neck and standing up in alarm. "What did you do?" he yelled at Louise.

"Nothing," she said. "Are you okay?"

The young man stumbled away from Louise, his eyes wild with fear. "You stabbed me! You stabbed me!"

Louise opened her gloved hands palms up and said, "No, I didn't. What's wrong?"

The young woman rushed to her colleague. "Michael, what is wrong?"

Dennis noticed both of them had foreign accents and were, as Louise had predicted, completely confused by these unfolding events.

Suddenly the young man sagged and Louise rushed to help the woman lead him to a large brown leather chair. She turned to Louise. "What did you do to him? And him?" she said, pointing at the doorman, who had slumped sideways onto the couch. His eyes were closed, and he was snoring lightly.

Dennis stepped behind the woman, grabbed her arm and put the tip of the silencer against her temple.

"Come," he said, pulling her to the small counter.

Louise rushed to the front door and slid two large bolts to lock it. Then she closed the two cloth curtains on either side of the huge Victorian-era door. She joined Dennis and the woman behind the small counter.

"How many guests do you have?" Dennis asked.

The woman shook her head violently and said nothing. Dennis could not tell whether she was frightened of them or someone else, but her eyes kept darting to the two cell phones on the counter.

Louise pulled a gun out of her pocket with her left hand and placed the silencer against the woman's nose, of all things, and said, "How many?"

"Three," the woman said.

"Where?" Louise said.

The woman pointed to a hallway behind them, her long arm shaking violently.

"Dennis!" Louise said.

He remembered his task.

"Where is the recording equipment?" Dennis said.

"No recordings. Not allowed."

Louise pressed barrel against her nose again.

"Tell me where the recordings are made," Dennis persisted.

"No recording. We don't have. Please."

Louise rolled her eyes.

"You have recording equipment here. We know you do. Your clients don't think you do, but we know you do. One last time. Where is it?"

Before the woman could finish saying "No recording," Louise lowered her pistol and shot the woman in the top of her right foot, the silencer partially muffling the sound. Dennis jumped nearly as far as the woman did, but the woman went down in a scream, grabbing her leg.

"Louise!" Dennis said. "What the hell are you doing?"

"We need to get to the recording device, Dennis. We're being recorded right now, and we need to destroy it or we'll probably go to prison. Get this lady off her ass to lead you to where the recording equipment is. I'm going to look for Judy, and I don't want you to be with me if I find her. I thought I told you that. Get moving!"

Dennis leaned down and put his hand over the wounded woman's mouth.

"Shut up," he said, suddenly feeling buoyed by Louise's ferocity and the thought that she might find Judy. If she was here, he knew it would be better if Louise found her first.

Dennis jerked the woman to her feet, though she could barely walk. The woman whimpered her way down a small, carpeted hallway, leaving a thin trail of blood.

She stopped in front of a door and leaned against the opposite wall, her eyes closed in pain.

"Here?"

"Yes," she said.

The door was locked.

"Keys, please."

"No keys."

Dennis pointed his weapon at her other foot. She yelped and put her hands together as if praying. "They do not give us keys! We don't have. I tell you the truth. Please!"

Oddly, Dennis believed her. He tried to test the door's strength by shoving it with his shoulder. It was solid.

"Shit," he said.

Dennis had never shot a lock off of a door, like they did in movies. He did not know how to do this and wished briefly that Louise were next to him, because she seemed capable of anything.

He stood back from the door, aimed at the keyhole and pulled the trigger. Nothing happened.

"Son of a bitch!" he yelled as he fingered off the safety.

The pop of the silenced 32-caliber was loud but barely dented the keyhole. He fired again as the woman slid to the floor and cried. He shoved the door with his shoulder, but it remained firm.

He flipped the safety back on, slid the gun into his coat pocket and reached around inside to the small of his back and pulled out the 9 mm. This time the pop was louder, and he aimed for the area above the keyhole but below the knob. Wood splinters shot into the air, and he fired two more times in quick succession.

This time the door gave a little bit when he hit it with his shoulder. He took a more severe angle at the lock and fired, splintering more pieces of wood. But the door barely budged.

"Damnit, damnit, damnit!" he yelled. He took a deep breath to calm down, gave the whimpering woman a glare and then leaned to look at the lock more closely. He realized that he would never open the door by shooting the lock mechanism itself but looked at the wood molding around the door where the lock bolt sat inside the wall.

He stood back, flinched, and shot three rounds into the molding at the area where he thought the bolt would be housed in the wall. He reared back and threw his right shoulder against the door, and it moved several inches as the wood split on the molding and old wall plaster gave way. But it still would not open completely.

Dennis reared back and flew at the door with his shoulder. The door gave way, with pieces of drywall and wood falling to the floor. He flipped on a light switch and illuminated a small den that held a desk and two laptop computers. He pulled the power cords out of the computers and put the laptops into a small bag Louise had given him.

The crying women let out a bigger moan as Louise poked her head in.

"Judy?" Dennis asked.

She shook her head.

He sagged. Louise stepped in and took the bag.

"Keep an eye on her and the hallway," she said. He stepped outside and kneeled next to the woman.

"You'll be all right," he said, looking at her nylon-stockinged foot. It had a small hole in the top. "Bullet went right through. You'll be fine. Don't worry. We'll be out of here soon."

But the tall blond woman continued to cry softly, rocking back and forth as she cradled the shin above her wounded foot.

Louise returned.

"Were other guests here?" Dennis asked.

"Yes, just as she said. Three customers and three women. They're all sleeping now, though I'm nearly out of pellets. Judy is not there, or your South African."

Louise kneeled down and grabbed the crying woman's chin in her gloved left hand.

"Where's the basement?"

The woman pointed to the foyer. "Other door. Is locked. Key is at front desk. I show you."

"Is someone down there?" Dennis asked, lifting her to her feet.

"Yes."

"Are women down there?"

"Yes, I think."

The woman could barely walk as she led them to the desk. Dennis stopped, picked her up and carried her to the desk, gently setting her on a stool.

"There," she said, pointed to a key ring.

Louise grabbed the keys. "Which one?"

She pointed to an old-fashioned skeleton key.

Louise grabbed the two cell phones on the counter and pocketed them. Then she reached into one of her coat pockets, pulled out a plastic zip tie, and spun the woman around on the stool. She tied her hands behind her back, spun her around again, pulled another tie out and bound her ankles together.

"Is that necessary?" Dennis asked.

"Jesus, Cunningham," she said, shaking her head.

They walked over to the basement door, and for the first time Dennis noticed Louise was visibly nervous. She took off her beret and jammed it into one of her coat pockets. She pulled off her right glove, and detached the palm pump and put it into her other coat pocket.

"Safety off?" she asked.

"Yes," he said.

"For the record, Dennis, basements are bad. I don't like this, but there's no other way in. Either we wait for your friend to come up or we go down and see what's there. I say we go down and get this over with. We don't have much more time with these guys," she said, pointing to the doorman and the young man. "That stuff is a sedative, not a poison."

"I say we go," Dennis said.

"Couple things to remember, so please pay attention. Try not to shoot me if we get separated, got that? I hate getting shot in the back by my own team."

"Yes."

"If someone has a gun in their hand, man or woman, shoot to kill. Aim for the middle of the chest. Got that?"

"Yes."

"If, by some strange act of fate, we find Judy, do not drop your guard. Getting her out may be more difficult than us getting in to this place. Okay?"

"Got it."

"Lastly, and I don't mean to be maudlin, Cunningham, but if I don't make it out, you'll personally — do you hear me? Personally — tell my husband Phil that I love him. I just wanted to use my skills again. I think he'll understand. Maybe he won't, actually, but tell him anyway."

"I don't like you talking this way, Louise. Better yet, you stay here and let me go down. I don't have a wife or much of a career left anyway. You stay. If I don't come up with Judy or Voorster, just call the cops and get out of here."

"You won't make ten minutes down there without help," she said. "We go together, and we go now."

Louise put the key in the lock and turned it slowly, the old locking mechanism making a loud sound.

"Careful," the wounded woman said from her stool. Dennis and Louise looked at the woman in alarm, but she just stared back, her eyes round and terrified.

CHAPTER 24

Voorster raced around the bed with such speed that Judy had barely moved when his snarling face and outstretched hands were in front of her.

She was not as frightened by him. She knew her chances of getting out of the building were almost zero and that she would die either by overdose or under a flurry of fists and boots.

So as Voorster lunged at her, she did something entirely instinctive, which explained why he was unprepared.

Judy lowered her head and thrust the crown of her skull into his face, catching him on the nose. The force of the collision rattled her neck, spine and ribcage, and his bulk forced the two of them back into the wall next to the bed.

She knew he was hurt.

He fell to his knees and held his face, cursing. She tried to scamper away across the bed and over the body of the small man, but Voorster grabbed her ankles and yanked them backward. Judy twisted her head sideways in anticipation of a fist, and he did not disappoint. The blow caught her on the back of the head, stunning her with a bright light and tingling down her right arm.

Let this be over soon, she thought. *I fought. They won. But at least I fought.* She felt another blow bounce off her left ear.

✦

The stairway was dimly lit, and Louise went first, though awkwardly on her prosthetic foot. Dennis cursed himself for involving her. Louise's request that he speak to her surviving husband was still bouncing around his head.

There were a dozen steps down the staircase, with a room at the bottom on the left. When Louise got to the last few steps, she stopped, leaned forward and peered into the room. She turned and shook her head.

Dennis followed her, his right hand now wet with perspiration around the handle of the 9 mm.

They found themselves in an open, cozy, furnished and carpeted room with several stuffed leather chairs, a couch, large coffee table and a large flat-screen TV.

A hallway led down to what appeared to be a room on the right.

The sounds of some activity, including crying, came from the room down the hall, and Louise gestured for Dennis to follow farther behind her.

And then it happened.

From upstairs they could hear pounding on the front door. It stopped and then started again, this time very loud.

They looked at each other, then again down the hallway to see if the pounding noise had been noticed. The knocking continued and then stopped abruptly as Dennis heard a strange rhythmic pounding on the floor above him. He looked at Louise and jerked his head upward, confused by the noise coming through the floor.

"Shit," he said. He pointed for her to continue down the hallway, turned and bounded up the steps.

✦

Judy expected a third and perhaps final blow to her listless head, but Voorster stopped and cursed wildly. She opened one of her eyes to see Voorster prying Agata's arms from around his neck, his face dripping blood down his nostrils onto his moustache and lips.

"Damn woman," he said, throwing Agata to the floor like she was a broom.

He turned back to Judy, and she watched in great wonder as he tried to decide which woman to beat first; the woman on the bed or the woman who had just climbed on his back and made a weak effort to stop him.

Before he could make up his mind, Judy heard a voice — a strange woman's voice — say, "Stop! You! I said stop!"

Confused, dazed from the blows to the head, and very sore, Judy managed to arch her head upside down on the bed to see a small blond woman in the doorway holding a gun. Judy looked back at Voorster.

"Get out of here," he said firmly. "You don't know what you're doing. Leave now and nothing will happen to you."

Judy looked back at the woman with the gun.

"Get down on your knees," the woman commanded.

"You get down on your bloody knees, you stupid bitch!"

Judy heard a sudden series of loud pops from elsewhere in the building, and then loud voices from far away.

Voorster took several steps toward the woman with the gun and yelled, "Get out of here!"

The woman fired and Voorster fell down, clutching his left leg. Judy realized the gun had a silencer. Confused and in pain, Judy lay on the bed, her head next to the shoulder of the now inert small man, and stared at the ceiling. She followed the path of her favorite ceiling crack, the one that looked like the Swan River that she remembered from geography class.

What a strange way to die, she thought. *I think someone is trying to save me. This is not Dennis.* She felt the rumpled bedsheet against her cheek and nuzzled it slightly, the only comfort she could find.

✦

Dennis got to the top of the stairs just as the tall blond woman had finished hopping across the floor, her legs bound by the plastic tie. The woman had used her teeth to pull back the first door bolt and was working on the second one.

"Stop!" Dennis said.

But she didn't stop and he weighed whether to shoot her. The second bolt clicked back unlocked and the huge door burst open, smashing the woman back and onto a small table.

Two men barreled through the front door, one large bald man and one even larger man with a blue wool knit cap on his head. Neither man carried a weapon, and they looked startled to see Dennis pointing a pistol at them from the stairwell.

One dove right and the other left.

Dennis shot twice at the man rolling to his right and was not sure whether he hit him. As he swung the gun to his left, that man had rolled behind one of the chairs next to the sedated doorman.

He heard a loud crack. The man on his right had pulled out a gun and fired several times, hitting the wall inches from Dennis's head. He retreated several steps down the stairs, stopped, propped himself on his knees and poked his head at floor level over the threshold.

The man on the right fired again as Dennis's face emerged. Dennis returned fire blindly as he dropped his head below the threshold. When he peered again above the threshold, the man to the right was lying face down on the floor. But the other man to his left now fired from behind the chair, and Dennis felt something slam into his shoulder and knock him backward, tossing him head over heels down the stairs. When he finished tumbling wildly, his head hit the corner of something, and he blacked out.

✦

Judy was amused by the scene in front of her. Agata had got to her feet and hid behind the woman with the gun. The woman with the gun kept telling Voorster to get on his knees and stop rolling around, but Voorster kept cursing at the woman.

Finally, the woman with the gun stepped up to Voorster and hit him twice across his head with the butt of the pistol, momentarily quieting him.

Judy looked back at the ceiling and idly wondered where the black bag was. She would like to have an injection, and the thought was very pleasing.

Agata raced out of the room, but screamed almost immediately and returned wild eyed.

"He's coming!" she said.

Judy didn't see the woman with the gun move deeper into the room, but she must have because into the doorway strode a huge man with a gun. He first pointed it at Judy and then swung it around at Voorster. The popping sound made Judy flinch, and she watched the big man collapse to the cold cement floor with a terrible fleshy sound.

"Is your name Judy?" the woman with the gun said, tugging at Judy's shoulder.

Judy nodded, but it was painful to do so.

"Please get up now. You, what's your name?"

"Agata."

"Agata. Help me get this woman up. We need to get out of here."

Judy felt Agata pulling her out of bed while the woman with the gun checked the pulse of the large man on the floor.

"Come," the woman with the gun said. "Hurry!"

As Judy made her way around the bed with assistance from Agata, she looked down at a snarling Voorster, who was bleeding profusely from both a leg wound and a broken nose. Agata continued to pull and tug Judy toward the doorway while the woman with the gun checked the hallway.

Judy stumbled over the man lying in the doorway, and noticed the gun next to him. She jerked away from Agata, picked up the gun, lurched several steps toward Voorster, shot him once in the head and dropped the gun.

"Oh, Christ," the blond woman with the gun said, looking back into the room. "Out! Now!"

Dennis felt Louise shaking him violently, yelling inches from his nose, "Get up now! Dennis, get up. Up!"

He was confused, crawling on all fours up the stairs with Louise and several women behind him. None of them appeared to be Judy — they were so thin and haggard. There was also something wrong with his right arm, and it felt wet and sticky underneath his coat.

The late afternoon sunlight blinded him as the group made their way to the van. Dennis felt like the entire group was blind, except for Louise, who shepherded them like sheep into the back of the van. They tumbled in on top of each other and lay there rolling around like logs while Louise raced through the streets of London, talking to someone on her cell phone.

"Louise," Dennis pleaded from the back, tumbling onto one of the women. "I don't feel well."

"Shut up, Dennis, you're fine. Sit still."

"Dennis?" a woman said in a weak, hoarse voice.

✦

She was mesmerized by how clean and soft the bedsheets were, and she nuzzled her pillow as if it were the biggest teddy bear in the world. Judy was happy, but her elation was offset by a darkness she could not control. Somewhere, lurking behind her happiness, was a feeling of anger, humiliation and shame. Her mind shuttled between the two extremes, and she had difficulty negotiating the path.

The hospital was clean, the professionals were kind and accommodating, and the medications were tolerable.

When Dennis was not there, she longed for him with a yearning that was almost painful.

But when he was there, sitting next to her and holding her hand, she felt uncomfortable and wished he would leave.

Her parents and son were on their way to London, and she wondered whether she would suffer the same confusing feelings of longing and revulsion. What was happening to her? She sometimes stole a glance at the wreckage of the skin and veins on the insides of her arms and wondered idly how it had happened.

And she still longed, albeit less frequently as the days passed, for another injection.

✦

"Just tell them everything, just as you remember it," Louise said. "Don't embellish or withhold anything. Just tell them how I got involved and what we did. Leave it at that. If you don't know the answer to something, just say you don't know. The key is not to lie. Got that?"

"Yes," Dennis said, cradling the phone to his ear. "But I can't divulge the existence of this NSA guy. I've got to cover that track."

"Why do you need to keep him out of it?"

"I promised him. And Freddie would expect me to keep him out of it."

"Well, I never brought him up, because I don't know anything about him officially."

"Let's leave it at that. Please don't mention him."

"Your call," she said.

"You okay?" he asked.

"Yes, I'm fine. We certainly caused a stir around here. Getting lots of messages from colleagues. Rumors spread quickly here at Langley. And how about your shoulder?"

"That was nothing; thank God you reminded me to wear the Kevlar. Big bruise, small wound. Nothing really. And you? Everything okay at home?"

"You're not allowed to know about my personal life," she said.

"Is he angry?" Dennis persisted.

"That would be an understatement."

"I'm sorry I got you involved in this thing."

"Listen, we've hashed this out already. It happened. I knew exactly what I was doing. I'll deal with consequences, and so will you. Which reminds me, how is Judy doing?"

"Much better. Guess the doctors have this withdrawal thing down pat. Still, she seems depressed at times. I'm having trouble breaking through to her."

"I can't believe how depraved some people are to do things like that. But as you said, she's a strong woman. Give her time."

"Yes, of course. She needs time."

"When are you meeting the investigators in London?" Louise asked.

"Tomorrow. What do you think will happen?"

"Nothing will happen."

"Nothing?" he said. "After the shootout, the deaths, the unauthorized use of agency weapons borrowed from a London safe house?"

"And the rescue of a kidnapped Australian policewoman, the smashing of a human trafficking ring and the killing of a high-value Interpol drug lord?" she added.

"Do you think those things balance out?" he asked. "They don't in my experience."

"They will if you tell them the truth tomorrow."

"Even your soliloquy in the van about being shunted aside from field work because of a disability?"

Silence.

"Louise?"

"Tell them everything, like I said."

"Should we keep these burners going?"

"Yes, for now."

◆

"You look exhausted," Judy said, sitting at a small table in her room. "Come sit next to me."

Dennis sat and tugged at his beard. "They grilled me for four hours. I tried not to lose my temper, but towards the end I was just beaten down and popped off a bit. They had someone from MI5 there, a woman from London Police, two guys from operations and one from OIG who I never met before. Relentless grilling."

"And it went all right?"

"Yes, I suppose so. You never know until some folks sit around a table somewhere in the bowels at Langley and make a decision. You'd like to think that they'll make a rational decision, but my experience is that the outcome is pretty arbitrary depending on who's running the meeting, who hates who, whether the Redskins won the day before, stuff like that."

"Who are the Redskins?"

He laughed. "A football team."

"My family will be here tomorrow. I'd like you to meet them."

"I told you I wanted to meet them. I can't wait."

"My mum was crying on the phone before they left. You'll pardon her if she's a little emotional. And Trevor, well, he's seventeen, and I never know how he's going to react to anything. And with the situation with his father and all."

"Not to worry, everything will be fine."

Judy reached out and put her hand over Dennis's on the tabletop.

"They say I have to stay here another couple of weeks or so. I guess they have to treat me like any other addict. They have group therapy sessions and individual therapy sessions. It's very overwhelming at times. I was jogging in a park in London, and the next thing you know…"

"We don't have to talk about it, Judy."

"Well, I need to talk about it. I realized that in our group session today. I've been feeling terrible at times, and confused."

"Maybe it's the drugs you're taking to fight the withdrawal."

"No, it's the shame."

"Shame? What shame."

"The shame for the things I did. Bad things."

Dennis grimaced. "Why do we need to talk about those things? You had no choice. Those were evil men."

"But I still feel shame, like I've done something really awful. I think people will look at me differently now. I think you will too."

"You're wrong. I told you that I'm moving to Australia, and we're going to live together. I'm not the poster child for proper relationships, but you're the person I want to be with, and I'll do whatever it takes to make it work."

Judy withdrew her hand and sighed.

"I think you've changed towards me," she said quietly, looking at her hands folded in her lap. "You're not the same."

"Please look up at me," he said.

"No, I can't stand those blue eyes of yours. It feels like you're looking right through me."

Dennis shifted in his seat; Judy looked out the window onto a rooftop next door.

"I have to go back to Washington," he said, standing up. "I'm going to leave right after I meet your family. There's a couple of things I need clear up in Langley, then I'm resigning. I'll fly back here and wait for you to get healthy, and we'll fly back to Perth. If you change your mind about anything, I'll support you. But I have no intention of leaving you."

He stood up, leaned down and kissed her gently on the lips, and left.

When she heard his steps disappear down the hall, she allowed herself to cry in short, stabbing sobs that seemed to stay lodged in her throat.

When Dennis entered her room the next day, every eye was red and watery. Emily, Judy's mother, a short, sturdy woman in her sixties, rushed over and hugged him ferociously.

"Thank you, thank you!" she cried. "You saved our poor Judy!"

Her husband Stevey gently pried Emily away and shook his hand vigorously. "My God, man, what a hero you are. Newspapers in Australia are covering this thing like it was the landing at Normandy! Blazing guns, shooting down these despicable men! We need more heroes like you, mate!"

"Oh, it was my colleague who did most of the heavy lifting," Dennis said quickly. "I was just a helper."

But Stevey would have none of it, and Dennis decided not to argue the point. He shook hands with the handsome and exceedingly tall Trevor, who looked stunned, confused, happy and sad — all at the same time.

Dennis sat with Judy, holding her hand while her parents circled around the room like celestial objects, animated in their pleasure at having their daughter back. Judy sat in middle of it all, gently rubbing Dennis's hand with her thumb and shrugging in mild embarrassment every now and then.

His office had been cleaned by the custodial staff, but it still smelled stale. He sat at his desk and felt comforted by the familiar squeak of chair springs as he leaned back and forward.

The phone rang.

"Hey, Stan," he said to a colleague. "Yeah, just got back into the office. Ha, well, news travels fast. Yes, quite a dustup over there. No, well, can't talk about that stuff, as you can imagine. Still awaiting word on what the Council of Doom will decide."

He chatted some more then hung up.

The phone rang again from the IG's office.

"Cunningham here," he said in a deeper, more officious tone. "In twenty minutes? Certainly."

He was not surprised to see Louise already at the table in Richardson's office. They nodded politely at each other. Two other people were at the table, a young man in his mid-thirties and an older, very thin, white-haired, severe looking woman in her fifties.

"We should just get down to business," Richardson said in his normal, convivial tone. Dennis could imagine him using the same bouncy, enthusiastic tone to announce his entire family had been murdered.

"Your unsanctioned activities in London have been reviewed and adjudicated by a steering committee, as is the policy here. Before we get down to the decision, I do want to say that while there was an obvious breach of protocol and professional guidelines, the end result was undeniably a good one. Still, we do have rules."

He turned to the older woman.

"The committee has taken all the factors into account in making our decision. It's not easy when we have to balance our rules and procedures against an outcome that was so positive. Still, we cannot sanction in any way the abrogation of duty and honor in rogue operations by employees of the agency…" At these words, Dennis stopped listening and stole a glance at Louise, who stared at the woman with that steely glare of hers.

Poor Louise, he thought. *She's going to get slammed on this, and it was all because of me. Me? I could give a shit what they do. But Louise, well, she cares about her job, her country and the agency.*

Which was why his self-absorption was jolted back to reality when he heard the older woman say, "While some of us were looking for more serious sanctions, the majority of the committee voted to take no action against either of you. At this time, that is. We could always choose to open the file later and press charges."

Richardson smiled, thanked the woman and young man, and escorted them out of his office.

Dennis stole a glance at Louise, but she kept her eyes on Richardson as he returned to the table.

"Well, that was a close one, wouldn't you say?" he said, sighing. "You know, I thought the two of you were going to be a good team, but boy was I mistaken. Louise, we've already had several discussions around this issue, and we don't need to go there again. On the other hand, Cunningham, you are just back from the UK, and we haven't spoken yet."

Dennis had his fingers intertwined on the mahogany table as if in a church pew and stared at them in a sign of abject penance mixed with profound confusion. He had been sure they were going to fire him or even incarcerate him.

"As we discussed at the beginning, you have a very influential bene-factor that pressed us to put you on a case. But so far we've managed to lose a highly valued member of the NSA's OIG to a horrible poisoning, we had an Australian policewoman abducted, tortured and rescued by the two of you in a shootout worthy of a Bourne movie. And we're no closer to finding out what happened to our deputy chief of station in London than before the two of you were given the case."

The intercom on Richardson' desk uttered a tone, and then his secre-tary said, "Director on line two, sir."

"Oh, crap," Richardson said, looking at his watch. He got up, went to his desk and grabbed the phone. Louise and Dennis exchanged glances; her face was blank, and Dennis knew enough about her already not to bother judging where she stood.

Richardson spoke on the phone for a few minutes then returned to the table and without sitting down, said, "So here's where we are: I've been ordered to close the Arnold investigation in exactly fourteen days. I would close it now, but the director is a little nervous about your benefactor, Cunningham. Do whatever you want on the case for two weeks, or do nothing for two weeks, I could care less. But the case is going to close, and you'll be on to other, more important tasks. Thank you."

✦

Louise shut the door to her office behind Dennis and then sat down. He vaguely remembered the first time he'd sat in her office, deciding that she was a lightweight talent that had been dumped out of operations. Now, sitting there with his legs folded, he kept conjuring up an image of Louise with her red beret sauntering toward the doorman in London.

"Do you remember why I let you go back to London?" she said, skipping any hint of friendship or camaraderie.

"Um, yes. You told me that you'd let me go back to search for Judy if I'd continue to work on the Arnold case."

"And did you work on the Arnold case?"

"A bit. Yes I did."

"I don't think so," she said. "I think you didn't give a shit about the Arnold case when you went back."

Dennis stirred in his chair. "Probably didn't do a lot."

"But you did get Judy out of her mess, correct?"

"I think you got Judy out of her mess. I was more or less a bystander."

"Well, that's where I'm going with this, Cunningham," she said as she tilted her head minutely back and forth like a blonde metronome, her straight hair swinging. "You need to break the Arnold case. You have two weeks."

He cleared his throat. "Louise, I'm resigning today. I've had it. Judy is very fragile right now and needs some stability. I'm moving to Australia, and I'll give this relationship a try."

While he thought he'd seen the many mysterious sides of Louise, he was unprepared for what emerged.

"You will not fucking resign, Dennis, until you tell me what happened to Arnold! You think I was a little fierce with our good friends in that high-end London flophouse? Well, you have no fucking idea how fierce I can be with you. You understand?"

"Louise!" he said, startled.

"Don't you fucking 'Louise' me," she said, her blue eyes now mostly a shade of Arctic iceberg. "I knew how to get that woman Judy out of the building. I was trained to do that. I am good at it. I can't figure this Arnold thing out. But you can. That's something you're good at. And I need this Arnold case badly to prove I can get back into operations. I'm not going to be so crass as to say you owe me one, but, well, you fucking owe me one."

"Okay," Dennis said quietly. "Okay. Got it." He stood up, turned and put his hand on the doorknob but stopped.

Without turning to face her, he said, "Ambition is a wonderful thing, Louise, but it can change people. And for the record, I don't think this organization deserves your profound loyalty."

He left the door open, but when he got back to his own office, he closed his door and called Peter Harbaugh, his mentor, father figure and wise old man. Dennis needed some wisdom in this moment.

✦

Judy hated the group therapy sessions, and she knew why: they were all addicts that had chosen their path to addiction. Judy had been kidnapped and forcibly turned into an addict. She did not choose to shoot heroin or snort Vicodin; they did. Besides, she was a policewoman who arrested people like this.

Still, there was something they had in common. The young woman named Cynthia with soft brown eyes and short, curly hair sitting across from Judy best summed it up.

"I can't get it out of my mind," Cynthia said. "I mean, I know we're not supposed to talk about it, but I loved the feeling I got from that stuff. I know it was killing me, but the high was so good, so brilliant, really. And I miss it. I'm not ashamed to say it."

"There is nothing wrong with admitting the power of these drugs, Cynthia," the session leader Derrick said. "I think everyone here can relate to that feeling. But that blissful feeling is fleeting and destructive. You said yourself you stole heirloom jewelry from your mother to pay for the drugs. It's important to acknowledge not just the bliss, but the pain it causes."

Judy thought of Agata, who was at another treatment center, and hoped they would not deport the poor woman afterwards.

And she thought of Dennis and wondered if he could accept a damaged woman, a woman who deep down was ashamed at her love affair with the injection; the junk that gave her such an enormous high that no man could compete with. Or so she worried.

CHAPTER 25

So is it true?" Harbaugh asked.

"True in what sense?" Dennis said.

"Did you bust into that whorehouse in London and shoot it out?"

"Peter, how long have you been retired from the agency? Maybe eight years? How in the hell do you hear stuff like this?"

"You're not answering. Is it true?"

They sat in a Starbucks on Wisconsin Avenue in northwest Washington, D.C. The sound of hissing cappuccino steamers melded with the hip music piped into the crowded seating area.

"Kind of true, I guess. Louise did all the heavy lifting. I was along for the ride."

"God, that woman is something else. With a prosthetic foot, she goes on an unauthorized mission to save some poor women from human traffickers. Be surprised if she doesn't end up running the Operations Directorate one day."

"Louise is indeed a piece of work. I'm kind of confused about her, to be honest. She's a complex person. And ambitious."

"And what's wrong with a little ambition? You've always been charmingly unambitious, Dennis. But people like Louise are needed in this business. Remember, it's a business, like Starbucks or Walmart. And businesses need leaders."

"Mmm. Not sure I'm quite there, Peter, and might never be. This is a mission for me to get things right and keep the agency within the limits of the law. You'd be surprised how this business, as you call it, operates more like the mafia than a police force."

"Ah, there's the cynic coming out," Peter laughed.

"Well, speaking of the cynic, can I ask you something?"

"Shoot."

"Last time we met, you warned me about the Arnold case in London. Why did you do that? I've been given two more weeks on the case, and then they're closing it down. I keep getting the feeling that everyone except me knows what's going on, but no one is talking."

Harbaugh took a sip of his coffee and frowned briefly as he considered the question.

"I know nothing specific about the Arnold case, especially since I've been out of the agency for many years, as you pointed out."

"But you had a strong opinion about it earlier."

"Yes, I did, and I still do."

"Can't you be a tiny bit more specific?"

Harbaugh leaned back in his chair as a young mother pushed an expensive stroller the size of the Taj Mahal past them.

"It's simply instinct; there's no data points or intel that I have. I'm sure you understand that. Just a feeling. Deputy chiefs of station don't just go missing, and in London of all places. Just doesn't happen. And not a peep, a body or a hint. Something strange is going on. We'll probably never know."

"That's it?"

"I'm afraid so, Dennis. And do you remember what I told you the last time we met? I think I drew a silly diagram for you. I said there was the professional organization that actually runs the intelligence business, and there was the public group of elected officials that think they run the intelligence business. But of course they don't. And I said that you, being in the IG's office, well, you were in this netherworld between the two entities."

"I remember the drawing well," Dennis said. "I've thought about it a lot."

"Well, the thing to remember about this netherworld is that anyone in there can easily be squashed. There's no one to protect you, because you don't have a constituency. You're a problem for at least one of the entities at any given time, and maybe both, like you might be now. Just not a great place to be."

"And Arnold? You think he's never going to be found?"

"I didn't say that. I'm saying that someone knows exactly where he is, but there's a reason they're not telling you or anyone else. Think about it. Didn't you lose someone already from the NSA?"

"Yes. Freddie, a good man. Terrible death."

"Have they found Freddie's killer yet?"

"No."

"And they never will."

"Your point?"

"My point, dear Dennis, is that one of the entities that I drew on the napkin knows exactly where the killer is, and they're not going to do anything about it, or else you would have heard about it by now."

"God, Peter, talking to you sometimes gives me a headache."

"I'm fond of you, Dennis, and want you to succeed. But I worry about you as well."

Dennis looked at Peter closely.

"Is that a warning? Do you think this case is that sensitive?"

Harbaugh shrugged. "Just a guess. From an old man."

✦

The Heathrow Express was not crowded, and Dennis watched the gray buildings blur past through the tinted glass of the train car. He was nervous about seeing Judy; the last time he saw her she had not been well.

How could things have changed so quickly? he thought. *One moment I'm talking about moving to Australia to live with this incredible woman, and the next moment she's been kidnapped, turned into an addict and been forced into the sex trade. Is there anything left of the original Judy? Is there anything left of us?*

He reached for his phone as it vibrated in his jacket.

"Hello, Ian."

"Dennis, my good fellow. Are you back in the States?"

"No, in London. Heading to Paddington. What's up?"

"Well, do you remember those ghastly bodies the police found outside of London?"

"Yes. Did you catch anyone yet?"

"No, not yet. But the police did get the tiniest of leads, though, and I thought I'd mention it to you."

"What lead?"

"Ah, well, there was a more recent body."

"Yes, I remember that detail particularly well."

"Well, the fellow — the police presume it was a man who did this — made an error and did not notice a rather distinctive mole on the inside of the woman's thigh. They appear to have removed something from her back, which they think was probably a tattoo."

"Maybe it's the jet lag, Ian, but I'm not getting why you're calling me on this case. We have nothing to do with these murders, or interest in them."

"Ah, but that's why I'm calling. You see, there was a missing person's report made out by a Serbian couple that emigrated here about ten years ago. Their twenty-year-old daughter went missing, and in the report they're asked to list any identifying features, and they listed a long, vertical mole on this inside of their daughter Andjela's left thigh."

"And?"

"And, well, the police think this body is indeed Andjela, and they're just waiting on a DNA match. But here's the part that I thought you'd be interested in. This woman Andjela, who was quite attractive, was a waitress at a restaurant in Mayfair that was owned by your Ukrainian fellow Pavlychko. Isn't he the one you were looking for?"

"Shit. Yes. Ian, can you do me a big favor?"

"I'll try."

"Ask the police to test this woman's body for radiation."

"I beg your pardon?"

"Radiation. Can they test her body for traces of radiation? It's very important."

"I'll try, if you think it's that important."

"Yes, I do."

✦

"My God, you look great," Dennis said as he wrapped his arms around Judy and squeezed. They kissed awkwardly and sat at the small round Formica table in her room.

"Dennis, can I come stay with you?" she blurted. "At your hotel? I need to get out of here. Derrick says it would be okay. I just need to keep coming to some sessions here."

"Of course you can. When can you leave?"

"Now!" she said, pointing to two travel bags. "Right bloody now. But you have to talk to Derrick first."

"Well, let's talk to Derrick."

"Did I hear my name?" said someone from the doorway.

Dennis turned to see a very short, thin man with bushy reddish-blond eyebrows and curly dirty blond hair pointing up haphazardly like a pile of steamed milk on a cappuccino.

"You must be Dennis?" he said, walking forward and holding out his hand.

They shook hands, and he asked Dennis and Judy to sit at the table.

"Typically, we like our patients to stay a minimum of thirty days, but given the progress of Judy and the unusual nature of her addiction, well, it may be possible for her to leave earlier. But I must ask you to follow some very strict rules, Dennis. First, no alcohol and prescription drugs should be left in your hotel room, Judy must continue to attend sessions here and you should consider avoiding alcohol in general until Judy is stronger. These drug mixtures nowadays are extremely powerful and can wreak havoc on the brain's chemistry. It is not a matter of volition or willpower; the brain has changed and needs time to heal. Judy never asked for this problem, of course, but she must own it, and she needs a strong, supportive partner to help her."

"I'm the guy, then," Dennis said.

"You'll make sure she attends her sessions here?"

"Of course."

"Then you're good to go, Judy."

✦

The cold air stung at Judy's cheeks, but she was so thrilled to be walking freely through Green Park that she did not mind. Her eyes watered slightly as the wind whipped, so she burrowed into Dennis's shoulder.

"I feel badly that I missed Christmas," Judy said. "I sent Trevor some late presents, but I still feel so bad about it. It's already January."

"Judy, you were in a hospital, for God's sake," he said.

"I still feel awful."

"Well, you didn't miss much. I don't celebrate Christmas, or New Year's, or anything for that matter, so doesn't make much difference to me."

"You talk like that, but you really do care about things," she said, pressing her head into the shoulder of his wool coat. "I know that much about you."

"Did I tell you that you sound like my therapist?"

"I thought you stopped seeing her."

"I think she fired me or something like that."

"Can they do that?"

"Well, she said that we didn't have much more to talk about and that I was about as well as I was going to get. Or something. I don't know. I can't believe we have to pay people to listen to our crap and then look at the clock on the wall every fifty minutes and say, 'Oops, our time is up today.'"

Judy laughed. "My gruff little Yank."

But it was the freedom that made her smile; she had been imprisoned in a basement in London for almost a month, then imprisoned in a hospital for almost three weeks and was now free. She could walk through a park, go to a film, eat at a restaurant, visit a museum ... and fight the urge to seek comfort in that tiny syringe. Would this fight go on forever? She did not like the way her thoughts would inexorably wander back to the thrill — as perverse as it was — of watching the small man plunge the needle into her vein.

"... and now it's less than two weeks, and I can't seem to crack this thing."

"What was that, Dennis? I'm sorry, I was daydreaming a little."

"Oh, nothing. Just complaining about this damn case. I can't find a thread to follow. Sometimes just walking around I can sort of stumble onto something. At least in the past it worked that way. I feel like my brain is dead or withered. God."

That's how I feel, Judy thought, wiping a small cold-generated tear from her eye. *Like I have a dead brain.*

✦

Dennis walked around the hotel room in his boxer shorts and tee shirt, trying to contain his agitation. There were only two things he wanted right now, and they gnawed at him like a squirrel scratching to get out of his stomach. He wanted a drink, and he wanted to have sex with Judy, neither of which was an option. Dennis had kept away from alcohol at Derrick's suggestion, and Judy had made it clear that she was not ready for sex, though she was as beautiful and desirable as ever.

"Why do you keep flying around like a bumblebee?" she asked from the bed as she watched a police drama on BBC One. "You're making me dizzy."

"Oh, I don't know," he lied, sitting down on the edge of the bed. "Just trying to get my head around this damned Arnold case."

"Well, at least you have something to get excited about," she said. "I used to get engulfed by investigations. Now, well, I don't know what they'll assign me to when I get back. And I don't even know if I want to go back into that building again or even work for the AFP. Heaven knows what they'll say about me behind my back: 'Poor Judy, such a shame. Did you hear what happened to her? They turned her into a drug-addicted sex slave.'"

"Stop saying things like that! Who gives a shit what they think? People will say whatever they want, but it means absolutely nothing. You're a terrific policewoman with great instincts and skills. The hell with other people's stupid thoughts."

She turned off the television and stared at the black screen for a moment.

"You've been so nice to me," she said softly. "Sometimes when I just start crying, you hold me and don't say anything. You don't judge me. You even try to distract me, I noticed, when I get moody. You've been wonderful, but I don't think I deserve it. I don't think I'm giving anything back."

"Nonsense."

"I'm feeling depressed again."

"Well, let's see if we can break that train of thought," he said, shifting around on the bed to face her. "Why don't you help me on this Arnold case?"

"Me?"

He looked around the room, got off the bed, kneeled down and looked under the bed, then stood up. "I don't see anyone else in the room."

"How in bloody hell would I help you find this missing department head or whatever he is?"

"A deputy chief of station."

"All right, him. How would I help you?"

"I'm missing something. It's right there in front of me, but it's this tiny little key that I cannot find. You could help me find it. Besides, you need something to sink your teeth into. Be good for you and for me."

"I know nothing about your intelligence community," she laughed. "Except what I've seen in the movies. They all seem to lie and cheat each other and then double-cross the people they just cheated."

"Exactly. That's all you need to know."

"I'll think about it," she said.

"Well, think fast, I'm running out of time. Louise has already called me twice."

"Mmm. I think I'm a little jealous of Louise."

"Huh?"

"She is a formidable person. Fearless. I can't believe what she did to get me out of that house. And she even lied about who shot Voorster. Why did she do that?"

"I think she didn't want you to have to answer to the police on that. I never asked, she just did it."

"That's what I mean. She's amazing."

"Let's not deify that woman, if you don't mind."

"Do you think she's attractive? I thought she was quite attractive."

Dennis got off the bed.

"Enough about Louise! Ugh. She'll never be my type, if that's what you're driving at. She's a real pain in the ass and just a little too ambitious for my liking. You, on the other hand, are my type: beautiful, mysterious, brilliant and you talk with a funny accent. Plus you have that little up-turned nose that is so cute. And now it's time for bed. Your job starting tomorrow morning is to solve the Arnold case."

"Perhaps," she said, turning off the light as Dennis got under the covers.

Dennis snuggled behind her and put his arm around her waist.

After several minutes she said softly, "Do you think I'm getting better?"

"Of course I do."

"How can you tell?"

"You're being a pain in ass, that's how I can tell."

She laughed and turned around to face him in the dark.

"You are such a darling to put up with me."

"You bet I am."

She laughed again, moved her face against his and kissed him softly.

"I need another one of those if you have one handy," he said.

She kissed him again, withdrew, and then kissed him yet again, this time longer. They parted only inches, their breaths mingling.

"You're a handsome devil," she said. "I'm glad you shaved."

"Devil, yes; handsome, not so much."

She leaned forward, pulled him closer and kissed him hard and did not let up; a minute later, after grappling under the sheets, it was as if a switch was turned on and the two went at each other with a fervor that took even Dennis by surprise.

CHAPTER 26

O
ut of the question?" Dennis yelled into the phone. "Are you kidding me, Chandler? Since when do you have the right to restrict an investigation by OIG?"

"You go right back to your boss Richardson there in Langley and ask him," Chandler said. "I've been told your investigation is nearly over and that we no longer are required to submit personnel to questions from you or turn over any data whatsoever."

"That's bullshit."

"No sir, it's not. Goodbye."

Dennis pushed the disconnect button on his phone and threw it onto the bed.

"This is ridiculous. Louise tells me to continue the investigation, but no one's cooperating any longer. You can't investigate if you don't have access. This goddamn investigation has been a bust from the beginning. Not to mention it got Freddie killed. My God, I feel so damn stupid."

Judy put down the newspaper she was reading and walked over to Dennis, who was sitting at the small hotel desk.

"Give me your notebook," she said, sitting at the edge of the bed. "And a pen."

"You can't read my writing," he said lamely. "I can barely read it myself."

"I'm not going to read your handwriting; I'm going to write. Give it to me."

He reached over, picked up the small black moleskin notebook and one of the hotel pens and gave them to her.

"Draw me a picture," he said, "of a donkey — that's me — wandering in a desert looking for a drink of water."

"Silly, I'm not going to draw. I'm going to ask you some questions."

Dennis put his hands on top of his head, leaned back in the chair and said, "Please do. I need a diversion. I'm going nuts."

"All right then, let's go over your visit to Menwith Hill. Is that okay?"

"Sure."

"Let's start from the moment you and Fred drove up to the gate."

Judy was surprised at how much she liked this process. She knew how to keep prodding and poking an interviewee, looking for inconsistencies or some hint of a missing element. She had done it so many times before, only this time she was not trying to break down a suspect; she was trying to test a man's memory and assemble a consistent narrative.

They did this for forty-five minutes, until Dennis could not sit any longer.

"I don't know how you did it," he said, standing, "but you made me feel like I was hiding something. Like I was lying. How did you do that?"

"Are you lying?" She laughed.

"No! It's just that you made me feel that way. You policewomen are horrible."

"Well, let's take a break. Then I want to go over your notes from the video you watched."

"Maybe you're taking this assignment a little too seriously," Dennis said.

"You told me I needed to sink my teeth into something."

"You're like a terrier. You sink your teeth in and then you don't let go."

"But I'm happy doing this. I feel like my brain is working again. It's exciting."

Dennis looked at Judy for a long time.

"What?" she said.

"How did we end up like this, you and I?" Dennis said, wrinkling his forehead.

"What do you mean?"

"I met you on an investigation in Western Australia less than two years ago, and it's been a strange mix of boredom when we're not together and complete, utter chaos when we are together. And what you just went through makes my stomach churn. So here we are in a small hotel room in London. I can't tell if we're about to enter the boredom phase or the chaos phase."

Judy turned and looked at the bright light coming from the gauzy white window curtains. In the street below she could hear the mechanical voices of the city calling: the deep-throated chug of the diesel-powered buses; the high-pitched whine of the passenger cars and cabs. She sighed.

"Do you think we're going to make it?" she said.

"Make what?"

"You know, as a couple?"

"I think so."

"You just think? I was hoping you would just say 'yes, we'll make it.'"

Dennis stood up, stretched and put his hands on top of his head and left them there.

"I don't think I'm good for you," he said. "I cause too much trouble. People die around me or get injured. Or abducted. You don't know how hard it is to look at you sometimes and realize how guilty I feel for bringing you to London and exposing you to that creep Voorster."

"Oh, Dennis, you had no control over that. You're just being ... well, I don't know what."

"Every time I look at you I'm reminded of how I made a beautiful woman suffer so badly."

"Dennis! Stop talking like that."

He dropped his hands to his side.

"I can't help it. My therapist said I was a professional self-flagellator."

"That sounds vaguely obscene," she said.

Dennis chuckled and then sighed. "I do better when I'm on a mission and solving things. This Arnold thing is a mess. One guy I liked a lot — which is unusual, because I don't have a lot of friends — is already dead. I've got Louise breathing down my neck — why does she care so much about this stupid case? And now it looks like the ops people are just going to stall until the clock runs out. And there's you."

"What about me?" Judy said, eyeing him closely.

"I feel like I'm not helping you whatsoever."

"Now you sound depressed," she said. "Stop it. You're being too negative. Sit down and let's go over your notes from your visit to Menwith Hill."

"I can't sit any longer," he said.

"Sit!" she said, pointing to the chair.

Dennis fell into the chair, and Judy picked up where they had left off, running him through every minute detail of the visit to the NSA listening post in the north of England.

✦

"How did you guess she was contaminated?" Ian said.

"It's a long story," Dennis said, sitting across from his MI5 friend in small coffee shop.

"I'm afraid you'll have to tell me," Ian said.

"I'm not supposed to be discussing this."

"Don't insult me, Dennis."

Dennis leaned forward and placed his open palm on the small table. "Give me your phone."

"My mobile?"

"Yes."

Ian wrinkled his forehead, drew the small phone out of the inside of his tweed jacket and put it in Dennis's hand.

Dennis removed his phone and took both of them up to the man behind the counter.

"Can you please put these into your refrigerator for a few minutes?"

"You want me to put them in the fridge?" the proprietor said.

"Yes," Dennis said, taking out a five-pound note and laying it on the counter. "Just for a few minutes."

The man picked up the two phones, turned, and opened the glass door of the refrigerator behind him, pushed two soft drinks aside, and put the phones down on the rack. He turned back to Dennis and shrugged.

"Dennis, was that necessary?" Ian asked. "Do you really think someone's listening in to our conversation using mobile phones?"

"Ian, how long have we known each other?"

"Lord, I don't know. Perhaps ten years. Sometimes with you it seems much longer."

Dennis laughed.

"Even for a cynic like me, I know they can listen in whenever they want. So I take precautions. You should too."

"A bit paranoid these days, are we, Dennis?"

"You're either being purposefully misleading, or you're too naïve, Ian."

"Ah. Well perhaps you and I are a bit of both."

"Mmm," Dennis said. "Ian, I think you know exactly why there was radiation on this woman and where it came from and why she was exposed. What I can't figure out is why you're acting like you don't know those things."

Ian looked down at his paper cup full of tepid tea as if straining to read something.

"Well, the thing is, we don't know what you Yanks are up to. A bit baffling, actually."

"Can you be a bit more specific?" Dennis said.

"This Arnold disappearance. And all this silliness about Pavlychko. I mean, you folks know perfectly well what happened. But you act like it's a mystery. And they send you and that poor fellow who gets poisoned. Just baffling. Why would you fellows do that? I suppose that's the question. I mean, it's been clear for some time that you Yanks don't really trust us Brits. You think we leak like a sieve and are penetrated with Russian moles, but this latest bit of tomfoolery has us completely, utterly confused. It's delicate to even ask, if you know what I mean."

Dennis scratched his now clean shaven chin and did his very best to appear composed, knowledgeable and in charge, even though he was confused, increasingly angry and not at all in charge.

"Ian, you know that I work for the Office of the Inspector General for the agency. I've never been in operations in Langley, and in fact those people hate folks like me for meddling in their private wars and vendettas. Sometimes they send us on wild goose chases, like this case, just to show they're open and transparent, which of course they're not."

Ian smiled. "So you do know?"

"Of course I know," Dennis smiled, lying through his teeth. "That's what makes this so amusing and tragic. Took me a while, mind you, to get my arms around it."

✦

"Yes, Trevor, I'm coming home very soon. Perhaps next week. I miss you terribly," Judy said, cradling the phone to her ear with her shoulder as she pulled change out of her purse and handed it to the man behind the counter. "I love you too. Ta."

Judy took her coffee to a countertop and stool that looked out onto London in rush hour.

A cold front from the northwest had swept through the previous night, sending temperatures down and wind gusts up. Judy watched the hapless Londoners slide by the window bundled up in overcoats, scarves and hats, looking more like miserable Russian soldiers massing for the attack at Stalingrad.

She was happy, or at least she told herself that she was happy. But there was so much that was unknowable, and it drained her, even in her best moments. Could she reenter her old job at the AFP with enough dignity and brush off the gossip and patronizing smiles? Would Dennis, the gruff Yank who seemed to find trouble everywhere, be content sitting idle in Perth, Western Australia? And would she be able to rebuild her life without drugs? She still harbored a perverse urge every now and then for just a bit of the pleasure those damned injections had inflicted upon her.

Judy took a sip of lukewarm coffee and let her mind wander as it did these days, her attention switching randomly from items as diverse as her attraction to a passerby's silk scarf to an image of Trevor competing in a track meet.

Then a fleeting image of a man passing through a metal detector flashed, followed by a memory of trip she had taken to Singapore with her former husband when they were young. Then the image of the metal detector returned. It stayed with her for a while longer, then dissipated.

Judy frowned, sat up straight and refocused in a more purposeful way on the image of a man walking through a metal detector. She spilled her coffee slightly as she bolted from the stool and raced back to the hotel.

✦

"He's in Russia," Dennis said, slowly enunciating every word. "Friggin' Russia. He defected!"

"No," Judy said. "That can't be right."

"That's what Ian told me. I acted like I knew what the hell he was talking about, and little by little he just let it out."

"Dennis, I know that I'm not fully aware of America's intelligence community, but there's something wrong with this information. Perhaps you misunderstood him."

Judy sat on the corner of the hotel bed facing Dennis, who sat at the small desk with his hands on top of his head. She thought he was trying to hold his head tight so it would not explode; she could hear the anger in his voice.

And he had grown more paranoid. When he returned to the hotel room, he took her phone and his and put them in the small hotel refrigerator, then he unplugged the hotel telephone. Lastly, he had gone around the hotel room with a device he purchased recently at a London specialty shop that could pick up radio frequencies, presumably from an eavesdropping apparatus.

"Russia," Dennis repeated, as if in wonder.

"How do they know he's in Russia?" she asked.

"Ian said they've picked up his voice print, in English, on routine scans of Russian phone exchanges. They were confused, of course, but if it was true, they wanted to look like heroes to the Yanks. So they pinpointed his mobile signal and sent someone in on the ground to verify. Sure enough, every day Arnold seems to go to his favorite coffee shop, called The Grind, in a section of Moscow called Patriarshiye Ponds. So the Brits turned it over to the London station here expecting accolades or something, and Chandler said 'Thank you very much,' and left it at that."

"So Chandler knows that Arnold is in Russia, but he never told you?"

"Seems that way."

"I don't get it, Dennis. This is much too strange for me to understand. This fellow Arnold, an important member of the US intelligence service, goes missing in London. The CIA investigates several times, and they claim not to know where he is."

"And then an influential member of the House of Representatives suddenly presses the OIG to look further into the missing person, and they request me," Dennis said, continuing the narrative. "And this congressman meets privately with me and keeps hinting that I'm not actually solving the case."

Judy continued, "But when you finally do come up with a lead — this Ukrainian fellow — someone poisons your fellow investigator. And probably you, too, if you would have joined him that night."

Dennis stood up, walked to the window and looked at the gray London skyline.

"Funny, but Ian was trying to get me to tell him what was going on with this Arnold charade, but I acted like it was too sensitive to discuss. He laughed and asked whether I felt silly running around like I didn't know what happened to Arnold."

"What did you tell him?"

"I told him it was embarrassing, but such is the work we do."

Dennis walked over to the desk and was about to sit down then abruptly swiveled toward Judy.

"You know what really pisses me off?"

"I'm afraid to ask," Judy said.

"I'm guessing that this Ukrainian thing had nothing to do with Arnold. It was a bum lead that got Freddie killed. Shit, what a mess this thing was from the start."

Judy and Dennis looked at each other, their eyes moving slightly as they processed the information.

"And I thought I had an interesting tidbit," Judy said. "Big bloody surprise that is."

"What tidbit?"

"Oh, nothing. Silly stuff."

"Come on, must have been something important."

"Not exactly," Judy said, standing up and stretching. "Feel like going for a walk? This room seems so small sometimes."

"Sure, but only if you tell me your tidbit."

"Ah, well," Judy said, sitting down on the bed again. "I looked through the notes of my extensive interrogation of a Mr. Dennis Cunningham. And I noticed that when you and your pal Fred visited Menwith Hill, you were forced to go through a metal detector and then a hand-held metal detector afterwards."

"Yeah, so?"

"But when I reviewed my notes of what you said you saw on the video of Arnold's last visit to Menwith Hill, you never mentioned him going through a metal detector. You only said he was wanded. Or that's what you said, anyway."

Dennis cocked his head in thought.

"Yeah, that's true. I wonder why he didn't go through the metal detector? That's odd. Why didn't Freddie and I pick that up before? Hell, maybe that's what he was talking about. He said we had missed something on the video, but he couldn't figure it out."

"It's probably nothing, but I thought you'd be proud of me," Judy chuckled. "Until you showed up with the Russia connection."

"But wait. Why would someone at such a top-secret facility be waved through a metal detector? Why would someone not go through a metal detector?"

"For health reasons?" Judy said.

"What health reasons?"

"I don't know. I thought if you had a pacemaker, you can't go through a metal detector. Or that's what I remember."

Dennis leaned forward, turned on his laptop and let it go through its security protocols while he got up and kissed Judy on the lips.

"You are a smart one."

"Well, let's not get too far ahead of ourselves."

"No, let's do just that. A little warning bell is ringing somewhere. You might have just found what we're looking for."

"Ha. I thought you just found what you're looking for. Arnold defected and is doing quite well in Russia."

"Hell, that's the easy part, assuming it's true. The hard part is why is the agency hiding it?"

"Well, they're apparently only hiding it from you and your boss."

"And the congressman. Or maybe not. Shit!" Dennis stopped walking toward the bathroom, turned and stared wide-eyed at Judy. "Hello?" Judy said. "Why are you staring at me like that?"

"I don't know how I could have missed it. Nearly everyone knows what happened to Arnold but me and the OIG. The agency knows but doesn't want it to leak out; MI5 and MI6 know about it and told the agency, but they are confused about why the agency persists in looking for him; and my pal Representative Barkley knows what happened to Arnold, but he can't do anything about it except prod me into uncovering it officially."

"You Yanks are so bloody strange."

✦

"I'm sure glad you're driving," Dennis said. "I just can't get this left side thing down. Why is it that you folks have to drive on the left?"

"It's a legacy of the Poms," Judy said. "Every country that they stole or conquered, they now drive on the left. India, South Africa, Australia. Just not Canada, which is part French anyway. About one-third of the world drives on the left. So get used to it. You Yanks can't have everything your way."

"We can't?"

"No, sir." She laughed. "Though I know you try."

They drove north on the M1 from London. It was a sunny but blustery cold day, the wind sometimes shunting the small rental car a little sideways.

"Did we have to leave our phones back at the hotel? I feel naked without my mobile phone."

"I know naked, and you're not naked," Dennis said.

"But really, no phones?"

"I told you I have a burner. We have a phone."

"I won't ask you again, but do you really think you can bluff your way into Menwith Hill?"

"Well, one of the charming weaknesses of the US intelligence business is that there are so many of these services and contractors running around the globe that no one can keep track of them. Chandler told me I couldn't see the video of Arnold's last visit, but he only has a copy given to him by the NSA. And the NSA doesn't talk to the London Station at this level. They have a shared mutual distrust of each other. So my guess is that Chandler hasn't told Sorenstam at Menwith Hill that they cut me off."

"Have you told Louise what you're up to?"

Dennis grimaced. "Why would I tell her anything?"

"Isn't she your boss?"

"Yes, of course she is. But that doesn't mean she needs to know every single thing I do. All she wants is results. And a promotion."

"You really don't like her much, do you?"

He sighed and watched the gray Midlands countryside slide by. "That's not entirely true. She's more complex than I thought. I can't tell if I trust her."

"Why don't you trust her?"

"Well, she came from operations. We don't have folks transfer in to OIG from operations. I know that doesn't sound like much, but it's odd. And there's just something about her I don't get. It's either that or a tumor I have that's undiagnosed."

"Oh, stop it. Those complaints of her seem kind of flimsy to me. And I'm biased, since she saved my life."

He smiled. "Yes, of course. Don't pay attention to me."

✦

"You're not on the list," the RAF guard said.

Dennis looked up at the machine gun slung around the man's shoulder.

"I'm not responsible for your lists. That's your job. I'm here to see Nathan Sorenstam. Call him."

The front gate at Menwith Hill sported a one-story brick building to the left of two large metal gates. In the middle of the gates sat a small brick-and-glass gatehouse.

The soldier looked down at him and scanned the interior of the car but said nothing.

"Hello," Dennis said. "Anyone home? Do the robots here speak, or do they just stare?"

The soldier turned around and spoke to a man inside the gatehouse. He could not hear what they said, but the man turned and pointed to an area outside the fence line.

"Park over there."

"For how long?"

"Park."

Dennis backed up and pulled into a parking space. He shut off the engine.

Judy waited for Dennis to return at a pub they'd found in the nearby town of Darley Head. He had given Judy the burner in case she needed to reach anyone, and especially if he didn't return at all.

✦

"What are you doing here?" Sorenstam said over the phone at the front gate.

"I'm here to see the video," Dennis said. "You were supposed to be notified. It's not my fault you folks don't have your shit together."

"I can't just let you in, Cunningham. This is a secure facility, and you know that. You need to go through Fort Meade, and Chandler needs to sign off on it."

"I did both of those things, so cut the crap and let me in. Obstructing an investigation looks bad on a personnel file, Sorenstam."

Dennis could hear Sorenstam's breath skittering across the mouthpiece.

"Give the phone to the officer," Sorenstam said.

Dennis handed it to the RAF guard inside the shack.

The man listened for a few seconds and then said, "Right."

"Leave your car where it is and proceed to that building there," he said, pointing to a two-story brick building twenty yards inside the fence line. "You'll need to go through security. Then wait and someone will get you."

Dennis walked to the building and shivered a little from the cold northerly wind.

Inside the building, he went through the same security screening as before. An RAF soldier asked for identification. Dennis placed the fingers of his right hand on a small glass-covered box while it scanned his fingerprints. He was photographed and then asked to remove any metal objects and place them in a bin. He walked through a metal detector. After that he was hand-searched by a husky soldier and was finally wanded again by another soldier.

After regaining his belt, wallet, watch, coins, notepad and pen, he was directed to a small waiting area. He was given a lanyard with a plastic temporary picture pass to wear around his neck. Dennis sat for nearly twenty minutes and was about to commence some highly agitated complaining when a civilian came through a side door and asked whether he was Dennis Cunningham.

"Who else would I be?" Dennis showed him the pass.

The man wore a blue wool coat, had short brown hair and spoke with an American accent. He had no facial expression beyond mild annoyance. He held Dennis's temporary badge briefly then let it flop back onto his chest.

"Come," he said, walking back out the door he'd come through.

They drove in silence about a quarter mile back to the building he and Fred had visited earlier.

Dennis followed him into a waiting area, where his fingertips were again scanned and his badge was scanned.

"Wait," the man said, pointing to a chair.

"Are you allowed to use more than one-syllable words?" Dennis said.

"No," the man said.

"That's good," Dennis said. "Good stuff. Love it."

✦

This time Dennis waited nearly thirty minutes. He prayed that Sorenstam had not bothered to call Fort Meade or Chandler. If so, Judy would need the phone to rent a car, since Dennis would be held incommunicado and probably flown back in handcuffs.

The trip back to Menwith Hill was the kind of high-stakes gamble that Dennis loved making; he had no idea what he was looking for, but something compelled him to break all the rules to try to find out what Freddie said they missed.

Miraculously, Judy had easily agreed to the plan and even insisted on going along for the ride. He wondered idly whether she was fully recovered from her ordeal, because she would have typically tried to convince him to avoid outlandish behavior, like being arrested at a US intelligence base.

This time she agreed it was the only way to discover what Freddie thought was missing. And she liked the idea of getting out of London.

As Dennis waited, he grew increasingly sullen and worried that his bluff hadn't worked.

Poor Judy, he thought. *How in the hell is she going to get back to London? Why would I put her through this much stress? Why can't I protect this woman instead of dragging her into my stupid battles?*

"Did I ruin your morning tea break?" Dennis asked Sorenstam when he was finally shown into his office. "You made me wait long enough."

"Oh, stop your bitching, Cunningham. I can't wait to be rid of you. What do you want here?"

"To see the Arnold video. I told you that."

"But you already saw it twice. Once here and once more in London."

"So what?"

"So why do you need to see it again? And why didn't you just ask Chandler? He has a copy."

"Maybe I don't want to tip Chandler that I'm seeing it again."

Sorenstam looked up at Dennis, who was still standing in front of his desk.

"I don't like this. Something doesn't sound right."

"I wouldn't worry about it if I were you. The best thing you could do is let me watch the video one last time and send me on my way."

"You're a reckless man, Cunningham. You already got one of our men killed."

Briefly — very briefly — Dennis considered launching himself across the desk.

"Show me the goddamn video so I can get out of here. And I want to see it in the room where Arnold sat the last time he was here. Hurry up. I can feel my body getting fried with all the microwaves you're producing up here."

"You're an asshole, Cunningham."

"Tell me something I don't know."

✦

Judy read the *Guardian*, then the *Sun*, and finally found a six-month-old edition of the glossy *Tatler*. She had already eaten lunch at the pub that was attached to an inn and then found a comfortable chair in a small waiting area.

She tried to convince herself that Dennis was all right; that he was not going to get into trouble, or worse, arrested. She would never tell him, but Judy had grown to despise the intelligence services that so immersed Dennis. She knew, despite his crude protestations, that he reveled in the dark passions of the business. It kept him from being depressed; it occupied his restless mind.

She wondered whether he would truly be happy in Perth, one of the most isolated cities of its size in the world. Even if he moved there, would he be traveling all the time for work? Would she be one of those 'work widows' that have boyfriends or husbands married to work?

Judy could smell the beer from the pub as it infiltrated the inn. What she wouldn't give for a glass of wine, a bright and citrusy New Zealand sauvignon blanc, or a hearty cabernet. She glanced down at her right wrist protruding from her maroon sweater. She could still make out several small scars where the small man had damaged veins.

What could a single glass of wine do to me? she thought. *They said I might be able to drink alcohol again, but only after a long wait.*

Judy put down the *Tatler* and made her way to the pub, clutching her purse tightly like it was a life preserver.

✦

Dennis made sure he sat with his back to the camera to duplicate Arnold's position in the video. He had been given a printed set of directions for the laptop in front of him and followed the steps to sign in as a visitor and to find the online folder with the video file. He was sitting in the exact chair, looking at the same screen that Arnold had looked at. He watched the video of Arnold's back as he appeared to look at the screen.

Dennis turned and looked back at the camera near the ceiling and realized that it was not situated on the ceiling but about two feet below it on the wall. The angle of the camera made it nearly impossible to see what was on the computer screen, and he guessed that was intentional.

The video droned on as Arnold appeared inert, shoulders flat, neck bent downward, arms not moving.

Then Arnold stood up, hunched over the laptop and seemed to do something with his left hand, but that was only conjecture since his body shielded his actions. Just as quickly, Arnold sat down and remained almost motionless for two full minutes. Then he keyed something into the computer, stood and left through the door to his left.

Dennis paused the video. He studied the small black laptop in front of him, and finally lifted it off the table. There were two cords attached, a power cord and an Ethernet cable. Dennis had been told that Wi-Fi was blocked in sensitive areas at Menwith Hill, so this laptop was only connected to the network though a standard Ethernet cable. There were no USB ports on the laptop.

Dennis put the laptop down and decided to wind the video back to the part where Arnold stood up and did something with his left hand.

What the hell is he doing? Dennis wondered. *He's very quick and seems to adjust something.*

Dennis hit "pause" again. He stood up and used his left hand to imitate Arnold's motion. At the back of the laptop, near the left corner, was the power supply plug. He made sure he shielded his actions from the camera by hunching forward like Arnold did.

With his left hand, he put his fingers around the power cord and pulled it out of the computer, knowing the battery would kick in. He stared at the metal tip of the cord for a second, then reinserted it and sat back down.

He stood again and used his left arm to reach around to the right rear of the computer, where the Ethernet cable attached. It was too cumbersome to do with his left hand, and Dennis could tell that the motion required for this behavior did not match Arnold's actions in the video.

He sat down again and looked at his watch. Sorenstam had given him only twenty-five minutes to review the video, and he had ten minutes left.

Think, Cunningham! he thought. *What the hell was Arnold doing in those fifteen seconds when he stood up? He couldn't have put anything into a USB port, because there are no USB ports; he couldn't have reached around to the Ethernet cable. It's the power cord. Maybe he had lost power? No, you idiot. He didn't lose power! Think!*

Dennis stood up abruptly, reached around to the power cable and removed it again. This time he pulled the shiny metal piece up to his face. It looked like any other battery charging cable he'd seen, except that it had a half-inch long black plastic cowling where the wire entered the metal tip. Then he tilted the laptop up to see the power plug on the computer. He ran his finger over the plug outlet on the laptop. He quickly reattached the power cable and sat down.

He had less than five minutes before he'd be escorted out of the building.

He ran his fingers through his hair, scratching the back of his head absently.

Damn, damn, damn, he thought. *Maybe Freddie was wrong. I mean, he was dying, for chrissakes!*

He stood up, reached around the back of the laptop with his left hand again, pulled out the power cord, ran his fingers over the jack and then the plug. He put the metal plug up to his face quickly, shielding it from the camera with his body.

Dennis felt a charge of electricity; not the kind that came from the wall, but the kind that came from synapses. He fiddled with the cord.

"Christ," he said out loud, and then sat down.

CHAPTER 27

Dennis found the inn easily enough and painstakingly stayed to the left side and parked properly. Inside, he expected to see Judy dozing from boredom in one of the inn's armchairs, but she was not there.

Looking into the pub, almost as an afterthought, he saw Judy at the bar talking to the bartender. There was one older gentleman at the other end of the bar. It was 2:20 in the afternoon.

"Hey there," he said, sitting next to Judy, eyeing her half-full glass of white wine.

"Gidday, Yank." She smiled. "How was your mission?"

Dennis shot a glance at the white-haired, thin bartender.

"Been here long?" he asked.

"No, not long, have I, Bob?" she said to the bartender.

"Bob, is it?" Dennis said.

"Yes, that's Bob. Bob this is Dennis. He's a Yank, but he's a bit of all right."

"Nice to meet you, Dennis," Bob said. "Can I get you something to drink?"

"Um, no, but thank you. We need to get going."

"Right then," the barman said, walking toward the register.

"Can't we stay a little longer?" Judy pleaded. Her eyes were a little glassy, and she smiled an odd, distant smile.

"No. We really must get going. How many have you had?"

"How many what?"

"Glasses of wine?"

"Oh, perhaps three."

"Mmm."

"I was bored," she said. "And worried. You always worry me."

"I'm sorry, I don't mean to worry you."

"But you do."

"I'm sorry. Can we leave, please?" Dennis said.

"Can I finish my wine?"

"If you must."

"I must."

✦

Judy slept most of the ride back to London, waking now and then to reposition herself.

When they were an hour away from the city, she roused herself.

"I don't feel well," she said.

"I'm sure you'll feel better in a while."

"I think I was drunk," she said. "I used to be able to drink three glasses of wine without a problem. Now it feels like I drank three bottles."

"That's okay. Derrick said you need to be careful, remember?"

"I remember."

They drove in silence.

"Do you want me to drive?" Judy asked. "You're not going very fast."

"I'd love it if you would drive, to be honest, but not if you're not feeling well."

"Pull over when you get a chance," she said, running her fingers through her hair. "I need to do something other than feel bloody awful."

✦

"What the devil is that?" Judy said in the hotel room, standing in the bathroom doorway, drying her hair with a towel.

Dennis had bent the small table lamp down six inches off the desktop and was using a pen to gently push around a thin shaft of shiny metal with a black cap at one end.

"It's a metal tip for a laptop power cord."

"Where did you get it?"

"At Menwith Hill."

"Why did you take it?"

"It didn't seem like it belonged there. Or that's what I thought."

"Do they know you took it?"

"No. At least I don't think so."

She stopped rubbing her hair.

"Dennis, that seems a bit rash, doesn't it? Just pulling something off a computer and stealing it?"

"Well, 'stealing' is a strong word. I borrowed it. Maybe this has something to do with what Arnold was doing during his last visit there. Or maybe it's nothing. Just seemed strange to me. So I took it."

She walked over, clad in the hotel's terrycloth robe, and peered over Dennis's shoulder.

"How are you feeling?" he asked, looking up at her.

"A little embarrassed, perhaps, but fine otherwise."

"Headache?"

"Mostly gone. Shame, on the other hand, lasts longer."

"I wouldn't worry about it, Judy. You're a strong woman."

"Everyone says that."

"Everyone's right."

They were silent for a moment.

"What is it again?" Judy asked. "That tiny thing."

"The end of a power cord, the piece that connects it to the back of a computer. Only it's a duplicate. I don't know whether Arnold added this on purpose or whether the NSA puts these things on themselves for some cyber-security purpose."

"I'm lost. What are you talking about?"

Dennis reached over to his laptop and pulled the power cord out of the back. He held it under the table lamp.

"See that plug right there?"

"Yes."

"Well, these are pretty much universal for laptops. And the Menwith Hill computer had the same setup. But when I pulled the power cord out of the computer, I noticed that the plug on the end of the power cord had a black plastic collar, which I've never seen before. Right before my time was up there, out of desperation, I just started to fiddle with the plug, and it slid off the end of the cord, showing another plug. Look. I'll show you."

Dennis picked up the piece from Menwith Hill, and using his laptop's power cable, showed how his power cable could be inserted into the back of it.

"I think it's an extension of some sort. I'm not going to plug my cord into it, but I'm thinking that this piece from Menwith Hill was slipped onto the real power cord by Arnold and quickly reinserted into the laptop. I mean, you can hardly tell it's there."

"Are you sure this isn't some kind of filter thing the NSA put on?"

"No, I'm not sure. I just need to have someone look at this and tell me."

"Who do you know?"

✦

Dennis sat in the bar and waited, taking the opportunity to sip a single malt without having it on his breath around Judy. While he wasn't worried about her brief relapse into drinking, he didn't want to make it harder for her.

After forty minutes he grew restless. He was sipping this third Scotch when the tall man sat down next to him. He asked the bartender for a menu and looked it over.

"What do you want?" the man said, speaking into the menu.

"Advice."

"Are you clean?"

"Of devices? Or just clean of thought?"

"Devices."

"Yes."

"I can't help you any more. Stop contacting me." He put down the menu and stood up.

"What's this?" Dennis said, pushing over a bar napkin with the miniature power plug from Menwith Hill resting on top.

The tall man leaned over and looked at the power plug for nearly thirty seconds, then sat down.

"Where did you get this?"

"Would be better if I didn't tell you."

"Try again."

"Menwith Hill. Stuck on the end of a laptop power cord. You ever see anything like this before?"

The man stared at it in silence for at least a minute; the raucous sounds of the pub offered a strange counterpoint to his rapt concentration.

"No," he finally answered.

"Do you think it's a filter put on by you folks?"

"Maybe. I'm not a hardware guy."

"I think our missing agency employee slipped this onto a laptop at Menwith Hill right before he disappeared."

The man could not take his eyes off the small plug.

"Would you mind taking it and telling me what it is? Maybe you could do some analysis."

"No," he said, pushing the napkin back to Dennis. "Stay away from me."

"Fred said you could help me."

"Fred's dead."

"Thanks a lot," Dennis said.

The man stood up just as the bartender asked if he wanted a drink. Dennis grabbed the plug off the napkin and stood up next to the man. With his left hand he grabbed the man's coat lapel, and with his right he dropped the plug into the man's coat pocket.

"You've got to help me," he said.

"Go away, you idiot," the man said, yanking Dennis's hand from his lapel.

✦

"Did you really put it in his coat?"

"Yes, I did."

"But it's so small, he'll never know it's there. What the point of that?"

"Well, when he gets this postcard he'll know it's in his coat. I'm betting that his curiosity will drive him nuts. If not, well, not much more I can do with that damn thing."

Dennis finished the postcard, put a stamp on it and said, "Let's take a walk through this cold town."

"Can we take our mobile phones out of the fridge? I'd like to call Trevor."

"Sure."

They walked two blocks, where he put the postcard into a Royal Mail slot.

The weather was unusually nice for January, and they walked for at least a mile before Dennis's phone rang.

"Ugh. It's Louise," he said to Judy, grimacing.

"Stop being so negative about her," Judy said.

"Well then, you talk to her."

Dennis put the phone to his ear.

"Hey, Louise."

"What's going on over there?"

"I'm working on the case. I have two days left. Making some progress."

"Were you going to fill me in on the progress?" she asked.

"Yeah, but it's a long shot, and I don't want to raise expectations."

"How could you possibly raise expectations on this investigation?"

"You have a point, Louise. I think I'll be able to give you something tomorrow."

"You bullshitting me like you normally do?"

"Nope," he said.

"How is Judy doing?"

"Nice of you to ask. She's doing well."

"So nothing else is going on?"

"What are you driving at, Louise?"

"Something unusual happened today."

"Okay, I'm waiting."

"Got a call from the IG," she said.

"Okay, good for you."

"No, not good. I never get a call directly from the IG. I get a call from Sandy, the IG's executive deputy, but never from the IG."

"So maybe Sandy was on vacation."

"Let me finish, Dennis. So the IG asked what was going on with the investigation. He said he'd just got a call from the director asking about a status update."

"The director of the CIA wanted a status update?" Dennis said, looking sideways at Judy, who was stamping her feet in the cold. "Since when does he give a shit about this thing? I thought he wanted it shut down?"

"Uh-huh," Louise said. "Which gets me back to you. Did anything happen there? My guess was it was you, but maybe not."

"I can't talk like this, Louise. I don't trust these phones."

"I'm flying out tomorrow. Same hotel room?"

"Yes. Is that really necessary?"

"I'll text when I land."

"Okay."

"What was that about?" Judy said, pulling Dennis along the street. "I'm freezing."

Dennis told Judy about the impending visit.

"Wait," Judy said, stopping Dennis. "That plug thing you took. Did that have anything to do with the sudden interest by the director?"

Dennis did not answer but kept looking over Judy's shoulder into the distance, trying to put the pieces together.

"I don't know," he said. "Now I'm cold. Let's get going."

They walked briskly back to the hotel, heads bent forward into the slight breeze.

✦

"Ha!" Judy said. "He had an ICD."

Dennis was sitting on the bed, his back against the headboard, reading his notes. Judy sat at the desk, perusing Dennis's computer.

"What?"

"His medical files show Arnold had an ICD. Did you and Freddie know that?"

Dennis tilted his head down and looked over his reading glasses.

"What?"

"I said, did you know Arnold had an implantable cardioverter defibrillator?"

"No, what are you talking about?"

"Didn't you read Arnold's medical files? I'll bet Freddie read them. Did he say anything about this?"

"No, he didn't, or at least I don't remember. But I don't even know what that thing is you're talking about. Something to do with the heart?"

"The only reason I know about it is that my dad might have needed one, but they put in a pacemaker instead."

"Did Arnold have a bad heart?"

"Says here that he was diagnosed with something called hypertrophic cardiomyopathy when he was forty-nine years old. And they put in an ICD then. He's had it for a few years."

"Is that why he didn't go through the metal detector?"

"Has to be. I'm looking it up now on the web, and you are not supposed to go through metal detectors. So yes, that's why he avoided them at Menwith Hill."

Dennis slid off the bed, walked over and sat down next to Judy.

"So what do these ICD things look like? Are they big or small?"

Judy looked back at the computer and started searching the web. After twenty minutes they stopped.

"So these things are maybe seventy-five millimeters tall, forty millimeters wide and fourteen or so deep. They have circuitry inside and wire leads going to the heart," Dennis said. "That's pretty big."

"Do you think he might have hidden that plug you found next to his ICD so that he could get it through security?" Judy said.

"But how would he do that?"

"Well, you were there several times. If Arnold did not go through the metal detector, but only got wanded, then the wand would have picked up the ICD in his chest, no?"

"I think so."

"And we saw how small that plug was. What if he simply taped it to his chest over the ICD, and it was masked by all the electronics in the device? Or maybe he had it inserted under his skin, and that's what he was doing in the bathroom stall."

"Mmm, I don't see why not. But we don't even know if that stupid thing is anything important."

"When did you say the postcard will get to your mystery man?"

"Tomorrow. Then either he gets curious or he doesn't."

"And your time is up on this case the day after tomorrow?"

"Officially, yes."

"What are you going to tell Louise when she gets here tomorrow?"

"Guess I'll tell her everything."

"Even what Ian said about Arnold being picked up on phone traffic in Moscow?"

"Not that. I'm going to hold that one. I'm having a hard time trusting her for some reason."

"What is it with you and that woman? Did she do something to you?"

"Judy, I'm just saying that people's motives in this business are not so linear. I know that's hard to understand, but it's the truth. Louise is from an operations background. But those people are trained liars."

"God, what a business you're in."

✦

"You just took it?" Louise said, leaning forward across the small coffee table.

"Yes, just like I said. Pulled it off the power cord, saw that it was some kind of extension and brought it back."

"And you gave it to this NSA employee that Kaczka turned you on to?"

"Yes."

"But this guy doesn't even know you gave it to him?"

"Well, like I said, I think he knows now. Hopefully he'll try to figure out what it is."

"Let's just say he does figure out what it is, and he wants to tell you. How will he tell you if you don't know who he is?"

"He contacts me."

"How does he do that? And what is the address you send the postcard to?"

"I'm not going to tell you."

Louise closed her eyes in what Dennis took to be an attempt to control her fury and leaned back in her chair. Her bright white-blond hair swung against the top of her fashionable navy pea coat.

She opened her eyes and focused her gaze above his head, biting the inside of her bottom lip.

"I have no idea how you have held this job for so long," she said. "You're insolent, disobedient and a royal pain in the ass. These aren't qualities highly prized by OIG."

"No, they're more highly prized by folks in operations," Dennis said.

"I'm not in operations any longer, and you know that. Jesus, Cunningham, you are a piece of work. So we have one more day on this case, then it's shut down. And I say we because I'm on this case too, in case you forgot. I'm your boss, remember?"

"You asked me to come back and solve the case. I'm doing that. Let me do my work. You'll have everything when the time is up."

"You won't come clean with what you have, and somewhere back at Langley warning bells are going off about this case. I'm not the brightest bulb, but you may need more friends than you know."

"Mmm."

She got up and walked out of the shop.

Dennis stared at his coffee cup, turning it in small motions, as if it was the dial of a radio.

✦

It was after 1:00 p.m. when Dennis got out of the elevator and walked toward his room. On the floor in front of his room was a glossy multi-colored brochure for an Indian restaurant. But it was the white sticky note on the front that caught his attention.

He picked it up, used his key swipe and entered the room. Judy was on the bed reading a book.

"Did you hear anyone at the front door?" Dennis asked.

"No, why?"

"I found this." He waved the brochure.

"Is that from your mystery man?"

"Maybe. But it's blank. And the paper color is different."

Judy got off the bed, and Dennis put it on the desk. They stared at it silently.

"I think it's from him," he said. "I just don't know what it means."

"Why didn't he just do what he normally does with these notes?" she said.

"Don't know. Maybe he's scared. Or maybe it's not him after all. Maybe it's just Louise screwing with me."

"She'd do that?"

"Everything is on the table right now."

They continued to stare.

Dennis slowly peeled the note off the brochure and held it up to the light, looking for writing.

"There's nothing here. I'm not sure it's him. Could be someone else who's trying to trick me. But what's the trick?"

"Don't ask me why," Judy said, sitting down. "I think this is him. He's trying to tell you something. You've said before that he's very cautious about electronic surveillance. That he doesn't trust technology, that he says old-school street craft is all that works nowadays, correct?"

"Yes, that's true."

"So, think old-school. What could this blank sticky mean?"

Dennis pulled at his earlobe and frowned, sitting down in the other chair.

"Jeez, I can't think. What does white mean? I surrender?"

"No. Why go through all the trouble to have some kid or bellman deliver this to your door just to say that?" she said. "Think harder."

"It's a restaurant brochure. An Indian restaurant. I don't like Indian food."

"That's not it," she said. "When he first sent the brochure from St. Paul's, what did he do?"

"Well, he highlighted letters, or words, or symbols to get his message across. And we pretty much put it together. It was sort of simple, really. Kind of Boy Scouty, if you get where I'm going. It was the complete opposite of what you'd expect from a modern cryptographer."

They stared at the brochure for a long time.

Dennis cocked his head slightly.

"Where was this sticky note when I pulled it off the brochure? I mean exactly where? I can't remember."

"I think it was right there." She pointed to a spot under a picture of a dish of chicken.

"No, I thought it was there," Dennis said pointing to a spot an inch away.

He picked up the brochure and held it an angle under the lamp so that he could look closely at the glossy coating for evidence of an adhesive.

"Right there," he said. "You were right. Let's put it back."

He slowly put the sticky back, and again they stared at it.

Above the sticky was a picture of a yellow bowl of rice with vegetables.

"It's a lemon rice dish," Judy said. "Says so here."

Dennis leaned back in his chair, again pulling on his earlobe.

"Something is resonating…"

"Rice?" Judy asked.

"No. Lemon."

Silence.

"Lemon. Huh."

Dennis twisted his head and looked at Judy.

He picked up a pen and put two lines on the brochure to mark the position of the sticky and then peeled it off.

"Come on," he said, walking to the bathroom.

He spread a white hand towel on the sink counter then put the sticky note down.

"Use this pen on the corner of the paper to hold it down. I'm going to use your hair blower on it, and I don't want it to blow away."

"I don't get it," she said.

"Neither do I. But it's worth a try."

Dennis picked up the hair dryer, looked around at the controls and turned it to medium, then cranked it up. The sound of the blower filled the room.

"Ready?" he yelled.

She nodded.

He lowered the nozzle until it was eight inches from the fluttering paper. Judy was forced to stab the corner to stop it flying away. After twenty seconds he turned it off and put his face next to the paper.

"It's hot in here," Judy said.

He smiled. "Think we got it."

He turned the blower on again and trained it on the paper.

Judy bent over and began to make out some numbers emerging.

✦

The bar smelled of stale beer, perfume and fried food. Dennis sat as near as he could to the stool he typically sat in. He ordered a single malt and toyed with it while waiting for his visitor.

The sticky note had had a set of numbers on it, written in lemon juice. It was a very old method of using invisible ink that had been popular for children in the early 1960s playing make-believe secret agent. It was dumb but painfully simple. The acid in the juice turned brown when it was heated gently, so writing could be seen on white paper.

The number sequence on the paper suggested a date and time, which happened to be that night. Dennis expected to meet his mystery man at the bar at the appointed time. Either that or Louise would be there. Or his friend from the Ukraine.

After thirty-five minutes of Dennis being jostled by the dense, after-work crowd of revelers, the bartender leaned forward and smiled.

"You Dennis?"

"Yes, why?"

"Here you go, mate." He handed Dennis a ticket.

Dennis looked at it. "What is Ministry of Sound?" he asked the grinning bartender.

"Dance club. Doesn't get going until later tonight. You must have an admirer."

"Who gave this to you?"

"Cabbie. Had clear directions he repeated about ten bloody times. Man of your description will sit near one of these stools at such and such time. He's a Yank named Dennis. Give him the bloody ticket. And here's ten quid for your work."

"How far away is the club from here?" Dennis asked.

"A ways; just tell the cabbie where you're going. No worries."

Dennis thanked him and looked at the ticket.

A dance club? Really? I'm getting a little pissed off at this guy, Dennis fumed. He looked at his watch; the ticket stated the club opened at 10:30 p.m. What the hell was he going to do until then? He called Judy using one of the two new burners he had purchased; he did not trust Louise's burner any longer.

"Perhaps he just wants to make sure you're not being followed?" she said. "And a dance club will be loud and distracting, with lights and music. Good cover, I suppose."

"I think it's stupid," Dennis said.

"What if it's not him?" she said. "You've got me feeling paranoid now. What if it's that Ukrainian bloke? You need to be careful, Dennis. The more I think about it, the less I like this meeting."

"I think it's our mystery man; it's something a nerd would think up. Hell, I don't know. I'll just go and hope for the best."

"Please be careful, Dennis."

"I don't dance."

"Not what I mean, and you know it."

"Maybe Louise is dying to dance with me."

"Stop it."

"I'll call you afterward, though it may be late."

"I'll be up."

✦

The line to get into Ministry of Sound was easily a block and half long at 10:00 p.m., and Dennis felt completely out of his element. The average age of the people in line was about twenty-five, and they were decked out in flashy clothing. Hulking bouncers monitored the door, and as they finally started letting people in, Dennis panicked. Maybe going in was a bad idea.

As an older single male, he stood out like a palm tree on the Arctic tundra. He could already hear the thumping music vibrating through his clothes from outside and wondered if the noise might disguise foul play directed against him. More importantly, he studied the front of the long line for evidence of his mystery man but could see nothing as he inched forward.

"ID, granddad?" the bouncer asked. Dennis dug out his wallet, and the bouncer looked at it with a flashlight. "Tourist, eh?"

"Yes, I guess."

"Put your wallet and phone in your front pockets, otherwise you'll have them taken."

"Thanks for the tip."

The club was enormous, with a long bar on one side facing a dance floor. No one was dancing now, because the show hadn't started, but the music was so loud that Dennis cringed. He made his way to the bar and shouted out that he wanted a beer.

Leaning against the bar, he waited.

And waited. The show started at 11:00 p.m., with a DJ on the stage, a video screen behind him and hundreds of colored laser light variations shooting above and around the crowd of dancers.

At eleven thirty Dennis began to feel not only stupid but tired. The music was so loud that his head ached. The bass notes from the huge speakers made his shirt flutter. There appeared to be more women than men in the club, and many looked like models, with short skirts and long torsos.

Finally, at 11:45, he guessed he had been made to look like a fool and wondered vaguely whether he had been purposely lured away from Judy.

He found a far corner of the dance hall and called her.

"Are you all right?" he asked. "Is everything all right?"

"Yes, of course it is. Why? And I can barely hear you."

"Don't answer the door if anyone knocks."

"No one is going to knock, Dennis."

"Just promise me that."

"I promise. What's going on there?"

"Nothing. Absolutely nothing. I'm coming back now."

"That's disappointing."

"What did you say?"

"I said, IT'S DISAPPOINTING."

"Yes, very. Home soon. Bye."

Dennis made his way past the flashing lasers, drunks, Ecstasy-fueled dancers and wandering bouncers to the front door. The winter air felt nice for once, and he made his way to a stand of taxis. The first one in line started his car as Dennis got near. As he reached for the door he felt a man brush past him.

"Come!" the man said. It was the mystery man in a long, herringbone wool coat.

Dennis followed as the man walked quickly down Southwark Bridge Road. Few people were on the street, and his natural caution had him glancing left and right and occasionally even behind him. Soon the mystery man was twenty yards ahead of Dennis, though he never looked back.

And suddenly he was gone.

Dennis stopped. A car went by. A young couple walked toward him. He strained to see ahead, but the man had simply vanished. He decided to advance slowly past dark storefronts and morose, lonely street lamps. Nothing. The man had vanished.

"Hssst."

Dennis looked into an alley to his right. The mystery man's face shone briefly in the glare of a street lamp then disappeared again into the dark alley.

Dennis walked closer but stopped.

"I'm not going in there. Come out and let's talk."

Nothing.

"Did you hear me?" he said. "I'm not going in there. You come out."

Nothing.

Dennis felt a cold river of fear run up his spine, and he quickly scanned the street around him. He backed away from the alley entrance.

"Get in here or I'll fucking shoot you right there," the man hissed from the alley.

Dennis stood his ground. Was the mystery man alone? He was a software engineer, not an assassin, for chrissakes. Or was he?

Shit, Dennis thought. *What's your guess, Cunningham? Is this guy a problem or is he just scared shitless?*

Dennis stepped into the alley and was instantly grabbed by the neck and slammed up against the brick wall. A cold pistol barrel was pressed against his forehead.

"You fucker. You set me up."

"Calm down," Dennis said. "And get that gun out of my face. I don't think you know how to use it."

"I ought to just kill you after what you did."

"Did what?"

"Put that device in my pocket, you stupid shit. Could get me sent to prison for fifty years."

"Hey, would you just calm down a bit," Dennis said. "Let's talk like adults."

The man suddenly shot a glance to his left at the sidewalk and dropped the pistol to his side as three young men walked by. They saw Dennis and the mystery man in the shadows and chuckled as they passed by.

"Poofters," Dennis heard one of the men say.

And just as quickly the barrel was back onto Dennis's forehead.

"Jeez," Dennis said. "Would you please put that friggin' thing down? You're pretty high-strung right now, and I'd hate to lose the top of my head because an alley cat rubbed against your leg."

"Asshole," the man said, putting the pistol in his coat pocket. "It's still pointed at you."

"Fine. So you have a gun on me. I got it. I'm scared. But why are you so scared?"

"I'm not scared."

"Well, it's a damn good imitation."

"Fuck you."

"Yeah, well, can we get past the salutations and talk about something more useful? Like the device. What is it?" Dennis asked.

"You know exactly what it is."

"Hello? Mr. NSA cryptographic wizard. Anyone home? I have no fucking idea what that stupid thing is. I put it in your pocket because I thought you could tell me. I think it has something to do with Freddie's death, but I don't know. Thought you'd help me figure it out. Instead you're freaking out and sticking a gun to my head. Not sure Freddie would be sanctioning this approach."

The man, who was easily a foot taller than Dennis, stood back a few feet and peered down at Dennis.

"Where did you get it?"

"The plug?"

"Yes."

"I told you. Menwith Hill."

"Fuck!"

Silence. A cab drove down the street, and Dennis could see the strain in the man's face as the light from the street lamp splashed his face again.

"Well, what is it?" Dennis said.

"It's a node in a PLC network."

"Umm, I have no idea what you're talking about. Can you just humor me a bit?"

"It's a surveillance device. Part of a network. It's not the whole network. Just a node."

"Well, was it there on purpose? Is it ours?"

"No, it's not fucking ours." The man gave a short and vicious snort of derision.

"I'm getting confused," Dennis said. "What is it exactly?"

"It's a PLC node, and its only job is to eavesdrop."

"What's a PLC?"

"Power Line Communications."

"I have no idea what you're talking about."

"PLCs use the powerlines in a house or building to move data around. They're like normal data networks, only they don't use Ethernet cables or Wi-Fi. They use the copper wires and power outlets to do the same thing."

"They can do that?"

"Of course they can fucking do that."

"Okay, so this is going to sound stupid, but stick with me. I pulled this thing off a laptop power supply cable at Menwith Hill. Make sense?"

"Yes. It was put there to mask the device. Unless you look closely, you can't tell it was added on."

"How can something this small be so important?"

"I said it was a node, not the entire system. The hub and repeaters are elsewhere on the electrical system. Do you have access to the repeater?"

"No. I wouldn't know a repeater if it hit me in the face. What makes you so worried about this device?"

"First, it looks like Russian hardware. Second, it's been tampered with."

Dennis sighed and rubbed his forehead where the barrel of the man's gun had created a neat, small, depressed circle.

"Okay. This device was used to eavesdrop on a computer or computer network. But it wasn't attached to the Ethernet cable on the computer. Instead it was attached to the power cord. That right?"

"Yes."

"And you're saying that the power line can be used to do the same thing as an Ethernet network or Wi-Fi system, only it uses standard power lines?"

"Yes. It's new and experimental. Never seen anything like this, but the device was using the power lines to push data."

"What kind of data?"

"Whatever was going on with that computer."

"That's hard to believe," Dennis said.

"Don't believe it then."

"Okay, fine. So this device was just a node, right?"

"I told you that already."

"You mentioned a repeater. Would the repeater collect this data and pass it along?"

"Yes."

"What would a repeater look like?" Dennis asked.

"My guess is you wouldn't be able to see it. It was probably slipped behind the power outlet. Maybe a network of repeaters."

"So this network of nodes and repeaters would capture data, then what?"

"Then send it somewhere for capture."

A large group of young people could be heard laughing hysterically nearby, and Dennis and the man stood farther back in the alley until the group passed.

"This PLC network — whatever the hell it's called — would be a secret surveillance system? Is that what you're saying?" Dennis asked.

"Could be."

"Is it possible that Menwith Hill didn't know this PLC system was listening in?"

"Not just possible, it's likely," the man said.

"Can you tell who might be listening in, you know, from the device I gave you?"

"Something's wrong with the node you gave me."

"What do you mean?"

"It's been tampered with. I told you already."

"Yes, you did. But I didn't understand what you meant."

"This is the last time I'm going to respond to one of your postcards. This is much more serious than you know. This meeting tonight was for Fred. But no more."

"Hey," Dennis said, grabbing the man's arm as he tried to walk away. "Come on. What do you mean tampered with?"

"Jesus, do your ears work at all, you old fart? I told you: the hardware looks Russian, but it was tampered with and an additional chip was added."

"Why would someone do that?"

"You figure it out. Now get your fucking hands off me."

✦

Judy sat on the bed in her flannel pajamas and yawned.

"Perhaps it's the late hour, or my befuddled brain, but I'm a tad lost in all this."

"He said that little device had been tampered with. He pulled it apart under a microscope and toyed with the chip inside. Said the original chip was connected to another chip that seemed to have been added later."

"Devil's advocate here: so what? What does any of this mean? Who tampered with what and why?"

"He didn't know, and I don't think he wanted to know. He said it was one of the strangest things he'd ever seen and thought I was being naïve in pursuing this."

"What did he do with the little plug you gave him?"

"Said he crushed it with a hammer then flushed it down the toilet."

"Think he actually did that?"

"Yeah. He was scared shitless."

"I'm going to bed," Judy said. "Look, it's 1:12 a.m. Come on."

"I have a headache," Dennis said, rubbing his temples.

"You've been knocked around a bit, poor fellow," she said. "Come to bed."

"I don't know if it was the music, or the gun, but my head's throbbing."

CHAPTER 28

The phone rang incessantly until Dennis heard it go to voicemail. Then the burner Louise had given him started up again.

"Christ," he said, stumbling out of bed. "Hello?"

"This is day zero," Louise said. "We're out of time. The investigation officially ends tonight at midnight Eastern time. You were holding back yesterday until the project was closed. So the project is nearly closed, and we need to meet for a debrief."

Dennis could hear Judy pull the pillow over her head to deaden the sound.

"How about tonight? Let's have dinner."

"Sounds cozy. And a dumb delaying tactic. How about now? I got another call from the IG."

"You're kidding?"

"Nope. 'What's going on with the Arnold thing?' he asked."

"Dinner. Please, Louise. We'll clear the air then. Promise."

She didn't say goodbye but just hung up.

"God, what a pain in the ass she is."

✦

After breakfast they decided to take a long walk, but not before Dennis put nearly all the mobile phones he had into the hotel safe.

Bundled up, they walked out of the hotel onto the crowded sidewalk, dodging the rush-hour pedestrians. Dennis walked no more than twenty steps with Judy when a well-dressed man coming toward him on the right suddenly stumbled and veered into his path.

The man wore a pinched cap and held a traditional hard, black brief-case in his right hand. As the man stumbled, he flung out the arm holding the briefcase wildly to get his balance, and Dennis felt the corner of it slap against his rib cage.

The man gathered himself and muttered, "My word, man. I'm so sorry. Are you all right?"

"Yes, yes," Dennis said, grimacing. As they walked on Judy asked if he was okay.

"I'm fine, I just can't wait to get out of this city."

They walked for thirty minutes until they arrived at a small park.

"Son of a bitch," Dennis said, rubbing his lower chest. "That bastard caught me good. Probably cracked a couple of ribs."

"You poor fellow, you can't catch a break," Judy said, rubbing his gloved hand. "I'm so glad your assignment is over." She was afraid to ask about his plans to move to Australia. *Why press him now? He wouldn't back out now, would he?* she thought.

Back at the hotel Dennis kept complaining about his ribs. Judy thought he was really complaining about meeting with Louise that evening. She knew he was paranoid about Louise's true motives, which further complicated his decision to turn over what he knew about Arnold in Moscow, and the purloined eavesdropping device from Menwith Hill.

"For heaven's sake, Dennis, show me your ribs."

Dennis took off his sweater vest, then his shirt.

"Right here, can you see anything? A bruise?"

Judy put her face six inches from his rib cage.

"I can make out a small bruise, or at least I think so. Oh, what's this? There's a tiny bit of blood."

She rubbed her hand over the tiny spec. "Does that hurt?"

"Sort of. Of all the damn things to happen, this idiot trips and falls into me, breaking a bunch of ribs."

"Now Dennis, you don't know if you have broken ribs. You'd have trouble breathing. It's just a bruise."

✦

During lunch Dennis barely ate his food and Judy worried about his meeting with Louise. He was clearly distracted and agitated.

At 2:35 p.m., Dennis complained to Judy that he didn't feel well. She checked his forehead and said he felt warm.

"I'll go purchase a thermometer," she said.

"No, forget it. I'm fine.'

At 4:20 he threw up for the first time. Judy did her best to comfort him, but he seemed very warm, especially around his ribs.

At 5:00 p.m. he threw up until there was nothing left in his stomach. She went out and purchased a thermometer, aspirin and athletic drinks with electrolytes.

His temperature hit 103 degrees at 5:45 p.m. and Judy began to walk around the room, wondering what to do. She knew he was supposed to meet Louise in several hours, but he could not make that appointment.

She tried to coax Dennis into explaining how to get in touch with Louise, but Dennis became increasingly sullen and sleepy. His breathing was labored.

At six thirty he was dry-heaving in his bed, and his temperature had spiked to 104 degrees.

She called the front desk and asked for an ambulance.

✦

The small waiting room was empty except for Judy, who sat with a worn magazine on her lap, trying to focus on the captions underneath pictures of celebrities.

She had been at the hospital for over two hours, after Dennis was admitted to an isolation ward. They diagnosed him with something called methicillin-resistant staphylococcus aureus, or MRSA. She had never heard of it before, but the emergency room staff was extremely nervous and rushed Dennis to a special section away from patients and most staff.

A door swung open, and Judy saw a very young man in a lab coat walk over to her. He introduced himself as Dr. Ravishana.

"I'm afraid this is a very serious illness, and it is also contagious, so Mr. Cunningham must be isolated. He is being treated with very powerful antibiotics intravenously, and we hope to stop the infection from spreading."

"Can I see him?"

"That is not advisable right now. He is sleeping. We have his fever under control. Please remember that this is a serious bacterial infection that is resistant to most of our drugs. You should make sure that you take a very hot shower this evening and wash yourself with a disinfectant soap. I'm sorry to be so rigid, but it is contagious. Please let us know immediately if you start feeling sick and develop a fever."

"I assume you have new antibiotics that can target this infection," she said.

"Presumably, yes. But there is some confusion about the exact type of bacteria he is infected with."

"What confusion?"

"Well, the swab sample we examined in our lab is a little different than what we've seen before."

Judy noticed the physician was exceedingly polite but had no facial affect, neither a wan smile nor a knowing frown of sympathy or concern. The blank expression worried her.

"Do you think he's going to be all right?"

"We certainly hope so, but until we find the correct antibiotics, the bacteria will continue to affect him."

"Affect him how?"

"It is attacking his liver and kidneys."

"Well, stop it then! You must be able to do something! This is a modern hospital, isn't it? We're in London, for god's sake!"

"I assure you we're doing everything possible to help Mr. Cunningham. Please understand that."

"I want to see him right now. I demand to see him." Judy could feel the rush of helplessness and fear wash over her, and it reminded her vaguely of the dark time in the cement basement room.

The physician sighed and said, "All right, but only for a brief period. You must wear protective clothing and are not allowed to touch him. Do you understand that?"

"Yes."

"And please do not reach any false conclusions about his health simply by looking at him. He is being well cared for and is being given intravenous antibiotics and other drugs."

✦

Judy wore a gown, gloves and a paper breathing mask, but none of it helped when she caught a glance of Dennis.

She gulped. Dennis lay in a bed enveloped in wires and tubes. He wore a clear plastic breathing mask. Several machines beeped in the background as his heartbeat and respiration were monitored on small video screens.

His eyes were closed, and he seemed not to breathe.

"Is he alive?" she yelled through her mask to the physician.

"Yes, of course he is. Please, don't be alarmed. He is breathing and fighting this infection as well as can be expected."

"He looks frail."

"He's very sick."

Her eyes welled up so fast that she did not have time to fight the sob.

The doctor quickly led Judy out of the room then had a nurse help her remove the protective clothing and studiously monitor her hand-washing.

Judy was led back to the waiting room, exhausted, sad and angry. Though she had never met the other person in the waiting room, she knew who it was.

Louise walked over and sat next to Judy.

"How is he?" Louise asked.

"Not well." Judy was angry at Louise for no other reason than that this small blond woman with ice-blue eyes was the embodiment of everything she hated about Dennis's employer.

"Can you tell me what happened to him?"

"How did you know he was here?" Judy asked.

"The hotel told me."

"I thought your surveillance teams or phone tracking satellites would have picked up his whereabouts."

Louise sighed. "I'm sorry, Judy. But I have to ask you what happened to him. It might be nothing or it might be important. Please help me."

"He doesn't trust you," she said, staring across the room. "And that means I don't trust you."

"Let's say he doesn't trust me, and you don't trust me. I still might be able to help. I've requested an agency physician who is on call 24/7 here in London to review the case as well, and he's on his way over now."

"Don't you dare let that doctor touch Dennis," Judy hissed, staring directly into Louise's face. "You can't wait to get him out of the way. You're all senseless killers. All of you."

Judy felt a huge tear roll down her right cheek, and she struck at it fiercely with the back of her right wrist.

Louise stood and walked several steps away, then returned and stood over Judy.

"You don't have to trust me, or like me, or do anything except tolerate me. But you need to do it for Dennis's sake. They won't answer any of my questions here because I don't have status as a family member, and he's too sick to be moved to a US facility. I need your help. Jesus, Judy, Dennis needs your help. Please look at me. Just answer a few questions. Please."

Judy glanced up and locked eyes with Louise. She hated her right now and had the desire to punch Louise in the throat then stomp her face when she went down.

"Control yourself," Louise said. "Dennis needs you to be strong."

Judy looked away across the room, as if she was standing on a hill looking down at a shadowed valley.

"When did Dennis show signs of being sick?" Louise asked.

Judy answered her questions in a monotone. She was a hostile witness and did nothing to hide her contempt.

After many questions, Louise suddenly sat down next to Judy.

"The man that stumbled into Dennis, had you seen him before?"

"No."

"Did the man stop to apologize or check on Dennis?"

"I already told you twice: the man said something like 'sorry, old man,' and kept walking."

"Was there anything on his ribcage when you looked at it back at the hotel?"

"I told you: there was a bruise near the bottom rib."

"And nothing else? No blood?"

"No blood. Well, there was a tiny fleck of blood. Probably from the corner of the briefcase. Or maybe Dennis was scratching it. It was tiny."

Louise stood up and left without speaking. After several minutes Judy turned and saw Louise talking to Dr. Ravishana outside the waiting room. Louise seemed to be grilling the doctor, who bent away at the waist from the small woman. Then the two of them disappeared, and Judy jumped up and followed them.

She caught up outside Dennis's isolation room.

"What are you doing?" Judy asked the doctor.

"I received a phone call from the medical director here, and he directed me to answer any and all questions about Mr. Cunningham's health this woman may have. This woman insists that she see Mr. Cunningham's chest area, and I am complying."

"Don't you dare let this woman touch him. Watch her closely."

"It's all right, Judy," Louise said. "You can watch me through the glass."

After donning the protective gear, they went in and Judy watched as the gloved doctor gently pulled back Dennis's hospital gown to expose the right side of his chest. Louise bent forward and then appeared to ask the doctor for something. He took out a small flashlight and shined it on Dennis's chest. Louise drew very close and looked at his chest.

Then she stood upright, turned and left the physician holding the flashlight. Judy watched Louise tear off the protective gear, wash her hands under the direction of a nurse and bolt down the hallway, reaching for her phone.

Judy returned to the waiting room. It was 11:32 p.m. The door opened behind her and the doctor returned.

"There is nothing you can do here. You should go home and rest. We will call you if we need to reach you for any reason."

"Don't let that woman touch him, do you hear me?"

"I won't let her touch him," he said.

✦

Judy stopped at the hotel bar and ordered a glass of red wine. She put it down in three long gulps then retired to her room.

She had purchased a strong antibacterial soap at a chemist on the way home. After taking a scalding shower and scrubbing religiously, she put on her pajamas and brushed her teeth. She stared at Dennis's toothbrush. It was his travel toothbrush that he insisted on putting back into its protective cap after each use. Judy had argued that it was better to let it dry first, but Dennis said he always did it this way and that he had not caught hoof and mouth disease yet. It was one of their silly little arguments. The memory of it left her feeling sad and lonely. She quickly went to bed and fell sound asleep.

The phone seemed to scream at her, and she knocked it off the bedside table trying to grab it. She used the charging cord as a tether and slowly pulled it toward her as she leaned over the bed.

"Hello?"

"Tthis is Dr. Ravishana. I wanted to update you on Mr. Cunningham's condition."

Judy said nothing.

"Ms. White, are you there?"

"Yes."

"I wanted to tell you that Mr. Cunningham is showing signs of improvement. We've adjusted our antibiotic regimen to better match his specific bacteria."

Judy looked at the clock. It was 7:12 a.m.

"Do you think this is just temporary?" Judy asked.

"When someone with MRSA gets the correct antibiotic treatment quickly, the patient can improve dramatically with minimal damage to their organs. We think he's on the way to a complete recovery. We appreciate Ms. Nordland's help on this."

"You didn't let her touch him, did you?"

"No, no, please calm down. She did not touch him. She helped us identify the correct regimen to treat him."

"She's not a doctor. What could she possibly know about regimens?"

"Well, she brought in an American doctor, who, in consultation with our medical director and the head of our infectious diseases department, procured a new experimental antibiotic that we did not have. Frankly, it's probably the reason he's doing so well now."

"You let those bastards touch him!" she screamed.

"Ms. White, you're overreacting. Please calm down. I know this has been a strain on you—." But Judy had already hung up and raced to get dressed.

CHAPTER 29

can't believe it," Judy said, standing next to Dr. Ravishana.

"He is doing well, but he will need time to recuperate," he said.

"Can he leave soon? Today or tomorrow?"

"Heavens, no. He's still quite sick. But we're pretty confident that he'll get through this."

"Can I see him?"

"Yes, but you know the rules. Please, no contact."

Judy moved within several feet of the bed and leaned forward. Dennis raised his head and looked at her, his bright blue eyes dimmed and pink around the edges.

"Hey," he said through his plastic mask.

"How you feeling, Yank?"

"Strong like bull," he said weakly through the mask.

"Bullshit. You look like hell," she said.

"Like bull," he said, closing his eyes.

Judy choked up, waved at Dennis, though his eyes were closed, turned quickly and left. She did not know why she was trying to hide her emotions from him. Perhaps she was trying to hide them from herself.

Judy was not surprised to find Louise in the waiting room.

Louise approached and sat down. The two women sat parallel to each other and faced forward, looking out the same large window into the gray sky.

"What did you do to him?" Judy asked without turning.

"Antibiotics. A new version."

"You Yanks have all the answers."

"Not all, just some."

They fell silent.

"Do you want to help Dennis and me?" Louise asked.

"I'll help Dennis but not you."

"He and I are on this assignment together, Judy. I'm sure you know that."

"I thought the assignment had run out of time," Judy said.

"He told you that?"

"Yes."

"Officially, it has been terminated. But Dennis and I were still trying to crack this thing."

"The Arnold case?"

"Yes. I wasn't sure how much he told you. This is a highly confidential and peculiar case. Dennis and I were committed to solving it."

"Well, it's over now. So Dennis can just relax and recuperate."

"You think Dennis is going to let this just go?" Louise asked, turning to face Judy.

Judy avoided the gaze and continued to stare out the window.

"Maybe," she said.

"I don't think so," Louise said. "You know he's going to jump right back into it, regardless of the rules. That's the way he is. I don't know him as well as you, but I know he's not going to let this go."

Judy shrugged.

"And that's why I'm asking for your help," Louise said. "You must know something about what Dennis was working on. I can't wait for him to get well and then wait for him to confide in me. It's clear that he was withholding things from me. He said as much. Maybe you could help me. Just tell me what he might know."

"Louise, he didn't trust you. As I already said before, I don't trust you. Why in God's name would I do something that he wouldn't approve of? Just because you're sitting in this room playing nice? Trying to take advantage of a woman who's scared for the man she loves? Please don't insult me."

The two women commenced their parallel positions, both silent and looking out the same window on the same rooftop view of a gray London winter sky. Judy became increasingly uncomfortable as the silence lingered. Finally, unable to stand it any longer, she stood up.

"Okay," Louise said.

Judy stopped. "Okay?"

"Yes, okay. I'll tell you."

"Tell me what?"

"Sit down and I'll tell you."

Judy sat down.

"Someone tried to kill Dennis," Louise said, rubbing her eyes with her fingertips, refocusing on the window.

"I don't understand. Are you suggesting it was the man who stumbled into Dennis?"

"It was the pinprick."

"Pinprick?"

"Yes. If you hadn't mentioned the little bit of blood you'd seen below his ribcage, it would never have occurred to me."

"I'm listening," Judy said.

"I started off my career at the agency in operations. Street work. Managing assets, running teams here and there. Dirty work, some of it."

"So?" Judy said.

"So, in this kind of work, we study the street craft of our opponents. I mean, everyone does it. It's like espionage graduate school. I know it sounds silly, but that's what we do. Some of the most famous cases of espionage and assassinations are studied and in some cases copied."

"I think I'm going to get some breakfast," Judy said, standing.

"In 1978 a Bulgarian named Markov was murdered in London by the Bulgarian Secret Police," Louise continued. "He was injected with a minuscule pellet that contained the poison ricin. The pellet was delivered by the tip of an umbrella."

Judy looked down at Louise, who continued to stare out the window.

"There have been lots of these outrageous assassinations over the years. Russians and Israelis are best known for their creativity; neither of those organizations have any adult supervision, so they do seem to have fun trying to kill people in the most inventive ways. The best methods, by far, are those that make the death look accidental or non-malicious."

Judy sat down.

"In 2004 one of our operatives in Rome got sick. He was involved in a very complicated surveillance program of a Syrian general who was purchasing chemical weapons on the private arms market. The agency guy died from a bacterial infection that at the time was considered unrelated to his espionage activities. I mean, people get infections and die all the time.

"In 2007 Israel took in a Syrian defector who had lots of stories to tell. One of them involved the use of Russians to kill an American intelligence official in Rome. The American had uncovered a plan by Syrian military to buy nerve gas from Russian arms dealers. The defector said the Russians sent a female agent to bump into our guy on the streets of Rome and accidentally prick him in the stomach area with a needle infected with a rare type of MRSA. When the Israelis reported the tip back to us from the defector, Langley didn't believe it.

"We get misinformation all the time; sometimes defectors are double agents, or they're fed misinformation without knowing it. It's a mess, but stick with me. Some analyst in Langley got curious and looked at the old autopsy photos of our dead agent in Rome. Sure enough, there was a little tiny pinprick on the left side of his stomach."

Louise raised her hands behind her neck, intertwined her fingers and left them there. She leaned back in the chair, still staring out the window.

"They exhumed the body of the agent who died in Rome. It was an unknown strain of MRSA. So we cloned it and developed an antibiotic protocol for it. Just in case the Russians got frisky with one of our people again."

Louise pulled her hands away from the back of her neck and pointed them at the ceiling as she stretched and yawned. She stood up, picked her purse off the chair, and said, "That's as far as I'm going with this. The rest of the math is up to you. If you feel like trusting me, let me know. Otherwise, you'll never hear from me again. And don't forget, when Dennis gets better, he'll jump back into this case, only he won't have protection or help from me. I'm getting reassigned."

As Louise walked out of the room, Judy noticed she had an odd gait.

"Wait," Judy said. "Maybe I can help."

"You're the only person right now that can help me figure out what Dennis knew," Louise said. "I think he has most of the pieces of the puzzle."

"Well, if you coax information out of me that harms Dennis, then I'll kill you, Louise."

"Wow, that's pretty intense."

Judy rubbed her eyes and bit the inside of her lip. "So Arnold is in Moscow. He defected."

"Bullshit," Louise said.

"And Dennis got back into Menwith Hill and stole something."

"How in the hell did he get inside there again?"

"I'm starving," Judy said. "I feel faint and I need food. Let's go to the cafeteria."

✦

Judy noticed that Louise had a very intense style of concentration. Over a simple breakfast in the cafeteria, she leaned in toward Judy's face and repeated questions.

What did the stolen device look like in precise detail?

Stainless steel with black plastic housing.

How many millimeters long was it?

Maybe twenty.

Did Dennis know for certain that Arnold sneaked the device in by inserting it under his skin near the ICD or did Dennis just guess?

A guess.

Who did Dennis talk to at MI5?

Judy did not know.

Was Judy sure that Dennis mentioned power line communications and nodes and repeaters?

Yes, that's what he said.

What was the neighborhood in Moscow where Arnold was seen?

Judy couldn't remember; only the name of the coffee shop: The Grind.

Did Dennis know why Chandler in the London station didn't report the tip from the Brits that Arnold was seen in Moscow?

He thought Chandler was either hiding something or was incompetent.

"I can't do this any longer, Louise," Judy said. "You're a very intense person, and it's exhausting having you interrogate me. I'm going up to the waiting room."

"We're moving him today," Louise said.

"What? You can't do that. He's sick."

"Did you not hear what I said happened to him, Judy? Someone tried to kill him. Did you not notice that two people who came closest to figuring out the Arnold disappearance were in someone's crosshairs? Fred Kaczka was poisoned and killed. Now Dennis. It's just a hunch, but the fact that Dennis probably disrupted the Russians' eavesdropping equipment at Menwith Hill upped the ante for them. You think I'm going to leave him here at a public hospital?"

"Where is he moving to?"

"A military hospital north of London. More controls. He'll be safe there."

"Can I visit him?"

"Of course. Maybe we can even move you into a room nearby. But I need to make a phone call first. I'll be right back. We need protection for Dennis right now."

Judy waited, toying with her cold coffee, anxious about the prospect of Dennis lying unprotected in the isolation room upstairs. And for the first time in a while, she felt homesick for her family and Perth. It would be midsummer there now, a perfect antidote to the gloomy London weather. Trevor was living with her parents and had called her again yesterday wondering when she was going to return.

"Very soon," she had told him. "Perhaps next week."

"Can I go with Jimmy and his family to Bunbury? You know Mrs. Wilson."

"Yes, I do. When are they going and for how long?"

"I think next week, and for a fortnight. I would love to go with them, Mum. Please?"

"Sure. Can you send me Mrs. Wilson's mobile phone number? I'll call her."

"You're the best, Mum."

✦

Louise returned twenty minutes later and sat down.

"I've arranged for some freelance protection for Dennis while he waits to be moved. Dr. Ravishana says he is doing well."

"I just want him out of this place," Judy said. "And out of this damn city. I've always loved London, but not anymore. I don't like its cellars, its pedestrians or its hospitals. I'll never come back."

"Can't say I blame you."

"So why did you ask me to wait for you? What do you want?"

"I've been thinking about what you told me," Louise said.

"Which part?"

"The part about Arnold in Russia."

"What about him?"

"Well, I'm officially off the case right now, as is Dennis. Even if I told the IG what I just learned, he'd tell me that it was too late and unverifiable and to forget it. He seems to be under a lot of pressure to end the case."

"I feel the same way."

"Now, on the other hand, if I could show proof to the IG that Arnold is in fact living happily in Moscow, well, that would be something he couldn't sweep under the rug."

"So just get one of your contractors in Russia to ID him and then pass it along."

"I can't do that," Louise said. "I have no resources in Russia to call on. That's not my area of expertise. Lebanon or Ankara, sure. I could roust up some folks there. But not Mother Russia. I'd even be willing to talk to Dennis's MI5 friend, but I don't know who he is, and Dennis would never tell me anyway. And let's not forget Chandler already knows, but he did not pass it up the chain of command. I'm not going to tip him off by asking for resources.

"I'd go myself," Louise continued, "but the FSB has me on file there and wouldn't let me breathe without surveillance the moment my name hit the flight manifest. But all we need is proof that Arnold is there in Moscow right now."

"I'm sure you could figure it out," Judy said.

"And then there's Dennis," Louise said.

"What about Dennis?"

"You and I both know that he's going to try to get proof of Arnold's presence in Moscow. I mean, he'll go crazy trying to do it. But he won't have any resources at his disposal, because he's off the case."

"Perhaps he'll get his MI5 friend to help out," Judy said.

"My guess is that his friend was an informal emissary from British intelligence, but they'll steer clear of getting into the middle of this mess."

"Louise, what are you driving at?" Judy asked.

"I'm simply trying to say that Dennis will do whatever he can to prove that Arnold is alive and well in Moscow, even if it means he goes over there himself."

"That's ridiculous."

"I didn't say it wasn't ridiculous, I'm saying that Dennis just can't help himself when he gets on the scent of something. You know that. I read the case file on the Australian mining case. You were there. He was brazen and reckless."

Judy could feel her face flush with anger, not because she thought Louise was incorrect, but because she knew Louise was manipulating her.

"As you Yanks say, cut the bullshit. What do you want?"

"Why don't you make a quick trip to Moscow?"

"What?!"

"Hang on. Just listen. You're not on any intelligence lists there, so you won't be watched. Aussies are known to be some of the world's most common tourists, so your visit won't send off any alarms. We know where Arnold goes for coffee daily. I've already verified that there's a coffee shop with that name."

"You did?"

"Yes. You just show up there for a day or two, waiting for him. I'll give you a small device to take video. Then you come back."

"You've lost your mind, Louise," Judy said, standing up.

"You're not listening closely," Louise said. "Dennis will try this stunt himself. You think that you can stop him, when he can't stop himself?"

Judy was so angry, she considered slapping Louise across that pale, jutting cheekbone of hers with enough strength to knock her off her chair.

Instead, she turned, walked out of the cafeteria and took the elevator up to see Dennis. Dennis the Menace. Dennis, the man who would not and could not let a case go unsolved. Reckless Dennis.

Dennis, the man she loved.

She put on the protective clothing and entered his room. His blue eyes brightened when he saw her; he broke into a wide smile that was hindered by the breathing mask.

"Hey," came his muffled greeting.

"You look good," she said, though in fact he looked terrible. He had lost weight, and his cheeks seemed hollowed out.

"I'm going home soon," he said.

"And where is home to you these days?" she laughed.

"Wherever you are."

"I like the sound of that."

"How are you and Louise getting along?"

"Fine."

"Watch out for her," he said.

"Yes, you told me already."

"Did she tell you anything about the Arnold case?"

"Good lord, what makes you think we talk about that?"

"I was just wondering."

"Besides, aren't you both off the case now?"

"Ha," he said, the plastic mask fogging slightly. "We'll see about that."

CHAPTER 30

So explain to me again how these glasses work," Judy said.

Louise held the fashionable horn-rimmed glasses in her hands and put them on. "You see these little metal decorative pieces on the front of the frames, here and there?" she said, pointing to the far left and right of the frames. "Those are tiny lenses. Don't worry, you can't tell by looking at them. You activate the video by doing this." She used the tip of her right forefinger and pressed on the bridge of the glasses across her nose, as if she were adjusting them slightly. "To stop shooting, just tap them again. Here, try it."

Judy put them on and noticed the lenses were actually clear and not magnified.

"Like this?" she said, pushing them up with her forefinger.

"Perfect. Don't forget to turn them off; the battery is very small. The important thing is to make sure you're looking at him from close up when you turn the camera on."

"Got it."

"Don't say anything to him, but if he does speak to you, simply tell him that you don't know how to order a black coffee."

"What if he continues to talk to me?"

"Just smile and ignore him."

"This feels weird. We have AFP blokes in W.A. that go undercover, but I never have. It's unnerving."

"Very simple stuff, Judy. You're a well-trained policewoman. You'll do great. Remember, make the reservations at the hotel I wrote down, then take a cab to the coffee shop or walk to it. It's not far from the hotel. Hang around the coffee shop and look for him. I've shown you at least five different pictures of Arnold. If you see him on any day and film him, return to the hotel and call this number. Please memorize it. Leave a voice-mail for Steve, saying you're bored and coming back to London.

"If you don't see him the first night, you need to contact us at exactly 9:20 p.m. Moscow local time. You call the same number and leave a message for Steve saying you miss him. If you don't call, that means something is wrong and we'll go into action. But don't worry, nothing will go wrong. You keep doing this for three days. If you don't see him on the final day, leave the same message with Steve that you're bored and returning. I'll contact you in London."

"But if I do see him on day one or two?"

"Judy. Pay attention, please. If you see him on any day and are able to film him up close, you make the call to Steve about being bored and return on the next British Airways direct flight. I'll meet you at Heathrow in the ladies' room inside the security area. It's right behind the Starbucks. Just come in, wash your hands, put the glasses on the counter and leave. I'll be washing my hands next to you."

"You make it sound so simple, but it seems complicated to me."

"You'll do fine. Not to worry."

"And after this the Arnold case will be closed, right? Dennis will be done with it?"

"The case will absolutely be closed. I don't know what else he has on his docket, but the Arnold case will be toast."

"And you won't tell him what I've done."

"Ha. He might be a little pissed off that I cracked the case. In fact, I guarantee he'll be pissed off. But I won't involve you."

"You folks are strange."

"Of course we are."

✦

The British Airways flight to Moscow's Sheremetyevo International Airport was three and a half hours. The moment Judy got on the plane she grew paranoid. Police work could be exhausting, shocking and sometimes dangerous, but this kind of work was draining and nerve-wracking.

Judy began to worry about everything. The two women seated next to her were British and on holiday, but she didn't know whether they were MI5 or MI6, or Russian FSB, or actually two British women on holiday.

She tried to nap but couldn't.

Louise had beseeched her to look happy and excited, as if she were experiencing a new country. She was instructed to answer any questions at the immigration checkpoint as simply as possible: smile and say little.

The weather was colder than she anticipated, and the air bit into her cheeks as she waited in line for a cab. The late afternoon air had a gray cast to it, like fine steel wool. Was it going to snow? Hardened snow piles lined the road. She had not brought boots.

The cabbie spoke halting English. "You English?"

"No, Australian."

"You come to work? Go to conference? Many conference in Moscow. Big city now. Important city. Many foreigners."

"No, taking a day or two to visit the city. A quick trip."

"Tourist. Good. Lots to see. July better."

"Ha. Yes, but only have time this week."

The cabbie tried to engage Judy in further conversation, but she gave monosyllabic answers until they got to the hotel. After setting up in her room, Judy went to the concierge and asked for the nearest coffee shop. He directed her to The Grind and said it was close enough to walk.

It was 4:20 local time, and the sun had started to set. The homes and apartments in the neighborhood were expensive-looking, and Judy was surprised at how many people were walking in the neighborhood. She kept her head down, having had the forethought to bring a wool hat and scarf.

The Grind was brightly lit up inside and full of young professionals sitting with their laptops and cell phones. The smell of coffee was strong and bracing when she walked in.

Judy tried her best to look like a confused Australian tourist, which she was, and not like a temporary untrained spy, which she was as well.

There were two women and a young man in the line in front of her; the man was too young to be Arnold. She wore her special glasses and nonchalantly tried to scan the café, but it was difficult and seemed unnatural, so she focused on the board with prices above the counter.

Soon there were several people behind her, and she tried to look askance to see if Arnold was there. Again, it was awkward to do so, and she gave up. When her turn came, she asked the young man behind the counter for a cappuccino and paid.

She grabbed a tall stool overlooking the busy street and waited, sometimes peering at a tourist guide. After forty-five minutes, with the coffee long consumed and the steamed milk hardened on the insides of the white porcelain mug, she stood up and walked back to the hotel.

The room service was adequate; she had a single glass of white wine. Louise had warned her that it was not impossible that her room might be bugged, so she was to act as normal as any Australian tourist would.

At 9:20 she made the obligatory call to Steve. *Good God, is every intelligence service in the world listening to my call to Steve? I prefer police work. At least I know who the bad guys are.*

At 7:10 the following morning Judy was back at The Grind. A strong wind from the northwest had made the walk very uncomfortable, and her eyes watered from the stinging cold.

The café was very busy, and she slid into the back of a long line. It shuffled slowly, and she wondered if the shop was understaffed or whether this was normal queuing practice in Russia.

At one point she turned sideways and noticed a gray-haired man of normal height standing two persons behind her. It was Arnold.

All right now, she thought. *Act normal.* But the more she thought about turning on the camera, she wondered how to do it without looking obvious. Perhaps she could say something to the man directly behind her, turn on the camera and film Arnold without actually looking at him. Louise hadn't told how her to manage that. *Shit, shit, shit.*

As the line shortened, Judy decided to act. She turned to face the young man behind her and pressed the bridge of the glasses.

"Excuse me, do you speak English?"

"Yes, a little bit," he said, holding up his forefinger and index fingers to show a tiny space between them.

Arnold thrust his face forward and said, "May I help you? I speak English."

"Ah, yes. I was wondering how you order a black coffee."

"Oh, these people speak English here. Just ask for black coffee."

"Thank you so much," Judy said, smiling. "I appreciate it."

The young man behind her shrugged and smiled.

Judy pressed the bridge of her nose to turn off the video. A minute later she asked the young woman behind the counter for a black coffee and paid. Standing off to the side, waiting for the coffee, Judy took an idle glance at Arnold in the line behind her.

He was gone. She scanned the coffee shop but could not see him.

She took her coffee to an open table and perused her tour guide. Every now and then she would look around but could not find him.

After forty-five minutes she left and walked the frigid sidewalk back to her hotel. She called and left the message for Steve about being bored.

The flight to Heathrow was bumpy, but she felt elation at helping Louise on the Arnold case. It had been as simple as Louise had predicted. She knew Dennis would be furious if he ever found out, but she was desperate. Dennis was intractable when it came to the hunt. Louise was right. So what if Louise got all the glory for cracking the Arnold case? At least Judy would have Dennis to herself.

At Heathrow, Judy found the woman's bathroom near the Starbucks, checked her watch and entered. It was busy with women of different nationalities moving in and out of the stalls, many dragging cumbersome roll-on suitcases.

Louise was nowhere to be seen, so Judy waited. Sure enough, Louise entered and went to an open sink and washed her hands. Judy washed her hands next to her and placed the glasses between them. Judy left, carrying her small overnight bag.

CHAPTER 31

J udy leaned forward and gently kissed Dennis on the lips. "They said I could do that now," she said. "Though you look a little weak, I'm sure you can handle a kiss."

Dennis lay in bed in his new hospital room. There were two security guards, one at the door, the other inside the room and monitoring everything the medical staff did.

"His name is Steven," Dennis said, nodding to the tall, middle-aged man with a receding hairline and pointed nose. "He's a bodyguard and physician. His job is to make sure no one tries to slip something in my IV. Right, Steven?"

Steven smiled and said nothing.

"And he barely talks to me," Dennis said. "I think they removed his tongue."

Steven chuckled and shook his head.

"Don't pay attention to him, Steven," Judy said. "He's like this all the time."

"Have you seen Louise?" Dennis said.

"No, why would I see her?" Judy asked.

"I don't know. Just thought I'd ask. She's disappeared. Or at least from me. Can't seem to reach her."

"Maybe she's traveling."

"No. She's been transferred. Got that confirmed by someone else in OIG. Strange."

"Doesn't that happen a lot?" Judy said.

"No, not really," Dennis said.

"Not really what?"

"People in OIG don't get reassigned out of the department. That's not normal."

"Well, does it matter? You told me that the investigation is closed. End of story."

"You think I'm going to just let this Arnold case go?"

Judy bit the inside of her lip. *Here he goes again*, she thought. *My God, Louise was right. Why can't he just give up on these lost causes? And what about us? Does our relationship even register with him anymore?*

"When are you getting discharged?" she asked.

"Maybe tomorrow. The doctor said there might be some damage to my liver, but he's not too worried."

"Your liver?"

"He told me that they'll need to keep an eye on it."

"I hope it's nothing serious."

"I'm not going to worry about it. They're flying me home tomorrow. Steven here and Casey, the guy outside, are to escort me back to Virginia. Then I'm free of them spying on me."

Judy looked at Steven, who rolled his eyes.

"You don't seem to trust anyone," she said.

"Only you."

Judy leaned in toward Dennis. "Are you going to join me in Perth, like we planned?"

"Of course. I just need to get back to Langley and get hold of Louise. Need to tell her about Arnold in Moscow. Maybe she'll help me reopen the case."

Judy felt a sickness sweep through her stomach and lodge in her throat. She started to speak and stopped, turned to Steven and said, "Do you mind if we speak privately?"

"I can't do that, ma'am," he said in a Southern drawl.

"Please, Steven? Just give me five minutes."

"No, ma'am. I'm sorry, but we can't do that."

"Can you at least stand over there in the doorway?"

Steven frowned, walked over to the doorway and said something to Casey. They both looked inside.

"Dennis," she said, sitting down on the edge of the bed. "I don't know how to say this, but I just realized that you have no intention of following me to Perth, or at least not any time soon. You're lost in one of your chases again. Nothing matters besides your chase, including me."

The sickness and disorientation of being hospitalized had muddled Dennis's perceptions, and he struggled to understand what Judy was talking about. Her eyes were watering, and he realized she was crying.

"Why are you crying?"

"Aren't you listening to me?" she said.

"Of course I am. But why are you crying?"

"Damnit, Dennis, you're not coming to Australia. And even if you did, you'd be off on another wild-goose chase as soon as you got there. Why has it taken me so long to understand this about you? What in God's name is wrong with me?"

She stood up and wiped her eyes. Dennis felt dull and languid. *Judy was crying, but why?* he thought. A tear slid down the middle of her right cheek, taking a fleck of dark mascara with it.

"Judy, I, I… "

She leaned forward, kissed him on his forehead and bolted from the room, pushing through the two men at the door.

"Steven," Dennis yelled. "Stop her."

Steven frowned at Dennis.

"Please, Steven?"

"Calm down, Cunningham," Steven said, entering the room. "You'll be in D.C. tomorrow. Everything's going to be fine. Try to chill."

✦

The condo smelled stale, and Dennis saw dust on every surface. He tried to open a window to let fresh air in, but the window resisted. After several exhausting attempts he shoved it open a few inches. The January air was cold and sharp, and he reflexively crossed his arms and went to the small kitchen and removed the items from his shopping bag.

He had been back in the States for two days, and though he was officially cleared to return to work, he was physically exhausted and emotionally drained.

During his illness in London, he lost track of time and hadn't known where he was sometimes. His dreams had been strange and violent. In one recurring dream a woman had stabbed him with a drinking straw, which in normal circumstances would be quite funny. But in his recurring dream, the woman meant to kill him and chased him relentlessly. The faster he tried to run away from her, the more his legs lost strength. The woman in the dream always caught him.

He was especially perplexed about Judy. Why had she burst into tears in his hospital room and returned to Perth? He had left more than a dozen voicemails on her cell phone and had written numerous emails and texts.

The only answer he'd gotten from her was a text that said simply:

"please leave me alone"

What had he done to her? He barely remembered his last conversation with her in the hospital about Louise and Arnold, but that was it.

He put a small container of orange juice in the refrigerator, along with milk, some cheese, eggs and a loaf of bread. Dennis always kept his bread in the fridge, otherwise it would go moldy given his sporadic travel and eating habits.

His cell phone hummed.

"Cunningham here."

"The IG will see you today at 3:45 p.m. Please be prompt. He has a 4:00 p.m. con call."

"Yes, I'll be there. Thanks."

He knew that fifteen minutes was a very short time to get the IG's attention on the Arnold case. Since his return to Langley, he'd done his best to figure out where Louise had moved to, but uncharacteristically, everything about her whereabouts was blocked. Even her email address had been changed, and he got bouncebacks stating the email address was no longer valid.

His fellow investigators in the office were as stumped as he was. They admitted that during her stint in OIG no one had gotten to know her well.

No one had heard of the Arnold case, which didn't surprise him.

Dennis was going to confront the IG to see if he could pry something out of him. It was a long shot, but he had no other options. He had even contacted Barkley's office to set up a meeting, but Morton, his chief of staff, said there was no record of the congressman ever speaking to Dennis.

Dennis reminded Morton that he and Morton met before, but the chief of staff said he had no recollection of that meeting.

"Please make sure that you follow protocols for contact with Representative Barkley," Morton warned Dennis. "It's not appropriate for an OIG staffer to contact the chairman directly. I'm sure I needn't remind you of that."

✦

"Come in," Richardson said, beaming that bright-white porcelain smile of his. "And again, I feel compelled to tell you how very sorry I am about your hospitalization in London. No one else in this department seems to get in harm's way like you, Dennis. But we're all so glad you're doing well."

"Thank you," Dennis said. "I appreciate your concern, and thank you for seeing me on such short notice."

"Not a problem," Richardson said. "You're our best investigator, and we want you safe and sound."

"Well, then if you don't mind, I just wanted to complete my investigation of the Arnold case with a brief verbal report to you."

Richardson's long face drew even longer in confusion.

"That case is closed. I'm sure you know that."

"Well, yes. I know it was closed. But I think I have some new information that you might be interested in."

"But the case is closed and solved," Richardson said. "Well, as solved as any of these complex cases are."

"I don't think so," Dennis said. "I'm afraid that Arnold didn't just disappear; he defected to Russia."

Richardson's eyes focused uncomfortably on Dennis's, and the silence was unnerving.

"And he didn't just defect, but he put Russian eavesdropping devices into the NSA facility in Menwith Hill. He allowed the Russians to tap into the NSA's data. It was a major breach."

Richardson continued to stare with what Dennis took to be a mixture of confusion and concern.

"We know all of that," Richardson said.

"You do?"

"Of course. Louise broke the case for us while you were sick."

"She did?"

"Yes. It's a very sordid tale, unfortunately. Arnold had a gay lover and fell so madly in love that he flipped. Planted some new kind of surveillance tools in the NSA facility north of London and took off for Moscow. Of course, you know this information is of the highest clearance. It's a terrible black mark on our operations group, and the London station in particular. But Louise, God bless her, was able to piece it together just when the deadline for the investigation hit. And once she discovered one of those things — a 'node' or something — the breach was found. And apparently Arnold disappeared in Moscow. Our folks are looking for him everywhere. We'll get him one day. That is, unless Putin and his thugs simply disappear him first. And your part will never be forgotten. Louise reported that you were integral to drawing out Arnold's handlers, though you and that poor fellow Kaczka from the NSA got the worst of it. She told us that the Russians were so convinced you were going to find out about the eavesdropping operation, they tried to take you out."

Dennis felt a pressure in his chest that he thought might be a heart attack. But he realized it was anger, the burning kind of coal-fired anger that even scared him at times.

His lips were dry, and he licked them to make them operable.

"Which reminds me, how are you feeling?" Richardson asked. "You look a little pale."

"I'm fine. Guess the infection and antibiotics played havoc with some organs, especially my liver. But I'm fine."

"Well, that's great then."

"By the way, where is Louise? I can't seem to find her."

"Oh, she's been transferred. Sorry to see her go."

"Yes, but I can't seem to contact her. I get bouncebacks on emails to her."

"Oh, that. She's been detailed to a special operations unit that's incommunicado. I'm sorry. I don't think I'd even be able to contact her."

"Who does she report to?"

"Ah, Cunningham," Richardson said in a patronizing gesture of concern. "I don't know the answer to that. It's over. You and Louise did a brilliant job on this one. Relax. Get healthy. You still look a little peaked. Take some time off."

"Mr. Richardson," the intercom at his desk squawked. "You have that con call in three minutes."

Richardson stood and extended his hand to Dennis. "Welcome back. Great job you and Louise did. Please take your time getting up to speed here. We want you healthy and focused for more projects."

✦

While it was common for individuals to be transferred within the agency, it was unusual for an employee to disappear without a trace. Louise had managed to do so.

Dennis asked around to his colleagues and friends in other sections, and no one seemed to know who she was, except that Louise Nordland was associated with something heroic in Lebanon several years earlier.

Richardson said Louise had been assigned to a special operations unit, but in agency parlance, that could be almost any fly-by-night, hare-brained project. Analysts and operational people often fell off the grid during special projects and returned later with a shrug and a wink to their colleagues.

Still, Louise's disappearance infuriated Dennis. It was clear, at least to him, that Louise had used Dennis's work in breaking the Arnold case to advance her career and get herself back to operations. But how did she find out about the defection? And the eavesdropping equipment?

Taking credit for his work was only part of his outrage; equally upsetting was how she had discovered the parts of the puzzle he had not told her.

He knew he was obsessing over Louise. He stopped going to work regularly and had not been given any new assignments yet. Dennis peppered his friends and contacts with questions about Louise's whereabouts as he looked for any lead. He wanted to confront her, though he was also aware that none of this mattered in the greater scheme of things. People exaggerated their accomplishments at work all the time — even fudged the truth to do so.

So the call was not a total surprise.

"Mr. Cunningham?"

"Yes, this is him."

"Inspector General Richardson would like to speak to you. Please hold on."

Dennis waited for several minutes.

"Cunningham, how are you?"

"Fine sir, how are you?"

"Just fine, thanks. Hope you're taking it easy. I've asked the team not to give you any assignments just quite yet."

"Thank you, sir."

"I hope you don't mind, but well, I have an awkward question to ask you."

Dennis knew where this was going.

"Go right ahead sir."

"Ah, well then. It's come to my attention that you have been devoting an extraordinary amount of time and energy to seek information on the whereabouts of Louise Nordland. Is that true?"

"Gee, I have been trying to figure out where she moved to. She has gone dark."

"Yes, but I thought I mentioned that she was transferred to a special operations group. These groups often go off the grid for a reason."

"I just wanted to contact her. I mean, we never said our goodbyes. I wanted to thank her for her help in London. She saved my life."

"She's a courageous woman, Cunningham. One of our best. I'm sure Louise appreciates your concern. But I've been asked to, well, have you cease trying to contact her. I know this is uncomfortable. But can I get your acknowledgement that you'll stop trying to track her down?"

"I suppose so. I didn't think I was breaking any rules."

"So we agree then?"

"Yes, we agree. I'm sorry that I've caused any trouble for you."

"Not at all, Cunningham. I'm glad we've had this conversation. I think we're all set then."

"Yes, we are. Thanks for the call."

✦

"Dennis, I thought you knew that our clinical relationship is over," Dr. Forrester said. She was sitting across from him in her small armchair. "We terminated therapy many months ago. The only reason I agreed to see you again was that you said you were in crisis."

"I know you said we were not making much progress, but I thought I could still see you."

"Dennis, I must say that you don't look well. You seem to have lost some weight, and you look tired. Are you sleeping properly?"

"Sort of."

"When you said you were in crisis, did you mean that you might be capable of hurting yourself or others?"

"No. Well, maybe I'm pissed off at one person in particular, but I don't think I'd hurt her."

Forrester's face tightened. "Are you talking about the woman in Australia you had a relationship with? My notes said you had a romantic relationship with a woman named Judy and were considering breaking up with her."

"No, not Judy. She's fine. Or I think she's fine. Another person. A woman I worked with."

"So you're not in danger of hurting yourself or this other woman?"

"No, I don't think so."

"That doesn't sound definitive, Dennis. 'I don't think so' is not the correct answer."

"Sorry, you're right, Dr. Forrester. I'm not going to hurt anyone."

"Then what is your crisis? Why did you keep calling my answering service?"

"It's just that I feel like everything is spinning out of control. I was involved in a very complex investigation, and someone I liked a lot was killed. Then Judy was abducted in London. God, what a horrible mess that was. Then someone tried to kill me, and I was hospitalized. And worst of all, the woman I was working with stole my investigation and took credit for the whole thing while I was sick."

Dr. Forrester looked down at the notebook in her lap and used her left hand to rub her temple. She sighed.

"Dennis, I'm not in a position to delve into your issues right now. My only goal is to ascertain whether you are capable of hurting yourself or someone else. You don't seem to be at risk of doing that. But I strongly encourage you to contact one of the approved therapists on the agency's list. It's important that you start seeing someone again soon."

"But I want to see you."

"No, Dennis. I don't see a clinical benefit in us continuing to work together. There are times when the therapeutic relationship becomes more habitual and less productive, and that's why we ended the therapy."

"But I'm in crisis," Dennis said. "Can't you see that?"

"To be honest, you've been in turmoil since we started with therapy. You're like a lot of my agency clients — though I'm breaking some rules in saying that — you're in a constant state of turmoil and crisis. If you think it's exhausting to be in your line of work, you should try to sit here and listen to the endless tales of anxiety, trauma and depression."

"I'm sorry," Dennis said slowly. "As usual, I don't take in other people's concerns. Just my own. I guess you'd call that a theme."

"Dennis, you seem to thrive on crises. I'm not suggesting that is the basis of a calm and rewarding life, but too many of your colleagues are wired the same way. I suspect that your employer collects these individuals like moths drawn to a flame. In the past, if I'm not mistaken, your instincts have been your salvation. So, until you find another therapist, trust your instincts, stop self-medicating with alcohol and try to lower your guard and let others into your life. And our time is up today."

CHAPTER 32

P hil Nordland was the lead he was looking for.

Perhaps Dennis was getting old, or perhaps the bacterial infection had damaged his brain cells, but Dennis remembered that Louise's husband's name was Phil and he worked as an analyst at the National Security Council.

The NSC's list of employees was not readily available, but it was much less sacrosanct than other intelligence lists. Yet it took him less time than he imagined to find a "P. Nordland" living in Vienna, Virginia, including an address. Who needed spies when you had Google to work with?

He drove by the address one afternoon to find a large, expensive suburban home with a two-car garage. The style was modern colonial, with all trappings of what passed for wealth in the Washington suburbs: huge lawn, manicured landscaping and a white fence separating it from the neighbors.

On the second evening Dennis drove by, the house was lit up. He did not slow down and was careful not to gawk. The following night, he drove by using a small video camera to case the place out.

He rented a car the third day to mix things up and drove by the Nordland house twice, once in the early morning and once again at dinnertime. Both times the garage doors were shut, but there was definitely activity in the house. Was Louise overseas on another assignment? Was this the P. Nordland who was married to Louise Nordland? Dennis guessed it was, but he needed verification.

On the following Saturday, Dennis drove by the Nordland household at 9:30 a.m. and caught the garage door opening. He sped down the block, pulled into someone's driveway and turned off the car. In his rear-view mirror he watched a late model jet-black Audi A6 slide by with Louise Nordland driving.

After she passed he started the car, backed up and followed the Audi to a mall. He saw Louise park in front of a Whole Foods and enter it. He parked nearby, pulled on a blue wool cap and wraparound sunglasses. He walked idly around the parking lot, keeping an eye on his watch. If she was shopping, he guessed it would take her about a half hour.

He was startled when she emerged a few minutes later carrying a small grocery bag, walking quickly to her car. The sun was bright and uncharacteristically warm on the February morning.

Louise walked up to her driver's side door at the same moment Dennis came from behind her. The Audi beeped as Louise hit the key fob, but she stopped as she reached for the door handle and whipped around to see Dennis. He was shocked at how well honed her street craft skills were.

"Jesus Christ," she said. "What the fuck are you doing here?"

Dennis pulled his right hand out of his coat pocket and briefly displayed a pistol.

"Really? Are you serious, Cunningham?"

"Get in the back seat," he said. "Don't screw around, Louise. I'm pretty crazy right now, and you don't want to test me."

She closed her eyes to compose herself, sighed and opened them again to stare at Dennis. He was thankful for the sunglasses, because her eyes were painfully blue and focused on the middle of his forehead.

"Get in, Louise. Please don't do anything stupid. I just have a couple of questions to ask. Then I'm gone. You'll never see me again."

"I'll never see you again because you'll be in prison or dead."

"Get in."

She sneered with a twist of her small mouth and opened the back door. As she slid in, Dennis slid in behind her and shut the door.

Louise refused to look at him; she stared coldly at the back of headrest in front of her, the small grocery bag on her lap.

"How did you figure out that Arnold was in Moscow?" he said. "I never told you that."

She continued to stare and did not speak.

"At first I figured you for someone so desperate for advancement and glory that you'd steal someone else's work and claim it for your own. But something's wrong with that narrative, though it's taken me a long time to figure it out."

"Go figure this out," she said, raising the middle finger of her right hand.

Dennis ripped off his sunglasses and the wool cap.

"Look at me, Louise," he said. "Look. You think my skin looks a little strange?"

Louise turned and looked, then turned away again.

"I'm jaundiced, Louise. Yeah, my liver is dying, thanks to the London infection. I'm on a donor list. I'm depressed and angry and feeling reckless right now. If I shot you, I'd just shoot myself and that would be the end of it."

She turned and stared at his face for a long time.

"What do you want, Cunningham? I mean, what can I possibly tell you? Unstable men with guns really, really bother me."

"You lied every step of the way. I just didn't figure it out until recently."

"You are crazy. You should see someone in employee assistance."

"Goddamnit, Louise, I'll show you crazy!" Dennis pulled the pistol out and pointed it at her forehead.

"Stop it!" she yelled.

He thrust the gun back into the coat pocket, took a quick glance around the nearby cars and put his sunglasses back on.

"Again," he said, regaining his breath, "how did you know Arnold was in Moscow?"

"I always knew he was in Moscow."

"No, you didn't; I never told you."

"You told Judy, and she told me."

"She may have told you, but I think you knew all along."

"So what if we knew?"

"Quit screwing around, Louise. How much did you know?"

Louise readjusted the grocery bag in her lap, and the crinkling of thick paper was the only sound in the cold car. A thin white stream of condensation shot forward when she exhaled.

"Arnold was caught in a honey trap, and he alerted the London station. It was decided he should go along and get trapped to see what the Russians wanted. The Russians still think homosexuality is a criminal offense or something. We, as you know, don't give a shit."

Dennis stared at the left side of Louise's pale face.

"More," he said.

"So Arnold finds out his handlers want him to place eavesdropping devices at Menwith Hill. Some newfangled network using power outlets."

"The NSA would never go along with that," Dennis said.

Louise turned toward Dennis.

"You've got me for five minutes, Cunningham. You want me to continue, or are you going burn your five minutes with commentary?

"Go."

"As you noted, the NSA would never go along with it, so the agency decides not to tell them."

"Mmm," Dennis said.

"Arnold was trained to install the tiny devices — there were several he put throughout the building — but we altered the Russian equipment to send along some bogus data."

"Presumably along with real data being scooped from NSA," Dennis said.

"The NSA has terabytes on terabytes of data they never look at. Don't worry about those idiots."

"Why the bogus data?"

"You're not authorized to know that."

"Goddamnit, Louise! I swear to God I'll blow your brains out if you try that shit with me one more time."

For the first time, Dennis noticed Louise's mouth twitch into a small circle, and her eyes grow smaller. She was finally nervous.

"We decided to take out a senior member of the FSB's cyber warfare unit. Guy named Vasiliev. Total maniac; we think he's bipolar. But brilliant. Caused us a lot of trouble. So we took a gamble. Fed bogus information into their eavesdropping network to make it look like Vasiliev was an MI6 mole."

"Why the hell would the IG send me and Freddie back to look for Arnold, if operations knew all along where he was?"

"First, the IG doesn't know shit. And secondly, that asshole Barkley got wind of the whole thing, or part of the thing, and decided to force the IG to use the unstable asshole sitting next to me right now to bust it open. Somehow he thought you were rogue enough to figure it out, and if you surfaced it, he didn't have to leak it to the press. But all you did was completely screw it up by tracking down Arnold's Ukrainian handler and confronting him. We don't know how you and your pal sniffed out the Ukrainian. We think it's an NSA leak, and when we find the bastard we'll fry him."

"Pavlychko was Arnold's handler," Dennis said. "He freaked out when we showed up at his door, and given the importance of the Menwith Hill project, he poisoned Freddie to stop us."

"He was actually ordered to kill the both of you as fast as possible."

"Wouldn't it have been nice of you to let Freddie and I know we were on someone's hit list?"

"By the time the order was decoded, Freddie was poisoned. You were supposed to be with him that night as well. Too bad you missed out on your dose of the polonium. A couple of us thought it was a real tragedy you didn't join your friend that night."

"Now look who's the asshole," he said. "Freddie was a good man."

"A lot of good men and women don't make it. And for the record, your five minutes are up." She reached for the door handle.

"Please don't open that door, Louise," he said, his voice cracking. "Please. I don't want to hurt you."

Again, he noticed her mouth constrict into a small circle and her eyes tighten at the corners. She sat back and stared sullenly at the headrest.

"Soon I'm going to call your bluff, and you're going to either shoot me or not shoot me," she said. "Talk quick, because I'm about to get out of the car."

"You were a goddamn mole for operations working against the OIG. Finally figured it out this week."

"Oh, grow up, Cunningham."

"If you folks didn't want me to bust open the Arnold case, why the hell did you send me back with time running out?"

"Wasn't my idea. Someone thought that Barkley would finally let up if you came back empty."

"And the part about you getting Judy out of that basement?"

"That was not authorized. For the record, I got a very fucking big demerit for that one. But what can I say? It happened. I took out some real, low-level scum and saved your girlfriend. Maybe you'd thank me for that instead of flipping out in a parking lot in a Virginia suburb. I was told you're always thirty seconds from losing it, and now I'm seeing the dark side up close and personal."

"Last question: I know I'm wrong about this, but I have to ask. I heard from a contact in MI5 that Judy traveled to Moscow for two days when I was in the hospital. Any truth to that? Doesn't sound like Judy, but it does sound like you."

"Nope, not me. Don't know anything about that. Can't be true."

Dennis had been enraged when Ian broached it and refused to believe it. Surely Judy would have told him afterward. Sending a defenseless woman into the lion's den of Russian espionage was something even Louise was not capable of.

But the more he thought about it, the more uncertain he became. His paranoia and rattled brain would not let it rest. The only certainty he could muster was that Louise was very much like him —capable of doing anything in pursuit of a mission she believed in.

"You sent her to Moscow."

"Don't be an idiot."

"She told me," he lied.

"I don't think so. She must be confused. You know what kind of condition she was in after the abduction. And then your illness threw her for a loop. Nothing against that woman, but she was compromised by a lot of trauma."

"She taped your conversation."

Louise flicked her head toward Dennis and then returned to face the armrest. The bag crinkled in her lap as she grasped it. A thick vapor stream accompanied a sigh.

"You're lying."

Dennis said nothing and waited. It didn't take long.

"We needed to get Arnold out as soon as the FSB arrested Vasiliev," Louise said. "The extraction protocol was very old-school. Arnold was to visit a particular coffee shop nearly every day. One day, someone would look at him with a very distinctive pair of eyeglasses that Arnold had memorized. The messenger would press the bridge of the glasses with their forefinger. At that point Arnold was to say something to the messenger. If the messenger said anything about ordering a black coffee, that was the order for him to get out immediately. He was in Poland twenty-four hours later and is back in the US as we speak."

Dennis tried to calm himself, but he could feel the anger turning his cheeks red and felt his palm sweat around the handle of the pistol.

"You sent that poor woman on a dangerous mission like that? Out of the blue? Did she know what she was doing?"

"No, she would never have gone if she knew she was just a messenger. She thought she was photographing him and returning with evidence he was alive. So you wouldn't try to do it yourself."

"Louise, she could have been arrested!"

"She wasn't, so stop worrying."

"But you didn't give a shit about how fragile she was. Didn't any of you people think about that?"

"We use the tools we have at hand, Cunningham. Someone suggested that she would be the perfect messenger, since she had no idea she was a messenger. So we took a gamble. She was perfect. It worked. End of story."

"I bet you suggested they use Judy," Dennis said.

Louise shrugged and reached for the door handle.

"Hey!" Dennis said, reaching for her left arm.

"Fuck off," she said as the door flew open.

She turned to see Dennis pointing the pistol at her forehead.

He pulled the trigger without a hint of reflection or concern about the consequences.

✦

Judy tried to cool down, but the workout was more strenuous than she had anticipated. Even after a shower, she was still perspiring slightly as she sat in the lounge area of the health club in Perth's Kings Park drinking sparkling water with a slice of lemon.

"My heavens, your arms look sculpted, Jude," her friend Cilla said, sitting across from her. "You're embarrassing all your friends with your workout routine. Have mercy on us."

Judy laughed and looked out the huge windows of the health club onto the tennis courts. It was 10:00 a.m., but the summer heat of February was building to a boil already, and Judy was looking to relax on this Sunday morning. Her son Trevor was at City Beach with some friends.

"So you're going to see your new flame again tonight?"

"Yes, he's quite charming," Judy said. "I'm new at this dating game."

"He's divorced?"

"Two children; amicable, as he describes it."

"I gather he's quite handsome," Cilla said. "Does he have another divorced handsome friend who's looking for companionship?"

"Oh, for heaven's sake, Cilla. You've been happily married for fourteen years. Stop it."

"Just mucking around. A woman can muck around, you know."

Judy laughed and took a long sip of water. She looked outside at a spirited doubles match. "I don't like tennis. Did I tell you that? Seems so boring."

"Can I help you?" Cilla said.

Judy turned to look at Cilla, who was staring at someone standing behind Judy. She twisted around to see a gaunt but smiling man.

"I was hoping to say hello to Judy," Dennis said.

Cilla shot Judy a glance then looked up at Dennis, then back to Judy.

"Um, I gather you're Dennis," Cilla said. "Judy doesn't have many Yank friends."

Dennis came around from behind Judy and shook Cilla's hand.

"Glad to meet you."

"What are you doing here?" Judy asked.

"Gee, everybody says that to me. Do I surprise people that much?"

"Really, Dennis," she said. "What are you doing here?" She shook her head and looked at the tiny effervescent bubbles bursting from the mouth of her glass.

"Nice to meet you, Dennis," Cilla said, standing. "Call me later, Judy?"

Judy nodded.

"Can I sit?" Dennis asked.

Judy shrugged.

"I'll take that for a yes. You look great."

"What are you doing here?" she said, this time with a touch of exasperation. "Can't you leave me alone?"

"I found an apartment here in the city. Charming place."

"Oh, lord," she said, sitting upright. "You can't be serious. That's stalking, Dennis. You can't stalk me. I won't stand for it."

"I'm not stalking. Who said I'm stalking? I told you I'd move to Perth. So here I am. I moved to Perth. Now it's your turn. You want me to stay, I stay. You want me to go, I go."

Judy looked at the floor, closed her eyes and slowly shook her head back and forth.

"You look great," Dennis said again.

"Stop it."

"Well, if I've come this far, sold my condo and put all my belongings in storage back in the States, you could at least tell me what you want me to do."

"Go away."

"Well, that's a bummer," he said. "I was kind of hoping you'd be glad to see me."

"I am glad to see you. And I'd be just as glad not to see you. You confuse me, Dennis. And I can't be around a man who confuses me so much. And you seem to attract trouble. I can't take any more trouble in my life. I've pieced my simple life together again in sleepy little old Perth. I have a life again. I'm dating a nice man. My son seems normal. Things are returning to normal. Nothing about you is normal. I can't do it, Dennis."

"Mmm. Another man. It was only a matter of time. I'm not surprised. Is he interesting?"

"Yes. Very."

"Is he funny like me?"

"Oh, stop it. And by the way, you're not funny. Cynical, snarling, suspicious and even paranoid sometimes. But not funny."

"Sometimes maybe?" he laughed.

"Okay. You are funny sometimes. But not often."

"See, I have some redeeming qualities."

She sighed. "Enough. I have to leave now. I'm not going to let you trick me into liking you."

"But I thought you liked me?"

"Of course I like you. I mean…whatever. I must go." She stood up, but Dennis remained seated.

"Thank you for going to Moscow. I'm ashamed that Louise tricked you into doing their dirty work."

Judy sat down. "She told you?"

"Actually, someone else did. Then I confronted her. She came clean. Admitted how she manipulated you into being a deliveryman for the CIA."

Judy winced. "I was photographing Arnold. She gave me special glasses, and I returned them to her. I did it so you wouldn't go. I knew you'd be angry. I thought maybe I could get you off your crazy mission to prove this man Arnold was in Moscow. But you disabused me of that soon enough. I tried, but you won't let things go."

"Louise lied to you."

"I found Arnold, just as she predicted, and photographed him."

"You didn't photograph him. You delivered a message from the Operations Directorate of the Central Intelligence Agency to an American double agent. The glasses were just glasses."

"But I returned them. She met me at Heathrow."

"She probably threw them in the trash as soon as you walked away."

"See, this is what I'm saying, Dennis. Damnit. I don't know what to believe! Are you saying she tricked me? Louise? I don't believe it!"

"Welcome to my world," he said, running his hand through his bristly hair. "I just knew something was wrong from the very beginning of this stupid Arnold case. Losing Freddie to those Russians was bad enough. But when I heard that Louise had tricked you into going to Moscow, I just flipped out. Lost it completely. I feel bad for what I did to her, but she deserved it."

Judy sat forward in her chair.

"What do you mean? What did you do to her?"

"I lost it. I mean, I just lost control. It happens. She had no business doing that you."

"Dennis, what did you do to her?"

"Louise?"

"Yes, of course, Louise!"

"I found where she lived. Then I followed her one day to a grocery store."

"Dennis, that's creepy!"

"Well, I just needed to confirm some things. God, she was tough. But I was prepared."

Judy stood up and moved to sit next to him.

"Dennis," she said. "Please tell me what you did to her."

"Well, to get her to admit everything, I had to make her think I was crazy. I mean, real crazy. So I stained my face and hands with a yellowish bronze tanning solution."

Judy looked confused.

"I told her I had liver failure and that it didn't matter if I lived or died. That if she didn't come clean I'd kill her."

"Is your liver failing?"

"No, of course not."

"But you threatened her?"

"Of course I did. I had a gun. Though to be honest, I don't think she gave a shit about the gun."

"Oh, God." Judy fell back in her chair. "Oh, God, help me."

"Well, the good news is that she told me everything, and it adds up. I get it. Clever stuff. I should have known that operations would plant people in our unit."

Judy sat up again, grabbed Dennis's right hand and folded her two hands around his. "Dennis, what did you do to Louise?"

"When?"

"When you confronted her. You said you had a gun."

"Oh, that. Well, when she finally confirmed that she used you to deliver the message to Arnold, well, I lost it."

"But what did you do to her?"

"I pulled out the stupid pistol, and before I knew what happened, I pulled the trigger."

Judy fell back into the chair, covering her eyes with her both hands. She let out a little sound. "My God, Dennis. You killed her."

Dennis grabbed her wrists and pulled them off her face.

"I didn't kill her. Who told you I killed her?"

"You did!"

"I said I shot her in the forehead."

She closed her eyes again and wiped away a small tear with her right hand.

"It was a squirt gun, for God's sake."

"A what?!" Judy shrieked. Several people nearby stopped and turned to look at them.

Dennis noticed their stares and tried to calm Judy.

"I didn't tell you it was a squirt gun?"

"No!"

"Sorry. I bought one of those fancy, authentic-looking squirt guns. They're illegal, but I found one online. The Chinese manufacture everything."

"You didn't kill her?"

"Why would I do that? I mean I admit to being really, really pissed off. But I wouldn't kill Louise."

Judy sprawled back in the chair, slouching awkwardly, and stared at the ceiling.

"So that was your plan, to threaten her into telling you everything? And then shoot her with a squirt gun?"

"No, silly. I didn't intend to squirt her. It just happened at the end."

"But she didn't know it was a squirt gun?"

"Hell, no," he said. "You should have seen her face when I pulled the trigger. We were in the back seat of her car."

"What did she do?"

"When?"

"Damnit, Dennis, when you squirted her in the face! What did she do?"

"Ah, well. Something I never expected from her. Kind of caught me off guard."

"What?"

"You know she's not that big, right? Maybe five foot two?"

"Yes, I met her. Remember?"

"Yeah, right. Well, I just stuck the gun about two inches from her forehead, and the water hit her right there," he said pointing to his forehead. "She jerked backward, then when she realized what had happened, she kind of closed her eyes and sat there for maybe five seconds."

"That's it?"

"No. Then she hit me. I still don't know how she did it, because I swear I never saw it coming. Her fist caught me right under my chin and nearly knocked me out. I saw honest to God stars. Next thing I know, I'm on the ground next to her car and she's peeling out of the parking lot. Some old man came over and asked if I needed help."

Judy sat forward again and clasped Dennis's right hand in her two hands. The two of them sat silently for several minutes, watching the muted doubles tennis match through the thick plate glass windows.

"Do you like tennis?" Dennis asked.

"Not particularly."

"Neither do I," he said. "Kind of boring."

She gently rubbed his hand.

After several minutes of silence she said, "A squirt gun."

"Yeah. I made one mistake, though."

"And that would be?"

"I should have put ink in the gun instead of water."

"Water was enough, Dennis."

"I suppose you're right."

OTHER BOOKS FROM KEITH YOCUM

Color of Blood

(BOOK 1 OF THE DENNIS CUNNINGHAM SERIES)

Dennis is glad to be back at work. His wife's death left him devastated but he'll do anything to lose himself into work at the Inspector General's office of the CIA. A brilliant, if prickly investigator, he's spent his career chasing down the Agency's thieves and liars. When his boss forces him to take a low-level assignment to investigate a missing employee in Australia, he soon finds that even in the red dust of the Outback, there is romance – and death – just a sweltering heartbeat away.

BUY IT FROM AMAZON TODAY

"Very intelligent. Expertly written and suspenseful as hell. I can see this coming to a Multiplex near you pretty soon." – *Robin, Amazon review*

"Awesome concept, title, cover. The writing is excellent. A great hook. What more can you ask for?" – *Susan, Amazon review*

"Yocum is an excellent story creator and teller and Color of Blood is definitely a top-of-the-pile find." – *Harry, Amazon review*

"This book was different than other spy stories which made for a great read." – *Ian, Amazon review*

"I love the thriller with unexpected ending. And this kept me intrigued until the end. I recommend it to everyone." – *Amparo, Amazon review*

Daniel

STRANGE THINGS HAPPEN IN WAR –
BUT THEN VIETNAM WAS ALWAYS DIFFERENT.

In January 1972, during the waning days of that sad war, a lone soldier crawled through the barbed wire and entered an isolated American firebase. He said his name was Daniel Carson, but could remember nothing else. A quick check found that a soldier with the same name and physical description was already buried at Arlington National Cemetery. So who was this new soldier named Daniel? Was he a crazy man, a common deserter or something else entirely? And why did he have such a profound effect on the unlucky company of grunts trying to survive the last days of the war?

As a fierce regiment of North Vietnamese regulars prepare to destroy the forgotten hilltop firebase, the odd little soldier named Daniel seems to have all the answers to their survival. Several years after the war, three survivors of the firebase meet in Washington, D.C. and, almost by accident, discover the shocking truth about Daniel.

Can you figure out the mystery of Daniel?

BUY IT FROM AMAZON TODAY

"If you like Dan Brown and Michael Crichton's style of historical/ mystery/supernatural well researched and fact-checked kind of writing, you'll like Keith Yocum's "Daniel", a novel set on the last functional firebase at the end of the Viet Nam war." – *Amazon review*

"I made the mistake of picking it up "for a few minutes" with about a third remaining unread one night when I was having difficulty sleeping at 2AM, and finished it at 6AM because I had to see if the author could resolve the mystery. He did, I wasn't disappointed, and you won't be either." – *Amazon review*

"This book was on my "recommended" list for a long time. Finally, for $2.99 who could resist. I can honestly say this is one of the best books I have ever read, and I have been reading voraciously for over sixty years." – *Amazon review*

"Haunting and intense, this book will stay with me for a long time." – *Amazon review*

"I'm not a Viet Nam vet, but I am an Iraq vet, and this work does a great job of depicting the chaos and confusion of armed conflict to my standards." – *Amazon review*

"I missed the fact that it is a true story. I just thought it was a well done novel based on the thoughts of a creative writer. I was pleased with the story and amazed that it was true. It is fascinating." – *Amazon review*

Titus

A Union soldier is found dead on the outskirts of camp, his neck sliced open from ear to ear. But when another and yet another soldier is found with his throat slit, an uneasy mood falls over the Union regiment.

Who is killing these soldiers, and what does the strange mark on the dead men's foreheads mean? A young Union lieutenant and an eccentric field surgeon are ordered to get to the bottom of the killings. Can the two officers unmask the killer's identity and motive before the fog of battle hides his identity forever?

BUY IT FROM AMAZON TODAY

KEITH YOCUM is a novelist living on Cape Cod. His career has oriented around publications and digital businesses. He has worked for *The Boston Globe* and *The New England Journal of Medicine*. He was also the founder of *NewsWest*, a chain of local newspapers in the Boston area that was sold to a competitor in the late 1980s. He is the author of four novels and welcomes feedback at www.keithyocum.com.

Made in the USA
Las Vegas, NV
20 January 2021